William Angus Knight, Leigh Hunt

Tales by Leigh Hunt

William Angus Knight, Leigh Hunt

Tales by Leigh Hunt

ISBN/EAN: 9783337024178

Printed in Europe, USA, Canada, Australia, Japan

Cover: Foto ©Andreas Hilbeck / pixelio.de

More available books at **www.hansebooks.com**

THE
TREASURE HOUSE OF TALES

BY

GREAT AUTHORS

———

LEIGH HUNT

& Achill.Paris

TALES

BY

LEIGH HUNT

NOW FIRST COLLECTED

WITH A PREFATORY MEMOIR

BY

WILLIAM KNIGHT, LL.D.
PROFESSOR OF MORAL PHILOSOPHY IN THE UNIVERSITY OF ST. ANDREWS

LONDON
WILLIAM PATERSON & CO.
1891

PREFATORY MEMOIR.

—o—

JAMES HENRY LEIGH HUNT was born in October 1784 at the village of Southgate, in the parish of Edmonton, Middlesex. The neighbourhood of the little village is full of associations to literary Englishmen. At Edmonton, Marlowe—the father of the British drama—was born. There Charles Lamb lies buried, with Coleridge not far off; and Steele, Arbuthnot, Akenside, Keats, and Shelley, all lived, at different times, at no great distance from it.

Hunt was of American extraction, his father having been originally a lawyer in Philadelphia; and his mother was the daughter of a Philadelphia merchant. Though destined for the clerical office, his father began life in the practice of the law. As a barrister, he took the side of the British Government in its dispute with America,—both making speeches, and writing pamphlets in its behalf,— and, in consequence, he not only became unpopular, but was exposed to violence. He was put in prison, and only escaped by bribing the sentinel in charge. Crossing the Atlantic with all speed, he entered the profession for which he had first been destined. As a clergyman he had a somewhat chequered career, and attained to no great distinction. Hunt's mother, Mary Shewell, was a woman of great nobility, generosity, and firmness of character.

There is little to record of his early years. In his *Autobiography*—one of the most delightful ever written—he tells us that, when a child, he was taken by his father to the Houses of Parliament. In the Commons he saw Mr. Pitt " sawing the air ; " and when his supporters cried " Hear, hear," he fancied they said " Dear, dear " in derision ! In the House of Lords, where he expected to see venerable conscript fathers, the members seemed generally insignificant. He was sent to school at Christ's Hospital, and he has given us a picture of that somewhat famous seminary, drawn with extreme vividness : " an old cloistered foundation, where a boy may grow up, as I did, among six hundred others, and know as little of the very neighbourhood as the world does of him." He refused to be a fag, and suffered some bullying in consequence. He speaks, however, of the genial comradeship of the boys, — no feeling of the difference of social rank being then known,—the dress, the lessons, the food, the daily routine, the cruel flogging master, Bowyer,—of whom Coleridge has also given us a picture,—all these are described in graphic detail. The boys used to assemble for church service, with a steward watching them; and when the passage in Scripture about "the unjust steward" came to be read, the whole school turned their eyes with general consent towards the unfortunate official! The books he greatly rejoiced in were Tooke's *Pantheon*, Lemprière's *Classical Dictionary*, and Spence's *Polymetis*. To the poets he was specially devoted. He says, "I am grateful to Christ's Hospital for having bred me up in old cloisters, for its having made me acquainted with the languages of Homer and Ovid, and for its having secured to me on the whole a well-trained and cheerful boyhood. It pressed no superstition upon me. It did not hinder my growing mind from making what excursions it pleased into the wide and healthy regions of general literature."

He went through the several stages of the school, and formed some very strong friendships. His description of the delights of boy-friendship among schoolfellows is wonderfully fine. A slight physical defect, a stammer (for which the cruel master, Bowyer, had once hit him), prevented him from going on to the University. He tells us that at the age of fifteen he was "first deputy Grecian, and had the honour of going out of the school in the same rank, at the same age, and for the same reason, as my friend Charles Lamb. The reason was that I hesitated in my speech. It was understood that a Grecian was bound to deliver a public speech before he left school, and to go into the

Church afterwards ; and, as I could do neither of
these things, a Grecian I could not be."

He left Christ's Hospital with keen regret, and
thereafter spent some time in "visiting his school
friends, hunting book-stalls, and writing verses."
These boyish verses his father collected and published in the year 1802, under the title of *Juvenilia*.
Hunt afterwards saw that the booklet was all but
absolutely worthless, and that he had been wasting
his powers in mere imitation for several years, while
he might have been studying Nature and the true
art of Poetry. Visiting some school friends, who
had gone to Oxford and Cambridge, he instinctively
caught the charm of these seats of learning, and
his subsequent descriptions of the Universities in
his *Autobiography* is noteworthy.

"Were I to visit the Universities now, I should
explore every corner, and reverently fancy myself
in the presence of every great and good man that
has adorned them ; but the most important people
to young men are one another ; and I was content
with glancing at the haunts of Addison and
Wharton in Oxford, and at those of Gray, Spenser,
and Milton in Cambridge. Oxford, I found, had
greatly the advantage of Cambridge in point of
country. You could understand well enough how
poets could wander about Ifiley and Woodstock ;
but when I visited Cambridge, the nakedness of
the land was too plainly visible under a sheet of
snow, through which gutters of ditches ran, like

ink, by the side of leafless sallows, which resembled
huge pincushions stuck on posts. The town,
however, made amends; and Cambridge has the
advantage of Oxford in a remarkable degree, as far
as regards eminent names. England's two greatest
philosophers, Bacon and Newton, and (according to
Tyrwhitt) three out of its four great poets, were
bred there, besides double the number of minor
celebrities. Oxford even did not always know 'the
good the gods provided.' It repudiated Locke;
alienated Gibbon; and had nothing but angry
sullenness and hard expulsion to answer to the
inquiries which its very ordinances encouraged in
the sincere and loving spirit of Shelley. Yet they
are divine places, both; full of grace, and beauty,
and scholarship; of reverend antiquity, and ever-
young nature and hope. Their faults, if of worldliness in some, are those of time and of conscience
in more; and, if the more pertinacious on those
accounts, will merge into a like conservative firmness, when still nobler developments are in their
keeping. So at least I hope; and so may the Fates
have ordained; keeping their gowns among them
as a symbol that learning is, indeed, something.
which ever learns; and instructing them to teach
love, and charity, and inquiry, with the same accomplished authority as that with which they have
taught assent."—*Autobiography*, ed. 1860, chap. v.
pp. 110, 111.

His boyish performance (the *Juvenilia*) was—

unfortunately for him — " successful everywhere, particularly in the metropolis." Taken to see Dr. Raine, the Master of Charterhouse, the latter told him to beware of authorship, adding " Sir, the shelves are full." Hunt says, " It was not till I came away that I thought of an answer which would have annihilated him—' Then, sir, we will make another.' " His grandfather, still living in America, urged him to come out to Philadelphia, where " he would make a man of him." He replied, " Men grow in England, as well as in America." When he was only seventeen years of age, he became engaged to Marianne Kent, who was only thirteen; and the very strength of his devotion to her led him to wish that she should carry on her studies on lines approved of, or even dictated by him. It was extremely foolish, and for a time the engagement was broken off in consequence.

About this time he became a volunteer, the possible invasion of Britain by Buonaparte giving, as he said, "a knock at the door of all England." At this time also, he got a situation as clerk in the War Office; but he admits that he was a bad clerk, and, feeling the task uncongenial, he entered definitely on the career of a pressman and publicist. He was unmethodical, and hopelessly unpunctual. He became so absorbed in the thing he had on hand —whether reading, conversation, or society—that he took no note of the lapse of time. Then the very simplest question in arithmetic was a puzzle to him.

He was absolutely incapable of working out the figures in a balance-sheet, and was as helpless in keeping books as one who has no ear for music is puzzled in listening to a symphony, or one who is colour-blind in distinguishing the shades of the spectrum.

In the year 1805, his brother John set up a paper called the *News;* and Leigh Hunt went to live with him, that he might write the theatrical criticism for it. Some of these criticisms, on the leading actors and actresses of the day, he afterwards revised, and issued as an appendix to a volume of *Critical Essays on the Performers of the London Theatres* (1807). He now definitely realized that his mission in life was to be that of a writer for the public. He felt that he had not been so much misdirected hitherto in the study of prose, as in that of poetry. Addison's papers in the *Spectator* became his standard, and in the Addisonian vein he wrote a series of articles for another contemporary paper called the *Traveller.* He describes himself at this time as a "glutton of books." Goldsmith, Fielding, Smollett, and Voltaire were amongst his favourite essayists and novelists. Amongst historians he chiefly admired Herodotus, Villani, Froissart, and Gibbon. Voltaire was, however, the author who most of all impressed him, and whom he chiefly admired for his healthy antagonisms to shams, his Carlyle-like hatred of all unveracities. His estimate of Voltaire is striking.

"It is a curious circumstance respecting the

books of Voltaire—the greatest writer upon the
whole that France has produced, and undoubtedly
the greatest name in the eighteenth century—that
to this moment they are far less known in England
than talked of ; so much so, that, with the exception
of a few educated circles, chiefly of the upper class,
and exclusively among the men even in those, he
has not only been hardly read at all, even by such
as have talked of him with admiration, or loaded
him with reproach, but the portions of his writings
that have had the greatest effect on the world are
the least known among readers the most popularly
acquainted with him."—*Autobiography*, chap. vii.
p. 142. Writing to a friend in 1805, he said of
Voltaire : " He is an author that perpetually delights
me, and has the felicitous art of uniting profound
philosophy with the most lively wit."

In 1808, while still a clerk in the War Office,
Leigh Hunt and his brother set up a new weekly paper
called the *Examiner*, of which they were to be joint
proprietors.   In this he continued the same kind
of theatrical criticism as in the *News*, but the main
object of the *Examiner* was to " assist in producing
reform in Parliament, liberality of opinion in
general, especially freedom from superstition, and
an infusion of literary taste into all subjects.   It
began," Hunt adds, " by being of no party, but
Reform gave it one."

The *Examiner* was a paper of high literary merit
and rare independence.   " Zeal for the public good

was a family inheritance," he says, "and this we thought ourselves bound to increase. As to myself, what I thought of more than either, was the making of verses. I did nothing for the greater part of the week but write verses and read books. I then made a rush at my editorial duties, took a world of superfluous pains in the writing, sat up late at night, and was a very trying person to compositors and newsmen." The *Examiner* was an organ of Constitutional Reform, was loyal to Church and State, and was opposed alike to Buonapartism and to Republicanism. While editing this paper Leigh Hunt made many literary acquaintances,—Thomas Campbell the poet, the two brothers James and Horace Smith, authors of the *Rejected Addresses*, Theodore Hook, Matthews the comedian, Fuseli the artist, and William Godwin. The editor of the *Examiner* could not fail to criticise the political characters of the period with some keenness; and, as might have been expected at that time, prosecutions for libel followed. Three of these, at the instance of the Tory Government, failed; the details it is needless to record. A fourth was, as we shall see, more serious. The way in which Hunt conducted the *Examiner*, however, brought him invitations to write for other papers. One reached him from 32 Fleet Street in March 1809, asking him to write on the state of the contemporary drama in the *Quarterly Review*. The letter is signed, " much your admirer and friend, John Murray."

In July 1809, Leigh Hunt was married to
Marianne Kent. They went to live at Beckenham.

In 1810, when the *Examiner* had been established for between two and three years, Leigh Hunt
and his brother started a new magazine, called the
Reflector. Charles Lamb was perhaps the most
distinguished contributor to this magazine. Hunt
himself contributed the *Feast of the Poets*, a *jeu
d'esprit* suggested by Sir John Suckling's *Session of
the Poets.* "Apollo gives the poets a dinner, and
many verse-makers who have no claim to the title
present themselves, and are rejected." In these
verses Hunt dealt several severe blows at the Tories;
but it was not as Tories that he assailed them. We
find in the *Autobiography* the following significant
sentence :—

"Every party has a right side and a wrong.
The right side of Whiggism, or Radicalism, is the
love of liberty, the love of justice,—the wish to see
fair play to all men, and the advancement of knowledge and competence. The wrong side is the wish
to pull down those above us, instead of the desire
of raising those who are below. The right side of
Toryism is the love of order and the disposition to
reverence and personal attachment; the wrong side
is the love of power for power's sake, and the determination to maintain it in the teeth of all that is
reasonable and humane."—Chap. xii. p. 217, 218.

In his *Feast of the Poets* Hunt offended all the
literary parties of the time ; the eighteenth-century

formalists, by his objecting to the monotony of Pope's style, and those who sympathized with the Renaissance, by his laughing at Wordsworth, whose verses he had never read. He tells us, however, that, on becoming acquainted with Wordsworth, he was such an admirer that Byron accused him of making him popular about town. Hunt shared the fate of all honest and vigorous critics, viz. of offending almost every one in turn. The *Reflector* contained a severe article on His Royal Highness the Prince Regent, satirizing one of his conventional dinner-parties. This was of course much disliked, but it was an article on the Prince in the *Examiner* which brought Hunt into real trouble. The Regent had reversed the policy which he had advocated as Prince of Wales. The article upon him was bitter and contemptuous, but it was substantially true. When the Prince's health had been proposed, and Sheridan had flattered him to the zenith, the company hissed. The *Morning Post* at once published an article of fulsome flattery, describing the "Mæcenas of the age" as an "Adonis in loveliness." To this the *Examiner* replied, giving a cold and clear comparison of the facts of the case with the flattering fictions of after-dinner oratory. It led to a prosecution by the Attorney-General, and to a verdict against Hunt and his brother, with the sentence of two years' imprisonment in separate jails, and the fine of £1000. Henry (afterwards Lord) Brougham conducted Hunt's defence. After the sentence, the brothers were told that if they would guarantee to abstain from all comments on the Prince Regent in future they would be pardoned; but they declined to do so, and went to their respective prisons in February 1813.

Although there were things to be regretted, and sentences to be condemned in the *Examiner* article, to inflict so severe a punishment on a man of letters such as Hunt was a grave political blunder. It made him the hero of the hour, doing him ultimately much more good than harm. Hunt has himself told the story of his imprisonment in a graphic manner. His account of the gaoler, and his conversations with him, of his removal to more comfortable quarters within the prison, of the visits of his wife, and of his friends,— Charles Lamb and Thomas Moore, Lord Byron and Lord Brougham, Hazlitt and Cowden Clarke,—of the birth of his eldest girl in prison, of the books he read, and others that he wrote,—all are recorded in a most fascinating manner. The imprisonment had an element of romance in it. He was left a good deal to the freedom of his own will, and had many things supplied to him to mitigate the severity of his lot. The following is the account, from his own lips, of his confinement in prison :—

"I papered the walls with a trellis of roses; I had the ceiling coloured with clouds and sky; the barred windows I screened with Venetian blinds; and when my bookcases were set up with their busts, and flowers and a pianoforte made their appearance, perhaps there was not a handsomer room on that side the water. I took a pleasure, when a stranger knocked at the door, to see him come in and stare about him. The surprise on issuing from the Borough, and passing through the avenues of a gaol, was dramatic. Charles Lamb declared there was no other such room, except in a fairy tale.

"But I possessed another surprise; which was a garden. There was a little yard outside the room, railed off from another belonging to the neighbouring ward. This yard I shut in with green palings, adorned it with a trellis, bordered it with a thick bed of earth from a nursery, and even contrived to have a grass-plot. The earth I filled with flowers and young trees. There was an apple-tree, from which we managed to get a pudding the second year. As to my flowers, they were allowed to be perfect. Thomas Moore, who came to see me with Lord Byron, told me he had seen no such heart's-ease. I bought the *Parnaso Italiano* while in prison, and used often to think of a passage in it, while looking at this miniature piece of horti-culture :——

'Mio picciol orto,
A me sei vigna e campo o silvo o prato.'—BALDI.

My little garden,
To me thou'rt vineyard, field, and meadow, and wood.

"Here I wrote and read in fine weather, some-

b

times under an awning. In autumn my trellises were hung with scarlet runners, which added to the flowery investment. I used to shut my eyes in my arm-chair, and affect to think myself hundreds of miles off.

"But my triumph was in issuing forth of a morning. A wicket out of the garden led into the large one belonging to the prison. The latter was only for vegetables; but it contained a cherry-tree, which I saw twice in blossom. I parcelled out the ground in my imagination into favourite districts. I made a point of dressing myself as if for a long walk; and then, putting on my gloves, and taking my book under my arm, stepped forth, requesting my wife not to wait dinner if I was too late. My eldest little boy, to whom Lamb addressed some charming verses on the occasion, was my constant companion, and we used to play all sorts of juvenile games together.

.   .   .   .

"When I sat amidst my books, and saw the imaginary sky overhead, and my paper roses about me, I drank in the quiet at my ears, as if they were thirsty."—*Autobiography*, chap. xiv. p. 238.

From his Surrey gaol Hunt wrote some delightful letters. He sent a list of Greek words to his boy Thornton, who was at the seaside with his mother, that he might begin the knowledge of the language early, in a colloquial fashion. His description of the flowers in his garden—the Persian lilac, the

rhododendron, the apple blossom, and all the lesser
flowers, is charming; as well as his account of his
many visitors, amongst whom were Haydon and
James Mill.   Writing in August 1846, Hunt said :
" Besides the fine, my imprisonment cost me several
hundred pounds, in monstrous *douceurs* to the gaoler,
for liberty to walk in the garden, for help towards
getting me rooms in the hospital, for fitting up of
said rooms, or rather converting them from dirty
wash-houses into comfortable apartments."

On the day on which he left prison, Keats wrote
the following sonnet :—

> " What though, for showing truth to flatter'd state,
>   Kind Hunt was shut in prison, yet has he,
>   In his immortal spirit, been as free
> As the sky-searching lark, and as elate.
> Minion of grandeur ! think you he did wait ?
>   Think you he nought but prison-walls did see,
>   Till, so unwilling, thou unturn'dst the key ?
> Ah, no ! far happier, nobler was his fate !
> In Spenser's halls he strayed, and bowers fair,
>   Culling enchanted flowers ; and he flew
> With daring Milton through the fields of air :
>   To regions of his own his genius true
> Took happy flights.   Who shall his fame impair
>   When thou art dead, and all thy wretched crew ? "

He was set at liberty in February 1815, and went
at once to live in the Edgeware Road, because his
brother's house was in the neighbourhood.   There
Byron and Wordsworth came to visit him.   His
account of Wordsworth may be quoted, as it is full
of character, and casts as much light on the writer
as on the man he writes about.

"Mr. Wordsworth had a dignified manner, with a deep and roughish but not unpleasing voice, and an exalted mode of speaking. He had a habit of keeping his left hand in the bosom of his waist-coat; and in this attitude, except when he turned round to take one of the subjects of his criticism from the shelves (for his contemporaries were there also), he sat dealing forth his eloquent but hardly catholic judgments. In his "father's house" there were not "many mansions." He was as sceptical on the merits of all kinds of poetry but one, as Richardson was on those of the novels of Fielding.

"Under the study in which my visitor and I were sitting was an archway, leading to a nursery-ground; a cart happened· to go through it while I was inquiring whether he would take any refresh-ment, and he uttered, in so lofty a voice, the words, 'Anything which is *going forward*,' that I felt inclined to ask him whether he would take a piece of the cart. Lamb would certainly have done it.

.   .   .   .

"I did not see this distinguished person again till thirty years afterwards, when, I should venture to say, his manner was greatly superior to what it was in the former instance; indeed, quite natural and noble, with a cheerful air of animal as well as spiritual confidence; a gallant bearing, curiously reminding me of the Duke of Wellington, as I saw him walk-ing some eighteen years ago by a lady's side, with no unbecoming oblivion of his time of life. I observed, also, that the poet no longer committed himself in scornful criticisms, or, indeed, in any criticisms whatever, at least as far as I know.

. . . .

" But certainly I never beheld eyes that looked so inspired or so supernatural. They were like fires half - burning, half - smouldering, with a sort of acrid fixture of regard, and seated at the farther end of two caverns. One might imagine Ezekiel or Isaiah to have had such eyes."—*Autobiography*, chap. xv. p. 248, 249.

After a visit to Shelley at Marlow, Hunt went to live at Hampstead, in the spring of 1816; and there he finished his most important poem, and the work with which his genius is perhaps most definitely associated, *The Story of Rimini*. It was written in what he himself called his "first manner"—not his best, he thought; but here his own judgment was as far astray as Milton's was in deciding the relative merits of *Paradise Lost* and *Paradise Regained*. *The Story of Rimini* had been begun at Hastings, more than a year before his imprisonment; but the great part of it had been written in prison. He afterwards thought it unfortunate that he had selected the subject of "Dante's famous episode," thus inviting a comparison or involuntary contrast with the prevailing poet of Italy. His poem was published in 1816, and was very soon afterwards republished in Boston and Philadelphia.. In its conception and execution, Hunt was inspired by Boccaccio and Ariosto, as well as by Dante, and, whatever its minor defects may be, there can be little doubt that he helped to emancipate the literature of his time from the trammels of conventionality, almost as much as Wordsworth had done in another direction. He had gone back from the monotonous pomp and stilted artificiality of Pope to the naturalness of Chaucer as recast by Dryden. Dryden, in fact, was his chief master. He says, "I could not rest till I had played on his instrument." There may be much in *The Story of Rimini* that is capricious, and even incongruous; but it excels in pathos, and has the free sweep of successful narrative art. In some things he even excelled Dryden, and in comparing himself with his master, he justly said that he had "a more southern insight into the beauties of colour." Those who know *The Story of Rimini* will recall the passage descriptive of a May morning at Ravenna :—

> The sun is up, and 'tis a morn of May
> Round old Ravenna's clear-shown towers and bay.
> A morn, the loveliest which the year has seen,
> Last of the spring, yet fresh with all its green ;
> For a warm eve, and gentle rains at night,
> Have left a sparkling welcome for the light,
> And there's a crystal clearness all about ;
> The leaves are sharp, the distant hills look out ;
> A balmy briskness comes upon the breeze ;
> The smoke goes dancing from the cottage trees ;
> And when you listen, you may hear a coil
> Of bubbling springs about the grassy soil ;
> And all the scene, in short—sky, earth, and sea,
> Breathes like a bright-eyed face that laughs out openly.

'Tis nature, full of spirits, waked and springing ;
The birds to the delicious time are singing,
Darting with freaks and snatches up and down,
Where the light woods go seaward from the town ;
While happy faces, striking through the green
Of leafy roads, at every turn are seen ;
And the far ships, lifting their sails of white
Like joyful hands, come up with scattery light,
Come gleaming up, true to the wished for day,
And chase the whistling brine, and swirl into the bay.
Already in the streets the stir grows loud
Of expectation and a bustling crowd.
With feet and voice the gathering hum contends,
The deep talk heaves, the ready laugh ascends ;
Callings, and clapping doors, and curs unite,
And shouts from mere exuberance of delight ;
And armed bands, making important way,
Gallant and grave, the lords of holiday ;
And nodding neighbours, greeting as they run,
And pilgrims, chanting in the morning sun.

Charles Lamb's judgment on *Rimini* was most
cordial, and another friend described it as the work
of a mind " bearing between Byron, Wordsworth,
and Dryden,—catching from each, and winding
itself up into a whole of its own."

The *Autobiography* at this period contains many
interesting anecdotes of Shelley, Keats, Charles
Lamb, and Coleridge, and a great deal of suggestive
and incisive criticism of the merits of these poets.
Hunt was now one of that brilliant set of men of
letters in the metropolis who flourished during the
first quarter of the present century, and which included, in addition to the poets just named, other
writers scarcely less distinguished, such as Procter,
Haydon, Hazlitt, Reynolds, Dilke, and Cowden
Clarke ; and we soon find his influence telling even

on the literary work of some of them. Probably
of all his contemporaries, it was toward Shelley that
he was at this time chiefly drawn. In proportion
to the abuse of the orthodox writers of the hour
was the cordial defence and enlightened criticism
of *Prometheus Unbound* in the pages of the *Examiner*.
Both men were dissenters from the traditions of the
majority, on some important subjects; while both
were ardent lovers of liberty, and of the public good,
as against privilege and tyranny. About this time
Hunt started another weekly paper, called the
Indicator, which contained some admirable essays.
It was not well supported, however, and had but a
short lease of life.

Very soon after his release from prison, however,
Leigh Hunt had to battle with accumulated adversity. The sky became overcast with cloud on
every side, and his affairs were embarrassed. His
own health, and that of his wife, grew feeble,
while the circulation of the *Examiner* fell off.
A different policy from that which it advocated
was now dominant in Europe. Shelley, who was
living on the Continent, and who had often invited
Hunt to visit him there, renewed his request; and
a definite proposal was made by Shelley and Byron
together, that he should take up his residence in
Italy, in order that the three might advocate in
concert a line of liberal policy which could not be
so easily carried out in England. "Put your music
and your books on board a vessel," wrote Shelley,

"and you will have no more trouble." Shelley's
account of the proposal, in his *Letters from Italy*,
shows that Byron was the originator of it. He
(Byron) had first offered it to Thomas Moore, but
the proposal fell through. He then wished the
triple arrangement with himself, Shelley, and Hunt.
Shelley very generously declined to share the profit
of any scheme in which Byron and Hunt had the
chief part, wishing only to be a link of connection
between them. In a characteristic letter to Shelley,
written from Hampstead in September 1821, Hunt
begins, "We are coming," and ends, "Italy, Italy,
Italy, where we hope soon to grasp the hands of
the best friends in the world." His account of the
voyage, setting out from the Thames on November
16, 1821, and only getting as far as Dartmouth
by the 22nd of December! starting again from Ply-
mouth in May 1822, and reaching Italy in June!
—a voyage not inaptly compared to that of Ulysses
—is very graphically told in the *Autobiography*.

Nothing, however, in Hunt's career was more
injudicious, or more unfortunate, than his acceptance
of this proposal to leave England for Italy. To
work in literary co-partnership with so fitful and
unpractical a man as Byron—the periodical they
were to edit together, and which was to be called
the *Liberal*, not yet having any existence—was the
most foolish thing he ever attempted, with the possible exception of the subsequent publication of his
book on *Lord Byron and his Contemporaries*. The

Hunts landed at Leghorn in July, and there they
were joined by Shelley—a most joyous meeting.
They went together to visit Byron at Monte Nero.
Shelley had already taken the Palazzo Villa Franca
on the Lung' Arno at Pisa for him; and there the
friends all met.   Thornton Hunt recalls to us
Shelley's reading aloud some passages from Plato
to his father, and his taking leave shortly afterwards, in his yacht *Don Juan*, on the fatal voyage
to Lerici, to bring Mrs. Shelley over.   The dreadful result of that voyage is known to every one.
Shelley's death was an appalling calamity to Hunt.
He wrote to Mary Shelley, " I belong to those
whom Shelley loves, and all · that which it is
possible for me to do for them now and ever is
theirs.   I will grieve with them, endure with them,
and, if it be necessary, work for them, while I have
life."

Shelley's death was also a death-blow to the
Liberal.   Four numbers appeared, and these contained Shelley's translation of the May-Day Night
in *Faust,* and Byron's *Vision of Judgment,* with
others of his poems.   More than half of the papers,
however, were written by Hunt, although he did not
reckon them among his best efforts.   He thought
them even dull.   The truth is, that he was far
from well during all of that year.   In 1820 Byron
went from Italy to Greece, leaving Hunt at Genoa
to manage the *Liberal,* and his own affairs, as best
he could.   A radical incongruity of taste and tem-

perament already divided the two poets; but it
deserves to be recorded that—although Hunt and
Byron separated—the former described the *Vision
of Judgment* as "the best satire since the days of
Pope. Churchill's satires compared with it are as
bludgeons compared with steel of Damascus."

Hunt stayed on in Italy for two years. He
subsequently found the climate suit him well, and
during his residence he translated Radi's *Bacco in
Toscana*, and wrote a work, which he afterwards
published in England, viz. the *Religion of the Heart.*
He lived for the most part at Genoa, and his descriptions of that city are delightful. The same is
true of what he says of Florence and other Tuscan
towns, as well as of Italy in general, *e.g.*: "You
learn for the first time in this climate what *colours*
really are. No wonder it produces painters." . . .
"Italy is a wonderful nation, always at the head
of the world in some respects, great or small, and
equally full of life."

He returned to England in 1825, and lived first
at Highgate. One reason for his return was a
family difference with his brother John, as to their
respective proprietary rights in the *Examiner.* The
difference was settled by arbitration, but the decision
having been in Leigh Hunt's favour, the brothers
became estranged; and years afterwards, when
family feeling brought them together again, the
whole difference was seen, as is so often the case,
to have had no deeper root than a mutual mis-

understanding.   On his return, he says: "I took possession of my old English scenery and my favourite haunts, with a delight proportionate to the difference of their beauty from beautiful Italy. For a true lover of nature does not require the contrast of good and bad in order to be delighted; he is better pleased with harmonious variety.   He is content to wander from beauty to beauty, not losing his love for the one because he loves the other.   A variation in a fine theme of music is better than a good song after a bad one.   It retains none of the bitterness of fault-finding. . . .   In England I was at home; and in English scenery I found my old friend, 'pastoral,' still more pastoral."   He soon resumed his old literary acquaintanceships with Lamb, Campbell, and others; and made new ones.   Mary Shelley wrote telling him that, as her husband intended to leave him a legacy of £2000, she had made a will leaving him that amount.

Some lines he wrote about this time, which he called "Gipsy June," record the delights which he found in his native country in that month.   Here is an extract from them:—

> Oh! could I walk round the earth
> With a heart to share my mirth,
> With a look to love me ever,
> Thoughtful much, but sullen never,
> I could be content to see
> June and no variety,
> Loitering here and living there,
> With a book and frugal fare,

With a finer gipsy-time
And a cuckoo in the clime,
Work at morn and mirth at noon,
And sleep beneath the sacred moon.

Hunt's book on Lord Byron is certainly a regrettable performance. Although it is entirely just in much of its criticism, he should have left that criticism to others. He had been Byron's friend; and, with all his faults, Byron had been kind to him in many ways. The attack provoked natural and obvious rejoinders, under which its author winced.

Domestic sorrows crowded on Hunt at this time. One of the most touching letters he ever wrote was in September 1827, after the death of one of his boys. He said: "There is nothing worth contesting here below, except who shall be kindest to one another. There seems to be something in these moments [of loss] by which life recommences with the surviving,—I mean we seem to be beginning, in a manner, the world again, with calmer if with sadder thoughts; and, wiping our eyes, and readjusting the burden on our backs, to set out anew on our roads, with a greater wish to help and console one another."

During the next ten years Hunt's life in London was a series of failures rather than a record of successes. The *Chat of the Week* was a semi-literary, semi-artistic journal, which was suppressed by the Stamp Office very soon after its appearance, because it was published without a stamp, and yet gave " news." Nothing could better illustrate the unpracticality of Hunt's work. The *Chat of the Week* was followed in 1831 by the *Tatler*. The difficulty of combining literature with an epitome and criticism of passing events is considerable ; and it required qualities which Hunt did not possess. The *Tatler* was followed by the *London Journal*, and the *Monthly Repository*.

Each of these were literary meteors in the social and political firmament. Vivid insight, sparkling criticism, wide knowledge, and extensive sympathy, were seen in all of them ; but Hunt seems to have been incapable not only of managing business details himself, but also of knowing how others could help him. In the *Tatler* he had the assistance of Barry Cornwall ; in the *Repository* that of Walter Savage Landor ; but no amount of assistance from the most gifted writers of the day could have kept those magazines alive for any length of time. Hunt had none of the tact and the give-and-take policy which are essential in order to work with literary assistants. The *London Journal* was started in partnership with Charles Knight. It promised well, but the labour devoted to it was greater than the return. Hunt's want of a sense of the proportion of things led him to spend time on details, and in verifying them, out of all proportion to the value of the result obtained. His original works, however, were better than his serials, and they were relatively more successful. *Captain Sword and Captain Pen* (1839)—a poem in which he contrasts the achievements of war and of peace—was excellent. In 1840 he edited a collection of the plays of Wycherley, Congreve, Vanbrugh, and Farquhar; and in the same year published an original drama which he called the *Legend of Florence*. This play was for a time admitted to the stage, and was performed at Covent Garden theatre with success. It was followed by his comedy, *Lovers' Amazements*. A narrative poem, the *Palfrey*, appeared in 1842, when he became for the first time a contributor to *The Edinburgh Review*.

In 1833 Hunt had gone to live in Upper Cheyne Row, Chelsea, which was his residence for seven years. There he wrote *The Year of Honeymoons*, for the *Bull's Court Magazine* (1833). His residence in Chelsea was marked by much suffering and domestic embarrassment. He left it in 1840, and removed to Kensington, where he stayed eleven years. It was at Kensington that he began to write for the *Edinburgh*. He was not a Radical of the extreme democratic type. He disliked the exclusiveness of the Tories, but he as cordially disliked the loud utterances of the demagogue.

For more than a quarter of a century Leigh Hunt had undergone a severe struggle with misfortune and embarrassment. The annuity from the Shelley family, received by him in 1844, and a civil list pension, secured by Lord John Russell in 1847,—amounting together to £350 per annum, —enabled him, however, to devote his remaining

years to literary works, which are quite as delightful
as any of his earlier efforts. Sir Percy Shelley, the
son of his old friend, set aside for him £120 a year,
believing that in so doing he was carrying out his
father's wishes. Mary Shelley, in writing to Hunt
of her son's intentions in 1844, describes to us
" the accomplishment of one of the million generous
desires of Shelley's heart—a practical embodiment
of that poetry, which was lost to this world just as
it was becoming happily associated with its realities."
Hunt's literary work, while residing in Kensington,
was very versatile. The titles of his books will show
the fertility of his mind, and the variety of his
labour :—*Ralph Esher* (1844); *Imagination and
Fancy* (1844) ; *Wit and Humour* (1846); *Stories
of the Italian Poets* (1846); *Men, Women, and
Books* (1847); *A Jar of Honey from Mount Hybla*
(1848); *The Town, its Memorable Characters and
Events* (1848); *A Book for a Corner* (1849); the
Autobiography (1850); *Table Talk* (1851); *The Old
Court Suburb* (1855), descriptive of Kensington ;
and his *Stories in Verse*, published in the same year.
These are memorials of twelve years' literary toil
and productiveness, almost rivalling the work of
Southey. Like Southey, he was a man of letters,
whose home was his library. The *Autobiography* is
an extremely interesting psychological study. It is
less a chronicle of events than a record of the
impressions and ideas which events made upon
him. Hunt's correspondence from Kensington,

as reproduced by his son Thornton, is very interesting.

Of his daily manner of life, his son tells us that he " habitually came down too late to breakfast, and he was no sooner seated sidewise at the table than he began to read. After breakfast he repaired to his study, where he remained till he went out to take his walk. He sometimes read at dinner, though not always. At some periods of his life he would sleep after dinner ; but usually he retired from the table to read. He read at tea-time, and all the evening read or wrote "—not the most agreeable domestic companion, one should say ! " He was rather tall, as straight as an arrow, and looked slenderer than he really was. His hair was black and shining, and slightly inclined to wave ; his head was high, his forehead straight and white, his eyes black and sparkling, his general complexion dark. There was in his whole carriage and manner an extraordinary degree of life. . . . Few men were more attractive in society, whether in a large company or over the fireside. His manners were peculiarly animated ; his conversation, varied, ranging over a wide field of subjects, was moved and called forth by the response of his companion, be that companion philosopher or student, sage or boy, man or woman ; and he was equally ready for the most lively topics, or for the gravest reflections. With such freedom of manners he combined a courtesy that never failed, and a considerateness that fascinated even strangers. . . .

His seclusion arose from no dislike to society. To his very latest days he preferred to have companions with him; but it was necessary to be surrounded by his books. He used to ascribe this propensity to his two years' seclusion in prison. . . . Perhaps the mastering trait in his character was a conscientiousness, which was carried even to extremes. . . . No man ever lived who was more prepared to make thorough work with the practice of his own precepts; and his precepts were always noble in their spirit, charitable in their construction. . . . To promote the happiness of his kind, to minister to the more educated appreciation of order and beauty, to open more widely the door of the library, and more widely the window of the library looking out upon Nature,—these were the purposes that guided his studies, and animated his labour to the very last." This is high praise, but, making allowance for filial exaggeration, it is doubtless not unmerited. Another sentence from his son Thornton's preface to his father's correspondence may be quoted: "It was stedfast fidelity to the principle of hopeful industry in cultivating the best influences of life that so specially endeared Leigh Hunt even to those who never saw him personally."

There is little to record of the closing years of his life. He died at Outley in 1859.

In his literary work, with many mannerisms and some prolixity, Hunt is never dull, or prosaic, or commonplace. Great fertility of mind,

a genuine enthusiasm for literature, a happy art in
prose criticism, the note of absolute sincerity in all
he wrote, and a certain delicacy, even a felicity of
style,—all these are characteristic of Leigh Hunt.
Admirable alike as a translator, a critic, an essayist,
and a poet, his criticism is perhaps superior to his
poetry. With the single exception of his book
on Byron, it may be said that a healthy note is
invariably struck by him, and that a serene and
sympathetic spirit pervades his work from first to
last. It is the healthiness of his genius that gives,
to both his prose and his poetry, the sparkle which
they possess. I have already compared him with
Southey. As a man of letters—a writer of stories
in verse or prose—he was almost as industrious
as the laureate. Throughout his whole life his
thoughts were quite as much with the dead as with
the living; and he looked up with genuine reverence
to every great author to whom he owed a debt of
influence. *Appreciative sympathy* was the characteristic feature of his mind and heart, and it is
visible in all his works.

·WILLIAM KNIGHT.

CONTENTS.

—o—

TALES

THE FLORENTINE LOVERS.

At the time when Florence was divided into the two fierce parties of Guelfs and Ghibelines, there was great hostility between two families of the name of Bardi and Buondelmonte. It was seldom that love took place between individuals of houses so divided; but when it did, it was proportionately vehement, either because the individuals themselves were vehement in all their passions, or because love, falling upon two gentle hearts, made them the more pity and love one another, to find themselves in so unnatural a situation.

Of this latter kind was an affection that took place between a young lady of the family of Bardi, called Dianora d'Amerigo, and a youth of the other family, whose name was Ippolito. The girl was about fifteen, and in the full flower of her beauty and sweetness. Ippolito was about three years older, and looked two or three more on account of a certain gravity and deep regard in the upper part of his face. You might know by his lips that he could love well, and by his eyes that he could keep the secret. There was a likeness, as sometimes happens, between the two lovers, and perhaps this was no mean help to their passion; for as we find painters often giving their own faces to their heroes, so the more excusable vanity of lovers delights to find that resemblance in one another, which Plato said was only the divorced half of the original human being rushing into communion with the other.

Be this as it may (and lovers in those times were not
ignorant of such speculations), it needed but one sight of
Dianora d'Amerigo to make Ippolito fall violently in
love with her. It was in church on a great holiday. In
the South the church has ever been the place where
people fall in love. It is there that the young of both
sexes oftenest find themselves in each other's company.
There the voluptuous that cannot fix their thoughts on
heaven find congenial objects, more earthly, to win their
attention; and there the most innocent and devotional
spirits, voluptuous also without being aware of it, and
not knowing how to vent the grateful pleasure of their
hearts, discover their tendency to repose on beings that
can show themselves visibly sensible to their joy. The
paintings, the perfumes, the music, the Crucifix, the
mixture of pious aspiration and earthly ceremony, the
draperies, the white vestments of young and old, the
boys' voices, the giant candles, typical of the seraphic
ministrants about God's altar, the meeting of all ages and
all classes, the echoing of the aisles, the lights and
shades of the pillars and vaulted roofs, the very struggle
of daylight at the lofty windows, as if earth were at
once present and not present,—all have a tendency to
confuse the boundaries of this world and the next, and
to set the heart floating in that delicious mixture of
elevation and humility, which is ready to sympathize
with whatever can preserve to it something like its sensations, and save it from the hardness and definite folly
of ordinary life. It was in a church that Boccaccio, not
merely the voluptuous Boccaccio, who is but half known
by the half-witted, but Boccaccio, the future painter of
the Falcon and the Pot of Basil, first saw the beautiful
face of his Fiammetta. In a church, Petrarch felt the
sweet shadow fall on him that darkened his life for
twenty years after. And the fond gratitude of the local
historian of a tale of true love, has left it on record, that

it was in the church of St. Giovanni at Florence, and on the great day of Pardon, which falls on the 13th of January, that Ippolito de' Buondelmonte became enamoured of Dianora d'Amerigo.

When the people were about to leave church, Ippolito, in turning to speak to an acquaintance, lost sight of his unknown beauty. He made haste to plant himself at the door, telling his companion that he should like to see the ladies come out; for he had not the courage to say which lady. When he saw Dianora appear, he changed colour, and saw nothing else. Yet though he beheld, and beheld her distinctly, so as to carry away every feature in his heart, it seemed to him afterwards that he had seen her only as in a dream. She glided by him like a thing of heaven, drawing her veil over her head. As he had not had the courage to speak to her, he had still less the courage to ask her name; but he was saved the trouble.

"God and St. John bless her beautiful face!" cried a beggar at the door; "she always gives double of any one else."

"Curse her!" muttered Ippolito's acquaintance; "she is one of the Bardi."

The ear of the lover heard both these exclamations, and they made an indelible impression. Being a lover of books and poetry, and intimate with the most liberal of the two parties, such as Dante Alighieri (afterwards so famous) and Guido Cavalcanti, Ippolito, though a warm partizan himself, and implicated in a fierce encounter that had lately taken place between some persons on horseback, had been saved from the worst feelings attendant on political hostility, and they now appeared to him odious. He had no thought, it is true, of forgiving one of the old Bardi, who had cut his father down from his horse, but he would now have sentenced the whole party to a milder banishment than before; and to curse a female belonging to it, and that female Dianora!—he differed with the stupid fellow that had done it whenever they met afterwards.

It was a heavy reflection to Ippolito to think that he could not see his mistress in her own house. She had a father and mother living as well as himself, and was surrounded with relations. It was a heavier still that he knew not how to make her sensible of his passion; and the heaviest of all that, being so lovely, she would certainly be carried off by another husband. What was he to do? He had no excuse for writing to her; and as to serenading her under her window, unless he meant to call all the neighbours to witness his temerity, and lose his life at once in that brawling age, it was not to be thought of. He was obliged to content himself with watching, as well as he could, the windows of her abode, following her about whenever he saw her leave it, and with pardonable vanity trying to catch her attention by some little action that should give her a good thought of the stranger, such as anticipating her in giving alms to a beggar. We must even record, that on one occasion he contrived to stumble against a dog and tread on his toes, in order that he might ostentatiously help the poor beast out of the way. But his day of delight was church-day. Not a fast, not a feast did he miss; not a Sunday, nor a saint's-day.

"The devotion of that young gentleman," said an old widow lady, her aunt, who was in the habit of accompanying Dianora, "is indeed edifying; and yet he is a mighty pretty youth, and might waste his time in sins and vanities with the gayest of them." And the old widow lady sighed, doubtless out of a tender pity for the gay. Her recommendation of Ippolito to her niece's notice would have been little applauded by her family; but, to say the truth, she was not responsible. His manœuvres and constant presence had already gained Dianora's attention; and, with all the unaffected instinct of an Italian, she was not long in suspecting who it was that attracted his devotions, and in wishing very heartily that they might continue. She longed to learn who he was, but felt the same want of courage as he himself had experienced.

"Did you observe," said the aunt, one day after leaving church, "how the poor boy blushed, because he did not catch my eye? Truly, such modesty is very rare."

"Dear aunt," replied Dianora, with a mixture of real and affected archness, of pleasure and of gratitude, "I thought you never wished me to notice the faces of young men."

"Not of young men, niece," returned the aunt gravely; "not of persons of twenty-eight, or thirty, or so, nor indeed of youths in general, however young; but then this youth is very different; and the most innocent of us may look, once in a way or so, at so very modest and respectful a young gentleman. I say respectful, because when I gave him a slight courtesy of acknowledgment, or so, for making way for me in the aisle, he bowed to me with so solemn and thankful an air as if the favour had come from me, which was extremely polite: and if he is very handsome, poor boy! how can he help that? Saints have been handsome in their days—ay, and young, or their pictures are not at all like, which is impossible; and I am sure St. Dominic himself, in the wax-work— God forgive me!—hardly looks sweeter and humbler at the Madonna and Child, than he did at me and you, as we went by."

"Dear aunt," rejoined Dianora, "I did not mean to reproach you, I'm sure; but, sweet aunt, we do not know him, you know; and, you know"—

"Know!" cried the old lady; "I'm sure I know him as well as if he were my own aunt's son, which might not be impossible, though she is a little younger than myself; and if he were my own, I should not be ashamed."

"And who, then," inquired Dianora, scarcely articulat-
ing her words,—"who, then, is he?"

"Who?" said the aunt; "why, the most edifying
young gentleman in all Florence, that's who he is; and
it does not signify what he is else, manifestly being a
gentleman as he is, and one of the noblest, I warrant;
and I wish you may have no worse husband, child, when
you come to marry, though there is time enough to think
of that.   Young ladies, now-a-days, are always for knowing who everybody is, who he is, and what he is, and
whether he is this person or that person, or is of the
Grand Prior's side, or the Archbishop's side, and what
not; and all this before they will allow him to be even
handsome, which, I am sure, was not so in my youngest
days.   It is all right and proper, if matrimony is concerned, or if they are in danger of marrying below their
condition, or a profane person, or one that's hideous, or a
heretic; but to admire an evident young saint, and one
that never misses church, Sunday or saint's-day, or any
day, for aught that I see, is a thing that, if anything,
shows we may hope for the company of young saints
hereafter; and if so very edifying a young gentleman is
also respectful to the ladies, was not the blessed St.
Francis himself of his opinion in that matter?   And did
not the seraphical St. Teresa admire him the more for it?
And does not St. Paul, in his very epistles, send his best
respects to the Ladies Tryphœna and Tryphosa?   And
was there ever woman in the New Testament (with
reverence be it spoken, if we may say women of such
blessed females)—was there ever woman, I say, in the New
Testament, not even excepting Madonna and Magdalen,
who had been possessed with seven devils (which is not
so many by half as some ladies I could mention), nor
Madonna, the other poor lady, whom the unforgiving
hypocrites wanted to stone" (and here the good old lady
wept, out of a mixture of devotion and gratitude),—"was

there one of all these women, or any other, whom our Blessed Lord Himself" (and here the tears came into the gentle eyes of Dianora) "did not treat with all that sweetness, and kindness, and tenderness, and brotherly love, which, like all His other actions, and as the seraphical Father Antonio said the other day in the pulpit, proved Him to be not only from heaven, but the truest of all nobles on earth, and a natural gentleman born?"

We know not how many more reasons the good old lady would have given why all the feelings of poor Dianora's heart, not excepting her very religion, which was truly one of them, should induce her to encourage her affection for Ippolito. By the end of this sentence they had arrived at their home, and the poor youth returned to his. We say "poor" of both lovers, for by this time they had both become sufficiently enamoured to render their cheeks the paler for discovering their respective families, which Dianora had now done as well as Ippolito.

A circumstance on the Sunday following had nearly discovered them, not only to one another, but to all the world. Dianora had latterly never dared to steal a look at Ippolito, for fear of seeing his eyes upon her; and Ippolito, who was less certain of her regard for him than herself, imagined that he had somehow offended her. A few Sundays before she had sent him home bounding for joy. There had been two places empty where he was kneeling, one near him, and the other a little farther off. The aunt and the niece, who came in after him, and found themselves at the spot where he was, were perplexed which of the two places to choose; when it seemed to Ippolito, that by a little movement of her arm, Dianora decided for the one nearest him. He had also another delight. The old lady, in the course of the service, turned to her niece, and asked her why she did not sing as usual. Dianora bowed her head, and, in a minute or two afterwards, Ippolito heard the sweetest voice in the world, low indeed, almost to a whisper, but audible to him. He thought it trembled; and he trembled also. It seemed to thrill within his spirit, in the same manner that the organ thrills through the body. No such symptom of preference occurred afterwards. The ladies did not come so near him, whatever pains he took to occupy so much room before they came in, and then make room when they appeared. However, he was self-satisfied as well as ingenious enough in his reasonings on the subject, not to lay much stress upon this behaviour, till it lasted week after week, and till he never again found Dianora looking even towards the quarter in which he sat: for it is our duty to confess, that if the lovers were two of the devoutest of the congregation, which is certain, they were apt also, at intervals, to be the least attentive; and, furthermore, that they would each pretend to look towards places at a little distance from the desired object, in order that they might take in, with the sidelong power of the eye, the presence and look of one another. But for some time Dianora had ceased even to do this; and though Ippolito gazed on her the more steadfastly, and saw that she was paler than before, he began to persuade himself that it was not on his account. At length, a sort of desperation urged him to get nearer to her, if she would not condescend to come near himself; and, on the Sunday in question, scarcely knowing what he did, or how he saw, felt, or breathed, he knelt right down beside her. There was a pillar next him, which luckily kept him somewhat in the shade; and, for a moment, he leaned his forehead against the cold marble, which revived him. Dianora did not know he was by her. She did not sing; nor did the aunt ask her. She kept one unaltered position, looking upon her mass-book, and he thought she did this on purpose. Ippolito, who had become weak with his late struggles of mind, felt almost suffocated with his sensations. He was kneeling

side by side with her; her idea, her presence, her very
drapery, which was all that he dared to feel himself in
contact with, the consciousness of kneeling with her in
the presence of Him whom tender hearts implore for pity
on their infirmities, all rendered him intensely sensible of
his situation.   By a strong effort, he endeavoured to turn
his self-pity into a feeling entirely religious; but when
he put his hands together, he felt the tears ready to gush
away so irrepressibly, that he did not dare it.   At last
the aunt, who had, in fact, looked about for him, recognised
him with some surprise, and more pleasure.   She had
begun to suspect his secret; and though she knew who
he was, and that the two families were at variance, yet a
great deal of good-nature, a sympathy with pleasures of
which no woman had tasted more, and some considerable
disputes she had had lately with another old lady, her
kinswoman, on the subject of politics, determined her upon
at least giving the two lovers that sort of encouragement
which arises, not so much from any decided object we
have in view, as from a certain vague sense of benevolence, mixed with a lurking wish to have our own way.
Accordingly, the well-meaning old widow lady, without
much consideration, and loud enough for Ippolito to hear,
whispered her niece to "let the gentleman next her read
in her book, as he seemed to have forgotten to bring his
own."   Dianora, without lifting her eyes, and never
suspecting who it was, moved her book sideways, with a
courteous inclination of the head, for the gentleman to
take it.   He did so.   He held it with her.   He could
not hinder his hand from shaking; but Dianora's reflections were so occupied upon one whom she little thought
so near her, that she did not perceive it.   At length the
book tottered so in his hand that she could not but
notice it.   She turned to see if the gentleman was ill;
and instantly looked back again.   She felt that she herself was too weak to look at him, and, whispering to her

aunt, " I am very unwell," the ladies rose and made their
way out of the church. As soon as she felt the fresh air
she fainted, and was carried home; and it happened, at
the same moment, that Ippolito, unable to keep his feelings to himself, leaned upon the marble pillar at which
he was kneeling, and groaned aloud. He fancied she had
left him in disdain. Luckily for him, a circumstance of
this kind was not unknown in a place where penitents
would sometimes be overpowered by a sense of their
crimes; and though Ippolito was recognised by some,
they concluded he had not been the innocent person they
supposed. They made up their minds in future that his
retired and bookish habits, and his late evident suffering,
were alike the result of some dark offence; and among
these persons, the acquaintance who had cursed Dianora
when he first beheld her, was glad to be one; for,
without knowing his passion for her, much less her
return of it, which was more than the poor youth knew
himself, he envied him for his accomplishments and
popularity.

Ippolito dragged himself home, and after endeavouring
to move about for a day or two, and to get as far as
Dianora's abode — an attempt he gave up for fear of
being unable to come away again—was fairly obliged to
take to his bed. What a mixture of delight with
sorrow would he have felt, had he known that his
mistress was almost in as bad a state! The poor aunt,
who soon discovered her niece's secret, now found herself
in a dreadful dilemma; and the worst of it was that,
being on the female side of the love, and told by Dianora
that it would be the death of her if she disclosed it to
" *him*," or anybody connected with him, or, indeed, anybody at all, she did not know what steps to take. However, as she believed that at least death might possibly
ensue if the dear young people were not assured of each
other's love, and certainly did not believe in any such

mortality as her niece spoke of, she was about to make
her first election out of two or three measures which she
was resolved upon taking, when, luckily for the salvation
of Dianora's feelings, she was surprised by a visit from the
person whom of all persons in the world she wished to
see—Ippolito's mother.

The two ladies soon came to a mutual understanding,
and separated with comfort for their respective patients.
We need not wait to describe how a mother came to the
knowledge of her son's wishes, nor will it be necessary
to relate how delighted the two lovers were to hear of one
another, and to be assured of each other's love. But
Ippolito's illness now put on a new aspect; for the
certainty of his being welcome to Dianora, and the
easiness with which he saw his mother give way to his
inclinations, made him impatient for an interview.
Dianora was afraid of encountering him as usual in
public; and he never ceased urging his mother, till she
consented to advise with Dianora's aunt upon what was
to be done. Indeed, with the usual weakness of those
who take any steps, however likely to produce future
trouble, rather than continue a present uneasiness, she
herself thought it high time to do something for the poor
boy; for the house began to remark on his strange
conduct. All his actions were either too quick or too
slow. At one time he would start up to perform the
most trivial office of politeness, as if he were going to .
stop a conflagration; at another, the whole world might
move before him without his noticing. He would now
leap on his horse as if the enemy were at the city gates;
and next day, when going to mount it, stop on a sudden,
with the reins in his hands, and fall a-musing. "What
is the matter with the boy?" said his father, who was
impatient at seeing him so little his own master; "has he
stolen a box of jewels?" for somebody had spread a report
that he gambled, and it was observed that he never had

any money in his pocket. The truth is, he gave it all
away to the objects of Dianora's bounty, particularly to
the man who blessed her at the church door. One day,
his father, who loved a bitter joke, made a young lady,
who sat next him at dinner, lay her hand before him
instead of the plate; and, upon being asked why he did
not eat, he was very near taking a piece of it for a
mouthful. "Oh, the gallant youth!" cried the father;
and Ippolito blushed up to the eyes, which was taken
as a proof that the irony was well founded. But
Ippolito thought of Dianora's hand, how it held the book
with him when he knelt by her side; and, after a little
pause, he turned and took up that of the young lady, and
begged her pardon with the best grace in the world.
"He has the air of a prince," thought his father, "if he
would but behave himself like other young men." The
young lady thought he had the air of a lover; and as
soon as the meal was over, his mother put on her
veil and went to seek a distant relation called Gossip
Veronica.

Gossip Veronica was in a singular position with regard
to the two families of Bardi and Buondelmonti. She
happened to be related at nearly equal distances to them
both; and she hardly knew whether to be prouder of the
double relationship, or more annoyed with the evil countenances they showed her, if she did not pay great
attention to one of them, and no attention to the other.
The pride remained uppermost, as it is apt to do; and
she hazarded all consequences for the pleasure of inviting
now some of the young de' Bardi, and now some of the
young de' Buondelmonti; hinting to them when they
went away, that it would be as well for them not to say
that they had heard anything of the other family's visiting
her. The young people were not sorry to keep the matter
as secret as possible, because their visits to Gossip Veronica
were always restrained, for a long time if anything of the

sort transpired; and thus a spirit of concealment and intrigue was sown in their young minds, which might have turned out worse for Ippolito and Dianora, if their hearts had not been so good.

But here was a situation for Gossip Veronica! Dianora's aunt had been with her for some days, hinting that something extraordinary, but, as she hoped, not unpleasant, would be proposed to the good Gossip, which for her part had her grave sanction; and now came the very mother of the young Buondelmonte to explain to her what this intimation was, and to give her an opportunity of having one of each family in her house at the same time! There was a great falling off in the beatitude when she understood that Ippolito's presence was to be kept a secret from all her visitors that day, except Dianora; but she was reconciled on receiving an intimation that in future the two ladies would have no objection to her inviting whom she pleased to her house, and upon receiving a jewel from each of them as a pledge of their esteem. As to keeping the main secret, it was necessary for all parties.

Gossip Veronica, for a person in her rank of life, was rich, and had a pleasant villa at Monticelli, about half a mile from the city. Thither, on a holiday in September, which was kept with great hilarity by the peasants, came Dianora d'Amerigo de' Bardi, attended by her aunt, Madonna Lucrezia, to see, as her mother observed, that no "improper persons" were there;—and thither, before daylight, let in by Signora Veronica herself, at the hazard of her reputation and of the furious jealousy of a young vine-dresser in the neighbourhood, who loved her good things better than anything in the world except her waiting-maid, came the young Ippolito Buondelmonte de' Buondelmonti, looking, as she said, like the morning star.

The morning star hugged and was hugged with great

good-will by the kind Gossip, and then twinkled with impatience from a corner of her chamber window till he saw Dianora. How his heart beat when he beheld her coming up through the avenue! Veronica met her near the garden gate, and pointed towards the window, as they walked along. Ippolito fancied she spoke of him, but did not know what to think of it, for Dianora did not change countenance, nor do anything but smile good-naturedly on her companion, and ask her apparently some common question. The truth was, she had no suspicion he was there; though the Gossip, with much smirking and mystery, said she had a little present there for her, and such as her lady-mother approved. Dianora, whom, with all imaginable respect for her, the Gossip had hitherto treated, from long habit, like a child, thought it was some trifle or other, and forgot it next moment. Every step which Ippolito heard on the staircase he fancied was hers, till it passed the door, and never did morning appear to him at once so delicious and so tiresome. To be in the same house with her, what joy! But to be in the same house with her, and not to be able to tell her his love directly, and ask her for hers, and fold her into his very soul, what impatience and misery! Two or three times there was a knock of some one to be let in; but it was only the Gossip come to inform him that he must be patient, and that she did not know when Madonna Lucrezia would please to bring Dianora, but most likely after dinner, when the visitors retired to sleep a little. Of all impertinent things, dinner appeared to him the most tiresome and unfit. He wondered how any thinking beings, who might take a cake or a cup of wine by the way, and then proceed to love one another, could sit round a great wooden table, patiently eating of this and that nicety; and, above all, how they could sit still afterwards for a moment, and not do anything else in preference,—stand on their heads, or toss the dishes

out of the window. Then the Festival! God only knew
how happy the peasantry might choose to be, and how
long they might detain Dianora with their compliments,
dances, and songs. Doubtless, there must be many lovers
among them; and how they could bear to go jigging
about in this gregarious manner, when they must all
wish to be walking two by two in the green lanes, was
to him inexplicable. However, Ippolito was very sincere
in his gratitude to Gossip Veronica, and even did his
best to behave handsomely to her cake and wine; and
after dinner his virtue was rewarded.

After dinner, when the other visitors had separated
here and there to sleep, Dianora, accompanied by her
aunt and Veronica, found herself, to her great astonishment, in the same room with Ippolito; and, in a few
minutes after their introduction to each other, and after
one had looked this way, and the other that, and one
taken up a book and laid it down again, and both looked
out of the window, and each blushed, and either turned
pale, and the gentleman adjusted his collar, and the lady
her sleeve, and the elder ladies had whispered one
another in a corner, Dianora, less to her astonishment
than before, was left in the room with him alone. She
made a movement as if to follow them, but Ippolito said
something, she knew not what, and she remained. She
went to the window, looking very serious and pale, and
not daring to glance towards him. He intended instantly
to go to her, and wondered what had become of his fierce
impatience; but the very delay had now something
delicious in it.

At length he went up to her. She was still looking
out of the window, her eyes fixed upon the blue moun
tains in the distance, but conscious of nothing outside
the room. She had a light green and gold net on her
head, which enclosed her luxuriant hair without violence,
and seemed as if it took it up that he might admire the

white neck underneath. She felt his breath upon it; and, beginning to expect that his lips would follow, raised her hands to her head, as if the net required adjusting. This movement, while it disconcerted him, presented her waist in a point of view so impossible not to touch, that, taking it gently in both his hands, he pressed one at the same time upon her heart, and said, "It will forgive me, even for doing this." He had reason to say so, for he felt it beat against his fingers, as if it leaped. Dianora, blushing and confused, though feeling abundantly happy, made another movement with her hands, as if to remove his own, but he only detained them on either side. "Messer Ippolito," said Dianora, in a tone as if to remonstrate, though suffering herself to remain a prisoner, "I fear you must think me"—"No, no," interrupted Ippolito, "you can fear nothing that I think, or that I do. It is I that have to fear your lovely and fearful beauty, which has been ever at the side of my sick-bed, and, I thought, looked angrily upon me—upon me alone of the whole world." "They told me you had been ill," said Dianora, in a very gentle tone, "and my aunt perhaps knew that I—thought that I— Have you been very ill?" And, without thinking, she drew her left hand from under his, and placed it upon it. "Very," answered Ippolito; "do not I look so?" and, saying this, he raised his other hand, and, venturing to put it round to the left side of her little dimpled chin, turned her face towards him. Dianora did not think he appeared so ill, by a good deal, as he did in the church; but there was enough in his face, ill or well, to make her eyesight swim as she looked at him; and the next moment her head was upon his shoulder, and his lips descended, welcome, upon hers.

There was a practice in those times, generated, like other involuntary struggles against wrong, by the absurdities in authority, of resorting to marriages, or rather,

plightings of troth, made in secret, and in the eye of
Heaven. It was a custom liable to great abuse, as all
secrecies are; but the harm of it, as usual, fell chiefly on
the poor, or where the condition of the parties was
unequal. Where the families were powerful and on an
equality, the hazard of violating the engagement was, for
obvious reasons, very great, and seldom encountered; the
lovers either foregoing their claims on each other upon
better acquaintance, or adhering to their engagement the
closer for the same reason, or keeping it at the expense
of one or the other's repentance for fear of the consequences. The troth of Ippolito and Dianora was
indeed a troth. They plighted it on their knees, before
a picture of the Virgin and Child, in Veronica's bed-
room, and over a mass - book which lay open upon a
chair.

The thoughtless old ladies, Donna Lucrezia and the
other (for old age is not always the most considerate
thing in the world, especially the old age of one's aunt
and gossips), had now returned into the room where they
left the two lovers; but not before Dianora had consented
to receive her bridegroom in her own apartment at home,
that same night, by means of that other old good-natured
go-between, yclept a ladder of ropes.

Ippolito had noticed a ladder of ropes which was used
in his father's house for some domestic purposes. To say
the truth, it was an old servant, and had formerly been
much in request for the purpose to which it was now
about to be turned by the old gentleman himself. He
was indeed a person of a truly orthodox description,
having been much given to intrigue in his younger days,
being consigned over to avarice in his older, and exhibiting great submission to everything established always.
Accordingly he was considered as a personage equally
respectable for his virtues as important from his rank and
connections; and if hundreds of ladders could have risen

B

up in judgment against him, they would only have been
considered as what are called in England "wild oats;"—
wild ladders, which it was natural for every gentleman to
plant.

Ippolito's character, however, being more principled,
his privileges were not the same, and on every account
he was obliged to take great care. He waited with
impatience till midnight, and then, letting himself out of
his window, and taking the ropes under his cloak, made
the best of his way to a little dark lane which bordered
the house of the Bardi. One of the windows of Dianora's
chamber looked into the lane, the others into the garden.
The house stood in a remote part of the city. Ippolito
listened to the diminishing sound of the guitars and
revellers in the distance, and was proceeding to inform
Dianora of his arrival, by throwing up some pebbles,
when he heard a noise coming. It was some young men
taking a circuit of the more solitary streets, to purify
them, as they said, from sobriety. Ippolito slunk into
a corner. He was afraid, as the sound opened upon his
ears, that they would turn down the lane; but the hubbub
passed on. He stepped forth from his corner, and again
retreated. Two young men, loiterers behind the rest,
disputed whether they should go down the lane. One,
who seemed intoxicated, swore he would serenade "the
little foe," as he called her, if it was only to vex the old
one, and "bring him out with his cursed long sword."
"And a lecture twice as long," said the other. "Ah,
there you have me," quoth the musician; "his sword is—
a sword; but his lecture's the devil: reaches the other
side of the river—never stops till it strikes one sleepy.
But I must serenade." "No, no," returned his friend;
"remember what the Grand Prior said, and don't let us
commit ourselves in a petty brawl. We'll have it out of
their hearts some day." Ippolito shuddered to hear
such words, even from one of his own party. "Don't

tell me," said the pertinacious drunken man; "I remember what the Grand Prior said. He said, I must serenade; no, he didn't say I must serenade—but I say it; the Grand Prior said, says he,—I remember it as if it was yesterday,—he said—Gentlemen, said he, there are three good things in the world, love, music, and fighting; and then he said a cursed number of other things by no means good; and all to prove, philosophically, you rogue, that love was good, and music was good, and fighting was good, philosophically, and in a cursed number of paragraphs. So I must serenade." "False logic, Vanni," cried the other; "so come along, or we shall have the enemy upon us in a heap, for I hear another party coming, and I am sure they are none of ours." "Good again," said the musician, "love and fighting, my boy, and music; so I'll have my song before they come up." And the fellow began roaring out one of the most indecent songs he could think of, which made our lover ready to start forth and dash the guitar in his face; but he repressed himself. In a minute he heard the other party come up. A clashing of swords ensued, and, to his great relief, the drunkard and his companion were driven off. In a minute or two all was silent. Ippolito gave the signal—it was acknowledged; the rope was fixed; and the lover was about to ascend, when he was startled with a strange diminutive face, smiling at him over a light. His next sensation was to smile at the state of his own nerves; for it was but a few minutes before, that he was regretting he could not put out the lantern that stood burning under a little image of the Virgin. He crossed himself, offered up a prayer for the success of his true love, and again proceeded to mount the ladder. Just as his hand reached the window, he thought he heard other steps. He looked down towards the street. Two figures evidently stood at the corner of the lane. He would have concluded them to be the two men returned, but for their profound

silence. At last one of them said out loud, "I am certain
I saw a shadow of somebody by the lantern, and now you
find we have not come back for nothing. Who's there?"
added he, coming at the same time down the lane with
his companion. Ippolito descended rapidly, intending to
hide his face as much as possible in his hood and escape
by dint of fighting, but his foot slipped in the ropes, and
he was at the same instant seized by the strangers. The
instinct of a lover, who above all things in the world
cared for his mistress's reputation, supplied our hero with
an artifice as quick as lightning. "They are all safe,"
said he, affecting to tremble with a cowardly terror; "I
have not touched one of them." "One of what?" said
the others; "what are all safe?" "The jewels," replied
Ippolito; "let me go, for the love of God! and it shall be
my last offence, as it was my first." "By all the saints
in the calendar," exclaimed the enemy, "a Buondelmonte!
and no less a Buondelmonte than the worthy and very
magnificent Messer Ippolito Buondelmonte! Messer Ippolito, I kiss your hands. I am very much your humble
servant and thief-taker. By my faith, this will be fine
news for to-morrow."

To-morrow was indeed a heavy day to all the Buondelmonti, and as merry a one to all the Bardi, except poor
Dianora. She knew not what had prevented Ippolito
from finishing his ascent up the ladder; some interruption it must have been, but of what nature she could not
determine, nor why he had not resumed his endeavours.
It must have been nothing common. Was he known?
Was *she* known? Was it all known? And the poor
girl tormented herself with a thousand fears. Madonna
Lucrezia hastened to her the first thing in the morning
with a full, true, and particular account. Ippolito de'
Buondelmonti had been seized in coming down a rope
ladder from one of the front windows of the house, with
a great drawn sword in one hand and a box of jewels in

the other. Dianora saw the whole truth in a moment, and from excess of sorrow, gratitude, and love, fainted away. Madonna Lucrezia guessed the truth too, but was almost afraid to confess it to her own mind, much more to speak of it aloud ; and had not the news, and the bustle, and her niece's fainting furnished her with something to do, she could have fainted herself very heartily, out of pure consternation. Gossip Veronica was in a worse condition when the news reached her; and Ippolito's mother, who guessed, but too truly, as well as the others, was seized with an illness, which, joining to the natural weakness of her constitution, threw her into a stupor, and prevented her from attending to anything. The next step of Madonna Lucrezia, after seeing Dianora out of her fainting fit, and giving the household to understand that the story of the robber had alarmed her, was to go to Gossip Veronica and concert measures of concealment. The two women wept very sincerely for the poor youth, and admired his heroism in saving his mistress's honour; but, with all their good-nature, they agreed that he was quite in the right, and that it would be but just to his magnanimity and to their poor dear Dianora to keep the secret as closely. Madonna Lucrezia then returned home, to be near Dianora, and help to baffle inquiry, while Gossip Veronica kept close indoors, too ill to see visitors, and alternately praying to the saint her namesake, and taking reasonable draughts of Montepulciano.

In those days there were too many wild young men of desperate fortunes to render Ippolito's confession improbable. Besides, he had been observed of late to be always without money; reports of his being addicted to gambling had arisen; and his father was avaricious. Lastly, his groaning in the church was remembered, under pretence of pity; and the magistrate (who was of the hostile party) concluded, with much sorrow, that he must have more sins to answer for than they knew of, which in so young a man was deplorable. The old gentleman had too much reason to know that in older people it would have been nothing remarkable.

Ippolito, with a grief of heart which only served to confirm the bystanders in their sense of his guilt, waited in expectation of his sentence. He thought it would be banishment, and was casting in his mind how he could hope some day or other to get a sight of his mistress, when the word Death fell on him like a thunderbolt. The origin of a sentence so severe was but too plain to everybody; but the Bardi were uppermost that day; and the city, exhausted by some late party excesses, had but too much need of repose. Still, it was thought a dangerous trial of the public pulse. The pity felt for the tender age of Ippolito was increased by the anguish which he found himself unable to repress. "Good God!" cried he, "must I die so young? And must I never see—must I never see the light again, and Florence, and my dear friends?" And he fell into almost abject entreaties to be spared; for he thought of Dianora. But the bystanders fancied that he was merely afraid of death; and, by the help of suggestions from the Bardi partizans, their pity almost turned into contempt. He prostrated himself at the magistrate's feet; he kissed his knees; he disgusted his own father; till, finding everything against him, and smitten at once with a sense of his cowardly appearance and the necessity of keeping his mistress's honour inviolable, he declared his readiness to die like a man, and at the same time stood wringing his hands, and weeping like an infant. He was sentenced to die next day.

The day came. The hour came. The Standard of Justice was hoisted before the door of the tribunal, and the trumpet blew through the city, announcing the death of a criminal.

Ippolito issued forth from the prison, looking more like a young martyr than a criminal. He was now perfectly quiet, and a sort of unnatural glow had risen into his cheeks, the result of the enthusiasm and conscious self-sacrifice into which he had worked himself during the night. He had only prayed, as a last favour, that he might be taken through the street in which the house of the Bardi stood; for he had lived, he said, as everybody knew, in great hostility with that family, and he now felt none any longer, and wished to bless the house as he passed it. The magistrate, for more reasons than one, had no objection; the old confessor, with tears in his eyes, said that the dear boy would still be an honour to his family, as surely as he would be a saint in heaven; and the procession moved on. The main feeling of the crowd, as usual, was that of curiosity, but there were few, indeed, in whom it was not mixed with pity; and many females found the sight so intolerable, that they were seen coming away down the streets, weeping bitterly, and unable to answer the questions of those they met.

The procession now began to pass the house of the Bardi. Ippolito's face, for an instant, turned of a chalky whiteness, and then resumed its colour. His lips trembled, his eyes filled with tears; and, thinking his mistress might possibly be at the window, taking a last look of the lover that died for her, he bowed his head gently, at the same time forcing a smile, which glittered through his watery eyes. At that instant the trumpet blew its dreary blast for the second time. Dianora had already risen on her couch, listening, and asking what noise it was that approached. Her aunt endeavoured to quiet her with her excuses; but this last noise aroused her beyond control; and the good old lady, forgetting herself in the condition of the two lovers, no longer attempted to stop her. "Go," said she, "in God's name, my child, and Heaven be with you."

Dianora, her hair streaming, her eye without a tear, her cheek on fire, burst, to the astonishment of her kindred, into the room where they were all standing. She tore them aside from one of the windows with a preternatural strength, and, stretching forth her head and hands, like one inspired, cried out, "Stop! stop! it is my Ippolito! my husband!" And, so saying, she actually made a movement as if she would have stepped to him out of the window; for everything but his image faded from her eyes. A movement of confusion took place among the multitude. Ippolito stood rapt, on the sudden, trembling, weeping, and stretching his hands towards the window, as if praying to his guardian angel. The kinsmen would have prevented her from doing anything further; but, as if all the gentleness of her character was gone, she broke from them with violence and contempt, and, rushing downstairs into the street, exclaimed, in a frantic manner, "People! dear God! countrymen! I am a Bardi; he is a Buondelmonte; he loved me; and that is the whole crime!" and, at these last words, they were locked in each other's arms.

The populace now broke through all restraint. They stopped the procession; they bore Ippolito back again to the seat of the magistracy, carrying Dianora with him; they described in a peremptory manner the mistake; they sent for the heads of the two houses; they made them swear a treaty of peace, amity, and unity; and, in half an hour after the lover had been on the road to his death, he set out upon it again, the acknowledged bridegroom of the beautiful creature by his side.

Never was such a sudden revulsion of feeling given to a whole city. The women who had retreated in anguish came back the gayest of the gay. Everybody plucked all the myrtles they could find, to put into the hands of those who made the former procession, and who now formed a singular one for a bridal; but all the young women fell in with their white veils; and, instead of the funeral dirge, a song of thanksgiving was chanted. The very excess of their sensations enabled the two lovers to hold up. Ippolito's cheeks, which seemed to have fallen away in one night, appeared to have plumped out again faster; and if he was now pale instead of high-coloured, the paleness of Dianora had given way to radiant blushes which made up for it. He looked, as he ought,—like the person saved; she, like the angelic saviour.

Thus the two lovers passed on, as if in a dream tumultuous but delightful. Neither of them looked on the other; they gazed hither and thither on the crowd, as if in answer to the blessings that poured upon them; but their hands were locked fast; and they went like one soul in a divided body.

THE BEAU MISER, AND WHAT HAPPENED TO HIM AT BRIGHTON.

THERE was a man of the name of Kennedy, who was well known to the people of fashion in our childhood, but with whose origin, pretensions, or way of living, nobody was acquainted. That he was rich was certain, for he wore the most precious stones on his fingers, and was known to keep a great deal of money at a banker's. He was evidently very fond of the upper circles, and for some time was admitted into their parties. He was now and then at the opera; oftener at routs and balls; and always went to Court, when he could get there.

We have heard him described. He was a very spare man, not much above thirty, of the middle height, with eyes a little shut and lowering, a small nose, and a very long chin. But he dressed extremely well; had a softness of manners amounting to the timid; and paid exceeding homage to every person and thing of any fashionable repute.

All this, for some time, procured him a good reception; but at last people began to wonder that, though he got invitations from everybody, he gave none himself. It was not even known that he ever made a present, or had a person home with him even to a luncheon or a cup of tea. Twice he gave a great dinner, at which it was owned there was a profusion of everything; but, though it was not at a tavern, it was not at his own place of abode; and the people of the house knew nothing about him.

All this gave rise to a suspicion that he was a miser; and people soon contrived to have pretty strong proofs of it. In vain the least bashful of his acquaintances admired the beauty of his numerous rings; in vain others applied to him for loans of money, some by way of trial, and others from necessity; in vain his movements were watched by the more idle and gossiping; in vain hints were thrown out and questions asked, and his very footsteps pursued. His rings were all keepsakes; he always had no money just then; he referred for his lodgings to a hotel where he occasionally put up, perhaps for that very purpose; and a curious fellow, who endeavoured to follow him home one night, was led such an enormous round through street after street, and even suburb after suburb, that he gave up the point with an oath.

After this his acquaintance grew more and more shy of him. They gradually left off inviting him to their houses, some from mercenary disappointment, some from a more generous disgust, others because the rest did so; and at last, just after a singular adventure which happened to him at Brighton, he totally disappeared.

Everybody took him for a madman on that occasion. He had not been at the place above a day or two, and was seen during that time walking about the beach very thoughtfully, with an air of sorrow, owing, it was conjectured, to his having put himself to the expense of travelling without obtaining his expected repayment, for nobody invited him. But be this as it may, he was seen, one morning, running in the most violent manner across the Steyne, and crying out "Fire!" His face was as pale as death; he seemed every now and then, in the midst of his haste, to be twitched and writhed up with a sort of convulsion; and his hat having blown off by the wind, no wonder he was thought seized with a frenzy. Yet when he arrived at his lodging, there was no fire, nor even a symptom of it.

The suspicion of his being out of his wits was rendered still stronger by a rumour which took place the same day; for the servants of the family which he used to visit most, and in which he was paying his addresses to a young lady, declared that not many minutes after the uproar about the fire, he came to their master's house, through the by-ways, with a coalheaver's hat on. And the assertion was confirmed by some tradesmen who had seen him pass, and by some boys who had followed him with shouts and nicknames.

The mystery supplied the world with talk for more than a week, when at length it was explained through the family we have just mentioned. Kennedy, it seems, was really a miser, and had inherited the estates of a third or fourth cousin, whose name he took. He had had little or no acquaintance with his kinsman before he found himself his heir. His father was a petty overseer somewhere or other at a distance from London; and the cousin whose estates he succeeded to, was the son of a general officer in the East India Service. The cousin had had a son whom he sent abroad to follow his grandfather's profession; but, receiving the news of his death a little before his own, he sickened the faster, and, being in a state of great weakness and despondency, left his estates to his next heir, without having much heart to inquire what sort of person he was. The fortunate young overseer quitted his shop immediately, and, coming up to town, had occasion to wait on a young lady, to whom his cousin's son had been attached. It was to give her a lock of her lover's hair, and a gold watch which his father sent her with it in token of his own regard for her. A little note accompanied them, which she showed one day with the tears in her eyes, though she was then happy enough :—

"I leave you no money, my dear child. I am dying, and you are wealthy enough, and money is not the thing wanted by either of us. Just before I received the news of my poor boy's death, he sent me this lock of his hair for you, to show you how glossy and healthy. . . . Excuse me, my love; the tears blot out what I was going to write; and so they ought. But I know well enough that the kind-hearted, generous girl who was worthy of him, will think I pay her a greater compliment in leaving her only what belonged to her Charles, than if I had sent her all the money which he ever possessed. The next heir, I am told, is a good young man, and he is poor, with a number of poor relations. The watch was Charles's when a boy. My father gave it me, and I to him, and he used to say that he would— God in heaven bless you, my poor, sweet girl! prays your old   CHARLES KENNEDY."

The consequence of the new heir's visiting Miss Cameron was his falling in love with her—if such a miser as he turned out to be could be said to fall in love. But though she could not help pitying him at first, as she afterwards said, it was only on account of his strange habits, which she soon detected, and which, she saw, would make him ridiculous and unhappy wherever he went. He soon tired and disgusted her. After a very unequivocal repulse one day, which seemed to make him prodigiously thoughtful and unhappy, he came in the evening, with a mixture of cold triumph and uneasiness in his aspect, at which Miss Cameron said she could hardly forbear laughing, even from a feeling of bitterness. She saw that he expected to make an impression on her of some sort; and so he did, for, taking an opportunity of speaking to her alone, he drew out of his waistcoat pocket, with much anxiety, the first present his wealth had ever made her, a fine diamond pin —a very fine one, she confessed it was. It was clear that he thought this irresistible; and nothing could exceed his surprise when she refused him peremptorily once more and the pin with him. She owned that her sense of the

ridiculous so far surmounted her other feelings as to give
her a passing inclination to accept the diamond, as she
knew very well that he had reckoned on its returning to
him by marriage.   But her contempt recovered itself;
and her disgust and scorn were completed by his mention-
ing the words " Mrs. Kennedy," which brought so noble
and lamented a contrast before her, and visited her so
fiercely with a sense of what she had lost, that she quitted
the room with a sort of breathless and passionate murmur.

This was but the day before the adventure of the fire.
She was almost inclined on the latter occasion to think
him mad, as others did, especially when he once more
appeared before her, shuffling in a ludicrous manner, with
something in his hand which he wished to conceal, and
which she found afterwards was the hat.   He would not
have ventured to appear before her again; but the truth
was, that her father, who was but an ordinary sort of
monied man, and not very delicate, did not interfere as he
ought to prevent her being thus persecuted.   But not only
was the mystery explained to her next day; it was the
most important one of both their lives.

On the morning when Kennedy was frightened by the
fire, he was standing very thoughtfully by the Ship Inn,
near the sea-side, when he was suddenly clapped by somebody on the shoulder.   He turned round with a start, and
saw a face which he knew well enough.   It was that of a
gentleman who, riding once, when a youth, by the place
where he lived, had saved him from drowning in a little
piece of water.   Some mischievous companions had hustled
him into it, not knowing how far their malicious joke
might have gone.   When he was pulled out, and had
recovered from his first fright, he thanked the young
gentleman in as warm a way as he could express; and,
taking fourpence-halfpenny out of a little leathern bag,
offered it him as a proof of his gratitude; the young
gentleman declining it with a good-natured smile, thinking

the offer to be the effect of mere simplicity; but the lads who were looking on, and who had helped to get him out when told of the danger, burst out into taunting reproaches of the fellow's meanness, and informed his preserver that he had at least three shillings in the other fob of his leathern bag, besides silver pennies. So saying, they wrenched it out of his hands, in spite of his crying and roaring; and one of them, opening it, shook out, together with the water, five shillings in sixpences, and the silver pennies to boot. The young gentleman laughed and blushed at the same instant, and, not knowing well what to do, for he longed to give the young miser a lesson, and yet thought it would be unjust to share the money between the lads, who had nearly drowned him, said to him, "I am not the only one to whom you are indebted for being saved, for it was the screams of those little girls there which brought me to you, and so, you know," continued he, with a laugh, which the others joined, "they ought to be rewarded as well as myself. Don't you think so?" "Yes, sir," mumbled the young hunks, half frightened, and half sulky. The young gentleman then divided all the silver but a shilling among the little girls, who dropped him a hundred curtseys; and, giving the fourpence-halfpenny to the boy who had been most forward in helping, and least noisy in accusing, rode off amidst the shouts of the rest.

It was the first time the two had met since. "I believe," said the stranger with a sort of smile, "I have had the honour of meeting you before?"

"The same, sir," answered the other, "at your service. I believe, sir—I think—I am sure "—

"Yes, sir," returned the stranger, "it was I who played you that trick with your bag of sixpences."

"Oh, dear sir," rejoined the other, half ashamed at the recollection, and admiring the fashionable air of his preserver, "I am sure I had no reason to complain. Been abroad, sir, I presume, by a certain brownness of complexion, not at all unbecoming?"

"Yes, sir," said the gentleman, smiling more and more; "I hope you have been as lucky at home as some of us who go abroad?"

"Why, yes, sir; I have a pretty fortune, thank Heaven, though at present—just now"—

"Oh, my dear sir," interrupted the stranger, with a peculiar sort of look, in which animal spirits and a sense of the ridiculous seemed predominant, "I can wait—I can wait."

"Can wait, sir?"

"Yes, sir; I know what you mean : you have a sort of liberal yearning, which incites you to make me an acknowledgment for the little piece of service I was enabled to render you. But I am not poor, sir; and, indeed, should decline such a thing from any but a man of fortune, and upon any other score than that of relieving his own feelings; so that I can very easily wait, you know, for an opportunity more convenient to you, when I shall certainly not hesitate to accept a trifle or so,—a brilliant—or a diamond seal,—or any little thing of that sort."

"Bless me, sir! you are very good. But you see, sir, you—you—see — I am very sorry, sir, but no doubt—in the fashionable circles—but at present I have an engagement."

"Ah, sir," said the stranger, with a careless air, and giving him a thump on the shoulder which made him jump, "pray do not let me interrupt you. I only hope you are not lodging in — in — what's the name of the street?"

"North Street?—I tried the Steyne, but"—

"Ah! North Street."

"Why so, sir, pray?" asked the other, with an air of increasing fidget and alarm, and looking about him.

"Why, sir, an accident has just happened there."

"An accident! Oh, my dear sir, you know those sort of things cannot be helped."

"No, sir; but it's a very awkward sort of accident, and the lodger, I understand, is from home."

"How, sir,—what lodger—what accident? What is it you mean, dear sir?"

"Why, look there, my good friend, look there!—there they are removing them—removing the goods; a fire has broken out."

Kennedy seemed petrified. There was a great crowd in the street to which the stranger pointed, occasioned by a scuffle with a puppet-show man. The boys were shouting, and the little moveable Punch-theatre tumbled about in the top of the fray, looking in the distance like a piece of bedstead, or some other sort of goods.

"There they are," continued the stranger; "now they take away the bedstead—now they bring the engines—now they are conveying out something else. The smoke—don't you see the smoke?"

"O Lord! I do, I do!" exclaimed the miser, who saw nothing but his own imagination, and his boxes of brilliants carried off. He turned deadly pale, then red, then pale again, and, seeming to summon up a convulsive strength, sprang off with all his might, and rushed across the Steyne like a madman.

When he arrived at his lodgings he found the street empty, and the house quite cool, and, being anxious to make the best and quickest of his story with his mistress and her father, went there as instantly as possible; but first, in a great hurry, he borrowed a hat of his landlord, who, half in haste also, and half in joke, gave him one of his coal-meter's, which he unconsciously put on.

Scarcely had he astonished the young lady, and set his foot again out of doors, than he encountered the stranger

who played him the joke. His first impulse was to be
very angry, but he wanted courage to complain, and,
recollecting his first adventure with his preserver, would
have passed by under pretence of not seeing him. He
was stopped, however, by the elbow.

"My dear sir," exclaimed the stranger, with his old
smile, "I rejoice to find that all was safe.   Pray,"
continued he, changing his aspect, and looking grave and
earnest, "you know the various families at Brighton; I
have found just now that there is one here that will save
me a journey to London — the name is Cameron — can
you tell me where they live? There is a person of the
name of Kennedy also, who, I understand, is here too;
but that doesn't signify at present; pray tell me if you
know where the Camerons are?"

"There, there, sir," answered the other, almost frightened out of his wits, and anxious to get away;—"there,
two or three doors off."

The stranger dropped his arm in an instant, and in an
instant knocked at the door.   With almost as much
speed poor Kennedy returned to his lodging. We know
not what he was thinking about, but he surprised the
landlord with his exceeding hurry to be gone; and gone
he would have been much sooner than he was, if it had
not been for a dispute about a bill, which he was in the
midst of contesting when a footman came from the
Camerons requesting his presence immediately upon
important business.

The poor miser's mortifications were not to cease by
the way. The footman, upon being admitted to him,
turned out to be the same person who was riding as a
footboy behind the young gentleman when the latter
came up to help him out of the water.

"Good God, sir!" says the man, who had something
of his master's look about him; "I beg your pardon, but are
you the Mr. Kennedy who has got my master's fortune?"

The other had been agitated already; but the whole truth seemed to come upon him as fast as if it would squeeze the breath out of his body, and, muttering a few indistinct words, he motioned to the footman that he would go with him. He then looked about in a bewildered manner for his hat, and, taking up the coal-heaver's, which, in spite of some other feelings, made the footman turn aside to hold his own to his mouth, he dropped it down again, and, turning as pale as a sheet, fell back into a chair.

The footman, after administering a glass of water, called up the landlord, and begging him, in a respectful manner, to take care of the gentleman, to whom he would fetch his master, hastened back to inform the latter, who, comparing the accounts of his old acquaintance with the Camerons', has already guessed the secret, to the great wondering of all parties.

You have, doubtless, been guessing with him; and it is easy to fancy the remainder. There had been a false return of the young soldier's death in accounts from the army in India. He had been taken prisoner, and when he obtained his liberty, learnt, with great grief and surprise, that his father had died under the impression that he was dead also, and had left his property to unknown heirs. The property would have been a very secondary thing, in his mind, for its own sake, and he was aware he could regain it, but his father's death afflicted him much, particularly under all the circumstances; and he felt so much anguish at the thought of what Miss Cameron must suffer, to whom he had plighted his faith but two years before, that it was with difficulty he held up against grief, and hurry, and a burning climate, so as not to fall into an illness; the very fear of which, and the delay that it would cause, was almost enough to produce it,—not to mention that it was possible his mistress, believing him dead, might too quickly enter into

engagements with another, though he did not suppose it
very likely. But we need not dwell upon these matters.
He found his mistress the same as ever; shed sweet-
bitter tears with her for his father, his own supposed
loss, and her grieving constancy; and, regaining his
fortune, settled an income upon the poor miser; which
the latter, remembering the adventure of the drowning,
could hardly believe possible.

JACK ABBOT'S BREAKFAST.

Animal Spirits—A Dominie Sampson Drawn from the Life—Many Things Fall Out between the (Breakfast) Cup and the Lip—A Magistrate Drawn from the Life—Is Breakfast ever to be Taken, or is it not?—The Question Answered.

" WHAT a breakfast I *shall* eat! " thought Jack Abbott, as he turned into Middle Temple Lane, towards the chambers of his old friend and tutor Goodall. "How I shall swill the tea! how cram down the rolls (especially the inside bits)! how apologise for 'one cup more!' But Goodall is an excellent old fellow—he won't mind. To be sure, I'm rather late. The rolls, I'm afraid, will be cold, or double-baked; but anything will be delicious. If I met a baker, I could eat his basket."

Jack Abbott was a good-hearted, careless fellow, who had walked that morning from Hendon, to breakfast with his old friend by appointment, and afterwards consult his late father's lawyer. He was the son of a clergyman more dignified by rank than by solemnity of manners, but an excellent person too, who had some remorse in leaving a family of sons with little provision, but comforted himself with reflecting that he had gifted them with good constitutions and cheerful natures, and that they would "find their legs somehow," as indeed they all did; for very good legs they were, whether to dance away care with, or make love with, or walk seven miles to breakfast with, as Jack had done that morning; and so they all got on accordingly, and clubbed up a comfortable maintenance for the

prebendary's widow, who, sanguine and loving as her
husband, almost wept out of a fondness of delight whenever she thought either of their legs or their affection.
As to Jack himself, he was the youngest, and at present
the least successful, of the brotherhood, having just
entered upon a small tutorship in no very rich family;
but his spirits were the greatest in the family (which is
saying much), and if he was destined never to prosper so
much as any of them in the ordinary sense, he had a
relish of every little pleasure that presented itself, and a
genius for neutralizing the disagreeable, which at least
equalized his fate with theirs.

Well, Jack Abbott has arrived at the door of his friend's
room.   He knocks; and it is opened by Goodall himself,
a thin, grizzled personage, in an old greatcoat instead of a
gown, with lanthorn jaws, shaggy eyebrows, and a most
bland and benevolent expression of countenance.   Like
many who inhabit Inns of Court, he was not a lawyer.
He had been a tutor all his life; and as he led only a
book-existence, he retained the great blessing of it—a
belief in the best things which he believed when young.
The natural sweetness of his disposition had even gifted
him with a politeness of manners which many a better-
bred man might have envied; and though he was a
scholar more literal than profound, and, in truth, had not
much sounded the depths of anything but his tea-caddy,
yet an irrepressible respect for him accompanied the
smiling of his friends; and mere worldly men made no
grosser mistake than in supposing they had a right to
scorn him with their uneasy satisfactions and misbelieving
success.   In a word, he was a sort of better-bred Dominie
Sampson—a Goldsmith, with the genius taken out of him,
but the goodness left—an angel of the dusty heaven of
bookstalls and the British Museum.

Unfortunately for the hero of our story, this angel of
sixty-five, unshaved, and with stockings down at heel,

had a memory which could not recollect what had been told him six hours before, much less six days. Accordingly, he had finished his breakfast, and given his cat the remaining drop of milk, long before his (in every sense of the word) late pupil presented himself within his threshold. Furthermore, besides being a lanthorn-jawed cherub, he was very short-sighted, and his ears were none of the quickest; so in answer to Jack's "Well—eh—how d'ye do, my dear sir?—I'm afraid I'm very late," he stood holding the door open with one hand, shading his winking eyes with the other, in order to concentrate their powers of investigation, and, in the blandest tones of *unawareness*, saying,—

"Ah, dear me—I'm very—I beg pardon—I really—pray who is it I have the pleasure of speaking to?"

"What! don't you recollect me, my dear sir? Jack Abbott. I met you, you know, and was to come and"—

"Oh! Mr. Abbott, is it? What—ah—Mr. James Abbott, no doubt—or Robert. My dear Mr. Abbott, to think I should not see you!"

"Yes, my dear sir; and you don't see now that it is Jack, and not James? Jack, your last pupil, who plagued you so in the Terence."

"Not at all, sir, not at all; no Abbott ever plagued me;—far too good and kind people, sir. Come in, pray; come in and sit down, and let's hear all about the good lady your mother, and how you all get on, Mr. James."

"Jack, my dear sir, Jack; but it doesn't signify. An Abbot is an Abbot, you know; that is, if he is but fat enough."

Goodall (very gravely, not seeing the joke). "Surely you are quite fat enough, my dear sir, and in excellent health. And how is the good lady your mother?"

"Capitally well, sir (*looking at the breakfast-table*). I'm quite rejoiced to see that the breakfast-cloth is not removed; for I'm horribly late, and fear I must have put you out; but don't you take any trouble, my good sir. The kettle, I see, is still singing on the hob. I'll cut myself a piece of bread and butter immediately; and you'll let me scramble beside you as I used to do, and look at a book, and talk with my mouth full."

Goodall. "Ay, ay; what! you have come to break-fast, have you, my kind boy? That is very good of you, very good indeed. Let me see—let me see—my laundress has never been here this morning, but you won't mind my serving you myself—I have everything at hand."

Abbott (apart, and sighing, with a smile). "He has forgotten all about the invitation! Thank ye, my dear sir, thank ye. I would apologise, only I know you wouldn't like it; and, to say the truth, I'm very hungry—hungry as a hunter—I've come all the way from Hendon."

"Bless me! have you indeed? and from Wendover too? Why, that is a very long way, isn't it?"

"Hendon, sir, not Wendover—Hendon."

"Oh, Endor—ah—dear me (*smiling*), I didn't know there was an Endor in England. I hope there is—he! he! —no witch there, Mr. Abbott; unless she be some very charming young lady with a fortune."

"Nay, sir, I think you can go nowhere in England and not meet with charming young ladies."

"Very true, sir, very true. England—what does the poet say? something about 'manly hearts to guard the fair.' You have no sisters, I think, Mr. Abbott?"

"No; but plenty of female cousins."

"Ah! very charming young ladies, I've no doubt, sir. Well, sir, there's your cup and saucer, and here's some fresh tea, and "—

"I beg pardon," interrupted Jack, who, in a fury of hunger and thirst, was pouring out what tea he could find in the pot, and anxiously looking for the bread; "I can do very well with this—at any rate to begin with."

"Just so, sir," balmily returned Goodall. "Well, sir, but I am sorry to see—eh, I really fear—certainly the cat —eh—what are we to do for milk? I'm afraid I must make you wait till I step out for some; for this laundress, when once she"—

"Don't stir, I beg you!" ejaculated our hero; "don't think of it, my dear sir. I can do very well without milk—I can indeed—I *often* do without milk."

This was said out of an intensity of a sense to the contrary; but Jack was anxious to make the old gentleman easy.

"Well," quoth Goodall, "I have met with such instances, to be sure; and very lucky it is, Mr.—a—John—James, I should say—that you do not care for milk; though I confess, for my part, I cannot do without it. But, bless me! heyday! well, if the sugar-basin, dear me! is not empty. Bless my soul! I'll go instantly—it is but as far as Fleet Street—and my hat, I think, must be under those pamphlets."

"Don't think of such a thing, pray, dear sir!" cried Jack, half leaping from his chair, and tenderly laying his hand on his arm. "You may think it odd; but sugar, I can assure you, is a thing I don't *at all* care for. Do you know, my dear Mr. Goodall, I have often had serious thoughts of leaving off sugar, owing to the slave trade?"

"Why that, indeed"—

"Yes, sir; and probably I should have done it, had not so many excellent men, yourself among them, thought fit to continue the practice, no doubt after the greatest reflection. However, what with these perhaps foolish doubts, and the indifference of my palate to sweets, sugar is a mere drug to me, sir—a mere drug."

"Well, but"—

"Nay, dear sir, you will distress me if you say another word upon the matter—you will indeed; see how I drink." (And here Jack made as if he took a hasty

gulp of his milkless and sugarless water.)   "The bread,
my dear sir—the bread is all I require ; just that piece
which you were going to take up.   You remember how I
used to stuff bread, and fill the book I was reading with
crumbs?   I dare say the old Euripides is bulging out with
them now."

"Well, sir—ah—em—ah—well, indeed, you're very
good, and, I'm sure, very temperate ; but, dear me!—well,
this laundress of mine—I must certainly get rid of her
thieving—rheumatism, I should say ; but *butter!* I vow I
do not"—

"BUTTER!" interrupted our hero, in a tone of the
greatest scorn.   "Why, I haven't eaten *butter* I don't
know when.   Not a step, sir, not a step.   And now, let
me tell you, I must make haste, for I've got to lunch with
my lawyer, and he'll expect me to eat something ; and in
fact I'm so anxious, and feel so hurried, that now I have
eaten a good piece of my hunk, I must be off, my good
sir—I must, indeed."

To say the truth, Jack's hunk was a good three days
old, if an hour ; and so hard,[1] that even his hunger and
fine teeth could not find it in the hearts of them to relish
it with the cold slop ; so he had made up his mind to
seek the nearest coffee-house as fast as possible, and there
have the heartiest and most luxurious breakfast that could
make amends for his disappointment.   After reconciling
the old gentleman, however, to his departure, he sat a
little longer, out of decency and respect, listening, with a
benevolence equal to his appetite, to the perusal of a long
passage in Cowley, which Goodall had been reading when
he arrived, and the recitation of which was prolonged by

[1] People of regular, comfortable lives, breakfasts, and conveniences,
must be cautious how they take pictures like these for caricatures.
The very letter of the adventure above described, with the exception
of a few words, has actually happened.   And so, with the same
difference, has that of the sheep and hackney-coach, narrated in the
Disasters of Carfington Blundell.

the inflictor with admiring repetitions, and bland luxuriations of comment.

"What an excellent good fellow he is!" thought Jack; "and what a very unshaved face he has, and neglectful washerwoman!"

At length he found it the more easy to get away, inasmuch as Goodall said he was himself in the habit of going out about that time to a coffee-house to look at the papers, before he went the round of his pupils; but he had to shave first, and would not detain Mr. Abbott, if he *must* go.

Being once more out of doors, our hero rushes back like a tiger into Fleet Street, and plunges into the first coffee-house in sight.

"Waiter!"

"*Yessir.*"

"Breakfast immediately. Tea, black and green, and all that."

"*Yessir.* Eggs and toast, sir?"

"By all means."

"*Yessir.* Any ham, sir?"

"Just so, and instantly."

"*Yessir.* Cold fowl, sir?"

"Precisely; and no delay."

"*Yessir.* Anchovy, perhaps, sir?"

"By all—eh?—no, I don't care for anchovy—but pray bring what you like; and above all, make haste, my good fellow—no delay—I'm as hungry as the devil."

"*Yessir*—coming directly, sir." ("Good chap, and great fool," said the waiter to himself.) "Like the newspaper, sir?"

"Thankye. Now, for heaven's sake"—

"*Yessir*—immediately, sir—everything ready, sir."

"Everything ready!" thought Jack. "Cheering sound! Beautiful place a coffee-house! Fine *English* place—everything so snug and at hand—so comfortable—so

easy—have what you like, and without fuss. What a
breakfast I *shall* eat! And the paper too—hum, hum
(*reading*)—Horrid Murder—Mysterious Affair—Express
from Paris—Assassination—intense. Bless me! what
horrible things—how very comfortable! What toast
I— Waiter!"

Waiter, from a distance—" *Yessir*—coming, sir."

In a few minutes everything is served up—the toast
hot and rich—eggs plump—ham huge, etc.

"You've another slice of toast getting ready," said Jack.
" *Yessir*."

"Let the third, if you please, be thicker; and the
fourth."

"Glorious moment!" inwardly ejaculated our hero.
He had doubled the paper conveniently, so as to read the
"Express from Paris" in perfect comfort; and, before he
poured out his tea, he was in the act of putting his hand
to one of the inner pieces of toast, when—awful visitation!—whom should he see passing the window, with
the evident design of turning into the coffee-house, but
his too-carelessly and swiftly-shaved friend Goodall. He
was coming, of course, to read the papers. Yes, such
was his horrible inconvenient practice, as Jack had too
lately heard him say; and this, of all coffee-houses in the
world, was the one he must needs go to.

What was to be done? Jack Abbott, who was not at
all a man of manœuvres, much less gifted with that sort
of impudence which can risk hurting another's feelings,
thought there was nothing left for him but to bolt; and
accordingly, after hiding his face with the newspaper
till Goodall had taken up another, he did so as if a
bailiff was after him, brushing past the waiter who had
brought it him, and who had just seen another person
out. The waiter, to his astonishment, sees him plunge
into another coffee-house over the way; then hastens
back to see if anything be missing; and, finding all safe,

concludes he must have run over to speak to some friend, perhaps upon some business suddenly called to mind, especially as he seemed "such a hasty gentleman."

Meanwhile, Jack, twice exasperated with hunger, but congratulating himself that he had neither been seen by Goodall, nor tasted a breakfast unpaid for, has ordered precisely such another breakfast, and has got the same newspaper, and seated himself as nearly as possible in the very same sort of place.

"*Now*," thought he, "I am beyond the reach of chance. No such ridiculous hazard as this can find me here. Goodall cannot read the papers in two coffee-houses. By Jove! was there ever a man so hungry as I am? What a breakfast I *shall* eat!"

Enter breakfast served up as before—toast hot and rich—eggs plump—ham huge, etc. Homer himself, who was equally fond of a repetition and a good meal, would have liked to re-describe it. "Glorious moment!" Jack has got the middle bit of toast in his fingers, precisely as before, when, happening to cast his eye at the door, he sees the waiter of the former coffee-house pop his head in, look him full in the face, and as suddenly withdraw it. Back goes the toast on the plate; up springs poor Abbott to the door, and, hardly taking time to observe that his visitant is not in sight, rushes forth for the second time, and makes out as fast as he can for a third coffee-house.

"Am I *never* to breakfast?" thought he. "Nay, breakfast I will. People can't go into three coffee-houses on purpose to go out again. But suppose the dog should have seen me! Not likely, or I should have seen him again. He may have gone and told the people; but I've hardly got out of the second coffee-house before I've found a third. Bless this confounded Fleet Street! Most convenient place for diving in and out coffee-houses! Dr. Johnson's street—'High tide of human existence'—ready breakfasts. What a breakfast I *will* eat!"

Jack Abbott, after some delay, owing to the fulness of the room, is seated as before—the waiter has *yessir'd* to their mutual content—the toast is done—Homeric repetition—eggs plump, ham huge, etc.

"By Hercules, who was the greatest twist of antiquity, what a breakfast I *will*, shall, must, and have now certainly *got* to eat! I could not have stood it any longer. Now, *now*, ᴋow, is the moment of moments."

Jack Abbott has put his hand to the toast.

Unluckily, there were three pair of eyes which had been observing him all the while from over the curtain of the landlord's little parlour; to wit, the waiter's of the first tavern, the waiter's of the second, and the landlord's of the third. The two waiters had got in time to the door of tavern the second, to watch his entrance into tavern the third; and both communicating the singular fact to the landlord of the same, the latter resolved upon a certain mode of action, which was now to develop itself.

"Well," said the first waiter, "I've seen strange chaps in my time in coffee-houses; but this going about, ordering breakfasts which a man doesn't eat, beats everything! and he hasn't taken a spoon or anything as I see. He doesn't seem to be looking about him, you see; he reads the paper as quiet as an old gentleman."

"Just for all the world as he did in our house," said the second waiter; "and he's very pleasant and easy-like in his ways."

"Pleasant and easy!" cried the landlord, whose general scepticism was sharpened by gout and a late loss of spoons. "Yes, yes; I've seen plenty of your pleasant and easy fellows—palavering rascals, who come, hail-fellow-well-met, with a bit of truth mayhap in their mouths, just to sweeten a parcel of lies and swindling. 'Twas only last Friday I lost a matter of fifty shillings' worth of plate by such a chap; and I vowed I'd nab the next. Only let him eat one mouthful, just to give a right o' search, and see how I'll pounce on him."

But Jack didn't eat one mouthful! No; not even though he was uninterrupted, and really had now a fair field before him, and was in the very agonies of hunger. It so happened that he had hardly taken up the piece of toast above mentioned, when, with a voluntary (as it seemed) and strange look of misgiving, *he laid it down again !*

"I'm blessed if he's touched it, after all!" said waiter the first. "Well, this beats everything! See how he looks about him! He's feeling in his pockets, though.".

"Ah, look at that!" says the landlord. "He's a precious rascal, depend on't. I shouldn't wonder if he whisked something out of the next box; but we'll nab him. Let us go to the door."

Mr. Abbott—Jack seems too light an appellation for one under his circumstances—looked exceedingly distressed. He gazed at the toast with a manifest sigh; then glanced cautiously around him; then again felt his pockets. At length he positively showed symptoms of quitting his seat. It was clear he did not intend eating a bit of this breakfast, any more than of the two others.

"I'll be hanged if he ain't going to bolt again!" said the waiter.

"Nab him!" said the landlord.

The unhappy, and, as he thought, secret Abbott makes a desperate movement to the door, and is received in the arms of this triple alliance.

"Search his pockets!" cried the landlord.

"Three breakfasts, and ne'er a one of 'em eaten!" cried first waiter.

"Breakfasts afore he collects his spoons!" cried second.

Our hero's pockets were searched almost before he was aware, and nothing found but a book in an unknown language and a pocket-handkerchief. He en-

couraged the search, however, as soon as his astonishment
allowed him to be sensible of it, with an air of bewildered
resignation.

"He's a Frenchman," said first waiter.

"He hasn't a penny in his pockets," said second.

"What a villain!" said the landlord.

"You're under a mistake—you are, upon my soul!"
cried poor Jack.   "I grant it's odd; but"—

"Bother and stuff!" said the landlord; "where did
you put my spoons last Friday?"

"Spoons!" echoed Jack; "why, I haven't eaten even
a bit of your breakfast."

By this time all the people in the coffee-room had
crowded into the passage, and a plentiful mob was
gathering at the door.

"Here's a chap has had three breakfasts this morning,"
exclaimed the landlord, "and eat ne'er a one."

"Three breakfasts!" cried a broad, dry-looking gentleman in spectacles, with a deposition-taking sort of face;
"how could he possibly do that? and why did you serve
him?"

"Three breakfasts in three different houses, I tell you,"
said the landlord; "he's been to *my* house, and to *this*
man's house, and to *this* man's; and we've searched him,
and he hasn't a penny in his pocket."

"That's it!" exclaimed Jack, who had in vain tried to
be heard; "that's the very reason."

"What's the very reason?" said the gentleman in
spectacles.

"Why, I was shocked to find just now that I had left
my purse at home, in the hurry of coming out, and"—

"Oh! oh!" cried the laughing audience: "here's the
policeman; he'll settle him."

"But how does that explain the two other breakfasts?"
returned the gentleman.

"Not at all," said Jack.

"Impudent rascal!" said the landlord. Here the police-man is receiving a by-explanation, while Jack is raising his voice to proceed.

"I mean," said he, "that *that* doesn't explain it; but I can explain it."

"Well, how, my fine fellow?" said the gentleman, hushing the angry landlord, who had meanwhile given our hero in charge.

"Don't lay hands on me, any of you!" cried our hero; "I'll go quietly anywhere, if you let me alone; but first let me explain."

"Hear him, hear him!" cried the spectators; "and watch your pockets."

Here Jack, reasonably thinking that nothing would help him out if the truth did not, but not aware that the truth does not always have its just effect, especially when of an extraordinary description, gave a rapid but reverent statement of the character of his friend in the neighbour-hood, whose breakfast had been so inefficient; then an account (all which excited laughter and derision) of his going into the first coffee-house, and seeing his friend come in (which, nevertheless, had a great effect on the first waiter, who knew the old gentleman), and so on of his subsequent proceedings,—a development which suc-ceeded in pacifying both the waiters, who had, in fact, lost nothing; so, coming to an understanding with one another, they slipped away, much to the anger and astonishment of the landlord. This personage, whose whole man, since he left off his active life, had become affected with drams and tit-bits, and whose irritability was aggravated by the late loss of his spoons, persisted in giving poor unbreakfasted Jack in charge, especially when he found that he would not send for a character to the friend he had been speaking of, and that he had no other in town but a lawyer, who lived at the end of it. And so off goes our hero to the police-office.

"You, perhaps, any more than my irritable friend here, don't know the sort of literary old gentleman I have been speaking of," said Jack to the policeman, as they were moving along.

"Can't say I do, sir," said the policeman, a highly respectable individual of his class, clean as a pink, and dull as a pikestaff.

"No, nor no one else," said the landlord. "Who's a man as can't be sent for? He's neither here nor there."

"That's true enough," observed Jack; "he's in Rome or Greece by this time, at some pupil's house; but, wherever he is, I can't send to him. With what face could I do it, even if possible, in the midst of all this fuss about a breakfast?"

"Fuss about white broth, you mean?" said the landlord; "my Friday spoons are prettily melted by this time; but Mr. Kingsley will fetch all that out."

"Then he will be an alchemist cunninger than Raymond Lully," said our hero. "But what is your charge, pray, after all?"

"False pretences, sir," said the policeman.

"False pretences!"

"Yes, sir. You comes, you see, into the gentleman's house under the pretence of eating breakfast, and has none; and that's false pretences."

"That is, supposing I intended them to be false."

"Yes, sir. In course I don't mean to say as—I only says what the gentleman says. Every man by law is held innocent till he's found guilty."

"You are a very civil, reasonable man," said our warm-hearted hero, grateful at this unlooked-for admittance of something possible in his favour; "I respect you. I have no money, nor even a spoon to beg your acceptance of; but pray take this book. It's of no use to me; I've another copy."

"Mayn't take anything in the execution of my office,"

said the man, giving a glance at the landlord, as if he might have done otherwise had he been out of the way. "Thank'ee all the same, sir; but ain't allowed to have no *targiwarsation*."

"Yet your duties are but scantily paid, I believe," said Jack. "However, you've a capital breakfast, no doubt, before you set out?"

"Not by the reg'lations, sir," said the policeman.

"But you have by seven or eight o'clock?" said Jack, smiling at his joke.

"Oh, yes, tight enough, as to that," answered the policeman, smiling; for the subject of eating rouses the wits of everybody.

"Hot toast, eggs, and all that, I suppose?" said Jack, heaving a sigh betwixt mirth and calamity.

"Can't say I take eggs," returned the other; "but I takes a bit o' cold meat, and a good lot o' bread and butter." And here he looked radiant with the reminiscence.

"Lots of bread and butter," thought Jack; "what bliss! I'll have bread and butter when I breakfast, not toast—it's more hearty—and, besides, you get it sooner: bread is sooner spread than toasted—thick, thick—I hear the knife plastering the edge of the crust before it cuts. Agony of expectation! When *shall* I breakfast?"

"The office!" cried the landlord, hurrying forward; and in two minutes our hero found himself in a crowded room, in which presided the all-knowing and all-settling Mr. Kingsley. This gentleman, who died not long after policemen came up, was the last lingering magistrate of the old school. He was a shortish, stout man, in powder, with a huge vinous face, a hasty expression of countenance, Roman nose, and large lively black eyes; and he always kept his hat on, partly for the most dignified reason in the world, because he represented the sovereign magistracy, and partly for the most undignified, to wit, a cold

in the head; for to this visitation he had a perpetual
tendency, owing to the wine he took over-night, and the
draughts of air which beset him every morning in the
police-office. Irritability was his weak side, like the
landlord's; but then, agreeably to the inconsistency in
that case made and provided, he was very intolerant of
the weakness in others. To sum up his character, he was
very loyal to his king; had a great reverence for all the
bygone statesmen of his youth, especially such as were
orators and lords; indeed, had no little tendency to suppose all rich men respectable, and to let them escape too
easily if brought before him, but was severe in proportion
with what are called "decent" men and tradesmen; and
very kind to the poor; and if he loved anything better
than his dignity, it was a good bottle of port and an ode
of Horace. He had not the wit of a Fielding or Dubois;
but he had a spice of their scholarship, and while taking
his wine, would nibble you the beginnings of half the
odes of his favourite poet, as other men do a cake or
biscuit.

To our hero's dismay, a considerable delay took place
before the landlord's charge could be heard. Time flew,
hunger pressed, breakfast drew further off, and the son of
the jovial prebendary learned what it was to feel the
pangs of the want of a penny, for he could not buy even
a roll. "Immortal Goldsmith!" thought he; "poor
Savage! amazing Chatterton! pathetic Otway! fine old
lay-bishop Johnson! venerable, surly man! is it possible
that you ever felt this? felt it to-morrow too, and next
day, and next day! Ill does it become *me* then, Jack
Abbott, to be impatient; and yet, O table-cloth! O thick
slices! O tea! when *shall* I breakfast?"

The case at length was brought on, and the testimony
of the absent witnesses admitted by our hero with a nonchalance which disgusted the magistrate, and began to
rouse his bile. What irritated him the more was that

he saw there would be no proving anything, unless the
criminal (whom for the very innocence of his looks he
took for an impudent offender) should somehow or other
commit himself; which he thought not very likely.   In
fact, as nothing had been eaten, and nothing found on the
person, there was no real charge ; and Mr. Kingsley had
a very particular secret reason, as we shall see presently,
why he could not help feeling that there was one point
strongly in the defendant's favour.   But this only served
to irritate him the more.

"Well, now, you sir—Mr. What's-your-name," quoth
he, in a huffing manner, and staring from under his hat;
"what is your wonderful explanation of this very extraordinary habit of taking three breakfasts—ch, sir ? You
seem mighty cool upon it."

"Sir," answered our hero, whose good-nature gifted
him with a certain kind of address, "it is out of no disrespect to yourself that I am cool.   You may well be
surprised at the circumstances under which I find myself;
but in addressing a gentleman and a man of understanding,
and giving him a plain statement of the facts, I have no
doubt he will discover a veracity in it which escapes eyes
less discerning."

Here the landlord, who instinctively saw the effect
which this exordium would have upon Kingsley, could not
help muttering the word "palaver," loud enough to be heard.

"Silence !" exclaimed the magistrate.   "Keep your
vulgar words to yourself, sir.   And hark'ee, sir, take your
hat off, sir ! How dare you come into this office with your
hat on ? "

"Sir, I have a very bad cold, and I thought that in a
public office "—

"Sir," returned Kingsley, who was doubly offended at
this excuse about the cold, "think us none of your
thoughts, sir. Public office ! Public-house, I suppose
you mean. Nobody wears his hat in this office but

myself, and I only do it as the representative of a
greater power. Hat, indeed! I suppose some day or
other we shall all have the privilege of my Lord Kinsale,
and wear our hats in the royal presence."

Jack gave his account of the whole matter, which,
from a certain ignorance it exhibited of the ways of the
town, did appear a little romantic to his interrogator ;
but the latter, besides knowing our hero's lawyer, was
not unacquainted with the character of Goodall, "who,"
said he, "is known to everybody."

"Probably, sir," observed the landlord; "but for that
reason may not this person have heard of him, and so pretend to be his acquaintance? He calls himself Abbott,
but that is not the name in the French book he's got
about him."

"Let me see the book," cried Kingsley. "French
book! It is a Latin book, and a very good book too,
and an Elzevir. '*E libris Caroli Gibson*, 1743.' A
pretty age for the person before us truly—a very hale,
hearty young gentleman, some ninety years old, or thereabouts." (Here a laugh all over the office, which,
together with the sight of the Horace, put Kingsley into
the greatest good-humour.) "You are thinking, I guess,
Mr.—a—Abbott, of the '*Odi profanum vulgus*,' I take
it; and wishing you could add, '*et arceo*.'"[1]

"Why, to tell you the truth," answered Jack, "I cannot deny a wish to that effect; but my main thought, for
these five hours past, has been rather of the '*Nunc est
bibendum*,'[2] only substituting teacups for goblets."

"Very good, sir, very good; and doubtless you admire
the '*Persicos odi*,' and the '*Quid dedicatum*,' and that
beautiful ode, the '*Vides ut altá*'?"[3]

"I do, indeed," said Jack; "and I trust that one of

---

[1] "I hate the profane vulgar,—and drive them away."

[2] "Now for drinking."

[3] Various beginnings of other odes.

your favourites, like mine, is the '*Integer vitæ scelerisque purus*'?"

"'*Non eget Mauri jaculis, neque arcu,*'

(added Kingsley, unable to avoid going on with the quotation),

"'*Nec venenatis gravidâ sagittis,*
Fusce, pharetrâ,'

There's something very charming in that '*Fusce, pharetrâ,*' —so short and pithy, and elegant; and then the pleasant, social familiarity of *Fusce.*"

"Just so," said Jack; "you hit the true relish of it to a nicety!"

"*Fussy fair-eater!*" muttered the landlord. "A great deal more *fuss* than *fair eating.* My time's lost—that's certain."

Kingsley could not resist a few more returns to his favourite pages; but suddenly recollecting himself, he looked grand and a little turbulent, and said,—

"Well, Mr. — a — Landlord — What's-your-name,— what's the charge here, after all? for, on my conscience, I cannot see any; and, for my part, I thoroughly believe the gentleman; and I'll give you another reason for it, besides knowing this Mr. Goodall. It may not be thought very dignified in me to own it, but dignity must give way to justice—'*Fiat justitia, ruat cælum*'—and to say the truth I, I myself, Mr. Landlord—whatever you may think of the confession — came from home this morning without remembering my purse."

In short, the upshot was, that the worthy magistrate, seeing Bidds' impatience at this confession, and warming the more towards his Horatian friend, not only proceeded to throw the greatest ridicule on the charge, but gave Jack a note to the nearest tavern-keeper, desiring him to furnish the gentleman with a breakfast at his expense, and stating the reason why. He then proclaimed aloud, as he was directing it, what he had done; and added, that he should be very happy to see so intelligent and very innocent a young gentleman, whenever he chose to call upon him.

With abundance of acknowledgments, and in raptures at the now certain approach of the bread and butter, Jack made his way out of the office, and proceeded for the tavern.

"At *last* I have thee!" cried he internally, "O most fugacious of meals—what a repast I will make of it! What a breakfast I *shall* have! Never will a breakfast have been so *intensified*."

Jack Abbott, with the note in his hand, arrived at the tavern, went up the steps, hurried through the passage. Every inch of the way was full of hope and bliss. He sees the bar in an angle round the corner, and is hastening into it with the magical document, when, lo! whom should his eyes light on but the plaintiff, Bidds himself, detailing his version of the story to the new landlord, and evidently poisoning his mind with every syllable.

Our modest, albeit not timid, hero, raging with hunger as he was, could not stand this. A man of more confident face might not unreasonably have presented his note, and stood the brunt of the uncomfortableness; but Jack Abbott, with all his apparent thoughtlessness, had one of those natures which feel for the improprieties of others, even when they themselves have no sense of them; and he had not the heart to outface the vindictiveness of Bidds. To say the truth, Bidds, who was a dull fellow, had some reason to be suspicious; and Jack felt this too, and, retreating accordingly, made haste to take the long step to his lawyer's.

"Now, the lawyer," quoth he, soliloquizing, "I have never seen; but he was an intimate friend of my father's; so intimate, that I can surely take a household liberty with him, and fairly accept his breakfast, if he offers it, as of course he will; and I shall plainly tell him that I prefer breakfast to lunch; in short, that I have made up my mind to have it, even if I wait till dinner-time, or tea-time; and he'll laugh, and we shall be jolly, and so I shall get my breakfast at last. Exquisite moment! What a breakfast I *shall* have!"

The lawyer, Mr. Pallinson, occupied a good large house, with the marks of plenty on it. Jack hailed the sight of the fire blazing in the kitchen. "Delicious spot!" thought he; "kettle, pantry, and all that—comfortable; maid-servant too; hope she has milk left, and will cut the bread and butter. A home too—good family house. Sure of being comfortable there. Taverns not exactly what I took 'em for—not hospitable—not *fiducial*—don't trust; don't know an honest man when they see him. What slices!"

But a little baulk presented itself. Jack unfortunately rang at the *office*-bell instead of the *house*, and found himself among a parcel of clerks. Mr. Pallinson was out —not expected at home till evening—had gone to West-minster on special business—and at such times always dined at the Mendip Coffee-house. Jack, in desperation, fairly stated his case. No result but "Strange, indeed, sir," from one of the clerks, and a general look-up from their desks on the part of the others. Not a syllable of "Won't you stop, sir?" or "The servant can easily give you breakfast;" or any of those fond succedaneums for the master's presence, which our hero's simplicity had fancied. Furthermore, no Mrs. Pallinson existed, to whom he might have applied; and he had not the face to ask for any minor goddess of the household. Blush-ing, and stammering a "Good-morning," he again found himself in the wide world of pavement and houses. He had got, however, his lawyer's direction at the coffee-house, and thither accordingly he betook himself, retracing great part of his melancholy steps.

Had our hero, instead of having passed his time at college and in the country, been at all used to living in London, he would have set himself down comfortably at once in this or any other coffee-house; ordered what he pleased, and despatched a messenger in the meanwhile to anybody he wanted. But, under all the circumstances, he was resolved, for fear of encountering further disappointment, to endure whatsoever pangs remained to him for the rest of the time, and wait till he saw his solicitor come in to dinner. In vain the waiters gave him all encouragement—"Knew Mr. Pallinson well"— "a most excellent gentleman" — had "recommended many gentlemen to their house."— "Would you like anything, sir, before he comes?"— "Like to look at the paper?" And the paper was laid, huge and crisp, before him.

"Ah!" thought Jack, with a sigh, "I know that sound—no, I'll certainly wait. Five o'clock isn't far off, and then I'm certain. What a breakfast I shall now have, when it *does* come. I'll wait, if I die first, so as to have it in perfect comfort."

At length five o'clock strikes, and almost at the same moment enters Mr. Pallinson. He was a brisk, good-humoured man, who had the happy art of throwing off business with the occasion for it; and he acknowledged our hero's claims at once, in a jovial voice, "from his likeness to his excellent friend, the prebendary."

"Don't say a word more, my dear sir—not a word; your eyes and face tell all. Here, John, plates for two. You'll dine, of course, with your father's old friend? or would you like a private room?"

Jack's heart felt itself at home at once with this cordiality He said he was very thankful for the offer of the private room, especially for a reason which he would explain presently. Having entered it, he opened into the history of his morning; and by laughing himself,

warranted Pallinson in the bursts of laughter which he
would have had the greatest difficulty to restrain. But
the good and merry lawyer, who understood both a joke
and a comfort to the depth, entered heartily into Jack's
whim of still having his breakfast, and it was accordingly
brought up—not, however, without a guarded explanation
on the part of the Westminster Hall man, who had a
professional dislike to seeing anybody committed in the
eyes of the ignorant; so he told the waiter that "his
friend here had got up so late, and kept such fashionable
hours, he must needs breakfast while himself was dining."
The waiter bowed with great respect; "And so," says the
shrewd attorney, "no harm's done; and now, my dear
Mr. Abbott, peg away."

Jack needed not this injunction to lay his hand upon
the prey. The bread and butter was now actually before
him; not so thick, indeed, as he had pictured to himself,
but there it was, real, right-earnest bread and butter; and,
since the waiter had turned his back, three slices could be
rolled into one, and half of the coy aggregation clapped
into the mouth at once. The lump was accordingly made,
the fingers whisked it up, and the mouth was ready
opened to swallow, when the waiter again throws open
the door—

"Mr. Goodall, sir."

"Breakfast is abolished with me," thought Jack;
"there's no such thing. Henceforward I shall not
attempt it."

The prebendary, the lawyer, and Goodall were all well
known to each other; but this is not what had brought
him hither. The waiter at his coffee-house, where he
went to read the papers, and where Jack had had his first
mischance, had returned home before the old gentleman
had finished his morning's journal, and told him what, to
his dusty apprehension, appeared the most confused and
unaccountable story in the world, of Mr. Abbott having

ordered three breakfasts and been taken to jail. In his benevolent uneasiness, he could hardly get through his day's work, which, unfortunately, called him so far as Hackney; but as soon as it was over, he hastened in a coach to Pallinson's, and coming there just after Jack had gone, had followed him, in less uneasiness of mind, to the tavern.

"Well, sir—eh, sir?—why, my dear Mr. Abbott—John—James, I should say—why, what a dance you have led me to find you out! and very glad I am, I'm sure, sir, to find you so comfortably situated, with our good friend here, after the story which that foolish, half-witted fellow, William, told me at the coffee-house. Well, sir—eh—and now—I beg pardon—but pray what is it, and can I do anything for you? I suppose not—eh—ah? for here's our excellent friend, Mr. Pallinson—*he* does everything of that sort—bailiff and house—yes, sir, and no doubt it's all right—only, if I *am* wanted, you'll say so; and so, sir—eh—ah—well—but don't let me interrupt your *tea*, I beg."

"Luckiest of innocent fancies!" thought our hero, relieved from a load of misgiving. "He thinks I'm at *tea!*"

Jack plunged again at the bread and butter, and at last actually realized it in his mouth. His calamities were over! He was in the act of breakfasting!

"I'm afraid, too," said Goodall,—"eh, my dear sir?—that the very sparing breakfast you took at my chambers—eh—ah—my, my dear Mr. John—must have contributed not a little to—to—yes, sir. Well, but pray now what was the trouble you had, of which that foolish fellow told me such flams? I'm afraid—yes, indeed—I've had great fears sometimes that he ventures to tell me stories—things untrue, sir."

"God bless him and you, both of you," thought Abbott. "You're a delicious fellow.—Why, my dear, good sir," continued he, always eating, and at the same time racking his brains for an invention,—" I beg your pardon—I'm eating a little too fast "—

Here he made signs of uneasiness in the throat.

" The fact is," said Pallinson, coming to the rescue (for he knew that the whole business would fade from Goodall's mind next day, or be remembered so dimly that the waiter would hear no more of it), "the fact is, Mr. Abbott met *me* in Temple Lane, where I had been summoned on business so early that I had not break-fasted ; and he said he would order breakfast for me at your coffee-house ; and I not coming, he came out to look for me, and found me discussing a matter at another tavern door, with a policeman, who had been sent for to take up a swindler ; and hence, my good sir, all this stuff about the jail and the two breakfasts, for there were only two ; but you know how stories accumulate."

" Very deplorably, indeed, sir," said Goodall ; "it always was so, and—eh—ah—yes, sir—I fear always will be."

" I beg pardon," interrupted Jack, " but may I trouble you for that loaf ? These slices are very thin, and I'm so ravenously hungry, that "—

" Glorious moment ! " The inward ejaculation was at last a true one. The sturdy slices beautifully made their appearance from under the sharp, robust-going, and butter-plastering knife of Jack Abbott. Even the hot toast was called for—Goodall having " vowed " he'd take his tea also, since they were all three met. The eggs were also contrived, and plump went the spoon upon their tops in the egg-cup. The huge ham furthermore was not want-ing. And then the well-filled and thrice-filled breakfast-cup ; — excellent was its strong and well-milked tea, between black and green, " with an eye of tawny in it ; " something with a body, although most liquidly refreshing. Jack doubled his thick slices ; he took huge bites ; he swilled his tea, as he had sworn in thought he would; and he had the eggs on one side of him, and the ham on the other, and his friends before him, and was as happy as a prince escaped into a foreign land (for no prince in possession knows such moments as these); and when he had at length finished, talking and laughing all the while, or hearing talk and laugh, he pushed the breakfast-cup aside, and said to himself,

"I'VE HAD IT!—BREAKFAST hath been mine!—And now, my dear Mr. Pallinson, I'll take a glass of your port."

GALGANO AND MADONNA MINOCCIA.

In the city of Sienna in Italy, famous for its sweet voices
and pleasant air, lived a sprightly and accomplished young
man of the name of Galgano, who had long loved in vain
the wife of one Signor Stricca.   He knew nothing of the
husband, except that he was what we call a respectable
man, and something or other in his mind prevented him
from making his acquaintance ; but he contrived to meet
the lady wherever he could at other men's houses, and to
let her know the extent of his admiration.   He wore her
colours at tournaments.   He played and sung to the
mandolin under her window when her husband was away.
He was always of her opinion in company, partly because
he was in love, and partly because their dispositions were
so alike that he really thought as she did.   One evening,
as a party sat out on a large wide balcony full of orange
trees, listening to music that was going on inside of the
house, Madonna Minoccia (such was the lady's name)
dropped a small jewel in one of the trees ; and as he was
helping her to find it, her sweet stooping face and spicy-
smelling hair appeared so lovely among the polished and
graceful leaves, that he could not but steal a kiss upon
one of her eyelids, adding, in a low and earnest voice,
" Forgive me, for I could not help it."

Whether the sincere and respectful manner in which
these words were uttered had any influence upon the lady's
mind, we cannot say ; but neither on this, nor on future
occasions when he sent her presents and letters, did she

return any answer, kind or unkind; nor did she show him a different countenance whenever they met. She only dropped her eyes a little more than usual when he spoke to her; but whether, again, this was owing to a wish to avoid looking at him, or to some little feeling of self-love, perhaps unknown to herself, and produced by the recollection of that irrepressible movement on his part, is not to be ascertained. Some ladies will say that she ought to have made a complaint to her husband, or spoken to the people whom he visited, or looked the man into the dust at once; and doubtless this would have settled the matter on all sides. But Madonna Minoccia was of so kind a disposition that she could not easily find it in her heart to complain of anybody, much less of a man who found such irresistible gentleness in her eye-lids. Besides, whatever may be thought of her vanity in this score, she was really so good, and innocent, and modest, that we know not how much it would have taken to convince her fully of any one's being really in love with her, or admiring her more than other ladies for qualities which she thought so many of them must have in common. In short, Madonna, though innocent, was not ignorant that gallantry was very common in Sienna. Her husband, who was a very honest, sincere-hearted man, had told her that all unmarried young men had their vagaries, and, as for that matter, many very grave-look-ing married people too; and she thought that if a husband whom she loved, and whose word she could rely on, set her an example nevertheless of conjugal fidelity, she could not do better than do her duty quietly and without ostentation, and think of these odd proceedings both as good-naturedly and rarely as possible.

Unfortunately for Galgano, this kind of temper was the worst thing in the world to make him leave off his love. He had habitually got a common notion of gallantry from the light in which it was generally regarded; but his

instinct was better. The subtlety of love made him discover what was passing in Minoccia's mind; and as he
had the elements of true modesty in him as well as herself, and would want much to be convinced that a woman
really loved him, whatever might be his affection for her,
or rather in proportion to the sincerity of it, he thought
that she only treated him as she would any other young
man who had paid her unwelcome attention. But then
to see how kind she still was,—to observe no change in
her, for all his unwelcomeness, but only such as might be
construed into a gentle request to him to forbear,—in
short, to meet with a woman who neither showed a
disposition to gallantry, nor resentment against the
manifestation of it, nor a coldness that might be construed into natural indifference, all this made him so
much in love, that he thought his very being failed him,
and wanted replenishing, if he was a day without seeing
her. He took a lodging opposite Signor Stricca's house;
and in order to indulge himself in looking at her without
being discovered, filled the window of his room with
orange trees. At times, when everything was still, and
the windows were open in the warm summer-time, he
heard her voice speaking to the servants. "It is the
same kind voice," said he, "always." At other times he
sat watching her through his orange trees as she read a
book or worked at her embroidery; and if she left off,
and happened to look at them (which he often moved
about with a noise for that purpose), it seemed as if her
face was coming again among the leaves. Then he thought
it would never come, and that he should never touch it
more; and he felt sick with impatience, and said to himself, "This is the way these virtuous people are kind, is it?"

It chanced that Signor Stricca took a house at a little
distance from Sienna, where his wife, who was fond of a
garden, from that time forth always resided. Galgano—
who was like a bird with a string tied to his leg—be sure,

flow after them. He found a room in a cottage just pitched like his former one. The orange trees were removed, and he recommenced his enamoured task, fully resolved, besides, to get intimate with Signor Stricca, and try what importunity could do in the country.

"I think," said Madonna Minoccia to her maid-servant, looking out of the window, "I can never turn my eyes anywhere but I see beautiful orange trees."

"Ah!" sighed Galgano, "the turning of those eyes! They ought always to light upon what is beautiful."

"I could swear," said Madonna, "if my husband would let me, that those were the very same oranges which belonged to our invisible neighbour at Sienna, only he must be too old a bachelor to change his quarters." And she began to sing a canzonet that was all over the country:—

> "Arancie, belle arancie,
> Pienotte come guancie"—

Here she suddenly stopped, and said, "I am very giddy to-day, to sing such lawless little rhymes; but the skies are so blue, and the leaves so green, they make me chant like a bird. I can see my husband now with a bird's eye. There he is, Lisetta, coming through the olive trees. Go and get me my veil, and I'll walk and meet him like a fair unknown."

"The invisible neighbour!" thought Galgano;— "is this coquetry now, or is it sheer innocence and vivacity! And the song of the oranges! I'll try, however; I'll look at her above the leaves."

Now the reader must be informed that Galgano himself was the author of this canzonet, both words and music, and was generally known as such. Whether Minoccia knew it we cannot determine; but Galgano thought that she could hardly have quite forgotten the adventure of the orange tree, especially as the song was calculated to call it to mind. The whole of the words amounted to this:—

> O oranges, sweet oranges,
> Plumpy cheeks that peep in trees,

The crabbed'st churl in all the south
Would hardly let a thirsty mouth
Gaze at ye, and long to taste,
Nor grant one golden kiss at last.
　La, la, la—la sol fa mi—
　My lady looked through the orange tree

Yet cheeks there are, yet cheeks there are,
Sweeter—O good God, how far!—
That make a thirst like very death
Down to the heart through lips and breath;
And if we asked a taste of those,
The kindest owners would turn foes.
　O la, la—la sol fa mi—
　My lady's gone from the orange tree.

Galgano, full of this modest complaint against husbands, and of Minoccia's knowledge of it, suddenly raised his head over the orange pots, and made a very bold yet courteous bow full in Madonna's astonished face. For it was astonished;—there was, unfortunately, no doubt of that. She resumed herself, however, with the best grace she could, and staying just long enough to drop one of her kindest though gravest curtseys, walked slowly from the window. After that he never saw her there again.

Galgano tried all the points of view about the house, but could only catch an occasional glimpse of her through the garden trees. He could not even meet with Signor Stricca, to whom he meant, under some plausible pretext, to introduce himself. At length, however, a favourable opportunity occurred. His dog, in scouring hither and thither, had darted into the front gate of the house, and seemed resolved not to be hunted out till he had made the full circuit of the grounds.

"My master, sir," said one of the servants, "bade me ask you if you would choose to walk in and call the dog out yourself?"

"I thank you," answered Galgano, who seemed to feel that he could not go in precisely because he had the best opportunity in the world; "I will whistle him to me over those palings there." He did so, and the dog presently appeared, followed by Signor Stricca and his household. The animal, in leaping to his master over the palings, hurt his leg; but nothing could induce Galgano to enter the house.

"Minoccia, my love," cried the host, "why do you not come up and entreat Signor Galgano to favour our home with his presence?"

The lady was approaching, when Galgano, lapping up the wounded dog in his cloak, hurried off, protesting that he had the rascalliest business in life to attend to, and that he would take the very earliest opportunity of repaying himself for his loss.

"There now," said Stricca to a little, coxcombical-looking fellow who was on a holiday visit to him; "there is one of the most accomplished gentlemen in all Italy, and yet he does not disdain to wrap up his bleeding dog in his silken coat. That," continued he to his wife, "is Signor Galgano, one of the finest wits in Sienna, and what is better, one of the most generous of men. But you must have seen him before."

"Yes," replied Madonna; "but I knew nothing of his generosity."

Her husband, like one generous man speaking of another, related twenty different instances in which Galgano had manifested his friendship and liberality in the most delicate manner; so that Minoccia, at last, almost began to feel the kiss in the orange tree stronger upon her eyelids than she did when it was stolen.

Galgano soon made his appearance in Signor Stricca's house, and could not but perceive that the lady suffered herself to look kinder at him than when he bowed to her out of the cottage window. He was beginning to congratulate himself, after the fashion of the young gallants among whom he had been brought up; but what per-

plexed him was the extremely affectionate attention she
paid her husband, and his perplexity was not diminished
by the very great kindness shown him by the husband
himself. Indeed, the kindness of both seemed to go
hand in hand ; so that our hero, having never yet been
taught that a lady to whom a stranger had shown attention
could do anything but favour him entirely, or laugh at or
insult him, was more than ever bewildered between his
respect for the husband and increasing passion for the
wife.

Galgano, though not in so many words, pressed his
suit in a manner that grew warmer every day. Minoccia
seemed more and more distressed at it, and yet her kindness appeared to increase in proportion. At length, one
afternoon, as they sat together in a summer-house, Galgano,
seeing her stoop her face into an orange tree, was so overcome with the recollection of the first meeting of their
faces, that he repeated the kiss, changing it, however, from
the eyelids to the lips ; and it struck him that she did
not withdraw as quickly as before, nor look by any
means so calm and indifferent. He accordingly took her
hand, in order to kiss it with a passionate gratitude, when
she laid her other hand upon his, and, looking at him
with a sort of appealing tenderness in the face, said,—

" Signor Galgano, I respect you for numberless generous
things I have heard of you ; and knowing as I do how
little what is called gallantry is thought of, I cannot deny
but that your present attentions to me and apparent
wishes do not hinder me from letting my respect run into
a kinder feeling towards you. Perhaps, so sweet to us is
flattery from those we regard, they have even more effect
upon me than I ought to allow. But, sir, there are
always persons, whether they act justly or unjustly themselves, who do think a great deal of this gallantry, and
who, if the case applied to themselves, would be rendered
very uncomfortable ; and, Signor Galgano, I have one of

the very best husbands in the world; and if I show any weakness towards another unbecoming a grateful wife, I do beseech you, sir,—and I pay you one of the greatest and most affectionate compliments under heaven,—that rather than do or risk anything the knowledge of which should pain him, you will help me with all the united strength of your generosity against my very self; otherwise" (here she fell into a blushing passion of tears), "it may be a hard struggle for me to call to mind what I ought respecting the happiness of others, while you are saying to me things that make me frightfully absorbed in the moment before me."

We leave the reader to guess how Galgano's attention to the appealing part of this speech was divided and hurt by the tenderness it avowed, and the opportunity it seemed to offer him. He passionately kissed the hand of the gentle Minoccia, and she did not hinder him, only she looked another way, drying up her tears; and he thought the turn of her head and neck never looked so lovely.

"And if it were possible," asked he, "that the opinions of good and generous men could be changed on this subject (not that it would become me to seek to change those of the man I allude to)—but if it were possible, and no bar were in the way of a small share of Minoccia's kindness, might I indeed then hope that she would not withdraw it?"

"Is it fair, Signor Galgano," said Minoccia, in a low but kind voice, "to ask me such a question, after the words that have found their way out of my lips?"

"And who, then, was the kindest of men or women,—next to yourself, dearest Minoccia,—that told you so many handsome and over-coloured things of your worshipper?"

"My husband himself," answered she; "he has long had a regard for your character, and at last he taught me to share it."

"Did he so!" exclaimed Galgona; "then, by heavens"
—He broke off a moment, and resumed in a quieter
tone: — "You, Madame Minoccia, who have a loving
and affectionate heart, and who confess that you have
been moved to some regard for me by qualities which you
know only by report, will guess what pangs that spirit
must go through which has been made dizzy by looking
upon your qualities day after day, and yet must tear
itself from a happiness in which it would plunge headlong. But, by the great and good God, which created
all this beauty around us, and you the most beautiful of
all beautiful things in the midst of it, I do love the
generosity, and the sincerity, and the harmony that keeps
them beautiful, so much more than my own will, that
although I think the happiness might be greater, it
shall never be said that Galgano made it less; and that
he made it less, too, because the generosity trusted him,
and the kind sincerity leaned on him for support. One
embrace, or I shall die." And Galgano not only gave,
but received, an embrace almost as warm as what he gave;
and Minoccia kissed his eyelids, and then, putting her
hand over them, and pressing them as if not to let him
see, suddenly took it off, and disappeared.

We know not how Signor Stricca received the account
of this interview at the time, for Madame Minoccia
certainly related it to him; but it is in the records of
Sienna, that years afterwards, while she was yet alive,
her husband became bound for Signor Galgano in a large
sum of money, as security, for an office which the latter
held in the State; and it appears by the dates in the
papers, that they were close neighbours as well as
friends.[1]

---

[1] This story (with the usual difference of detail) is from the Italian
novelists, and has been told in Painter's "Palace of Pleasure," one
of the storehouses of our great dramatic writers.

V

THE NURTURE OF TRIPTOLEMUS.

TRIPTOLEMUS was the son of Celeus, king of Attica, by his wife Polymnia. During his youth he felt such an ardour for knowledge, and such a desire to impart it to his fellow-creatures, that having but a slight frame for so vigorous a soul to inhabit, and meeting as usual with a great deal of jealousy and envy from those who were interested in being thought wiser, he fell into a wasting illness. His flesh left his bones; his thin hands trembled when he touched the harp; his fine warm eyes looked staringly out of their sockets, like stars that had slipped out of their places in heaven.

At this period an extraordinary and awful sensation struck, one night, through all the streets of Eleusis. It was felt both by those who slept and those who were awake. The former dreamt great dreams; the latter, especially the revellers and hypocrites who were pursuing their profane orgies, looked at one another, and thought of Triptolemus. As to Triptolemus himself, he shook in his bed with exceeding agitation; but it was with a pleasure that overcame him like pain. He knew not how to account for it; but he begged his father to go out, and meet whatever was coming. He felt that some extraordinary good was approaching, both for himself and his fellow-creatures; but revenge was never further from his thoughts. What was he to revenge? Mistake and unhappiness? He was too wise, too kind, and too suffering. "Alas!" thought he, "an unknown joy shakes me like a palpable sorrow; and their minds are but as weak as my body. They cannot bear a touch they are not accustomed to."

The king, his wife, and his daughters were out, trembling, though not so much as Triptolemus, nor with the same feeling. There was a great light in the air, which moved gradually towards them, and seemed to be struck upwards from something in the street. Presently two gigantic torches appeared round the corner; and underneath them, sitting in a car, and looking earnestly about, sat a mighty female, of more than ordinary size and beauty. Her large black eyes, with their gigantic brows bent over them, and surmounted with a white forehead and a profusion of hair, looked here and there with an intentness and a depth of yearning indescribable. "Chaire, Demeter!" exclaimed the king in a loud voice. "Hail, creative mother!" He raised the cry common at festivals when they imagined a deity manifesting himself; and the priests poured out of their dwellings with vestment and with incense, which they held trembling aloft, turning down their pale faces from the gaze of the passing goddess.

It was Ceres looking for her lost daughter Proserpina. The eye of the deity seemed to have a greater severity in its earnestness as she passed by the priests; but at sight of a chorus of youths and damsels, who dared to lift up their eyes as well as voices, she gave such a beautiful smile as none but gods in sorrow can give; and, emboldened with this, the king and his family prayed her to accept their hospitality.

She did so. A temple in the king's palace was her chamber, where she lay on the golden bed usually assigned to her image. The most precious fruits and perfumes burnt constantly at the door; and at first no hymns were sung but those of homage and condolence. But these the goddess commanded to be changed for

happier songs; and word was also given to the city that
it should remit its fears and its cares, and show all the
happiness of which it was capable before she arrived.
"For," said she, "the voice of happiness arising from
earth is a god's best incense. A deity lives better on the
pleasure of what it has created, than in a return of a part
of its gifts."

Such were the maxims which Ceres delighted to utter
during her abode at Eleusis, and which afterwards formed
the essence of her renowned mysteries at that place. But
the bigots, who afterwards adopted and injured them,
heard them with dismay; for they were similar to what
young Triptolemus had uttered in the aspirations of his
virtue. The rest of the inhabitants gave themselves up
to the joy from which the divinity would only extract
consolation. They danced, they wedded, they loved;
they praised her in hymns as cheerful as her natural
temper; they did great and glorious things for one
another: never was Attica so full of true joy and heroism: the young men sought every den and fearful place
in the territory, to see if Proserpina was there; and the
damsels vied who should give them most kisses for their
reward. "Oh, dearest and divinest mother!" sang the
Eleusinians, as they surrounded the king's palace at
night with their evening hymn,—"Oh, greatest and best
goddess, who, not above sorrow thyself, art yet above all
wish to inflict it, we know by this thou art indeed divine!
Would that we might restore thee thy beloved daughter,
thy daughter Proserpina, the dark, the beautiful, the
mother-loving, whom some god, less generous than thyself, would keep for his own jealous doating! Would
we might see her in thine arms! We would willingly
die for the sight—would willingly die with the only
pleasure which thou has left wanting to us."

The goddess would weep at these twilight hymns, con-
soling herself for the absence of Proserpina by thinking

how many daughters she had made happy. Triptolemus shed weaker tears at them in his secret bed, but they were happier ones than before. "I shall die," thought he, "merely from the bitter-sweet joy of seeing the growth of a happiness which I must never taste; but the days I longed for have arrived. Would that my father would only speak to the goddess, that my passage to the grave might be a little easier!"

The father doubted whether he should speak to the goddess. He loved his son warmly, though he did not well understand him; and the mother, in spite of all the goddess's kindness, was afraid lest in telling her of a child whom they were about to lose, they should remind her too forcibly of her own. Yet the mother, in an agony of alarm one day at a fainting fit of her son's, was the first to resolve to speak to her; and the king and she, with pale and agitated faces, went and prostrated themselves at her feet.

"What is this, kind hosts?" said Ceres; "have ye, too, lost a daughter?"

"No; but we shall lose a son," answered the parents, "but for the help of Heaven."

"A son!" replied Ceres; "why did you not tell me your son was living? I had heard of him, and wished to see him; but never finding him among ye, I guessed that he was no more, and I would not trouble you with such a memory. But why did ye fear mine, when I could do good? Did your son fear it?"

"No, indeed," said the parents; "he urged us to tell thee."

"He is the being I took him for," returned the goddess; "lead me to where he lies."

They came to his chamber, and found him kneeling upon the bed, his face and joined hands bending towards the door. He had felt the approach of the deity; and though he shook in every limb, it was a transport beyond fear that made him rise; it was love and gratitude. The goddess saw it, and bent on him a look that put composure in his shattered nerves.

"What wantest thou," said she, "struggler with great thoughts?"

"Nothing," answered Triptolemus, "if thou thinkest it good, but a shorter and easier death."

"What? Before thy task is done?"

"Fate," he replied, "seems to tell me that I was not fitted for my task, and it is more than done since thou art here. I pray thee, let me die, that I may not see every one around me weeping in the midst of joy at my disease, and yet not have strength enough left in my hands to wipe away their tears."

"Not so, my child," said the goddess, and her grand, harmonious voice had tears in it as she spoke,—"not so, Triptolemus; for my task is thy task, and even gods work with instruments. Thou hast not gone through all thy trials yet; but thou shalt have a better covering to bear them,—yet still by degrees. Gradual sorrow, gradual joy."

So saying, she put her hand to his heart, and pressed it; and the agitation of his spirit was further allayed, though he returned to his reclining posture for weakness. From that time the bed of Triptolemus was removed into the temple, and Ceres herself became his second mother. But nobody knew how she nourished him. It was said that she summoned milk into her bosom, and nourished him at her immortal heart, as though he had been newly born in heaven. But he did not grow taller in stature, as men expected. His health was restored; his joints were knit again, and stronger than ever; but he continued the same small though graceful youth; only the sicklier particles which he had received from his parents withdrew their wasting influence.

At last, however, his very figure began to grow and

expand.   Up to this moment he had only been an interesting mortal, in whom the stoutest and best made of his
father's subjects recognised something mentally superior.
Now he began to look in person, as well as in mind, a
demigod.   The curiosity of the parents was roused at this
appearance; and it was heightened by the report of a
domestic, who said that in passing the door of the temple
one night she heard a sound as of a mighty fire.   But
their parental feelings were also excited by the behaviour
of Triptolemus, who, while he seemed to rise with double
cheerfulness in the morning, always began to look melancholy towards nightfall.   For some hours before he retired
to rest he grew silent, and looked more and more thoughtful; though nothing could be kinder in his manners to
everybody, and the hour no sooner approached for his
retiring than he went instantly and even cheerfully.

His parents resolved to watch.   They knew not what
they were about, or they would have abstained, for Ceres
was every night at her enchantments to render their son
immortal in being as well as fame, and interruption
would be fatal.   At midnight they listened at the temple
door.

The first thing they heard was the roaring noise of fire,
as had been reported.   It was deep and fierce.   They
were about to retire for fear, but curiosity and parental
feeling prevailed.   They listened again; but for some
time they heard nothing but the fire.   At last a voice,
resembling their child's, gave a deep groan.

"It was a strong trial, my son," said another, in which
they recognised the melancholy sweetness of the goddess.

"The grandeur and exceeding novelty of these visions,"
said the fainter voice, "press upon me, as though they
would bear down my brain."

"But they do not," returned the deity, "and they
have not.   I will summon the next."

"Nay, not yet," rejoined the mortal; "yet be it as

thou wilt. I know what thou tellest me, great and kind mother."

"Thou dost know," said the goddess, "and thou knowest in the very heart of thy knowledge, which is in the sympathy of it and the love. Thou seest that difference is not difference, and yet is so ; that the same is not the same, and yet must be; that what is, is but what we see, and as we see it; and yet that which we see, is. Thou shalt prove it finally ; and this is the last trial but one. Vision, come forth."

A noise here took place, as of the entrance of something exceeding hurried and agonized, but which remained fixed with equal stillness. A brief pause took place, at the end of which the listeners heard their son speak, but in a voice of exceeding toil and loathing, and as if he turned away his head. "It is," said he, gasping for breath, "utmost deformity."

"Only to thine habitual eyes, and when alone," said the goddess, in a soothing and earnest manner;—"look again !"

"Oh, my heart !" said the same voice, gasping as with transport; "they are perfect beauty and humanity."

"They are only two of the same," said the goddess, "each going out of itself. Deformity to the eyes of habit is nothing but analysis; in essence it is nothing but oneness, if such a thing there be. The touch and the result is everything. See what a goddess knows, and see, nevertheless, what she feels,—in this only greater than mortals, that she lives for ever to do good. Now comes the last and greatest trial: now shalt thou see the real worlds as they are ; now shalt thou behold them lapsing in reflected splendour about the blackness of space; now shalt thou dip thine ears into the mighty ocean of their harmonics, and be able to be touched with the concentrated love of the universe. Roar heavier, fire ; endure, endure, thou immortalizing frame !"

"Yes, now, now," said the other voice in a superhuman tone, which the listeners knew not whether to think joy or anguish; but their minds were so much more full of the latter that they opened a place from which the priestess used to speak at the lintel, and looked in. The mother beheld her son stretched, with a face of bright agony, upon burning coals. She shrieked, and pitch darkness fell upon the temple and all about it.

"A little while," said the mournful voice of the goddess, "and heaven had had another life. O Fear! what dost thou not do? Oh, my all but divine boy," continued she, "now plunged again into physical darkness, thou canst not do good so long as thou wouldst have done, but thou shalt have a life almost as long as the commonest sons of men, and a thousand times more useful and glorious! Thou must change away the rest of thy particles, as others do; and in the process of time they may meet again under some nature worthy of thee, and give thee another chance for yearning into immortality; but at present the pain is done; the pleasure must not arrive."

The fright they had undergone slew the weak parents. Triptolemus, strong in body, cheerful to all in show, cheerful to himself in many things, retained, nevertheless, a certain melancholy from his recollections; but it did not hinder him from sowing joy wherever he went. It incited him but the more to do so. The success of others stood him instead of his own. Ceres gave him the first seeds of the corn that makes bread, and sent him in her chariot round the world to teach men how to use it. "I am not immortal myself," said he, "but let the good I do be so, and I shall yet die happy."

VI

THE FAIR REVENGE.

THE elements of this story are to be found in the old poem called "Albion's England."

Aganippus, king of Argos, dying without heirs male, bequeathed his throne to his only daughter, the beautiful and beloved Daphles. This female succession was displeasing to a nobleman who held large possessions on the frontiers; and he came for the first time towards the court, not to pay his respects to the new queen, but to give her battle. Doracles (for that was his name) was not much known by the people. He had distinguished himself for as jealous an independence as a subject could well assume; and though he had been of use in repelling invasion during the latter years of the king, had never made his appearance to receive his master's thanks personally. A correspondence, however, was understood to have gone on between him and several noblemen about the court; and there were those who, in spite of his inattention to popularity, suspected that it would go hard with the young queen when the two armies came face to face.

But neither these subtle statesmen, nor the ambitious young soldier Doracles, were aware of the effects to be produced by a strong personal attachment. The young queen, amiable as she was beautiful, had involuntarily baffled his expectations from her courtiers, by exciting in the minds of some a real disinterested regard, while others nourished a hope of sharing her throne instead. At least, they speculated upon becoming each the favourite minister; and held it a better thing to reign under that title and a charming mistress, than be the servants of a master, wilful and domineering. By the people she was adored; and when she came riding out of her palace, on the morning of the fight, with an unaccustomed spear standing up in its rest by her side, her diademed hair flowing a little off into the wind, her face paler than usual, but still tinted with its roses, and a look in which confidence in the love of her subjects, and tenderness for the wounds they were going to encounter, seemed to contend for the expression,—the shout which they sent up would have told a stouter heart than a traitor's that the royal charmer was secure.

The queen, during the conflict, remained in a tent upon an eminence, to which the younger leaders vied who should best spur up their smoking horses, to bring her good news from time to time. The battle was short and bloody. Doracles soon found that he had miscalculated his point, and all his skill and resolution could not set the error to rights. It was allowed that if either courage or military talent could entitle him to the throne, he would have had a right to it; but the popularity of Daphles supplied her cause with all the ardour which a lax state of subjection on the part of the more powerful nobles might have denied it. When her troops charged, or made any other voluntary movement, they put all their hearts into their blows; and when they were compelled to await the enemy, they stood as inflexible as walls of iron. It was like hammering upon metal statuary; or staking their fated horses upon spears riveted in stone. Doracles was taken prisoner. The queen, re-issuing from her tent, crowned with laurel, came riding down the eminence, and remained at the foot with her generals, while the prisoners were taken by. Her pale face kept as royal a countenance of composed pity as she could

F

manage while the commoner rebels passed along, aching
with their wounded arms fastened behind, and shaking
back their bloody and blinding locks for want of a hand
to part them. But the blood mounted to her cheeks
when the proud and handsome Doracles, whom she now
saw for the first time, blushed deeply as he cast a glance
at his female conqueror, and then stepped haughtily along,
handling his gilded chains as if they were an indifferent
ornament. "I have conquered him," thought she : " it
is a heavy blow to so proud a head ; and as he looks not
unamiable, it might be politic as well as courteous and
kind in me to turn his submission into a more willing one."
Alas ! pity was helping admiration to a kinder set of offices
than the generous hearted queen suspected. The captive
went to his prison, a conqueror after all; for Daphles
loved him.

The second night, after having exhibited in her manners a strange mixture of joy and seriousness, and signified to her counsellors her intentions of setting the
prisoner free, she released him with her own hands.
Many a step did she hesitate as she went down the
stairs ; and when she came to the door, she shed a full,
but soft, and as it seemed to her a wilful and refreshing
flood of tears, humbling herself for her approaching task.
When she had entered, she blushed deeply, and then,
turning as pale, stood for a minute silent and without
motion. She then said, "Thy queen, Doracles, has come
to show thee how kindly she can treat a great and
gallant subject, who did not know her ;" and with these
words, and almost before she was aware, the prisoner
was released and preparing to go. He appeared surprised, but not off his guard, nor in any temper to be
over-grateful.

"Name," said he, "O queen ! the conditions on which
I depart, and they will be faithfully kept."

Daphles moved her lips, but they spoke not. She

waved her head and hand with a deadly smile, as if
freeing him from all conditions; and he was turning to
go, when she fell senseless on the floor. The haughty
warrior raised her with more impatience than good-will.
He could guess at love in a woman; but he had but a
mean opinion both of it and her sex; and the deacly
struggle in the heart of Daphles did not help him to
distinguish the romantic passion, which had induced her
to put all her past and virgin notions of love into his
person, from the commonest liking that might flatter his
soldierly vanity.

· The queen, on awaking from her swoon, found herself
compelled, in very justice to the intensity of a true
passion, to explain how pity had brought it upon her.

"I might ask it," said she, "Doracles, in return;" and
here she resumed something of her queen-like dignity;
"but I feel that my modesty will be sufficiently saved by
the name of your wife; and a substantial throne, with a
return that shall nothing perplex or interfere with thee,
I do now accordingly offer thee, not as the condition of
thy freedom, but as a diversion of men's eyes and
thoughts from what they will think ill in me, if they
find me rejected." And in getting out that hard word,
her voice faltered a little and her eyes filled with tears.

Doracles, with the best grace his lately defeated spirit
could assume, spoke in willing terms of accepting her
offer. They left the prison; and his full pardon having
been proclaimed, the courtiers, with feasts and entertainments, vied who should seem best to approve their
mistress' choice; for so they were quick to understand
it. The late captive, who was really as graceful and
accomplished as a proud spirit would let him be, received
and returned all their attention in princely sort; and
Daphles was beginning to hope that he might turn a
glad eye upon her some day, when news was brought her
that he had gone from court, nobody knew whither.

The next intelligence was too certain. He had passed the frontiers, and was leaguing with her enemies for another struggle.

From that day gladness, though not kindness, went out of the face of Daphles. She wrote him a letter, without a word of reproach in it, enough to bring back the remotest heart that had the least spark of sympathy; but he only answered it in a spirit which showed that he regarded the deepest love but as a wanton trifle. That letter touched her kind wits. She had had a paper drawn up leaving him her throne in case she should die; but some of her ministers, availing themselves of her enfeebled spirit, had summoned a meeting of the nobles, at which she was to preside in the dress she wore on the day of victory, the sight of which, it was thought, with the arguments they meant to use, would prevail upon the assembly to urge her to a revocation of the bequest. Her women dressed her while she was almost unconscious of what they were doing, for she had now begun to fade quickly, body as well as mind. They put on her the white garments edged with silver waves, in remembrance of the stream of Inachus, the founder of the Argive monarchy; the spear was brought out, to be stuck by the side of the throne instead of the sceptre; and their hands prepared to put the same laurel on her head which bound its healthy white temples when she sat on horseback and saw the prisoner go by. But at sight of its twisted and withered green she took it in her hand, and looking about her in her chair with an air of momentary recollection, began picking it and letting the leaves fall upon the floor. She went on thus, leaf after leaf, looking vacantly downwards; and when she had stripped the circle half round she leaned her cheek against the side of her sick-chair, and, shutting her eyes quietly, so died.

The envoys from Argos went to the court of Calydon,

where Doracles then was, and, bringing him the diadem
upon a black cushion, informed him at once of the death
of the queen and her nomination of him to the throne.
He showed little more than a ceremonious gravity at the
former news, but could ill contain his joy at the latter,
and set off instantly to take possession. Among the
other nobles who feasted him was one who, having been
the particular companion of the late king, had become
like a second father to his unhappy daughter. The new
prince, observing the melancholy which he scarcely
affected to repress, and seeing him look occasionally up at
a picture which had a veil over it, asked him what the
picture was that seemed to disturb him so, and why it
was veiled.

"If it be the portrait of the late king," said Doracles,
"pray think me worthy of doing honour to it, for he was
a noble prince. Unveil it, pray. I insist upon it.
What! Am I not worthy to look upon my predecessors,
Phorbas?"

At these words he frowned impatiently. Phorbas, with
a trembling hand, but not for want of courage, withdrew
the black covering, and the portrait of Daphles, in all her
youth and beauty, flashed upon the eyes of Doracles. It
was not a melancholy face. It was drawn before misfortune had touched it, and sparkled with a blooming
beauty in which animal spirits and good-nature contended
for predominance. Doracles paused and seemed struck.

"The possessor of that face," said he inquiringly,
"could never have been so sorrowful as I have heard?"

"Pardon me, sir," answered Phorbas; "I was as
another father to her, and knew all."

"It cannot be," returned the prince.

The old man begged his other guests to withdraw a
while, and then told Doracles how many fond and
despairing things the queen had said of him, both before
her wits began to fail and after.

"Her wits to fail?" murmured the king. "I have known what it is to feel almost a mad impatience of the will, but I knew not that these—gentle creatures, women, could so feel for such a trifle."

Phorbas brought out the laurel-crown and told him how it was that the half of it became bare. The impatient blood of Doracles mounted, but not in anger, to his face, and, breaking up the party, he requested that the picture might be removed to his own chamber, promising to return it.

A whole year, however, did he keep it; and as he had no foreign enemies to occupy his time, nor was disposed to enter into the common sports of peace, it was understood that he spent the greatest part of his time, when he was not in council, in the room where the picture hung. In truth, the image of the once smiling Daphles haunted him wherever he went; and to ease himself of the yearning of wishing her alive again and seeing her face, he was in the habit of being with it as much as possible. His self-will turned upon him even in that gentle shape. Millions of times did he wish back the loving author of his fortunes, whom he had treated with so clownish an ingratitude; and millions of times did the sense of the impotence of his wish run up in red hurry to his cheeks, and help to pull them into gaunt melancholy. But this is not a repaying sorrow to dwell upon. He was one day, after being in vain expected at council, found lying madly on the floor of the room, dead. He had torn the portrait from the wall. His dagger was in his heart; and his cheek lay upon that blooming and smiling face, which, had it been living, would never have looked so at being revenged.

VII.

VER-VERT;[1] *OR THE PARROT OF THE NUNS.*

(FROM THE FRENCH OF GRESSET.)

" What words have passed thy lips ?"—MILTON.

INTRODUCTION.

THIS story is the subject of one of the most agreeable poems in the French language, and has the additional piquancy of having been written by the author when he was a Jesuit. The delicate moral which is insinuated against the waste of time in nunneries, and the perversion of good and useful feeling into trifling channels, promised to have an effect (and most likely had) which startled some feeble minds. Our author did not remain a Jesuit long, but he was allowed to retire from his order without scandal. He was a man of so much integrity, as well as wit, that his brethren regretted his loss as much as the world was pleased with the acquisition.

After having undergone the admiration of the circles in Paris, Gresset married, and lived in retirement. He died in 1777, beloved by everybody but the critics. Critics were not the good-natured people in those times which they have lately become; and they worried him, as a matter of course, because he was original. He was intimate with Jean Jacques Rousseau. The self-torment-ing and somewhat affected philosopher came to see him

---

[1] Sometimes written *Vert-Vert* (Green-green).

87

in his retreat; and being interrogated respecting his misfortunes, said to him, "You have made a parrot speak; but you will find it a harder task with a bear."

Gresset wrote other poems and a comedy, which are admired; but the Parrot is the feather in his cap. It was an addition to the stock of originality, and has greater right perhaps than the *Lutrin* to challenge a comparison with the *Rape of the Lock*. This is spoken with deference to better French scholars; but there is at least more of Pope's delicacy and invention in the *Ver-Vert* than in the *Lutrin;* and it does not depend so much as the latter upon a mimicry of the classics. It is less made up of what preceded it.

I am afraid this is but a bad preface to a prose translation. I would willingly have done it in verse, but after wistfully looking at a page or two with which I indulged myself, I renounced the temptation. Readers not bitten with the love of verse will hardly conceive how much philosophy was requisite to do this; but they may guess, if they have a turn for good eating and give up dining with an epicure.

I must mention, that a subject of this nature is of necessity more piquant in a Catholic country than a Protestant. But the loss of poor Ver-Vert's purity of speech comes home to all Christendom; and it is hard if the tender imaginations of the fair sex do not sympathize everywhere both with parrot and with nuns. When the poem appeared in France, it touched the fibres of the whole polite world, male and female. A minister of state made the author a present of a coffee-service in porcelain, on which was painted, in the most delicate colours, the whole history of the "immortal bird." If I had the leisure and the means of Mr. Rogers, nothing should hinder me from trying to outdo (in one respect) the delicacy of his publications, in versifying a subject so worthy of vellum and morocco. The paper should be

as soft as the novice's lips, the register as rose-coloured ;
every canto should have vignettes from the hand of
Stothard ; and the binding should be green and gold, the
colours of the hero.

Alas ! and must all this end in a prose abstract, and
an anti-climax !   Weep all ye little Loves and Graces, ye

> "Veneres Cupidinesque !
> Et quantum est hominum venustiorum."

But first enable us, for our good-will, to relate the story,
albeit we cannot do it justice.[1]

[1] There are two English poetical versions of the *Ver-Vert:* one
by Dr. Geddes, which I have never seen ; the other by John
Gilbert Cooper, author of the *Song to Winifreda.*   The latter is
written on the false principle of naturalizing French versification ;
and it is not immodest in a prose translator to say that it failed
altogether.   The following is a sample of the commencement :—

> " At Nevers, but few years ago,
>   Among the nuns o' the *Visitation,*
> There dwelt a Parrot, though a beau,
>   For sense of wondrous *reputation ;*
> Whose virtues and genteel address,
>   Whose figure and whose noble soul,
> Would have secured him from distress,
>   Could wit and beauty fate control.
> Ver-Vert (for so the nuns agreed
>   To call this noble *personage*),
> The hopes of an illustrious breed,
>   To India owed his *parentage.*"

CHAPTER I.

Character and Manners of Ver-Vert—His Popularity in the Convent, and the Life he led with the Nuns—Toilets and Looking-
glasses not unknown among those Ladies—Four Canary-birds
and two Cats die of Rage and Jealousy.

At Nevers, in the Convent of the Visitation, lived, not
long ago, a famous parrot. His talents and good temper,
nay, the virtues he possessed, besides his more earthly
graces, would have rendered his whole life as happy as a
portion of it, if happiness had been made for hearts like
his.

Ver-Vert (for such was his name) was brought early
from his native country; and while yet in his tender
years, and ignorant of everything, was shut up in this
convent for his good. He was a handsome creature,
brilliant, spruce, and full of spirits, with all the candour
and amiableness natural to his time of life; innocent
withal as could be: in short, a bird worthy of such a
blessed cage. His very prattle showed him born for a
convent.

When we say that nuns undertake to look after a
thing, we say all. No need to enter into the delicacy of
their attentions. Nobody could rival the affection which
was borne our hero by every mother in the convent,
except the confessor; and even with respect to him, a
sincere MS. has left it on record, that in more than one
heart the bird had the advantage of the holy Father.
He partook, at any rate, of all the pretty sops and
syrups with which the dear Father in God (thanks to
the kindness of the sweet nuns) consoled his reverend
stomach. Nuns have leisure: they have also loving
hearts. Ver-Vert was a legitimate object of attachment,
and he became the soul of the place. All the house
loved him, except a few old nuns whom time and the

toothache rendered jealous surveyors of the young ones. Not having arrived at years of discretion, too much judgment was not expected of him. He said and did what he pleased, and everything was found charming. He lightened the labours of the good sisters by his engaging ways,—pulling their veils, and pecking their stomachers. No party could be pleasant if he was not there to shine and to sidle about; to flutter and to whistle, and play the nightingale. Sport he did, that is certain; and yet he had all the modesty, all the prudent daring and submission in the midst of his pretensions which became a novice, even in sporting. Twenty tongues were incessantly asking him questions, and he answered with propriety to every one. It was thus, of old, that Cæsar dictated to four persons at once in four different styles.

Our favourite had the whole range of the house. He preferred dining in the refectory, where he ate as he pleased. In the intervals of the table, being of an indefatigable stomach, he amused his palate with pocket-loads of sweetmeats which the nuns always carried about for him. Delicate attentions, ingenious and preventing cares, were born, they say, among the nuns of the Visitation. The happy Ver-Vert had reason to think so. He had a better place of it than a parrot at court. He lay, lapped-up, as it were, in the very glove of contentment.

At bed-time he repaired to whatever cell he chose; and happy, too happy was the blessed sister whose retreat at the return of nightfall it pleased him to honour with his presence. He seldom lodged with the old ones. The novices, with their simple beds, were more to his taste; which, you must observe, had always a peculiar turn for propriety. Ver-Vert used to take his station on the agnus-box,[1] and remain there till the star of Venus rose

---

[1] A box containing a religious figure of a Lamb.

in the morning. He had then the pleasure of witnessing the toilet of the fresh little nun ; for, between ourselves (and I say it in a whisper), nuns have toilets. I have read somewhere, that they even like good ones. Plain veils require to be put on properly, as well as lace and diamonds. Furthermore, they have their fashions and modes. There is an art, a gusto in these things, inseparable from their natures. Sackcloth itself may sit well. Huckaback may have an air. The swarm of the little loves who meddle in all directions, and who know how to whisk through the grates of convents, take a pleasure in giving a profane turn to a bandeau, a piquancy to a nun's tucker. In short, before one goes to the parlour, it is as well to give a glance or two at the looking-glass. But let that rest. I say all in confidence. So now to return to our hero.

In this blissful state of indolence Ver-Vert passed his time without a care,—without a moment of *ennui*,—lord, undisputed, of all hearts. For him sister Agatha forgot her sparrows ; for him, or because of him, four canary-birds died out of rage and spite ; for him a couple of tom-cats, once in favour, took to their cushions, and never afterwards held up their heads.

Who could have foreboded, in the course of a life so charming, that the morals of our hero were taken care of, only to be ruined ! that a day should arise, a day full of guilt and astonishment, when Ver-Vert, the idol of so many hearts, should be nothing but an object of pity and horror !

Let us husband our tears as long as possible, for come they must : sad fruit of the over-tender care of our dear little sisters !

CHAPTER II.

Further Details respecting the Piety and Accomplishments of our
Hero—Sister Melanie in the Habit of Exhibiting them—A Visit
from him is requested by the Nuns of the Visitation at Nantes
—Consternation in the Convent—The Visit conceded—Agonies
at his Departure.

You may guess that, in a school like this, a bird of our
hero's parts of speech could want nothing to complete his
education. Like a nun, he never ceased talking, except
at meals; but at the same time, he always spoke like a
book. His style was pickled and preserved in the very
sauce and sugar of good behaviour. He was none of
your flashy parrots, puffed up with airs of fashion and
learned only in vanities. Ver-Vert was a devout fowl: a
beautiful soul, led by the hand of innocence. He had no
notion of evil; never uttered an improper word; but
then, to be even with those who knew how to talk, he was
deep in canticles, *Oremuses*, and mystical colloquies. His
Pax vobiscum was edifying. His *Hail, sister!* was not to
be lightly thought of. He knew even a *Meditation* or so,
and some of the delicatest touches out of *Marie Alacoque*.[1]
Doubtless he had every help to edification. There were
many learned sisters in the convent who knew by heart
all the Christmas carols, ancient and modern. Formed
under their auspices, our parrot soon equalled his instructors. He acquired even their very tone, giving it all
their pious lengthiness, the holy sighs, and languishing
cadences of the singing of the dear sisters, groaning little
doves.

The renown of merit like this was not to be confined
to a cloister. In all Nevers, from morning till night,
nothing was talked of but the darling scenes exhibited by
the parrot of the blessed nuns. People came as far as

[1] A famous devotee.

from Moulins to see him. Ver-Vert never budged out of
the parlour. Sister Melanie, in her best stomacher, held
him, and made the spectators remark his tints, his
beauties, his infantine sweetness. The bird sat at the
receipt of victory. And yet even these attractions were
forgotten when he spoke. Polished, rounded, brimful of
the pious gentilities which the younger aspirants had
taught him, our illustrious parrot commenced his recitation. Every instant a new charm developed itself; and
what was remarkable, nobody fell asleep. His hearers
listened; they hummed, they applauded. He, nevertheless, trained to perfection, and convinced of the
nothingness of glory, always withdrew into the recesses of
his heart, and triumphed with modesty. Closing his
beak, and dropping into a low tone of voice, he bowed
himself with sanctity, and so left his world edified. He
uttered nothing under a gentility or a dulcitude; that is
to say, with the exception of a few words of scandal or
so, which crept from the convent-grate into the parlour.

Thus lived, in this delectable nest, like a master, a
saint, and a true sage as he was, Father Ver-Vert, dear
to more than one Hebe; fat as a monk, and not less
reverend; handsome as a sweetheart; knowing as an
abbé; always loved, and always worthy to be loved;
polished, perfumed, cockered up, the very pink of perfection: happy, in short, if he had never travelled.

But now comes the time of miserable memory, the
critical minute in which his glory is to be eclipsed. O
guilt! O shame! O cruel recollection! Fatal journey,
why must we see thy calamities beforehand? Alas! a
great name is a perilous thing. Your retired lot is by
much the safest. Let this example, my friends, show
you, that too many talents, and too flattering a success,
often bring in their train the ruin of one's virtue.

The renown of thy brilliant achievements, Ver-Vert,
spread itself abroad on every side, even as far as Nantes.

There, as everybody knows, is another meek fold of the reverend Mothers of the Visitation,—ladies, who, as elsewhere in this country of ours, are by no means the last to know everything. To hear of our parrot was to desire to see him; and desire, at all times and in everybody, is a devouring flame. Judge what it must be in a nun.

Behold, then, at one blow, twenty heads turned for a parrot. The ladies of Nantes wrote to Nevers, to beg that this bewitching bird might be allowed to come down to the Loire, and pay them a visit. The letter is sent off; but when, ah, when will come the answer? In something less than a fortnight. What an age! Letter upon letter is despatched, entreaty on entreaty. There is no more sleep in the house. Sister Cecilie will die of it.

At length the epistle arrives at Nevers. Tremendous event! A chapter is held upon it. Dismay follows the consultation. "What! lose Ver-Vert! O heavens! What are we to do in these desolate holes and corners without the darling bird! Better to die at once!" Thus spoke one of the younger sisters, whose heart, tired of having nothing to do, still lay open to a little innocent pleasure. To say the truth, it was no great matter to wish to keep a parrot, in a place where no other bird was to be had. Nevertheless, the older nuns determined upon letting the charmer go—for a fortnight. Their prudent heads didn't choose to embroil themselves with their sisters of Nantes.

This bill, on the part of their ladyships, produced great disorder in the commons. What a sacrifice! Is it in human nature to consent to it? "Is it true?" quoth sister Seraphine:—"What! live, and Ver-Vert away!" In another quarter of the room, thrice did the vestry-nun turn pale; four times did she sigh; she wept, she groaned, she fainted, she lost her voice. The whole place is in mourning. I know not what prophetic finger traced the journey in black colours; but the dreams of the night

redoubled the horrors of the day. In vain. The fatal
moment arrives ; everything is ready ; courage must be
summoned to bid adieu.   Not a sister but groaned like a
turtle ; so long was the widowhood she anticipated.   How
many kisses did not Ver-Vert receive on going out!
They retain him ; they bathe him with tears ; his attractions redouble at every step.   Nevertheless, he is at
length outside the walls.   He is gone ; and out of the
monastery, with him, flies love !

CHAPTER III.

Lamentable State of Manners in the Boat which Carries our Hero
down the Loire—He becomes Corrupted—His Biting the Nun
that came to Meet him—Ecstasy of the other Nuns on hearing
of his Arrival.

THE same vagabond of a boat which contained the sacred
bird, contained also a couple of giggling damsels, three
dragoons, a wet-nurse, a monk, and two garçons : pretty
society for a young thing just out of a monastery !

Ver-Vert thought himself in another world.   It was no
longer texts and orisons with which he was treated, but
words which he never heard before, and those words none
of the most Christian.   The dragoons, a race not eminent
for devotion, spoke no language but that of the ale-house.
All their hymns to beguile the road were in honour of
Bacchus ; all their movable feasts consisted only in those
of the ordinary.   The garçons and the three new graces
kept up a concert in the taste of the allies.   The boatmen
cursed and swore, and made horrible rhymes ; taking care,
by a masculine articulation, that not a syllable should lose
its vigour.   Ver-Vert, melancholy and frightened, sat
dumb in a corner.   He knew not what to say or think.

In the course of the voyage, the company resolved to "fetch out" our hero. The task fell on Brother Lubin the monk, who, in a tone very unlike his profession, put some questions to the handsome forlorn. The benign bird answered in his best manner. He sighed with a formality the most finished, and said, in a pedantic tone, "Hail, Sister!" At this "Hail," you may judge whether the hearers shouted with laughter. Every tongue fell on poor Father Parrot.

Our novice bethought within him that he must have spoken amiss. He began to consider, that if he would be well with the fair portion of the company he must adopt the style of their friends. Being naturally of a daring soul, and having been hitherto well fumed with incense, his modesty was not proof against so much contempt. Ver-Vert lost his patience; and in losing his patience, alas! poor fellow, he lost his innocence. He even began, inwardly, to mutter ungracious curses against the good sisters, his instructors, for not having taught him the true refinements of the French language, its nerve and its delicacy. He accordingly set himself to learn them with all his might; not speaking much, it is true, but not the less inwardly studying for all that. In two days (such is the progress of evil in young minds) he forgot all that had been taught him, and in less than three was as off-hand a swearer as any in the boat. He swore worse than an old devil at the bottom of a holy water-box. It has been said, that nobody becomes abandoned at once. Ver-Vert scorned the saying. He had a comtempt for any more novitiates. He became a blackguard in the twinkling of an eye. In short, on one of the boatmen exclaiming, "Go to the devil," Ver-Vert echoed the wretch! The company applauded, and he swore again. Nay, he swore other oaths. A new vanity seized him, and, degrading his generous organ, he now felt no other ambition but that of pleasing the wicked.

G

During these melancholy scenes, what were you about,
chaste nuns of the convent of Nevers? Doubtless you
were putting up vows for the safe return of the vilest of
ingrates, a vagabond unworthy of your anxiety, who holds
his former loves in contempt. Anxious affection is in
your hearts, melancholy in your dwelling. Cease your
prayers, dear deluded ones; dry up your tears. Ver-Vert
is no longer worthy of you; he is a *raf*, an apostate, a
common swearer. The winds and the water-nymphs have
spoilt the fruit of your labours. Genius he may be still;
but what is genius without virtue?

Meanwhile, the boat was approaching the town of
Nantes, where the new sisters of the Visitation expected
it with impatience. The days and nights had never been
so long. During all their torments, however, they had
the image of the coming angel before them,—the polished
soul, the bird of noble breeding, the tender, sincere, and
edifying voice — behaviour, sentiments, — distinguished
merit—oh grief! what is it all to come to?

The boat arrives; the passengers disembark. A lay-sister
of the turning-box[1] was waiting in the dock, where she
had been over and over again at stated time, ever since
the letters were despatched. Her looks, darting over the
water, seemed to hasten the vessel that conveyed our hero.
The rascal guessed her business at first sight. Her prudish
eyes, letting a look out at the corner, her great coif, white
gloves, dying voice, and little pendent cross, were not to
be mistaken. Ver-Vert ruffled his feathers with disgust.
There is reason to believe that he gave her internally to
the devil. He was now all for the army, and could not
bear the thought of new ceremonies and litanies. However, my gentleman was obliged to submit. The lay-sister
carried him off in spite of his vociferations. They say he
bit her in going: some say in the neck, others on the arm.
I believe it is not well known where he bit her; but the

---

[1] A box at the convent gate, by which things are received.

circumstance is of no consequence. Off he went. The devotee was soon within the convent, and the visitor's arrival was announced.

Here's a noise ! At the first sound of the news, the bell was set ringing. The nuns were at prayers, but up they all jump. They shriek, they clap their hands, they fly. "'Tis he ! He is in the great parlour !" The great parlour is filled in a twinkling. Even the old nuns, marching in order, forget the weight of their years. The whole house was grown young again. It is said to have been on this occasion that Mother Angelica ran for the first time.

CHAPTER IV.

Admiration of the Parrot's new Friends converted into Astonishment and Horror—Ver-Vert keeps no Measures with his shocking Acquirements—the Nuns fly from him in Terror, and determine upon instantly sending him back, not, however, without Pity —His Return, and Astonishment of his old Friends—He is sentenced to Solitary Confinement, which restores his Virtue— Transport of the Nuns, who kill him with Kindness.

At length the blessed spectacle bursts upon the good sisters. They cannot satiate their eyes with admiring; and in truth, the rascal was not the less handsome for being less virtuous. His military look and *petit-maître* airs gave him even a new charm. All mouths burst out in his praise; all at once. He, however, does not deign to utter one pious word, but stands rolling his eyes like a young Carmelite. Grief the first. There was a scandal in this air of effrontery. In the second place, when the Prioress, with an august air, and like an inward-hearted creature as she was, wished to interchange a few senti-

ments with the bird, the first words my gentleman uttered,
—the only answer he condescended to give, and that, too,
with an air of nonchalance, or rather contempt, and like
an unfeeling villain, was, "What a pack of fools these
nuns are!"

History says he learned these words on the road.

At this *début*, Sister Augustin, with an air of the
greatest sweetness, hoping to make their visitor cautious,
said to him, "For shame, my dear brother." The dear
brother, not to be corrected, rhymed her a word or two,
too audacious to be repeated.

"Holy Jesus!" exclaimed the sister; "he is a sorcerer,
my dear mother! Just Heaven! what a wretch! Is this
the divine parrot!"

Ver-Vert, like a reprobate at the gallows, made no
other answer than by setting up a dance, and singing,
"Here we go, up! up! up!" which, to improve, he commenced with an "Oh, d—mme."

The nuns would have stopped his mouth; but he was
not to be hindered. He gave a buffoon imitation of the
prattle of the young sisters; and then shutting his beak,
and dropping into a palsied imbecility, mimicked the
nasal drawl of his old enemies, the antiques!

But it was still worse when, tired and worn out with
the stale sentences of his reprovers, Ver-Vert foamed and
raged like a corsair, thundering out all the terrible words
he had learned aboard the vessel. Heavens! how he
swore, and what things he said! His dissolute voice
knew no bounds. The lower regions themselves appeared
to open before them. Words not to be thought of danced
upon his beak. The young sisters thought he was talking
Hebrew.

Oh!—blood and 'ounds! Whew! D—mn! Here's
a h-ll of a storm!"

At these tremendous utterances all the place trembled
with horror. The nuns, without more ado, fled a thousand

ways, making as many signs of the cross. They thought
it was the end of the world. Poor Mother Cicely, falling
on her nose, was the ruin of her last tooth.

"Eternal Father!" exclaimed Sister Vivian, opening
with difficulty a sepulchral voice; "Lord have mercy on
us! Who has sent us this antichrist? Sweet Saviour!
What a conscience can it be which swears in this manner,
like one of the damned? Is this the famous wit, the
sage Ver-Vert, who is so beloved and extolled? For
Heaven's sake, let him depart from among us without
more ado."

"O God of love!" cried Sister Ursula, taking up the
lamentation; "what horrors! Is this the way they
talk among our sisters at Nevers? This their perverse
language! This the manner in which they form youth!
What a heretic! O divine wisdom, let us get rid of him,
or we shall all go to the wicked place together!"

In short, Ver-Vert is fairly put in his cage, and sent
on his travels back again. They pronounce him detestable, abominable, a condemned criminal, convicted of
having endeavoured to pollute the virtue of the holy
sisters. All the convent sign his decree of banishment;
but they shed tears in doing it. It was impossible not to
pity a reprobate in the flower of his age, who was unfortunate enough to hide such a depraved heart under an
exterior so beautiful. For his part, Ver-Vert desired
nothing better than to be off. He was carried back to
the river-side in a box, and did not bite the lay-sister
again.

But what was the despair, when he returned home, and
would fain have given his old instructors a like serenade!
Nine venerable sisters, their eyes in tears, their senses
confused with horror, their veils two deep, condemned
him in full conclave. The younger ones, who might have
spoken for him, were not allowed to be present. One or
two were for sending him back to the vessel; but the

majority resolved upon keeping and chastising him.
He was sentenced to two months' abstinence, three of
imprisonment, and four of silence.   No garden, no toilet,
no bed-room, no little cakes.   Nor was this all.   The
sisters chose for his jailer the very Alecto of the convent,
a hideous old fury, a veiled ape, an octogenary skeleton,
a spectacle made on purpose for the eye of a penitent.

In spite of the cares of this inflexible Argus, some
amiable nuns would often come with their sympathy to
relieve the horrors of the bird's imprisonment.   Sister
Rosalie, more than once, brought him almonds before
breakfast.   But what are almonds in a room cut off from
the rest of the world !   What are sweetmeats in captivity
but bitter herbs ?

Covered with shame and instructed by misfortune, or
weary of the eternal old hag his companion, our hero at
last found himself contrite.   He forgot the dragoons and
the monk, and, once more in unison with the holy sisters
both in matter and manner, became more devout than a
canon.   When they were sure of his conversion, the
divan reassembled, and agreed to shorten the term of his
penitence.   Judge if the day of his deliverance was a day
of joy !   All his future moments, consecrated to gratitude,
were to be spun by the hands of love and security.   O
faithless pleasure !   O vain expectation of mortal delight !
All the dormitories were dressed with flowers.   Exquisite
coffee, songs, lively exercise, an amiable tumult of pleasure,
a plenary indulgence of liberty,—all breathed of love and
delight ; nothing announced the coming adversity.   But,
O indiscreet liberality !   O fatal overflowingness of the
hearts of nuns !   Passing too quickly from abstinence to
abundance, from the hard bosom of misfortune to whole
seas of sweetness, saturated with sugar and set on fire
with liquours, Ver-Vert fell one day on a box of sweetmeats, and lay on his death-bed.   His roses were all
changed to cypress.   In vain the sisters endeavoured to

recall his fleeting spirit. The sweet excess had hastened
his destiny, and the fortunate victim of love expired
in the bosom of pleasure. His last words were much
admired, but history has not recorded them. Venus
herself, closing his eyelids, took him with her into the
little Elysium described by the lover of Corinna, where
Ver-Vert assumed his station among the heroes of the
parrot race, close to the one that was the subject of the
poet's elegy.[1]

To describe how his death was lamented is impossible.
The present history was taken from one of the circulars
composed by the nuns on the occasion. His portrait was
painted after nature. More than one hand gave him a
new life in colours and embroidery ; and Grief, taking up
the stitches in her turn, drew his effigies in the midst of
a border of tears of white silk. All the funeral honours
were paid him which Helicon is accustomed to pay to
illustrious birds. His mausoleum was built at the foot
of a myrtle ; and on a piece of porphyry environed with
flowers, the tender Artemisias placed the following
epitaph, inscribed in letters of gold :

> " O ye who come to tattle in this wood,
> Unknown to us, the graver sisterhood,
> Hold for one moment (if ye can) your tongues,
> Ye novices, and hear how fortune wrongs.
> Hush : or, if hushing be too hard a task,
> Hear but one little speech ; 'tis all we ask—
> One word will pierce ye with a thousand darts ;—
> Here lies Ver-Vert, and with him lie all hearts."

They say, nevertheless, that the shade of the bird is
not in the tomb. The immortal parrot, according to
good authority, survives in the nuns themselves ; and is
destined, through all ages, to transfer, from sister to
sister, his soul and his tattle.

[1] See OVID, *Liber Amorum*, book ii. Elegy 6.

VIII.

THE ADVENTURES OF CEPHALUS AND PROCRIS.

CEPHALUS, the son of Deioneus, king of Thessaly, married Procris, daughter of Pandion, king of Athens. They bound each other by a vow never to love anyone else. Cephalus, who was fond of hunting, suffered the wood-nymphs to be charming to no purpose; and Procris, waiting his return every day from the chace, scarcely had a civil answer for the most agreeable of the wood-gods.

Their security in each other's exclusive attachment was increased, if possible, by a passion which was conceived for Cephalus by Aurora, the Goddess of Morning. To think that the beaming eyes and rosy blushes of so charming a deity were upon him every morning to no purpose, was a high exaltation to the proud confidence which each reposed in the other. Procris, whom the very particular vow which they had entered into had begun to render a little too apt to be jealous, concluded that if he could deny a goddess, she need have no fear of the nymphs. All that disturbed her was lest Aurora should grow angry. Cephalus, on the other hand, whatever airs he might occasionally give himself on the strength of his fidelity, held it to be utterly impossible that his wife should for a moment forget the rejecter of a divinity.

Aurora, however, was not angry. She was too much

in love. Cephalus began to feel a softer pride when he
found that she still loved him secretly, and that she did
all in her power to gratify him. The dawns in Thessaly
had never been known to be so fine. Rosy little clouds,
floating in yellow light, were sure to usher in the day,
whatever it might turn out at noon. He had but to wish
for more air, and it came streaming upon his face. Did
he want light in a gloomy depth of the forest? Beams
thrilled through the twisted thickets, and made the
hunters start to see their faces so plainly. Some said
that a divine countenance was to be seen at these times,
passing on the other side of the trees and looking through.
It is certain that when Cephalus had lain down towards
noon to rest himself in a solitary place, he would see, as
he woke, a nymph suddenly departing from the spot,
whose hair shook out a kind of sunshine. He knew that
this was Aurora, and could not help being touched by so
delicate an affection.

By degrees, Cephalus began to think that Procris might
spare a little of so great a love; and as these wicked
thoughts stole upon him, he found Aurora steal nearer.
She came closer to him as he pretended to sleep, and
loitered more in going away. At length they conversed
again; and the argument which was uppermost in both
their minds soon got more and more explicit. We are
bound to believe that a goddess could reason more
divinely on the subject; but it must not be concealed,
that the argument which made the greatest impression
on Cephalus was one which has since been much in
fashion, though we cannot say a great deal for it. All
defences of love should proceed upon the kindest grounds,
or on none. The moment it refers to anything like
retaliation, or even to a justice which hazards such
feelings, it is trenching on the monstrous territory of
hate. Be this, however, as it may, Aurora one morning
did certainly condescend to finish a conversation with

saying, that she would not look to have her love returned unless Procris should first be found unfaithful.

The husband, in whose mind this suggestion seemed to awaken all his exclusive tenderness for his wife, readily accepted the alternative. But how was Procris to be tried? Aurora soon found an expedient. She changed the appearance of Cephalus to that of a young Phœnician merchant; filled his pockets with gold and jewels; hung the rarest gems from Ormus and the Red Sea in his turban; and seating him in a Sidonian car, drawn by white fawns, with a peacock standing beside him on the edge, sent him to offer all these bribes to Procris for her love. Cephalus turned a little pale at sight of the fawns; but his colour and even his gaiety returned in a minute; and taking a respectful farewell of the goddess, he shook the reins, and set off down the grassy valley that led to his home.

The fawns, with a yearning yet easy swiftness, wound along down the sides of the hill. Their snowy figures flashed in and out of the trees; the peacock's tail trailed along the air; the jewels sparkled in the stranger's turban. Procris, looking out of the window for her husband, wondered what illustrious unknown was coming. He is evidently coming towards her abode. It is the only one in the valley. He arrives, and making a respectful obeisance, alights and enters. He makes no request for admittance, but yet no fault is to be found with his easy gravity. He says, indeed, that he could not but come in, whether he would or no, for the fame of Procris' beauty and sweetness had reached him in Phœnicia; and as his father's great riches allowed him to travel at his leisure, he had brought a few trifles,— not as a return for the few hours' hospitality which he should presume upon,—by no means,—but solely as he had not wit or attraction enough of his own to leave any other memorial of his visit and homage. All this was somewhat too elaborate for the people in those days; but Cephalus, in his confidence, had become a little over-ingenious; and when he had done speaking, and had presented his splendid credentials, Procris thought that the accomplished stranger undervalued himself. A little obstacle presented itself. On giving her the peacock, the handsome stranger stooped his face with an air of confident but respectful pleasure and was about to kiss her. "How is this?" said Procris.

"We always do so in Phœnicia," said he, "when presents are received;" and without more ado he kissed her in a sort of formal and cabalistic manner, first on one cheek, then on the other, and lastly on the forehead. Procris submitted, purely because she did not know how to object to a Phœnician custom. But on his presenting a casket of gold, she demurred. He seemed to take no notice of this, but stooped as before and kissed her, not only on the cheeks and forehead, but on the lips. Procris blushed, and looked displeased. "We always do so in Phœnicia," said he, in a tone as if all offence must be done away by that explanation. Another casket succeeded, full of jewels, and much more precious than the last. Procris wondered whether any additional ceremony was to take place in return, and was about to decline the third present in some alarm, when the stranger, with as brief an indifference of voice as his gallantry could assume, observed, that all that was to be done for the third gift was to have the kiss returned,—slightly, it was true, but still returned:—it was always the way in Phœnicia. And he had scarcely spoken the words when he stooped as before and kissed her. Procris would sincerely have rejected to return the salute; but, as she said afterwards, she really had not time to consider. Besides, she persuaded herself that she felt relieved at thinking the casket was to be the last present; and so, giving a short glance at the window, the kiss was returned. A very odd, and not comfortable expression, passed over the face of the stranger, but very quickly. The only reason that Procris could conceive why he should look so, was that the salute might have been too slight.

"He is very generous, I own," thought she; "but these Phœnicians are strange people."

The stranger had now a totally different air. It was that of an excessive gaiety, in which respect was nevertheless strongly mingled.

"Having honoured me so far with your acquaintance," said he, "nothing remains but to close our Phœnician ceremonies of introduction with this trifle from the Red Sea." So saying, he took a most magnificent ruby from the front of his turban, and hitched it on the collar of her vest. "The hook," said he, "is of Phœnician crystal."

Procris's ears fairly tingled with the word Phœnician. She was bewildered; the ceremonies were indeed about to close, and this word somewhat relieved her; but she was going to demur in a more peremptory manner, when he said that all that was to be done on this final occasion was just to embrace him—slightly—in a sisterly way.

"It is not always done," said he: "the Tyre people, for instance, do not do it; but the Sidonians do; and, generally speaking, it is the closing custom in Phœnici"—and the final syllable was lost in a new kiss, against which she found it out of her power to remonstrate. In giving her at the same time a brief but affectionate embrace, he contrived to bring her arms about himself. He then bowed in the most respectful and grateful manner imaginable, and handed her to a seat.

Procris, with whom the ice had been thus broken, and who already thought herself half faithless to the strictness of her vow, scarcely knew whether to feel angry at the warmth, or piqued at the ceremonious indifference of the stranger. A sense, however, of gratified pride, and of his

extraordinary generosity, was the uppermost feeling in
her mind, and this led her to be piqued rather than
angry.   Luckily, she bethought herself of offering him
the hospitality of the house, which helped to divert her
confusion.   The milk and fruit were brought out; and
he tasted them, more, it seemed, out of politeness than
for want of refreshment.   Procris cast her eyes first up
the hill, and then at the fawns.   She wondered whether
the fawns and car would follow the other presents; but
upon the whole concluded they would not, unless the
traveller meant to stop, which was impossible; at least
in that house.   She made up her mind, therefore, to be
very angry in case he should offer the fawns; when he
interrupted any further reflections.

"Those fawns," said he, "came into my possession in
a remarkable manner.   They are fatal."

"Fatal!" echoed Procris.

"Not in a bad sense," returned the stranger smiling;
"I am destined to present them to some fair one (I know
not who she is), who shall honour me with the privileges
of a husband, and who is to be fairer than the goddess
that gave them me."

"A strange, impossible condition," said Procris; "but
who, pray, was the goddess?"

"Aurora."

The beautiful wife of Cephalus smiled victoriously at
the mention of that name.   She had already triumphed
over the divinity, and thought that this new test of
superiority was scarcely necessary.   The Phœnician, upon
seeing her turn her countenance, added significantly, "I
saw her just now, and must confess that it will take
something very extraordinary to surpass her; but I do
not conceive it actually impossible."

Procris longed to tell him of Aurora's unsuccessful
passion for Cephalus.   She asked how long it was since
he had seen the goddess.

"I saw her but now," said the stranger; "she was conversing in the forest here."

"Do you know with whom?" asked Procris.

"Oh, yes; it was your husband; and this reminds me that he told me to beg of you not to be alarmed, but he should not return till night-fall."

"Not till night-fall?" half murmured and half inquired the fair conqueror of Aurora.

Now this was wrong in Cephalus. He was led into the mention of his interview with Aurora by its being actually the case; but he need not have gone so far with the lesson she had taught him. We blush to say that it succeeded but too well. There is no necessity to pursue the detail further. Towards night-fall Procris gave anxious looks up the hill, and hoped (which was kind of her) that her husband might receive great pleasure from the present she intended to make him of the fawns.

"I think he is coming down the hill," said she.

"No," said the stranger.

"How can you tell," returned Procris, "with your face turned from the window?"

"Look at me," replied he, "and you will know."

Procris turned quickly, and looked him in the face. It was Cephalus himself. Astonishment, fear, shame, and a sense of the triumphant artifice of the goddess fell upon her at once. She uttered a loud shriek, and, tearing her vest from her husband's grasp, darted off into the woods

Cephalus, in his chariot of fawns, sought her a hundred ways in vain. He was at once angry and sorry, and Aurora found that her artifice had been of no use. She hoped, however, that time and the absence of his wife would mollify him; and, in the meanwhile, seeing how sullenly he turned aside whenever she ventured to become manifest, she tried to humble him a little. His skill became less super-eminent in the chace.   Other dogs ran faster than his, and other lances took truer aim.   The gloom of the forest was still enlightened for him, because she did not wish to let him know how she was trying him ; but the name of Cephalus suffered in its reputation. People began to say that Phalerus was as good as he.

He was sitting at home one evening in a melancholy manner, after an unsuccessful day's sport, when a beautiful female with a dog appeared at the door, and begged permission to rest herself.   The faintness of her voice interested our suffering huntsman.   He brought her in with great kindness, set refreshments before her, and could not help gazing with admiration on her lovely face, which, covered with blushes, looked with a particularly melancholy expression on the fruits and the bowls of cream.   He thought he distressed her, and began playing in a negligent manner with the dog.   The animal, at a slight snap of his fingers, darted up on his legs like lightning, and stood panting and looking eagerly towards the door.   Cephalus had the finest dogs in Thessaly, yet he doubted whether this was not finer than any of them. He looked at the female, and now saw that she was buskined up like a nymph of the chace.

"The truth flashes upon me," thought he ; "this is a fugitive nymph of Diana.   Her buskins and her blushes tell her whole story."

The fair stranger seemed first oppressed, and then relieved by his gaze.

"You guess," said she, "but too well, I fear, what has put me upon your kind hospitality.   But the other sex, especially where they are of the best natures, will be too kind to betray me.   I have indeed fled from the company of Diana, having been first left myself by a river-god who "— She blushed, and was silent.

"And this dog ?" inquired Cephalus, after reassuring her.

"It was my favourite dog in the chace," said she;
"now my faithful companion in flight. Poor Leilaps!"
And the dog, forgetting his vivacity in an instant, came
and lay at his mistress' feet as if he would have wound
about them. They were very beautiful feet.

"The river-god doubtless admired them," thought
Cephalus. But there was a something in her face more
touching than all the shapeliness in the world. It was a
mixture of the pensive and the pleasurable, which seemed
to say that if she had no cause for trouble she would
have been all tender vivacity.

"And whither are you going, fairest?" asked Cephalus.

"To Cyprus."

"To the temple of Venus?"

"To the temple of Venus," replied the beautiful
stranger, dropping her words and face as she spoke. "I
have made a new vow, which—a new vow"— And,
blushing more deeply, she was again silent.

"Which she shall be able to keep better than the
last," thought Cephalus.

She sat in a simple posture,—her back gently bending,
her knees together, her rosy face and languid eyes looking
down sideways between her dark heavy curls. She
moved the fingers of her right hand towards the dog, as
if snapping them; but it was done faintly, and evidently
only to do something. Cephalus thought she had a look
of Procris, and he did not pity her the less for that.

"But what are you to do with this dog?"

This, it seemed, was a very perplexing question. It
was a long time before Cephalus could get an answer;
but he was so kind and importunate, and really, with all
his love of hunting, appeared to be so much more
interested in the nymph than her companion, that at
length he did obtain a sort of understanding on the
subject. It was necessary to make a renouncement of
something highly valued by the professor, before a new

devotee could enter on the service of Venus. The
renouncement was to be made to one of the other sex;
and Cephalus, partly out of curiosity, partly out of
vanity, partly out of self-interest, and not a little out of
an interest of a better sort, contrived to discover that it
would be made, with no prodigious unwillingness, to
himself.

"Leilaps," said he. The dog started towards him as
if he knew his future master. The lady gave a gentle
laugh, and seemed much happier. The supper, that
evening, was upon a much easier footing than the
luncheon. The next morning, on waking, Cephalus
saw the face of Procris hanging over him. He would
have been more astonished had he not remembered
his own transformation; but he was nevertheless quite
enough so. Procris shook her head at him archly, then
kissed him kindly, then burst into tears, then declared
herself happy and forgiving as well as forgiven, and
neither of them ever passed a happier day in their
lives.

Procris' account of herself was partly true. Our informant [1] does not account for a proceeding which certainly
requires some explanation; but she had really gone to
the haunts of Diana, whose reception of her, though a
huntress, was what might have been expected. She
begged her, in very explicit terms, to withdraw. Procris,
however, though she could obtain no sympathy purely
on her own account, contrived to waken an interest in
the bosom of the divine virgin by telling her of the trick
played by Cephalus and Aurora. This she thought
abominable. She therefore wrought a counter-change in
the appearance of Procris; and giving her a hound out
of her own pack, sent her to practice artifice for artifice.
She regretted afterwards the having consented to interfere at all in such matters; but the impulse had engaged

[1] Hyginus Fabularum Liber. Cap. 189.

her to commit herself, and she was too proud and stately
to recall what she had done. Procris told all to her
husband; and the goddess was little aware how they
enjoyed the kind result of her anger at the expense of
her dignity.

It is on record that our married couple were never so
fond of each other, or so contented, as now. Procris, in
the gratitude of her joy, was not disposed even to quarrel
with Aurora, whom her husband no doubt saw occasionally. But it is not known whether he was kinder to her
than before. Procris was inclined to think not, as he
said nothing about it; so certain she had become of his
confidence. As to Cephalus, the praises of his wife by
his fellow-huntsmen gave him great pleasure, now that
he was sure of her loving him unrestrictedly.

What a pity that such a happy state of things was not
to last! But Procris had early been taught jealousy.
She had even identified it with a virtue; and by degrees,
as little fits of ill-temper were exchanged, and she began
to think less kindly of herself, she began to be uneasy
about others. Unfortunately for this return of her complaint, a little anxious busybody, whom she had been
accustomed to treat with contemptuous indifference,
perhaps to show it too much, came and said to her one
day, that as she knew she should not be mortifying her
with such pretty matters, she might tell her, as a piece
of news, that Cephalus was passionately and notoriously
in love with a beautiful nymph of the name of Aura.

"Aurora, you mean," said Procris scornfully.

"No, no," said the little snappish voice, "Aura, Aura;
I know it well enough; all Athens knows it, or else I
should not have repeated it. I am no tale-bearer; but I
hate to see a man pretending to be what he is not."

"Cephalus pretends nothing," said Procris.

"Oh, of course," said the gossip; "and mighty useful
it is to him, no doubt, to be so wanting in pretence.

But my maxim is : Be decent enough, at least, to appear virtuous."

"Yes," thought Procris; "and your whole life would be an exemplification of it, if you could hold your tongue." But the blow was struck. She despised the scandal, while she became its victim.

Procris, who was on a visit with Cephalus to her father, had heard of a spot in which he reposed himself every day after the chace. Here, it was added, the lady as regularly met him. He was even so impatient for her sight, that if she delayed a minute beyond the usual time he called upon her aloud in the fondest manner. "Come, come, sweet Aura," said he, "and cool this glow in my bosom."

Now his delight in the new spot, and the invocation also, were both very true ; only the informant forgot to mention, and Procris to remember, that although Aura was the name of a female, it also signified the fresh air.

One day Cephalus went as usual into his favourite haunt to enjoy its freshness, verdure, and seclusion. The place has been very prettily described by Ovid :

> "Est prope purpureos colles florentis Hymetti
> Fons sacer, et viridi cespite mollis humus.
> Sylva nemus non alta facit; tegit arbutus herbam ;
> Ros maris, et lauri, nigraque myrtus olent.
> Nec densæ foliis buxi, fragilesque myricæ,
> Nec tenues cytisi, cultaque pinus abest.
> Lenibus impulsæ Zephyris, auraque salubri,
> Tot generum frondes, herbaque summa tremunt."
> ART. AMAT. LIB. III. v. 687.

> Close by the flowery purple hill
> Hymettus, may be found
> A sacred fountain, and a plot
> Of green and lovely ground.

> 'Tis in a copse. The strawberry
> Grows blushing through the grass ;
> And myrtle, rosemary, and bay
> Quite perfume all the place.

Nor is the tamarisk wanting there;
  Nor clumps of leafy box;
Nor slender ctisus; nor yet
  The pine with its proud looks.

Touched by the zephyrs and sweet airs,
  Which there in balm assemble,
This little world of leaves and all
  The tops of the grass tremble.

Cephalus lay upon a slope of the velvet ground, his hands behind his head, and his face towards the balmy heaven. He little thought that Procris was near. She was lurking close to him behind some box-trees. She listened. There was not a sound but that of the fountain, the noise of whose splashes was softened by the trees that half-encircled it. She listened again, thinking she heard her husband speak. It was only the fervid bees, buzzing along from Hymettus, and murmuring as if disdainfully in her ear. A variety of feelings agitate her. Now she is sorry that she came, and would have given anything to be back again. Now she longs to know who her rival is. Now she is sorry again, and feels that her conduct is unworthy, let her husband's be what it may. Now she reassures herself, and thinks that he should have at least been ingenuous. Jealousy and curiosity prevail, and she still looks and listens. The air seems more than usually quiet, and the bees worry her with their officious humming. Cephalus leaps up, and plays idly with his javelin. Still nothing is said. Nobody appears. She expects the lady every minute to issue from the trees, and thinks how she shall confound her. But no one comes. At last her husband speaks. She parts the box-trees a little more, to listen the keener.

"Come, gentle Aura," cried he, as if in a tone of reproach; "come, and breathe refreshment upon me: thou scarcely stirrest the poplars to-day." Procris leaped up in an ecstasy of delight and remorse, and began tearing back the boughs to go to her husband. He starts up.

He thinks it a deer hampered in the thicket, and raises his javelin to dart it. Forbear, forbear, miserable man : it is thy more miserable wife! Alas! the javelin is thrown, and the wife pierced. Upon coming up to secure his prey, he finds, with a dumb despair, that it is Procris dying. She does not reproach him; she reproaches only herself. "Forgive me," said she, "dear Cephalus," pressing her cheek against his; "I was made wise in vain once, and I am now wise again too late. Forgive my poor jealous heart, and bless me. It weeps blood for its folly." And as she spoke, she sobbed aloud; and the penitent tears gushed away, as if to emulate the gushing of her heart. Cephalus, bewildered and agonized, uttered what kind and remorseful words his lips could frame, pressing her all the while gently to his heart. He saw that the wound was mortal, and it was quickly so. Her eyes faded away while looking at him; but opening her lips, she still made a yearning movement of them towards his. It reminded him of paying that affectionate office to the departing spirit, and, stooping with a face washed in tears, he put his mouth upon hers, and received at once her last kiss and breath.

IX.

THE DAY OF THE DISASTERS OF CARFINGTON BLUNDELL, ESQUIRE.

Description of a Penurious Independent Gentleman, Fond of Invitations and the Great—He takes his Way to a "Dining-out"—His Calamities on the Road—And on his Return.

CARFINGTON BLUNDELL, ESQUIRE, aged six-and-thirty, but apparently a dozen years older, was a spare, well-dressed, sickly-looking, dry sort of leisurely individual, of respectable birth, very small income, and no abilities. He was the younger son of the younger son of a younger brother; and, not being able to marry a fortune (which once, they say, nearly made him die for love), and steering clear, with a provoking philosophy, of the corkscrew curls and pretty staircase perplexities of the young ladies of lodging-houses, contrived to live in London upon the rent of half a dozen cottages in Berkshire.

Having, in fact, no imagination, Carfington Blundell, Esquire, had no sympathies, except with the wants and wishes of that interesting personage, Carfington Blundell, Esquire,—of whom he always bore about with him as lively an image in his brain as it was possible for it to possess, and with whom, when other people were of the least consequence to his inclinations, he was astonished that the whole world did not hasten to sympathize. On every other occasion the only thing which he had to do with his fellow-creatures, all and every of them, was, he thought, to leave them alone,—an excellent principle as far as con-

cerns their own wish to be so left, but not quite so much
so in the reverse instances; such, for example, as when
they have fallen into ditches, or want to be paid their
bills, or have a turn for delicate attentions, or under any
other circumstances which induce people to suppose that
you might as well do to them as you would be done by.
Mr. Blundell, it is true, was a regular payer of his bills;
and though, agreeably to that absorption of himself in the
one interesting idea above mentioned, he was not famous
for paying delicate attentions, except when he took a
fancy to having them paid to himself, yet, provided the
morning was not very cold or muddy, and he had a stick
with him for the individual to lay hold of, and could
reckon upon using it without soiling his shoes or straining
his muscles, the probability is that he might have helped
a man out of a ditch. As people, however, are not in the
habit of falling into ditches, especially about Regent
Street, and as it was not easy to conjecture in what other
instances Mr. Blundell might have deemed it fitting to
evince a sense of the existence of anything but his own
coat and waistcoat, muffins, mutton cutlet, and bed, certain
it is that the sympathies of others were anything but
lively towards himself; and they would have been less so
if the only other intense idea which he had in his head—
to wit, that of his birth and connections (which he pretty
freely overrated)—had not instinctively led him to hit
upon the precise class of acquaintances to whom his
insipidity could have been welcome.

These acquaintances, with whom he dined frequently
(and breakfasted too), were rich men of a grade a good
deal lower than himself; and to such of these as had not
"unexpectedly left town" he gave a sort of a quiet, particular, just-enough kind of a lodging-house dinner once a
year, the shoeblack in gloves assisting the deputy under-
waiter from the tavern. The friends out of town he paid
with regrets at their "lamented absence;" and the whole

of them he would have thought amply recompensed, even without his giving in to this fond notion of the necessity of a dinner on his part, by the fact of his eating their good things and talking of his fifth cousin, the Marquis,— a personage, by the way, who never heard of him. He did, indeed, once contrive to pick up the Marquis' glove at the opera, and to intimate at the same time that his name was Blundell; upon which the noble lord, staring somewhat, but good-humouredly smiling withal, said, "Much obliged to you, Mr. Bungle." As to his positive insipidity over the hock and pine-apples of his friends, Mr. Blundell never dreamt of such a thing; and if he happened to sit next to any wit, or other lion of the day, who seemed of consequence enough to compete with the merits of his presence, he thought it amply set off by his taste in having had such ancestors, and, indeed, in simply being that identical Mr. Blundell, who, in having no merits at all, was gifted by the kind providence of nature with a proportionate sense of his enjoying a superabundance of them.

To complete the idea of him in the reader's mind, his manners were gentlemanly, except that they betrayed now and then too nice a sense of his habiliments. His hat he always held in the best way adapted to keep it in shape; and a footman, coming once too softly into a room where he was waiting during a call, detected him in the act of dusting his boots with an extra-coloured handkerchief, which he always carried about with him for that purpose. He calculated that, with allowance for changes in the weather, it saved him a good four months' coach-hire.

Such was the acomplished individual who, in the month of May, in the year of our Lord one thousand eight hundred and twenty-seven, and in a "fashionable dress of the first water" (as Sir Phelim called it), issued forth from his lodgings near St. James', drawing the air through

his teeth with an elegant indifference, coughing slightly
at intervals out of emotion, and, to say the truth, as
happy as coat and hat, hunger, a dinner-party, and a
fine day could make him.   Had the weather been in the
smallest degree rainy, or the mansion for which he was
bound at any distance, the spectators were to understand
that he would have come in his own carriage, or at least
that he intended to call a coach ; but as the day was so
very fine, and he kept looking at every door that he passed,
as though each were the one he was about to knock at, the
conclusion to be drawn was that, having but a little way
to go, and possessing a high taste for superiority to appearances, it was his pleasure to go on foot.   Vulgar wealth
might be always making out its case.   Dukes and he could
afford to dispense with pretension.

The day was beautiful, the sky blue, the air a zephyr,
the ground in that perfect state for walking (a day or two
before dust), when there is a sort of dry moisture in the
earth, and people in the country prefer the road to the
path.   The house at which our hero was going to dine was
midway between the West End and the north-east ; and
he had just got half-way, and was in a very quiet street,
when, in the "measureless content" of his anticipations,
he thought he would indulge his eyesight with one or two
of those personal ornaments, the presence of which, on
leaving the house, he always ascertained with sundry
pattings of his waistcoat and coat pockets.   Having, therefore, again assured himself that he had duly got his two
pocket-handkerchiefs, his ring, his shirt-pin, his snuff-box,
his watch, and his purse *under* his watch, he first took off
a glove that he might behold the ring ; and then, with the
ungloved hand, he took out the snuff-box, in order that he
might as delicately contemplate the snuff-box.

Now, the snuff-box was an ancient but costly snuff-box,
once the possession of his grandmother, who had it from
her uncle, whose arms, flaming in *or* and *gules*, were upon

the lid ; and inside the lid was a most ingeniously-contrived portrait of the uncle's lady, in a shepherdess' hat and powdered toupee, looking, or to be supposed to be looking, into an actual bit of looking-glass.

Carfington Blundell, Esquire, in a transport of ease, hope, and ancestral elegance, and with that expression of countenance, the insipidity of which is bound to be in proportion to the inward rapture, took a pinch out of this hereditary amenity, and was in the act of giving a glance at his grand-aunt before he closed the lid, when a strange, respectably-dressed person, who seemed to be going somewhere in a great hurry, suddenly dashed against him, and, uttering the words, "With pleasure," dipped his fingers into the box, and sent it, as Carfington thought, half-way across the street.

Intense was the indignation, but at the same time highly considerate the movement of Mr. Blundell, who, seeing the "impertinent beast" turn a corner, and hearing the sound of empty metal dancing over the street, naturally judged it better to secure the box than derange his propriety further by an idle pursuit. Contenting himself, therefore, with sending an ejaculation after the vagabond to the purpose just quoted, and fixing his eye upon the affecting movable, now stationary, he delicately stepped off the pavement towards it, with inward congratulation upon its not being muddy, when imagine his dismay and petrifaction on lifting up, not the identical box, but one of the commonest order! To be brief, it was of pewter ; and upon the lid of it, with after-dinner fork, was scratched a question which, in the immediate state of Mr. Blundell's sensations, almost appeared to have a supernatural meaning, to wit, "How's your mother?"

Had it been possible for a man of the delicacy of Mr. Blundell's life and proportions to give chase to a thief, or had he felt it of the least use to raise a hue-and-cry in a gentlemanly tone of voice,—or, indeed, in any voice not incompatible with his character,—doubtless he would have done so with inconceivable swiftness; but, as it was, he stood as if thunderstruck; and in an instant there were a dozen persons about him, all saying, "What is it?" "Which?" "Who?"

Mr. Blundell, in his first emotions, hardly knew "what it was" himself; the "which" did not puzzle him quite so much, as often as he looked upon the snuff-box; but the "who" he was totally at a loss to conjecture, and so were his condolers.

"What—was it that chap as run agin you," said one, "jist as I was coming in at t'other end of the street? Lord love you! you might as well run arter last year. He's a mile off by this time."

"If the gentleman 'll give me a shilling," said the boy, "*I'll* run arter him."

"Get out, you young dog!" said the first speaker, "d'ye think the gentleman's a fool?"

"It is a circumstance," said Mr. Blundell, grateful for this question, and attempting a breathless smile, "which —might have—surprised—anybody."

"What *sort* of a man was it?" emphatically inquired a judicious-looking person, jerking his face into Mr. Blundell's, and then bending his ear close to his, as though he were deaf.

"I—declare," said Mr. Blundell, "that I can—hardly say, the thing was so very unexpected; but—from the glimpse I had of him, I should—really say—he looked like a gentleman" (here Mr. Blundell lifted up his eyebrows),—"not indeed a *perfect* gentleman."

"I daresay not, sir," returned the judicious-looking person.

"*What is* all this?" inquired a loud individual, elbowing his way through.

"A gentleman has been robbed," said the boy, "by another gentleman."

"Another gentleman?"

"Yes; not a *perfect* gentleman, he says, but highly respectable."

Here, to the equal surprise and grief of the sufferer, the crowd laughed and began joking with one another. None but the judicious-looking deaf individual seemed to keep his countenance.

"Well," quoth the loud man, "here's a policeman coming at the end of the street; the gentleman had better apply to him."

"Yes, sir," said the deaf friend, "that's your resource, and God bless you with it!" So saying, he grasped Mr. Blundell's hand with a familiarity more sympathizing than respectful, and, treading at the same time upon his toes in the most horrible manner, begged his pardon, and went away.

Mr. Blundell stooped down, partly to rub his toes, and partly to hide his confusion, and the policeman came up. The matter was explained to the policeman, all the while he was hearing the sufferer, by a dozen voices, and the question was put, "What sort of a man was it?"

"Here is a gentleman," said Mr. Blundell, "who saw him."

The policeman looked about for the witness, but nobody answered; and it was discovered that all the first speakers had vanished—loud man, boy, and all.

"Have you lost anything else, sir?" inquired the policeman.

"Bless me!" said Mr. Blundell, turning very red, and feeling his pockets; "I really—positively I do fear—that "—

"You can remember, sir, what you had with you when you came out?"

"*One* handkerchief," continued Mr. Blundell, "has certainly gone; and "—

"Your watch is safe," returned the policeman, "for it

is hanging out of your waistcoat. Very lucky you fastened it. Have you got your purse, sir ?"

"The purse was under the watch," breathed Mr. Blundell; "therefore I have no doubt that—but I regret to say—that I do not—feel my *ring*."

A laugh, and cries of "Too bad !"

"A man shook your hand, sir," said the policeman; "did you not feel it then ?"

"I did not, indeed," replied Mr. Blundell; "I felt nothing but the severity of the squeeze."

"And you had a brooch, I perceive."

The brooch was gone too.

"Why don't you run arter him," cried a very little boy in an extremely high and loud voice, which set the crowd in a roar.

The policeman, as speedily as he could, dispersed the crowd, and accompanied Mr. Blundell part of his way; whither the latter knew not, for he walked along as if he had taken too much wine. Indeed, he already doubted whether he should proceed to recruit himself at his friend's table, or avoid the shame of telling his story and return home. The policeman helped to allay his confusion a little by condolence, by promises of search, and accounts of daring robberies practised upon the most knowing; and our hero, in the gratitude of his heart, would have given him his card; but he now found that his pocket-book was gone ! His companion rubbed his face to conceal a smile, and received with great respect an oral communication of the address. Mr. Blundell, to show that his spirit as a gentleman was not subdued, told him there was half-a-crown for him on his calling.

Alone, and meditative, and astonished, and, as it were, half undone, Mr. Blundell continued his journey towards the dinner, having made up his mind that, as his watch-chain was still apparent, and had the watch attached to it, and as the disorder of his nerves, if not quite got rid of, might easily be referred to delicacy of health, he would refresh his spirits with some of that excellent port which always made him feel twice the man he was.

Nor was this judicious conclusion prevented, but rather irritated and enforced, by one of those sudden showers which in this fickle climate are apt to come pouring down in the midst of the finest weather, especially upon the heels of April. This, to be sure, was a tremendous one; though, by diverting our hero's chagrin, and putting him upon his mettle, it only made him gather up his determination, and look extremely counteractive and frowning. Would to heaven his nerves had been as braced-up as his face! The gutters were suddenly a torrent; the pavement a dancing wash; the wind a whirlwind; the women all turned into distressed Venuses de' Medici. Everybody got up in doorways, or called a coach.

Unfortunately no coach was to be had. The hacks went by insolently, taking no notice. Mr. Blundell's determination was put to a nonplus. The very door-ways in the street where he was, being of that modern, *skimping*, inhospitable penny-saving, done-by-contract order, so unlike the good old projecting ones with pediments and ample thresholds, denied security even to his thin and shrinking person. His pumps were speedily as wet through as if they had been made of paper; and what rendered this ruin of his hopes the more provoking was, that the sunshine suddenly burst forth again as powerful as the rain which had interrupted it. A coach, however, he now thought, would be forthcoming; and it would, at least, take him home again; while the rain, and " the previous inability to get one," would furnish a good excuse for returning.

But no coach was to be had so speedily, and meantime his feet were wet, and there was danger of cold. "As I *am* wet," thought Mr. Blundell, sighing, "a little motion, at all events, is best. It would be better, considering I am so, not to stop at all, nor perhaps get into a coach;

but then how am I to get home in these shoes and this highly evening-dress? I shall be a sight. I shall have those cursed little boys after me. Perhaps I shall again be hustled."

Bewildered with contending emotions of shame, grief, disappointment, anger, nay hunger, and the sympathy between his present pumps and departed elegancies, our hero picked his way as delicately as he could along the curb-stones, and, turning a corner, had the pleasure of seeing a hackney-coach slowly moving in the distance, and the man holding forth his whip to the pedestrians, evidently disengaged. The back of it, to be sure, was towards him, and the street long and narrow, and very muddy. But no matter. An object's an object; a little more mud could not signify; our light-footed sufferer began running.

Now runners unfortunately are not always prepared for corners, especially when their anxiety has an object right before it, and the haste is in proportion. Mr. Blundell, almost before he was aware of it, found himself in the middle of a flock of sheep. There was a hackney-coach also in the way; the dog was yelping, and leaping hither and thither; and the drover, in a very loud state of mind, hooting, whistling, swearing, and tossing up his arms.

Mr. Blundell, it is certain, could not have got into a position less congenial to his self-possession, or more calculated to commit his graces in the eyes of the unpropitiated. And the sheep, instead of sympathizing with him, as in their own distress they might (poetically) be supposed to do, positively seemed in the league to distress his stockings, and not at all to consider even his higher garment. They ran against him; they bolted at him; they leaped at him; or if they seemed to avoid him, it was only to brush him with muddier sides, and to let in upon his weakened forces the frightful earnestness of the dog, and the inconsiderate, if not somewhat suspicious, circumambiences of the coachman's whip.

Mr. Blundell suddenly disappeared.

He fell down, and the sheep began jumping over him! The spectators, I am sorry to say, were in an ecstasy.

You know, observant reader, the way in which sheep carry themselves on abrupt and saltatory occasions; how they follow one another with a sort of spurious and involuntary energy; what a pretended air of determination they have; how they really have it, as far as example induces and fear propels them; with what a heavy kind of lightness they take the leap; how brittle in the legs, lumpish in the body, and insignificant in the face; how they seem to quiver with apprehension, while they are bold in act; and with what a provoking and massy springiness they brush by you, if you happen to be in the way, as though they wouldn't avoid the terrors of your presence, if possible, or, rather, as if they would avoid it with all their hearts, but insulted you out of a desperation of inability. *Baas* intermix their pensive objections with the hurry, and a sound of feet as of water. Then, ever and anon, come the fiercer leap, the conglomerating circuits, the dorsal visitations, the yelps and tongue-lollings of the dog, lean and earnest minister of compulsion; and loud, and dominant over all, exult the no less yelping orders of the drover,—indefinite, it is true, but expressive, —rustical cogencies of *oo* and *ou*, the intelligible jargon of the Corydon or Thyrsis of Chalk-Ditch, who cometh, final and humane, with a bit of candle in his hat, a spike at the end of his stick, and a hoarseness full of pastoral catarrh and juniper.

Thrice (as the poets say) did Carfington Blundell, Esquire, raise his unhappy head out of the *mêlée*, hatless and mudded; thrice did the spectators shout; and thrice did he sink back from the shout and the sheep, in calamitous acquiescence.

"Lie still, you fool!" said the hackney - coachman, "and they'll jump easy."

"JUMP EASY!" Heavens! how strange are the vicissitudes of human affairs. To think of Mr. Blundell only but yesterday, or this evening rather,—nay, not an hour ago,—his day fine, his hopes immense, his whole life lapped-up, as it were, in cotton and lavender, his success elegant, his evening about to be spent in a room full of admirers; and NOW, his very prosperity is to consist in lying still in the mud, and letting sheep jump over him!

Then to be called a "fool":—"Lie still, *you fool!*"

Mr. Blundell could not stand it any longer (as the Irishman said); so he rose up just in time to secure a kick from the last sheep, and emerged amidst a roar of congratulation.

He got as quickly as possible into a shop, which luckily communicated with a back street; and, as things generally mend when they reach their worst (such at least was the consolatory reflection which our hero's excess of suffering was glad to seize hold of), a hackney-coach was standing close to him, empty and disengaged. It had just let a gentleman down next door.

Our hero breathed a great breath, returned his handkerchief into his pocket (which had been made a sop of to no purpose), and uttering the word "*accident*," and giving rapid orders where to drive to, was hastening to hide himself from fate and the little boys within the vehicle, when, to his intense amazement, the coachman stopped him.

"Hullo!" quoth the Jerveian mystery; "what are you arter?"

"Going to get in," said Blundell.

"I'm bless'd if you do," said the coachman.

"How, fellow! Not get in!" cried Mr. Blundell, irritated that so mean an obstacle should present itself to his great wants. " What's your coach for, sir, if it isn't to accommodate gentlemen; to accommodate *any*body, I may say ?"

Now it happened that the coachman, besides having had his eye caught by another fare, was a very irritable coachman, given to repenting or being out of temper all day for the drinking he solaced himself with overnight; and he didn't choose to be called " fellow," especially by an individual with a sort of dancing-master appearance, with his hat jammed in, his silk stockings untimely, and his whole very equivocal man all over mud. So jerking him aside with his elbow, and then turning about, with the steps behind him, and facing the unhappy Blundell, he thus, with a terrible slowness of articulation, bespoke him, the countenances of both getting redder as he spoke :

"And do you think now, Master 'Fellow,' or Fiddler, or Mudlark,—or whatsoever else you call yourself,— that I'm going to have the new seats and lining o' my coach dirtied, so as not to be fit to be seen, by such a TRUMPERY BEAST as *you* are ?"

"It is for light sorrows to speak," saith the philosopher; "great ones are struck dumb." Mr. Blundell was struck dumb ; dumber than ever he had conceived it possible for a gentleman to be struck. It is little to say that he felt as if heaven and earth had come together. There was *no* heaven and earth ; nothing but space and silence. Mr. Blundell's world was annihilated.

Alas! it was restored to him by a shout from the "cursed little boys." Mr. Blundell mechanically turned away, and began retracing his steps homeward, half conscious, and all a spectacle; the little boys following and preceding him, just leaving a hollow space for his advances, and looking back, as they jogged, in his face. He turned into a shop and begged to be allowed to wait a little in the back parlour. He was humanely accommodated with soap and water, and a cloth; and partly out of shame at returning through the gazes of the shopmen, he stayed there long enough to get rid of his tormentors. No great-coat, however, was to be had; no shoes that fitted; no stockings; and though he was no longer in his worst and wettest condition, he could not gather up courage enough to send for another coach. In the very idea of a coachman he beheld something that upturned all his previous existence: a visitation—a Gorgon—a hypochondria. "Don't talk to me like a death's-head," said Falstaff to Doll Tearsheet, when she reminded him of his age. Mr. Blundell would have said, "Don't talk to me like a hackney - coachman." The death's - head and cross-bones were superseded in his imagination by an old hat, wisp of hay, and arms akimbo.

Our hero had washed his hands and face, had set his beaver to rights, had effaced (as he thought) the worst part of his stains, and succeeded in exchanging his boot pocket-handkerchief for a cleaner one; with which, alternately concealing his face as if he had had a toothache, or holding it carelessly before his habiliments, he was fain, now that the day was declining, to see if he could not pick his way home again, not quite intolerably. It was a delicate emergency; but experience having somewhat rallied his forces, and gifted him with that sudden world of reflection which is produced by adversity, he bethought himself, not only that he must yield, like all other great men, to necessity, but that he was a personage fitted for nice and ultimate contrivances. He was of opinion, that although the passengers, if they chose to look at him, could not but be aware that he had sustained a mischance common to the meanest, yet, in consideration of his air and manners, perhaps they would not choose to look at him *very* much; or if they did, their surprise would be divided between pity for his mishap and admiration of his superiority to it.

Certainly the passengers who met him did look a good deal. He could not but see it, though he saw as little as he could help. How those who came behind him looked it would have been a needless cruelty to himself to ascertain; so he never turned his head. No little boys thought it worth their while to follow his steps, which was a great comfort; though whenever any observers of that class met him, strange and most disrespectful were their grins and ejaculations. "Here's a Guy!" was the most innocent of their salutes. A drunken sailor startled him with asking how the land lay about "Tower Ditch"? And an old Irishwoman, in explanation of his appearance to the wondering eyes of her companions, defined him to be one that was so fond of "crame o' the valley" that he must needs be "roulling in it."

Had "cabs" been then, Mr. Blundell would un-questionably have made compromise with his horror of charioteers, and on the strength of the mitigated deface-ments of his presence have risked a summons to the whip. As it was, he averted his look from every hackney-coach, and congratulated himself as he began nearing home— home, sweet even to the most insipid of the Blundells, and never so sweet as now, though the first thoughts of returning to it had been accompanied with agonies of mortification. "In a few minutes," thought he, "I shall be *seen* no more for the day (oh! strange felicity for a dandy!); in a few minutes I shall be in other clothes, other shoes, and another train of feelings—not the happiest of men, perhaps, retrospectively, but how blest in the instant and by comparison! In a few minutes all will be silence, security, *dryness*. I shall be in my arm-chair, in my slippers—shall have a fire; and I will have a mutton-cutlet, hot—and refresh myself with a bottle of wine my friend Mimpin sent me."

Alas! what are the hopes of man, even when he con-cludes that things *must* alter for the better, seeing that they are at their worst? How is he to be quite sure, even after he has been under sheep in a gutter, that things *have* been at their worst?—that his cup of calamity, full as it seemed, is not to be succeeded by, or wonderfully expanded into, a still larger cup, with a remaining draught of bitterness, amazing, not to have been thought of, making the sick throat shudder, and the heart convulse?

Scarcely had the sweet images of the mutton-cutlet and wine risen in prospect upon the tired soul of our hero, than he approached the corner of the street round which he was to turn into his own; and scarcely had he experienced that inward transport, that chuckle of the heart with which tired homesters are in the habit of turning those corners,—in short, scarcely had his entire person manifested itself *round* the corner, and his eyes lifted themselves up to behold the side of the blessed threshold, than he heard, or rather was saluted and drowned with a roar of voices the most huge, the most unexpected, the most terrific, the most weighty, the most world-like, the most grave yet merry, the most intensely stupefying, that it would have been possible for Sancho himself to conceive, after all his experience with Don Quixote.

It now struck Mr. Blundell that, with a half-conscious, half-unconscious eye, he had seen people running towards the point which he had just attained, and others looking out of their windows; but as they did not look at *him*, and everyone passed him without attention, how was he to dream of what was going forward; much more, that it had any relation to himself? Frightful discovery! which he was destined speedily to make, though not on the instant.

The crowd (for almost the whole street was one dense population) seemed in an agony of delight. They roared, they shrieked, they screamed, they writhed, they bent themselves double, they threw about their arms, they seemed as if they would have gone into fits. Mr. Blundell's bewilderment was so complete that he walked soberly along, steadied by the very amazement; and as he advanced, they at once, as in a dream, appeared to him both to make way for him, and to advance towards him; to make way in the particular, but advance in the mass; to admit him with respect, and overwhelm him with familiarity.

"In the name of heaven!" thought he, "*what can it all be?* It is impossible the crowd can have any connection with me in the *first* instance. I could not have *brought* them here; and my appearance, though unpleasant, and perhaps somewhat ludicrous, cannot account for such a perfect mass and conspiracy of astonishment. *What is it?*"

And all the way he advanced did Mr. Blundell's eyes, and manner, and whole person exhibit a sort of visible echo to this internal question of his—*What is it?*

The house was about three-quarters of the way up the street, which was not a long one; and it stood on the same side on which our unfortunate pedestrian had turned.

As he approached the denser part of the crowd, words began to develop themselves to his ear — "Well, this beats all!" "Well, of all the sights!" "Why, it's the man himself, the very man, poor devil!" "Look at his face!" "What the devil can he have been at?" "Look at the pianoforte man—he's coming up!"

Blundell mechanically pursued his path, mystified to the last depths of astonishment, and scarcely seeing what he saw. Go forward he felt that he must; to turn back was not only useless, but he experienced the very fascination of terror and necessity. He would have proceeded to his lodgings had Death himself stood in the doorway. Meantime up comes this aforesaid mystery, the pianoforte man.

"Here's a pretty business you've been getting us into," said the amazing stranger.

"What business?" ejaculated Mr. Blundell.

"What business? Why, all this here d—d business —all this blackguard crowd—and my master's ruined pianoforte. A pretty jobation I shall get; and I should like to know what for, and who's to pay me?"

"In the name of God!" said our hero, "what is it?"

"Why, don't you see what it is?—a *hoax*, and be d—d to it. It's a mercy I wasn't dashed to pieces when these rascals tipped over the pianoforte; and there it lies, with three of its legs smashed and a corner split. I should like to know what I'm to have for the trouble?"

"And I," said the upholsterer's man.

"And I," said the glass man.

"And this here coffin," said the undertaker.

There had been a hoax sure enough; and a tremendous hoax it was. A plentiful space before the door was strewed with hay, boxes, and baskets. There stood the coffin, upright, like a mummy; and here lay the pianoforte, a dumb and shattered discord.

Mr. Blundell had now arrived at his door, but did not even think of going in; that is to say, not instantly. He mechanically stopped, as if to say or do something: for something was plainly expected of him; but what it was he knew not, except that he mechanically put his hand towards his purse, and as mechanically withdrew it.

The crowd all the while seemed to concentrate their forces towards him — all laughing, murmuring, staring —all eager, and pressing on one another; yet leaving a clear way for the gentleman, his tradesmen, and his goods.

What was to be done?

Mr. Blundell drew a sigh from the bottom of his heart, as though it were his last sigh or his last sixpence; yet he drew forth no sixpence. Extremes met, as usual. The consummation of distress produced calmness and reflection.

"You must plainly perceive, gentlemen," said our hero, "that it could be no fault of mine."

"I don't know that," said the pianoforte man. The crowd laughed at the man's rage, and at once cheered him on, and provoked him against themselves. He seemed as if he did not know which he should run at first, — his involuntary customer or "the cursed little boys."

"Zounds, sir!" said the man, "you *oughtn't* to have been hoaxed."

"Oh! oh!" said the parliamentary crowd.

"I mean," continued he, "that none but some d—d disagreeable chap, or infernal fool, is ever treated in this here manner."

"Oh! oh!" reiterated the bystanders. "Come, that's better than the last."

"Which is the biggest fool?" exclaimed a boy, in that altitude of voice which is the most sovereign of provocations to grown ears.

The man ran at the boy, first making a gesture to our hero, as much as to say, "I'll be with you again presently." The crowd hustled the man back;—the undertaker had seized the opportunity of repeating that he "hoped his honour would consider his trouble;"—the glass man and the upholsterer were on each side of him;—and suddenly the heavy shout recommenced, for a new victim had turned the corner,—a stranger to what was taking place, —a man with some sort of milliner's or florist's box. The crowd doted on his face. First, he turned the corner with the usual look of indifferent hurry; then he began to have an inquiring expression, but without the least intimation that the catastrophe applied to himself; then the stare became wider, and a little doubtful; and then he stopped short, as if to reconnoitre—at which the laugh was prodigious. But the new comer was wise; for he asked what was the matter of the first person he came up with; and learning how the case stood, had energy enough to compound with one more hearty laugh, in preference to a series of mortifications. He fairly turned back, pursued by a roar; and oh! how he loved the corner, as he went round it! Every hair at the back of his head had seemed to tingle with consciousness and annoyance. He felt as if he saw with his shoulder-blades;—as if he was face to face at the back of his hat.

At length the misery and perplexity of Mr. Blundell reached a climax so insurmountable, that he would have taken out his second and (as he thought) remaining pocket-handkerchief, if even that consolation had been left him; for the tears came into his eyes. But it was gone! The handkerchief, however, itself, did not distress him. Nothing could touch him further. He wiped his eyes with the ends of the fingers of his gloves, and stood mute,—a perplexity to the perplexed,—a pity even to the "little boys."

Now tears are very critical things, and must be cautiously shed, especially in critical ages. In a private way, provided you have locked the door, and lost three children, you may be supposed to shed a few without detriment to your dignity; and in the heroical ages, the magnitude and candour of passion permitted tears openly, the feelings then being supposed to be equally strong in all respects, and a man to have as much right to weep as a woman. But how lucky was it for poor Blundell that no brother dandy saw him! His tormentors did not know whether to pity or despise him. The pianoforte man, with an oath, was going to move off; but, on

looking again at his broken instrument, remained and
urged compensation. The others expressed their sorrow,
but repeated, that they hoped his honour would consider them; and they repeated it the more, because
his tears raised expectations of the money which he
would be weak enough to disburse.

Alas! they did not know that the dislike of disburse-
ment, and the total absence of all sympathy with others
in our weeping hero (in this, as in other respects, very
different from the tear-shedding Achilles), was the cause of
all which they and he were at this moment enduring; for
it was the inability to bring out his money which kept
Mr. Blundell lingering outside his lodging, when he
might have taken his claimants into it; and it was the
jovial irascibility of an acquaintance of his, which, in
disgust at his evasion of dinner-givings, and his repeatedly
shirking his part of the score at some entertainments at
which he pretended to consider himself a guest, had
brought this astounding calamity to his door.

Happily for these "last infirmities" of a mind which
certainly could not be called "noble," there are hearts so
full of natural sympathy that the very greatest proofs of
the want of it will but produce, in certain extremities, a
pity which takes the want itself for a claim and a misfortune; and this sympathy now descended to Mr.
Blundell's aid, like another goddess from heaven, in a
shape not unworthy of it,—to wit, that of the pretty
daughter of his landlord, a little buxom thing, less handsome than good-natured, and with a heart that might
have served to cut up into cordial bosoms for half a
dozen fine ladies. She had once nursed our hero in
sickness, and to say the truth, had not been disinclined
to fall in love with him, and be made "a lady," half out
of pure pity at his fever, had he given her the slightest
encouragement; but she might as well have hoped to
find a heart in an empty coat. However, a thoroughly

good nature never entirely loses a sort of gratitude to
the object that has called forth so sweet a feeling as
that of love, even though it turn out unworthy, or the
affections (as in our heroine's case) be transferred elsewhere; and accordingly, in sudden bonnet and shawl,
and with a face blushing partly from shame and partly
from anger at the crowd, forth came the vision of pretty,
plump little Miss Widgeon (Mrs. Burrowes "as is to
be"), and tapping Mr. Blundell on the shoulder, and
begging the "other gentlemen" to walk in, said, in a
voice not to be resisted, "Hadn't you better settle this
matter in-doors, Mr. Blundell?   I daresay it can be done
very easily.

Blundell has gone in, dear reader; the other gentlemen
have gone in; the crowd are slowly dislodging; Miss
Widgeon, aided partly by the generosity of her nature,
partly by the science of lodging-house economy, and
partly by the sense and manhood of Mr. William
Burrowes, then present, a strapping young citizen from
Tower Hill, takes upon herself that ascendency of the
moment over Mr. Blundell due to a superior nature, and
settles the very illegitimate claims of the goods-and-
chattel bringers to the satisfaction of all parties, yea,
even of Mr. Blundell himself.   The balm of the immediate relief was irresistible, even though he saw a few
of his shillings departing.

What he felt next morning, when he woke, this
history saith not; for we like to leave off, according to
the Italian recommendation, with a *bocca dolce*, a sweet
mouth; and with whose mouth, even though it was not
always grammatical, can the imagination be left in better
company than with that of the sweet-hearted and generous
little Polly Widgeon?

X.

THE SHOEMAKER OF VEYROS.

A PORTUGUESE TRADITION.

In the times of the old kings of Portugal, Don John, a natural son of the reigning prince, was governor of the town of Veyros, in the province of Alentejo. The town was situate (perhaps is there still) upon a mountain, at the foot of which runs a river; and at a little distance there was a ford over it, under another eminence. The bed of the river thereabouts was so high as to form a shallow sandy place; and in that clear spot of water the maidens of Veyros, both of high rank and humble, used to wash their clothes.

It happened one day that Don John, riding out with a company, came to the spot at the time the young women were so employed; and being, says our author, "a young and lusty gallant," he fell to jesting with his followers upon the bare legs of the busy girls, who had tucked up their clothes, as usual, to their work. He passed along the river; and all his company had not yet gone by, when a lass in a red petticoat, while tucking it up, showed her legs somewhat high, and clapping her hand on her right calf, said, loud enough to be heard by the riders, "Here's a white leg, girls, for the Master of Avis.[1]

These words, spoken probably out of a little lively bravado, upon the strength of the governor's having gone by, were repeated to him when he got home, together

---

[1] An order of knighthood of which Don John was master.

with the action that accompanied them : upon which the
young lord felt the eloquence of the speech so deeply
that he contrived to have the fair speaker brought to him
in private; and the consequence was, that our lively natural
son and his sprightly challenger had another natural son.

Ines (for that was the girl's name) was the daughter of
a shoemaker in Veyros, a man of very good account, and
wealthy.   Hearing how his daughter had been sent for to
the young governor's house, and that it was her own light
behaviour that subjected her to what he was assured she
willingly consented to, he took it so to heart, that at her
return home she was driven by him from the house, with
every species of contumely and spurning.   After this he
never saw her more.   And to prove to the world and to
himself that his severity was a matter of principle, and
not a mere indulgence of his own passions, he never
afterwards lay in a bed, nor ate at a table, nor changed
his linen, nor cut his hair, nails, or beard ; which latter
grew to such a length, reaching below his knees, that the
people used to call him Barbadon, or old Beardy.

In the meantime his grandson, called Don Alphonso,
not only grew to be a man, but was created Duke of
Braganza, his father, Don John, having been elected to
the crown of Portugal ; which he wore after such noble
fashion, to the great good of his country, as to be sur-
named the Memorable.   Now, the town of Veyros stood
in the middle of seven or eight others, all belonging to
the young Duke, from whose palace at Villa Viciosa it
was but four leagues distant.   He therefore had good
intelligence of the shoemaker his grandfather ; and being
of a humane and truly generous spirit, the accounts he
received of the old man's way of life made him extremely
desirous of paying him a visit.   He accordingly went
with a retinue to Veyros ; and meeting Barbadon in the
streets, he alighted from his horse, bareheaded, and in the
presence of that stately company and the people, asked

the old man his blessing. The shoemaker, astonished at
this sudden spectacle, and at the strange contrast which
it furnished to his humble rank, stared in a bewildered
manner upon the unknown personage who thus knelt to
him in the public way, and said, "Sir, do you mock me?"

"No," answered the Duke; "may God so help me, as
I do not: but in earnest I crave I may kiss your hand
and receive your blessing, for I am your grandson, and
son to Ines your daughter, conceived by the king, my
lord and father."

No sooner had the shoemaker heard these words than
he clapped his hand before his eyes, and said, "God bless
me from ever beholding the son of so wicked a daughter as
mine was! And yet, forasmuch as you are not guilty of
her offence, hold; take my hand and my blessing, in the
name of the Father, and of the Son, and of the Holy
Ghost." So saying, he laid one of his old hands upon
the young man's head, blessing him; but neither the
Duke nor his followers could persuade him to take the
other away from his eyes; neither would he talk with
him a word more. In this spirit, shortly after, he died;
and just before his death he directed a tomb to be made
for him, on which were sculptured the tools belonging to
his trade, with this epitaph:

> "This sepulchre Barbadon caused to be made
> (Being of Veyros, a shoemaker by his trade),
> For himself and the rest of his race,
> Excepting his daughter Ines in any case."

The author says that he has "heard it reported by the
ancientest persons that the fourth Duke of Braganza,
Don James, son to Donna Isabel, sister to the King Don
Emanuel, caused that tomb to be defaced, being the
sepulchre of his fourth grandfather." [1]

[1] It appears by this that the Don John of the tradition is John the
First, who was elected king of Portugal, and became famous for his
great qualities; and that his son by the alleged shoemaker's daughter
was his successor, Alphonso the Fifth.

As for the daughter, the conclusion of whose story comes lagging in like a penitent, "she continued," says the writer, " after she was delivered of that son, a very chaste and virtuous woman ; and the king made her commandress of Santos, a most honourable place, and very plentiful ; to the which none but princesses were admitted, living, as it were, abbesses and princesses of a monastery built without the walls of Lisbon, called Santos, that is Saints, founded by reason of some martyrs that were martyred there. And the religious women of that place have liberty to marry with the knights of their order, before they enter into that holy profession."

The rest of our author's remarks are in too curious a spirit to be omitted. "In this monastery," he says, "the same Donna Ines died, leaving behind her a glorious reputation for her virtue and holiness. Observe, gentle reader, the constancy that this Portuguese, a shoemaker, continued in, loathing to behold the honourable estate of his grandchild, nor would any more acknowledge his daughter, having been a lewd woman, for purchasing advancement with dishonour. This considered, you will not wonder at the Count Julian, that plagued Spain, and executed the king Roderigo for forcing his daughter La Cava. The example of this shoemaker is especially worthy the noting, and deeply to be considered ; for, besides that it makes good our assertion, it teaches the higher not to disdain the lower, as long as they be virtuous and lovers of honour. It may be that this old man, for his integrity, rising from a virtuous zeal, merited that a daughter coming by descent from his grandchild, should be made Queen of Castile, and the mother of great Isabel, grandmother to the Emperor Charles the Fifth, and Ferdinando."

Alas ! a pretty posterity our shoemaker had in Philip the Second and his successors,—a race more suitable to his severity against his child, than his blessing upon his

grandchild. Old Barbadon was a fine fellow too, after his
fashion. We do not know how he reconciled his unforgiving conduct with his Christianity; but he had enough
precedents on that point. What we admire in him is
his showing that he acted out of principle, and did not
mistake passion for it. His crepidarian sculptures indeed
are not so well; but a little vanity may be allowed to
mingle with and soften such edge-tools of self-denial as
he chose to handle. His treatment of his daughter was
ignorant, and in wiser times would have been brutal,
especially when it is considered how much the conduct
of children is modified by education and other circumstances; but then a brutal man would not have accompanied it with such voluntary suffering of his own.
Neither did Barbadon leave his daughter to take her
chance in the wide world, thinking of the evils she might
be enduring, only to give a greater zest of fancied pity
to the contentedness of his cruelty. He knew she was
well taken care of; and if she was not to have the enjoyment of his society, he was determined that it should be
a very uncomfortable one to himself. He knew that she
lay on a princely bed, while he would have none at all.
He knew that she was served upon gold and silver, while
he renounced his old chestnut table,—the table at which
he used to sit. He knew, while he sat looking at his old
beard and the wilful sordidness of his hands, that her
locks and her fair limbs were objects of worship to the
gallant and the great. And so he set off his destitu-
tions against her over-possession, and took out the
punishment he gave her in revenge upon himself. This
was the instinct of a man who loved a principle, but
hated nobody,—of a man who, in a wiser time, would
have felt the wisdom of kindness. Thus his blessing
upon his grandchild becomes consistent with his cruelty
to his child; and his living stock was a fine one in spite
of him. His daughter showed a sense of the wound she

had given such a father, by relinquishing the sympathies
she loved, because they had hurt him ; and her son,
worthy of such a grandfather and such a daughter, and
refined into a gracefulness of knowledge by education,
thought it no mean thing or vulgar to kneel to the grey-
headed artisan in the street, and beg the blessing of his
honest hand.

XI.

RONALD OF THE PERFECT HAND.

[The following tale is founded on a Scottish tradition.
   It was intended to be written in verse; which will
   account for its present appearance.]

THE stern old shepherd of the air,
The spirit of the whistling hair,
The wind, has risen drearily
In the Northern evening sea,
And is piping long and loud
To many a heavy upcoming cloud,—
Upcoming heavy in many a row,
Like the unwieldy droves below
Of seals, and horses of the sea,
That gather up as drearily,
And watch with solemn-visaged eyes
Those mightier movers in the skies.

   'Tis evening quick;—'tis night:—the rain
Is sowing wide the fruitless main,
Thick, thick;—no sight remains the while
From the farthest Orkney isle,
No sight to sea-horse, or to seer,
But of a little pallid sail,
That seems as if 'twould struggle near,
And then as if its pinion pale
Gave up the battle to the gale.
Four chiefs there are of special note,
Labouring in that earnest boat;
Four Orkney chiefs, that yesterday
Coming in their pride away
From there smote Norwegian king,
Led their war-boats triumphing
Straight along the golden line
Made by morning's eye divine.

146

Stately came they, one by one,
Every sail beneath the sun,
As if he their admiral were
Looking down from the lofty air,
Stately, stately through the gold.—
But before that day was done,
Lo, his eye grew vexed and cold;
And every boat, except that one,
A tempest trampled in its roar;
And every man, except those four,
Was drenched, and driving far from home,
Dead and swift, through the Northern foam

Four are they, who wearily
Have drunk of toil two days at sea;
Duth Maruno, steady and dark,
Cormar, Soul of the Winged Bark;
And bright Clan Alpin, who could leap
Like a torrent from steep to steep;
And he, the greatest of that great band,
Ronald of the Perfect Hand.

Dumbly strain they for the shore,
Foot to board, and grasp on oar.
The billows, panting in the wind,
Seem instinct with ghastly mind,
And climb like crowding savages
At the boat that dares their seas.
Dumbly strain they, through and through,
Dumbly, and half blindly too,
Drenched, and buffeted, and bending
Up and down without an ending,
Like ghostly things that could not cease
To row among those savages.

Ronald of the Perfect Hand
Has rowed the most of all that band;
And now he's resting for a space
At the helm, and turns his face
Round and round on every side
To see what cannot be descried,
Shore, nor sky, nor light, nor even
HOPE, whose feet are lost in heaven.
Ronald thought him of the roar
Of the fight the day before,
And of the young Norwegian prince
Whom in all the worryings

And hot vexations of the fray,
He had sent with life away,
Because he told him of a bride
That if she lost him, would have died;
And Ronald then, in bitter case,
Thought of his own sweet lady's face,
Which upon this very night
Should have blushed with bridal light,
And of her downward eyelids meek,
And of her voice, just heard to speak,
As at the altar, hand in hand,
On ceasing of the organ grand,
'Twould have bound her, for weal or woe,
With delicious answers low:
And more he thought of, grave and sweet,
That made the thin tears start, and meet
The wetting of the insolent wave;
And Ronald, who though all so brave,
Had often that hard day before
Wished himself well housed on shore,
Felt a sharp impatient start
Of home-sick wilfulness at heart,
And steering with still firmer hand,
As if the boat could feel command,
Thrilled with a fierce and forward motion,
As though 'twould shoot it through the ocean.

"Some spirit," exclaimed Duth Maruno, "must pursue us, and stubbornly urge the boat out of its way, or we must have arrived by this time at Inistore."[1]　Ronald took him at his word, and turning hastily round, thought he saw an armed figure behind the stern.　His anger rose with his despair; and with all his strength he dashed his arm at the moveless and airy shape.　At that instant a fierce blast of wind half turned the boat round.　The chieftains called out to Ronald to set his whole heart at the rudder; but the wind beat back their voices, like young birds into the nest, and no answer followed it. The boat seemed less and less manageable, and at last to be totally left to themselves.　In the intervals of the wind they again called out to Ronald, but still received

[1] The old name for the Orkneys.

no answer. One of them crept forward, and felt for him through the blinding wet and darkness. His place was void. "It was a ghost," said they, "which came to fetch him to the spirits of his fathers. Ronald of the Perfect Hand is gone, and we shall follow him as we did in the fight. Hark! The wind is louder and louder: it is louder and many-voiced. Is it his voice which has roused up the others? Is he calling upon us, as he did in the battle, when his followers shouted after his call?"

It was the rocks of an isle beyond Inistore which made that multitudinous roaring of the wind. The chieftains found that they were not destined to perish in the mid-ocean; but it was fortunate for them that the wind did not set in directly upon the island, or they would have been dashed to pieces upon the rocks. With great difficulty they stemmed their way obliquely; and at length were thrown violently to shore, bruised, wounded, and half inanimate. They remained on this desolate island two days, during the first of which the storm subsided. On the third, they were taken away by a boat of seal-hunters.

The chiefs, on their arrival at home, related how Ronald of the Perfect Hand had been summoned away by a loud-voiced spirit, and disappeared. Great was the mourning in Inistore for the Perfect Hand: for the Hand that with equal skill could throw the javelin and traverse the harp; could build the sudden hut of the hunter; and bind up the glad locks of the maiden tired in the dance. Therefore was he called the Perfect Hand; and therefore with great mourning was he mourned; yet with none half as great as by his love, his betrothed bride Moilena: by her of the Beautiful Voice; who had latterly begun to be called the Perfect Voice, because she was to be matched with him of the Perfect Hand. Perfect Hand and Perfect Voice were they called; but the Hand was now gone, and the Voice sang brokenly for tears.

A dreary winter was it, though a victorious, to the people of Inistore. Their swords had conquered in Lochlin; but most of the hands that wielded them had never come back. Their warm pressure was felt no more. The last which they had given their friends was now to serve them all their lives. "Never, with all my yearning," said Moilena, "shall I look upon his again, as I have looked upon it a hundred times, when nobody suspected. Never." And she turned from the sight of the destructive ocean, which seemed as interminable as her thoughts.

But winter had now passed away. The tears of the sky at least were dried up. The sun looked out kindly again; and the spring had scarcely reappeared, when Inistore had a proud and gladder day, from the arrival of the young Prince of Lochlin with his bride. It was a bitter one to Moilena, for the prince came to thank Ronald for sparing his life in the war, and had brought his lady to thank him too. They thanked Moilena instead; and, proud in the midst of her unhappiness of being the representative of the Perfect Hand, she lavished hundreds of smiles upon them from her pale face. But she wept in secret. She could not bear this new addition to the store of noble and kind memories respecting her Ronald. He had spared the bridegroom for his bride. He had hoped to come back to his own. She looked over to the north, and thought that her home was as much there as in Inistore.

Meantime, Ronald was not drowned. A Scandinavian boat, bound for an island called the Island of the Circle, had picked him up. The crew, which consisted chiefly of priests, were going thither to propitiate the deities, on account of the late defeat of their countrymen. They recognised the victorious chieftain, who, on coming to his senses, freely confessed who he was. Instantly they raised a chorus, which rose sternly through the tempest. "We carry, said they, "an acceptable present to the gods.

Odin, stay thy hand from the slaughter of the obscure.
Thor, put down the mallet with which thou beatest, like
red hail, on the skulls of thine enemies. Ye other feasters
in Valhalla, set down the skulls full of mead, and pledge
a health out of a new and noble one to the King of Gods
and men, that the twilight of heaven may come late.
We bring an acceptable present; we bring Ronald of the
Perfect Hand." Thus they sang in the boat, labouring all
the while with the winds and waves, but surer now than
ever of reaching the shore. And they did so by the first
light of the morning. When they came to the circle of
sacred stones, from which the island took its name, they
placed their late conqueror by the largest, and kindled a
fire in the middle. The warm smoke rose thickly against
the cold white morning. "Let me be offered up to your
gods," said Ronald, "like a man, by the sword, and not,
like food, by the fire." "We know all," answered the
priests; "be thou silent." "Treat not him," said Ronald,
"who spared your prince, unworthily. If he must be
sacrificed, let him die as your prince would have died, by
this hand." Still they answered nothing but, "We know
all; be thou silent." Ronald could not help witnessing
these preparations for a new and unexpected death with
an emotion of terror, but disdain and despair were uppermost. Once, and but once, his cheek turned deadly pale
in thinking of Moilena. He shifted his posture resolutely,
and thought of the spirits of the dead, whom he was
about to join. The priests then encircled the fire and the
stone at which he stood with another devoting song; and
Ronald looked earnestly at the ruddy flames, which gave
to his body, as in mockery, a kindly warmth. The priests,
however, did not lay hands on him. They respected the
sparer of their prince so far as not to touch him themselves; they left him to be despatched by the supernatural
beings, whom they confidently expected to come down for
that purpose as soon as they had retired.

Ronald, whose faith was of another description, saw their departure with joy; but it was damped the next minute. What was he to do in winter-time on an island, inhabited only by the fowls and other creatures of the Northern Sea, and never touched at but for a purpose hostile to his hopes? For he now recollected that this was the island he had so often heard of, as the chief seat of the Scandinavian religion, whose traditions had so influenced countries of a different faith that it was believed in Scotland, as well as the Continent, that no human being could live there many hours. Spirits, it was thought, appeared in terrible superhuman shapes, like the bloody idols which the priests worshipped, and carried the stranger off.

The warrior of Inistore had soon too much reason to know the extent of this belief. He was not without fear himself, but disdained to yield to any circumstances without a struggle. He refreshed himself with some snow-water, and, after climbing the highest part of the island to look for a boat in vain (nothing was to be seen but the waves tumbling on all sides after the storm), he set about preparing a habitation. He saw at a little distance, on a slope, the mouth of a rocky cave. This he destined for his shelter at night; and, looking round for a defence for the door, as he knew not whether bears might not be among the inhabitants, he cast his eyes upon the thinnest of the stones which stood upright about the fire. The heart of the warrior, though of a different faith, misgave him as he thought of appropriating this mystical stone, carved full of strange figures; but half in courage, and half in the despair of fear, he suddenly twisted it from its place. No one appeared. The fire altered not. The noise of the fowl and other creatures was no louder on the shore. Ronald smiled at his fears, and knew the undiminished vigour of the Perfect Hand.

He found the cavern already fitted for shelter, doubtless by the Scandinavian priests. He had bitter reason to know how well it sheltered him ; for day after day he hoped in vain that some boat from Inistore would venture upon the island. He beheld sails at a distance, but they never came. He piled stone upon stone, joined old pieces of boats together, and made flags of the seaweed, but all in vain. The vessels, he thought, came nearer, but none so near as to be of use ; and a new and sickly kind of impatience cut across the stout heart of Ronald, and set it beating. He knew not whether it was with the cold or with misery, but his frame would shake for an hour together when he lay down on his dried weeds and feathers to rest. He remembered the happy sleeps that used to follow upon toil ; and he looked with double activity for the eggs and shell-fish on which he sustained himself, and smote double the number of seals, half in the very exercise of his anger ; and then he would fall dead asleep with fatigue.

In this way he bore up against the violences of the winter season, which had now past. The sun looked out with a melancholy smile upon the moss and the poor grass, chequered here and there with flowers almost as poor. There was the buttercup, struggling from a dirty white into a yellow ; and a faint-coloured poppy, neither the good nor the ill of which was then known ; and here and there by the thorny underwood a shrinking violet. The lark alone seemed cheerful, and startled the ear of the desolate chieftain with its climbing triumph in the air. Ronald looked up. His fancy had been made wild and wilful by strange habits and sickened blood ; and he thought impatiently, that if he were up there like the lark he might see his friends and his love in Inistore.

Being naturally, however, of a gentle as well as courageous disposition, the Perfect Hand found the advantage as well as the necessity of turning his violent impulses into noble matter for patience. He had heard of the dreadful

bodily sufferings which the Scandinavian heroes underwent from their enemies with triumphant songs. He
knew that no such sufferings, which were fugitive, could
equal the agonies of a daily martyrdom of mind; and he
cultivated a certain humane pride of patience, in order to
bear them.

His only hope of being delivered from the island now
depended on the Scandinavian priests; but it was a
moot point whether they would respect him for surviving, or kill him on that very account, out of a mixture
of personal and superstitious resentment. He thought
his death the more likely; but this, at least, was a
termination to the dreary prospect of a solitude for life;
and partly out of that hope, and partly from a courageous
patience, he cultivated as many pleasant thoughts and
objects about him as he could. He adorned his cavern
with shells and feathers; he made himself a cap and
cloak of the latter, and boots and a vest of seal-skin,
girding it about with the glossy sea-weed; he cleared
away a circle before the cavern, planted it with the best
grass, and heaped about it the mossiest stones : he strung
some bones of fish with sinews, and fitting a shell beneath
it, the Perfect Hand drew forth the first gentle music
that had been heard in that wild island. He touched it
one day in the midst of a flock of seals, who were basking in the sun; they turned their heads towards the
sound; he thought he saw in their mild faces a human
expression; and from that day forth no seal was ever
slain by the Perfect Hand. He spared even the huge
and cloudy-visaged walrusses, in whose societies he beheld a dull resemblance to the gentler affections; and his
new intimacy with these possessors of the place was
completed by one of the former animals, who having
been rescued by him from a contest with a larger one,
followed him about, as well as its half-formed and dragging
legs would allow, with the officious attachment of a dog.

But the summer was gone, and no one had appeared. The new thoughts and deeper insight into things, which solitude and sorrowful necessity had produced, together with a diminution of his activity, had not tended to strengthen him against the approach of winter; and autumn came upon him like the melancholy twilight of the year. He had now no hope of seeing even the finishers of his existence before the spring. The rising winds among the rocks, and the noise of the whales blowing up their spouts of water, till the caverns thundered with their echoes, seemed to be like heralds of the stern season which was to close him in against approach. He had tried one day to move the stone at the mouth of his habitation a little farther in, and found his strength fail him. He laid himself half reclining on the ground, full of such melancholy thoughts as half bewildered him. Things, by turns, appeared a fierce dream, and a fiercer reality. He was leaning and looking on the ground, and idly twisting his long hair, when his eyes fell upon the hand that held it. It was livid and emaciated. He opened and shut it, opened and shut it again, turned it round, and looked at its ribbed thinness and laid-open machinery; many thoughts came upon him, some which he understood not, and some which he recognised but too well; and a turbid violence seemed rising at his heart, when the seal, his companion, drew nigh, and began licking that weak memorial of the Perfect Hand. A shower of self-pitying tears fell upon the seal's face and the hand together.

On a sudden he heard a voice. It was a deep and loud one, and distinctly called out "Ronald!" He looked up, gasping with wonder. Three times it called out, as if with peremptory command, and three times the rocks and caverns echoed the word with a dim sullenness.

Recollecting himself, he would have risen and answered; but the sudden change of sensations had done what all his sufferings had not been able to do, and he found himself unable either to rise or to speak. The voice called again and again; but it was now more distant, and Ronald's heart sickened as he heard it retreating. His strength seemed to fail him in proportion as it became necessary. Suddenly the voice came back again. It advances. Other voices are heard, all advancing. In a short time, figures come hastily down the slope by the side of his cavern, looking over into the area before it as they descend. They enter. They are before him and about him. Some of them, in a Scandinavian habit, prostrate themselves at his feet, and address him in an unknown language. But these are sent away by another, who remains with none but two youths. Ronald has risen a little, and leans his back against the rock. One of the youths puts his arm between his neck and the rock, and half kneels beside him, turning his face away and weeping. "I am no god, nor a favourite of gods, as these people supposed me," said Ronald, looking up at the chief who was speaking to the other youth : "if thou wilt despatch me then, do so. I only pray thee to let the death be fit for a warrior, such as I once was." The chief appeared agitated. "Speak not ill of the gods, Ronald," said he, "although thou wert blindly brought up. A warrior like thee must be a favourite of heaven. I come to prove it to thee. Dost thou not know me? I come to give thee life for life." Ronald looked more stedfastly. It was the Scandinavian prince whom he had spared, because of his bride, in battle. He smiled, and lifted up his hand to him, which was intercepted and kissed by the youth who held his arm round his neck. "Who are these fair youths?" said Ronald, half turning his head to look in his supporter's face. "This is the bride I spoke of," answered the prince, "who insisted on sharing this voyage with me, and put on this dress to be the bolder in it." "And who is the other?" The *other*, with dried eyes, looked smiling into his, and intercepted the answer also. "Who," said the sweetest voice in the world, "can it be, but one?" With a quick and almost fierce tone, Ronald cried out aloud, "I know the voice;" and he would have fallen flat on the earth, if they had not all three supported him.

It was a mild return to Inistore, Ronald gathering strength all the way, at the eyes and voice of Moilena, and the hands of all three. Their discovery of him was easily explained. The crews of the vessels, who had been afraid to come nearer, had repeatedly seen a figure on the island making signs. The Scandinavian priests related how they had left Ronald there; but insisted that no human being could live upon it, and that some god wished to manifest himself to his faithful worshippers. The heart of Moilena was quick to guess the truth. The prince proposed to accompany the priests. His bride, and the destined bride of his saviour went with him, and returned as you heard; and from that day forth many were the songs in Inistore upon the fortunes of the Perfect Hand and the kindness of the Perfect Voice. Nor were those forgotten who forgot not others.

XII.

THE DAUGHTER OF HIPPOCRATES.

In the time of the Norman reign in Sicily, a vessel bound from that island for Smyrna was driven by a westerly wind upon the island of Cos. The crew did not know where they were, though they had often visited the island; for the trading towns lay in other quarters, and they saw nothing before them but woods and solitudes. They found, however, a comfortable harbour; and the wind having fallen in the night, they went on shore next morning for water. The country proved as solitary as they thought it; which was the more extraordinary, inasmuch as it was very luxuriant, full of wild figs and grapes, with a high uneven ground, and stocked with goats and other animals, who fled whenever they appeared. The bees were remarkably numerous, so that the wild honey, fruits, and delicious water, especially one spring which fell into a beautiful marble bason, made them more and more wonder at every step that they could see no human inhabitants.

Thus idling about and wondering, stretching themselves now and then among the wild thyme and grass, and now getting up to look at some specially fertile place which another called them to see, and which they thought might be turned to fine trading purpose, they came upon a mound covered with trees, which looked into a flat wide lawn of rank grass, with a house at the end of it. They crept nearer towards the house along the mound, still continuing among the trees, for

158

fear they were trespassing at last upon somebody's property. It had a large garden wall at the back, as much covered with ivy as if it had been built of it. Fruit-trees looked over the wall with an unpruned thickness; and neither at the back nor front of the house were there any signs of humanity. It was an ancient marble building, where glass was not to be expected in the windows; but it was much dilapidated, and the grass grew up over the steps. They listened again and again; but nothing was to be heard like a sound of men; nor scarcely of anything else. There was an intense noon-day silence. Only the hares made a rustling noise as they ran about the long hiding grass. The house looked like the tomb of human nature amidst the vitality of earth.

"Did you see?" said one of the crew, turning pale, and hastening to go.

"See what?" said the others.

"What looked out of window."

They all turned their faces towards the house, but saw nothing. Upon this they laughed at their companion, who persisted, however, with great earnestness, and with great reluctance at stopping, to say that he saw a strange hideous kind of face look out of window.

"Let us go, sir," said he, to the captain;—"for I tell ye what: I know this place now: and you, Signor Gualtier," continued he, turning to a young man, "you may now follow that adventure I have often heard you wish to be engaged in."

The crew turned pale, and Gualtier among them.

"Yes," added the man, "we are fallen upon the enchanted part of the island of Cos, where the daughter of—Hush! Look there!"

They turned their faces again, and beheld the head of a large serpent looking out of window. Its eyes were direct upon them; and stretching out of window, it lifted

back its head with little sharp jerks like a fowl, and so
stood keenly gazing.

The terrified sailors would have begun to depart
quicklier than they did, had not fear itself made them
move slowly.   Their legs seemed melting from under
them.

Gualtier tried to rally his voice.   "They say," said
he, "it is a gentle creature. The hares that feed right
in front of the house are a proof of it:—let us all
stay."

The others shook their heads, and spoke in whispers,
still continuing to descend the mound as well as they
could.

"There is something unnatural in that very thing,"
said the captain : "but we will wait for you in the
vessel, if you stay.   We will, by St. Ermo."

The captain had not supposed that Gualtier would
stay an instant; but seeing him linger more than the
rest, he added the oath in question, and in the meantime was hastening with the others to get away as fast
as possible.

The truth is, Gualtier was, in one respect, more
frightened than any one of them.   His legs were more
rooted to the spot.   But the same force of imagination
that helped to detain him, enabled him to muster up
a courage beyond those who found their wills more
powerful; and in the midst of his terror he could not
help thinking what a fine adventure this would be to
tell in Salerno, even if he did but conceal himself a
little, and stay a few minutes longer than the rest.
The thought, however, had hardly come upon him, when
it was succeeded by a fear still more lively, and he was
preparing to follow the others with all the expedition he
could contrive, when a fierce rustling took place in the
trees behind him, and in an instant the serpent's head
was at his feet. Gualtier's brain, as well as heart, seemed

to sicken, as he thought the monstrous object scented him like a bear; but despair coming in aid of a courage naturally fanciful and chivalrous, he bent his eyes more steadily, and found the huge jaws and fangs not only abstaining from hurting him, but crouching and fawning at his feet like a spaniel. At the same time, he called to mind the old legend respecting the creature, and, corroborated as he now saw it, he ejaculated with good firmness, "In the name of God and His saints, what art thou?"

"Hast thou not heard of me?" answered the serpent, in a voice whose singular human slenderness made it seem the more horrible.

"I guess who thou art," answered Gualtier: "the fearful thing in the island of Cos."

"I am that loathly thing," replied the serpent; "once not so."

And Gualtier thought that its voice trembled sorrowfully.

The monster told Gualtier that what was said of her was true: that she had been a serpent hundreds of years, feeling old age and renewing her youth at the end of each century; that it was a curse of Diana's which had changed her, and that she was never to resume a human form till somebody was found kind and bold enough to kiss her on the mouth. As she spoke this word, she raised her crest, and sparkled so with her fiery green eyes, dilating at the same time the corners of her jaws, that the young man thrilled through his very scalp.

He stepped back with a look of the utmost horror and loathing. The creature gave a sharp groan inwardly, and, after rolling her neck franticly on the ground, withdrew a little back likewise, and seemed to be looking another way.

Gualtier heard two or three little sounds as of a person weeping piteously, yet trying to subdue its voice;

L

and, looking with breathless curiosity, he saw the side of
the loathly creature's face bathed in tears.

"Why speakest thou, lady," said he, "if lady thou art,
of the curse of the false goddess Diana, who never was,
or only a devil?   I cannot kiss thee!" and he shuddered
with a horrible shudder as he spoke; "but I will bless
thee in the name of the true God, and even mark thee
with His cross."

The serpent shook her head mournfully, still keeping
it turned round.   She then faced him again, hanging
her head in a dreary and desponding manner.

"Thou knowest not," said she, "what I know.   Diana
both was, and never was; and there are many other
things on earth which are, and yet are not.   Thou canst
not comprehend it, even though thou art kind.   But the
heavens alter not, neither the sun, nor the strength of
nature; and if thou wert kinder, I should be as I once
was, happy and human.   Suffice it, that nothing can
change me but what I said."

"Why wert thou changed, thou fearful and mysterious
thing?" said Gualtier.

"Because I denied Diana, as thou dost," answered the
serpent; "and it was pronounced an awful crime in me,
though it is none in thee; and I was to be made a thing
loathsome in men's eyes.   Let me not catch thine eye,
I beseech thee; but go thy way, and be safe; for I feel
a cruel thought coming on me, which will shake my
innermost soul, though it shall not harm thee.   But I
could make thee suffer for the pleasure of seeing thine
anguish, even as some tyrants do; and is not that
dreadful?"   And the monster openly shed tears, and
sobbed.

There was something in this mixture of avowed cruelty
and weeping contradiction to it, which made Gualtier
remain in spite of himself.   But fear was still uppermost
in his mind, when he looked upon the mouth that was to

be kissed; and he held fast round a tree with one hand, and his sword as fast in the other, watching the movements of her neck as he conversed.

"How did thy father, the sage Hippocrates," asked he, "suffer thee to come to this?"

"My father," replied she, "sage and good as he was, was but a Greek mortal; and the great virgin was a worshipped goddess. I pray thee go."

She uttered the last word in a tone of loud anguish; but the very horror of it made Gualtier hesitate, and he said,—

"How can I know that it is not thy destiny to deceive the merciful into this horrible kiss, that then, and then only, thou may'st devour them?"

But the serpent rose higher at this, and, looking around loftily, said in a mild and majestic tone of voice:

"O ye green and happy woods, breathing like sleep! O safe and quiet population of these leafy places, dying brief deaths! O sea! O earth! O heavens, never uttering syllable to man! Is there no way to make better known the meaning of your gentle silence, of your long basking pleasures and brief pains? And must the want of what is beautiful and kind from others ever remain different from what is beautiful and kind in itself? And must form obscure essence? And human confidence in good from within never be bolder than suspicion of evil from without? O ye large-looking and grand benignities of creation, is it that we are atoms in a dream; or that your largeness and benignity are in those only who see them, and that it is for us to hang over ye till we wake you into a voice with our kisses? I yearn to be made beautiful by one kind action, and beauty itself will not believe me!"

Gualtier, though not a foolish youth, understood little or nothing of this mystic apostrophe; but something or

other made him bear in mind, and really incline to
believe that it was a transformed woman speaking to
him; and he was making a violent internal effort to
conquer his repugnance to the kiss, when some hares,
starting from him as they passed, ran and cowered
behind the folds of the monster: and she stooped her
head and licked them.

"By Christ!" exclaimed he, "whom the wormy grave
gathered into its arms, to save us from our corruptions, I
will do this thing; so may He have mercy on my soul,
whether I live or die; for the very hares take refuge in
her shadow."

And, shuddering and shutting his eyes, he put his
mouth out for her to meet; and he seemed to feel, in
his blindness, that dreadful mouth approaching; and he
made the sign of the cross, and he murmured internally
the name of Him who cast seven devils out of Mary
Magdalen, that afterwards anointed His feet; and in the
midst of his courageous agony he felt a small mouth fast
and warm upon his, and a hand about his neck, and
another on his left hand; and opening his eyes, he
dropped them upon two of the sweetest that ever looked
into the eye of man. But the hares fled, for they had
loved the serpent, and knew not the beautiful human
being.

Great was the fame of Gualtier, not only throughout
all the Grecian islands, but on both continents, and most
of all in Sicily, where every one of his countrymen
thought he had had a hand in the enterprise, for being
born on the same soil. The captain and his crew never
came again, for, alas! they had gone off without waiting,
as they promised. But Tancred, prince of Salerno, came
himself with a knightly train to see Gualtier, who lived
with his lady in the same place, all her past sufferings
appearing as nothing to her before even a month of love,
and even sorrowful habit having endeared it to her.

Tancred, and his knights, and learned clerks, came in a noble ship, every oar having a painted scutcheon over the rowlock; and Gualtier and his lady feasted them nobly, and drank to them amidst music in cups of Hippocras,—that knightly liquor afterwards so renowned, which she retained the secret of making from her sage father, whose name it bore. And when king Tancred, with a gentle gravity in the midst of his mirth, expressed a hope that the beautiful lady no longer worshipped Diana, Gualtier said, "No, indeed, sir;" and she looked in Gualtier's face, as she sat next him, with the sweetest look in the world, as who should say, "No, indeed:—I worship thee and thy kind heart."

XIII.

GODIVA.

THIS is the lady who, under the title of Countess of
Coventry, used to make such a figure in our childhood
upon some old pocket-pieces of that city. We hope she
is in request there still; otherwise the inhabitants deserve
to be sent *from* Coventry. That city was famous in
saintly legends for the visit of the eleven thousand
virgins,—an "incredible number," quoth Selden. But
the eleven thousand virgins have vanished with their
credibility, and a noble-hearted woman of flesh and blood
is Coventry's true immortality.

The story of Godiva is not a fiction, as many suppose
it. At least it is to be found in Matthew of Westminster,
and is not of a nature to have been a mere invention.
Her name, and that of her husband, Leofric, are mentioned in an old charter recorded by another early historian.
That the story is omitted by Hume and others argues
little against it; for the latter are accustomed to confound
the most interesting anecdotes of times and manners with
something below the dignity of history (a very absurd
mistake); and Hume, of whose philosophy better things
might have been expected, is notoriously less philosophical
in his history than in any other of his works. A certain
coldness of temperament, not unmixed with aristocratical
pride, or at least with a great aversion from everything
like vulgar credulity, rendered his scepticism so extreme
that it became a sort of superstition in turn, and blinded
him to the claims of every species of enthusiasm, civil as

well as religious. Milton, with his poetical eyesight, saw better, when he meditated the history of his native country. We do not remember whether he relates the present story; but we remember well, that at the beginning of his fragment on that subject, he says he shall relate doubtful stories as well as authentic ones, for the benefit of those, if no others, who will know how to make use of them, namely, the poets.[1] We have faith, however, in the story ourselves. It has innate evidence enough for us, to give full weight to that of the old annalist. Imagination can invent a good deal; affection more: but affection can sometimes do things, such as the tenderest imagination is not in the habit of inventing; and this piece of noble-heartedness we believe to have been one of them.

Leofric, Earl of Leicester, was the lord of a large feudal territory in the middle of England, of which Coventry formed a part. He lived in the time of Edward the Confessor; and was so eminently a feudal lord that the hereditary greatness of his dominion appears to have been singular even at that time, and to have lasted with an uninterrupted succession from Ethelbald to the Conquest,—a period of more than three hundred years. He was a great and useful opponent of the famous Earl Goodwin.

Whether it was owing to Leofric or not does not appear, but Coventry was subject to a very oppressive tollage, by which it would seem that the feudal despot enjoyed the greater part of the profit of all marketable commodities. The progress of knowledge has shown us how abominable, and even how unhappy for all parties, is an injustice of this description; yet it gives one an

[1] When Dr. Johnson, among his other impatient accusations of our great republican, charged him with telling unwarrantable stories in his history, he must have overlooked this announcement; and yet, if we recollect, it is but in the second page of the fragment. So hasty, and blind, and liable to be put to shame, is prejudice.

extraordinary idea of a mind in those times, to see it capable of piercing through the clouds of custom, of ignorance, and even of self-interest, and petitioning the petty tyrant to forego such a privilege. This mind was Godiva's. The other sex, always more slow to admit reason through the medium of feeling, were then occupied to the full in their warlike habits. It was reserved for a woman to anticipate ages of liberal opinion, and to surpass them in the daring virtue of setting a principle above a custom.

Godiva entreated her lord to give up his fancied right; but in vain. At last, wishing to put an end to her importunities, he told her, either in a spirit of bitter jesting, or with a playful raillery that could not be bitter with so sweet an earnestness, that he would give up his tax provided she rode through the city of Coventry, naked. She took him at his word. One may imagine the astonishment of a fierce unlettered chieftain, not untinged with chivalry, at hearing a woman, and that too of the greatest delicacy and rank, maintaining seriously her intention of acting in a manner contrary to all that was supposed fitting for her sex, and at the same time forcing upon him a sense of the very beauty of her conduct by its principled excess. It is probable that, as he could not prevail upon her to give up her design, he had sworn some religious oath when he made his promise; but be this as it may, he took every possible precaution to secure her modesty from hurt. The people of Coventry were ordered to keep within doors, to close up all their windows and outlets, and not to give a glance into the streets upon pain of death. The day came; and Coventry, it may be imagined, was silent as death. The lady went out at the palace door, was set on horseback, and at the same time divested of her wrapping garment, as if she had been going into a bath; then taking the fillet from her head, she let down her long and lovely tresses, which poured around her body like a veil; and so, with only her white legs remaining conspicuous, took her gentle way through the streets.[1]

What scene can be more touching to the imagination— beauty, modesty, feminine softness, a daring sympathy; an extravagance producing, by the nobleness of its object and the strange gentleness of its means, the grave and profound effect of the most reverend custom. We may suppose the scene taking place in the warm noon: the doors all shut, the windows closed; the Earl and his court serious and wondering; the other inhabitants, many of them gushing with grateful tears, and all reverently listening to hear the footsteps of the horse; and lastly, the lady herself, with a downcast but not a shamefaced eye, looking towards the earth through her flowing locks, and riding through the dumb and deserted streets, like an angelic spirit.

It was an honourable superstition in that part of the country, that a man who ventured to look at the fair saviour of his native town was said to have been struck blind. But the vulgar use to which this superstition has been turned by some writers of late times is not so honourable. The whole story is as unvulgar and as sweetly serious as can be conceived.

Drayton has not made so much of this subject as might have been expected; yet what he says is said well and earnestly:

> "Coventry at length
> From her small mean regard, recovered state and strength;
> By Leofric her lord, yet in base bondage held,
> The people from her marts by tollage were expelled;

---

[1] "Nuda," says Matthew of Westminster, "equum ascendens, crines capitis et tricas dissolvens, corpus suum totum, præter crura candidissima, inde velavit." See Selden's Notes to the *Polyolbion* of Drayton, song 13. It is Selden from whom we learn that Leofric was Earl of Leicester, and the other particulars of him mentioned above. The Earl was buried at Coventry, his countess most probably in the same tomb.

Whose duchess which desired this tribute to release,
Their freedom often begged. The duke, to make her cease,
Told her, that if she would his loss so far enforce,
His will was, she should ride stark naked upon a horse
By daylight through the street: which certainly he thought
In her heroic breast so deeply would have wrought,
That in her former suit she would have left to deal.
But that most princely dame, as one devoured with zeal,
Went on, and by that mean the city clearly freed."

XIV

THE ITALIAN GIRL.

THE sun was shining beautifully one summer evening, as if he bade sparkling farewell to a world which he had made happy. It seemed also by his looks as if he promised to make his appearance again to-morrow; but there was at times a deep breathing western wind, and dark purple clouds came up here and there like gorgeous waiters at a funeral. The children in a village not far from the metropolis were playing, however, on the green, content with the brightness of the moment, when they saw a female approaching, who gathered them about her by the singularity of her dress. It was not a very remarkable dress; but any difference from the usual apparel of their countrywomen appeared so to them; and crying out, "A French girl! a French girl!" they ran up to her, and stood looking and talking.

The stranger seated herself upon a bench that was fixed between two elms, and for a moment leaned her head against one of them, as if faint with walking; but she raised it speedily, and smiled with complacency on the rude urchins. She had a boddice and petticoat on of different colours, and a handkerchief tied neatly about her head with the point behind. On her hands were gloves without fingers; and she wore about her neck a guitar, upon the strings of which one of her hands rested. The children thought her very handsome. Anybody else would also have thought her very ill; but they saw nothing before them but a good-natured looking foreigner

and a guitar, and they asked her to play. "*Oh che bei
ragazzi!*" said she, in a soft and almost inaudible voice;
—"*Che visi lieti!*"[1] and she began to play. She tried to
sing, too; but her voice failed her, and she shook her
head smilingly, saying, "*Stanca! Stanca!*"[2] "Sing—
do sing," said the children; and, nodding her head, she
was trying to do so, when a set of boys came up and
joined in the request. "No, no," said one of the elder
boys; "she is not well. You are ill, a'nt you, miss?"
added he, laying his hand upon hers as if to hinder it.
He drew out the last word somewhat doubtfully, for her
appearance perplexed him; he scarcely knew whether to
take her for a strolling musician or a lady strayed from a
sick-bed. "*Grazie!*" said she, understanding his look:
"*troppo stanca! troppo!*"[3]

By this time the usher came up, and addressed her in
French; but she only understood a word here and there.
He then spoke Latin; and she repeated one or two of his
words, as if they were familiar to her.

"She is an Italian," said he, looking round with a
good-natured importance; "for the Italian is but a bastard
of the Latin." The children looked with the more wonder,
thinking he was speaking of the fair musician.

"*Non dubito,*" continued the usher, "*quin tu lectitas
poetam illum celeberrimum, Tassonem;*[4] *Taxum,* I should
say properly, but the departure from the Italian name is
considerable." The stranger did not understand a word.

"I speak of Tasso," said the usher,—"of Tasso."

"*Tasso! Tasso!*" repeated the fair minstrel,—"oh—
conosco—il Tàs-so;"[5] and she hung with an accent of
beautiful languor upon the first syllable.

"Yes," returned the worthy scholar; "doubtless your

[1] Oh, what fine boys! What happy faces!
[2] Weary! weary!
[3] Thanks: too weary! too weary!
[4] Doubtless you read that celebrated poet Tasso.
[5] Oh—I know—Tasso.

accent may be better. Then, of course, you know those classical lines :

> " Intanto Erminia infra l'ombrosy pianty
> D'antica selva dal cavallo—*what is it?*"

The stranger repeated the words in a tone of fondness, like those of an old friend :

> " Intanto Erminia infra l'ombrose piante
> D'antica selva dal cavallo è scorta ;
> Ne più governo il fren la man tremante,
> E mezza quasi par, tra viva e morta." [1]

Our usher's common-place book had supplied him with a fortunate passage, for it was a favourite one of her countrywomen. It also singularly applied to her situation. There was a sort of exquisite mixture of clearness in her utterance of these verses, which gave some of the children a better idea of French than they had had ; for they could not get it out of their heads that she must be a French girl. "Italian-French, perhaps," said one of them ; but her voice trembled as she went on, like the hand she spoke of.

"I have heard my poor cousin Montague sing those very lines," said the boy who prevented her from playing.

"Montague?" repeated the stranger very plainly, but turning paler and fainter. She put one of her hands in turn upon the boy's affectionately, and pointed towards the spot where the church was.

"Yes, yes," cried the boy ; "why, she knew my cousin. She must have known him in Florence."

"I told you," said the usher, " she was an Italian."

" Help her to my aunt's," continued the youth ; "she'll understand her.—Lean upon me, miss ;" and he repeated the last word without his former hesitation.

---

[1] Meantime in the old wood, the palfrey bore
Erminia deeper into shade and shade ;
Her trembling hands could hold him in no more,
And she appeared betwixt alive and dead.

Only a few boys followed her to the door, the rest
having been awed away by the usher. As soon as the
stranger entered the house and saw an elderly lady who
received her kindly, she exclaimed, " La Signora Madre,"
and fell in a swoon at her feet.

She was taken to bed, and attended with the utmost
care by her hostess, who would not suffer her to talk till
she had had a sleep. She merely heard enough to find
out that the stranger had known her son in Italy; and
she was thrown into a painful state of suspicion by the
poor girl's eyes, which followed her about the room till
the lady fairly came up and closed them.

" Obedient! obedient!" said the patient,—" obedient
in every thing: only the Signora will let me kiss her
hand;" and taking it with her own trembling one, she
laid her cheek upon it, and it stayed there till she had
dropt asleep for weariness.

<blockquote>
" Silken rest
Tie all thy cares up!"
</blockquote>

thought her kind watcher, who was doubly thrown upon
a recollection of that beautiful passage in Beaumont and
Fletcher by the suspicion she had of the cause of the
girl's visit. "And yet," thought she, "turning her eyes
with a thin tear in them towards the church spire, "he
was an excellent boy,—the boy of my heart."

When the stranger woke, the secret was explained;
and if the mind of her hostess was relieved, it was only
the more touched with pity, and indeed moved with
respect and admiration. The dying girl (for she evidently
was dying, and happy at the thought of it) was the niece
of a humble tradesman in Florence, at whose house young
Montague, who was a gentleman of small fortune, had
lodged and fallen sick during his travels. She was a
lively, good-natured girl, whom he used to hear coquetting
and playing the guitar with her neighbours; and it was

greatly on this account that her considerate and hushing gravity struck him whenever she entered his room. One day he heard no more coquetting, nor even the guitar. He asked the reason, when she came to give him some drink; and she said she had heard him mention some noise that disturbed him.

"But you do not call your voice and your music a noise," said he, "do you, Rosaura? I hope not, for I had expected it would give me strength to get rid of this fever and reach home."

Rosaura turned pale, and let the patient into a secret; but what surprised and delighted him was, that she played her guitar nearly as often as before, and sang too, only less sprightly airs.

"You get better and better, Signor," said she, "every day, and your mother will see you and be happy. I hope you will tell her what a good doctor you had."

"The best in the world," cried he; and as he sat up in bed, he put his arm round her waist, and kissed her.

"Pardon me, Signora," said the poor girl to her hostess; "but I felt that arm round my waist for a week after: aye, almost as much as if it had been there."

"And Charles felt that you did," thought his mother; "for he never told me the story."

"He begged my pardon," continued she, "as I was hastening out of the room, and hoped I should not construe his warmth into impertinence. And to hear him talk so to me, who used to fear what he might think of myself; it made me stand in the passage, and lean my head against the wall, and weep such bitter, and yet such sweet tears! But he did not hear them. No, madame, he did not know, indeed, how much I—how much I"—

"Loved him, child," interrupted Mrs. Montague; "you have a right to say so, and I wish he had been alive to say as much to you himself."

"Oh, good God!" said the dying girl, her tears flowing

away, "this is too great a happiness for me, to hear his own mother talking so." And again she lays her weak head upon the lady's hand.

The latter would have persuaded her to sleep again; but she said she could not for joy: "for I'll tell you, madam," continued she,—"I do not believe you will think it foolish, for something very grave at my heart tells me it is not so;—but I have had a long thought" (and her voice and look grew more exalted as she spoke), "which has supported me through much toil and many disagreeable things to this country and this place; and I will tell you what it is, and how it came into my mind. I received this letter from your son."

Here she drew out a paper which, though carefully wrapped up in several others, was much worn at the sides. It was dated from the village, and ran thus:

"'This comes from the Englishman whom Rosaura nursed so kindly at Florence. She will be sorry to hear that her kindness was in vain, for he is dying; and he sometimes fears that her sorrow will be greater than he could wish it to be. But marry one of your kind countrymen, my good girl; for all must love Rosaura who know her. If it shall be my lot ever to meet her in heaven, I will thank her as a blessed tongue only can.'

"As soon I read this letter, madam," continues Rosaura, "and what he said about heaven, it flashed into my head, that though I did not deserve him on earth, I might, perhaps, by trying and patience, deserve to be joined with him in heaven, where there is no distinction of persons. My uncle was pleased to see me become a religious pilgrim; but he knew as little of the world as I, and I found that I could earn my way to England better, and quite as religiously, by playing my guitar, which was also more independent; and I had often heard your son talk of independence and freedom, and commend me for doing what he was pleased to call so much kindness to others. So I played my guitar from Florence all the way to England, and all that I earned by it I gave away to the poor, keeping enough to procure me lodging. I lived on bread and water, and used to weep happy tears over it, because I looked up to heaven and thought he might see me. I have sometimes, though not often, met with small insults; but if ever they threatened to grow greater, I begged the people to desist in the kindest way I could, even smiling and saying I would please them if I had the heart; which might be wrong, but it seemed as if deep thoughts told me to say so; and they used to look astonished, and left off; which made me the more hope that St. Philip and the Holy Virgin did not think ill of my endeavours. So playing, and giving alms in this manner, I arrived in the neighbourhood of your beloved village, where I fell sick for a while, and was very kindly treated in an out-house; though the people, I thought, seemed to look strange and afraid on this crucifix—(though your son never did),—though he taught me to think kindly of everybody, and hope the best, and leave everything, except our own endeavours, to heaven. I fell sick, madam, because I found for certain that the Signor Montague was dead, albeit I had no hope that he was alive."

She stopped awhile for breath, for she was growing weaker and weaker, and her hostess would fain have had her keep silence; but she pressed her hand as well as she might, and prayed with such a patient panting of voice to be allowed to go on, that she was. She smiled thankfully, and resumed :

"So when—so when I got my strength a little again, I walked on and came to the beloved village, and I saw the beautiful white church-spire in the trees; and then I knew where his body slept, and I thought some kind person would help me to die, with my face looking towards the church, as it now does; and death is upon me even now; but lift me a little higher on the pillows, dear lady, that I may see the green ground of the hill."

She was raised up as she wished, and, after looking awhile with a placid feebleness at the hill, said, in a very low voice, "Say one prayer for me, dear lady; and if it be not too proud in me, call me in it your daughter."

The mother of her beloved summoned up a grave and earnest voice, as well as she might, and knelt, and said: "O Heavenly Father of us all, who, in the midst of Thy manifold and merciful bounties, bringest us into strong passes of anguish, which nevertheless Thou enablest us to go through, look down, we beseech Thee, upon this Thy young and innocent servant, the daughter—that might have been—of my heart, and enable her spirit to pass through the struggling bonds of mortality, and be gathered into Thy rest with those we love. Do, dear and great God, of Thy infinite mercy, for we are poor weak creatures, both young and old"—here her voice melted away into a breathing tearfulness; and, after remaining on her knees a moment longer, she rose and looked upon the bed, and saw that the weary smiling one was no more.

XV.

THE TRUE STORY OF VERTUMNUS AND POMONA.

WEAK and uninitated are they who talk of things modern as opposed to the idea of antiquity; who fancy that the Assyrian monarchy must have preceded tea-drinking; and that no Sims or Gregson walked in a round hat and trousers before the times of Inachus. Plato has informed us (and therefore everybody ought to know), that at stated periods of time everything which has taken place on earth is acted over again. There have been a thousand or a million reigns, for instance, of Charles the Second, and there will be an infinite number more: the toothache we had in the year 1811 is making ready for us some thousands of years hence; again shall people be wise and in love, as surely as the May - blossoms reappear; and again will Alexander make a fool of himself at Babylon, and Bonaparte in Russia.

Among the heaps of modern stories which are accounted ancient, and which have been deprived of their true appearance by the alteration of colouring and costume, there is none more decidedly belonging to modern times than that of Vertumnus and Pomona. Vertumnus was, and will be, a young fellow, remarkable for his accomplishments, in the several successive reigns of Charles the Second; and, I find, practised his story over in the autumn of the year 1680. He was the younger brother of a respectable family in Herefordshire; and, from his genius at turning himself to a variety of shapes, came to be called, in after-ages, by his classical name. In like manner, Pomona, the heroine of the story, being the goddess of those parts, and singularly fond of their scenery and productions, the Latin poets, in after-ages, transformed her adventures according to their fashion, making her a goddess of mythology, and giving her a name after her beloved fruits. Her real name was Miss Appleton. I shall therefore waive that matter once for all, and, retaining only the appellation which poetry has rendered so pleasant, proceed with the true story.

Pomona was a beauty like her name, all fruit and bloom. She was a ruddy brunette, luxuriant without grossness; and had a spring in her step, like apples dancing on a bough. It was no poetical figure to say of her, that her lips were cherries and her cheeks a peach. Her locks, in clusters about her face, trembled heavily as she walked. The colour called Pomona-green was named after her favourite dress. Sometimes in her clothes she imitated one kind of fruit and sometimes another, philosophizing in a pretty poetical manner on the common nature of things, and saying there was more in the smiles of her lovers than they suspected. Her dress now resembled a burst of white blossoms, and now of red; but her favourite one was green, both coat and boddice, from which her beautiful face looked forth like a bud. To see her tending her trees in her orchard (for she would work herself, and sing all the while like a milk-maid)—to see her, I say, tending the fruit-trees, never caring for letting her boddice slip a little off her shoulders, and turning away now and then to look up at a bird, when her lips would glance in the sunshine like cherries bedewed,— such a sight, you may imagine, was not to be had everywhere. The young clowns would get up on the trees for a glimpse of her, over the garden-wall; and swear she was like an angel in Paradise.

Everybody was in love with her. The squire was in

love with her; the attorney was in love; the parson was
particularly in love. The peasantry in their smock-frocks,
old and young, were all in love. You never saw such a
loving place in your life; yet somehow or other the
women were not jealous, nor fared the worse. The people
only seemed to have grown the kinder. Their hearts
overflowed to all about them. Such toasts at the great
house! The squire's name was Payne, which afterwards
came to be called Pan. Pan, Payne (Paynim), Pagan, a
villager. The race was so numerous that country gentlemen obtained the name of Paynim in general, as distinguished from the nobility; a circumstance which has not
escaped the learning of Milton:

> "Both Paynim and the Peers."

Silenus was Cy or Cymon Lenox, the host of the "Tun,"
a fat merry old fellow, renowned in the song as old Sir
Cymon the King. He was in love too. All the Satyrs,
or rude wits of the neighbourhood, and all the Fauns, or
softer-spoken fellows,—none of them escaped. There
was also a Quaker gentleman—I forget his name—who
made himself conspicuous. Pomona confessed to herself
that he had merit; but it was so unaccompanied with
anything of the ornamental or intellectual, that she could
not put up with him. Indeed, though she was of a loving
nature, and had every other reason to wish herself settled
(for she was an heiress and an orphan), she could not find
it in her heart to respond to any of the rude multitude
around her; which at last occasioned such impatience in
them, and uneasiness to herself, that she was fain to keep
close at home, and avoid the lanes and country assemblies,
for fear of being carried off. It was then that the clowns
used to mount the trees outside her garden-wall to get a
sight of her.

Pomona wrote to a cousin she had in town, of the name
of Cerintha:

"Oh, my dear Cerintha, what am I to do! I could
laugh while I say it, though the tears positively come
into my eyes; but it is a sad thing to be an heiress
with ten thousand a-year, and one's guardian just dead.
Nobody will let me alone. And the worst of it is, that
while the rich animals that pester me disgust one with
talking about their rent-rolls, the younger brothers force
me to be suspicious of their views upon mine. I could
throw all my money into the Wye for vexation. God
knows I do not care twopence for it. Oh, Cerintha! I
wish you were unmarried, and could change yourself into
a man, and come and deliver me; for you are disinterested and sincere, and that is all I require. At all events,
I will run for it, and be with you before winter; for here
I cannot stay. Your friend the Quaker has just rode by.
He says, 'verily,' that I am cold! I say verily he is no
wiser than his horse; and that I could pitch him after
my money."

Cerintha sympathized heartily with her cousin, but she
was perplexed to know what to do. There were plenty
of wits and young fellows of her acquaintance, both rich
and poor; but only one whom she thought fit for her
charming cousin, and he was a younger brother, as poor
as a rat. Besides, he was not only liable to suspicion on
that account, but full of delicacies of his own, and the
last man in the world to hazard a generous woman's dislike. This was no other than our friend Vertumnus.
His real name was Vernon. He lived about five miles
from Pomona, and was almost the only young fellow of
any vivacity who had not been curious enough to get a
sight of her. He had got a notion that she was proud.
"She may be handsome," thought he; "but a handsome
proud face is but a handsome ugly one to my thinking,
and I'll not venture my poverty to her ill-humour."
Cerintha had half made up her mind to undeceive him
through the medium of his sister, who was an acquaint-

ance of hers; but an accident did it for her. Vertumnus was riding one day with some friends, who had been rejected, when, passing by Pomona's orchard, he saw one of her clownish admirers up in the trees, peeping at her over the wall. The gaping, unsophisticated admiration of the lad made them stop.

"Devil take me," said one of our hero's companions, "if they are not at it still. Why, you booby, did you never see a proud woman before, that you stand gaping there, as if your soul had gone out of ye?"

"Proud," said the lad, looking down:—"a wouldn't say nay to a fly, if gentlefolks wouldn't teaze 'un so."

"Come," said our hero, "I'll take this opportunity, and see for myself."

He was up in the tree in an instant, and almost as speedily exclaimed, "God! What a face!"

"He has it, by the lord!" cried the others laughing: —"fairly struck through the ribs, by Jove. Look, if booby and he arn't sworn friends on the thought of it."

It looked very like it certainly. Our hero had scarcely gazed at her, when, without turning away his eyes, he clapped his hand upon that of the peasant with a hearty shake, and said, "You're right, my friend. If there is pride in that face, truth itself is a lie. What a face! What eyes! What a figure!"

Pomona was observing her old gardener fill a basket. From time to time he looked up at her, smiling and talking. She was eating a plum; and as she said something that made them laugh, her rosy mouth sparkled with all its pearls in the sun.

"Pride!" thought Vertumnus; "there's no more pride in that charming mouth than there is folly enough to relish my fine companions here.

Our hero returned home more thoughtful than he came, replying but at intervals to the raillery of those with him, and then giving them pretty savage cuts. He was more out of humour with his poverty than he had ever felt, and not at all satisfied with the accomplishments which might have emboldened him to forget it. However, in spite of his delicacies, he felt it would be impossible not to hazard rejection like the rest. He only made up his mind to set about paying his addresses in a different manner, though how it was to be done he could not very well see. His first impulse was to go to her, and state the plain case at once ; to say how charming she was, and how poor her lover, and that nevertheless he did not care twopence for her riches, if she would but believe him. The only delight of riches would be to share them with her. "But then," said he, "how is she to take my word for that?"

On arriving at home he found his sister prepared to tell him what he had found out for himself—that Pomona was not proud. Unfortunately she added that the beautiful heiress had acquired a horror of younger brothers. "Ay," thought he, "there it is. I shall not get her, precisely because I have at once the greatest need of her money and the greatest contempt for it. Alas, not yet so! I have not contempt for anything that belongs to her, even her money. How heartily could I accept it from her, if she knew me, and if she is as generous as I take her to be! How delightful would it be to plant, to build, to indulge a thousand expenses in her company! O those rascals of rich men, without sense or taste, that are now going about spending their money as they please, and buying *my* jewels and *my* cabinets, that I ought to be making her presents of. I could tear my hair to think of it.

It happened, luckily or unluckily for our hero, that he was the best amateur actor that had ever appeared. Betterton could not perform Hamlet better, nor Lacy a friar.

He disguised himself, and contrived to get hired in his lady's household as a footman. It was a difficult matter, all the other servants having been there since she was a

child, and just grown old enough to escape the passion
common to all who saw her. They loved her like a
daughter of their own, and were indignant at the trouble
her lovers gave her. Vertumnus, however, made out his
case so well that they admitted him. For a time all went
on smoothly. Yes; for three or four weeks he performed
admirably, confining himself to the real footman. Nothing
could exceed the air of indifferent zeal with which he
waited at table. He was respectful, he was attentive,
even officious; but still as to a footman's mistress, not as
to a lover's. He looked in her face as if he did not wish
to kiss her; said "Yes, ma'am," and "No, ma'am," like
any other servant; and consented, not without many pangs
to his vanity, to wear proper footman's clothes—namely,
such as did not fit him. He even contrived, by a violent
effort, to suppress all appearance of emotion, when he
doubled up the steps of her chariot, after seeing the finest
foot and ankle in the world. In his haste to subdue this
emotion, he was one day nigh betraying himself. He
forgot his part so far as to clap the door too with more
vehemence than usual. His mistress started, and gave a
cry. He thought he had shut her hand in, and, opening
the door again with more vehemence, and as pale as death,
exclaimed, "God of Heaven! What have I done to
her!"

"Nothing, James," said his mistress smiling; "only
another time you need not be in quite such a hurry."
She was surprised at the turn of his words, and at a certain air which she observed for the first time; but the
same experience which might have enabled her to detect
him, led her, by a reasonable vanity, to think that love
had exalted her footman's manners. This made her
observe him with some interest afterwards, and notice how
good looking he was, and that his shape was better than
his clothes; but he continued to act his part so well that
she suspected nothing further. She only resolved, if he

gave any more evidences of being in love, to despatch him
after his betters.

By degrees our hero's nature became too much for his
art. He behaved so well among his fellow-servants that
they all took a liking to him. Now, when we please
others, and they show it, we wish to please them more;
and it turned out that James could play on the *viol di
gamba.* He played so well that his mistress must needs
inquire "what musician they had in the house." "James,
madam."—A week or two after, somebody was reading a
play, and making them all die with laughter.—"Who is
that reading so well there, and making you all a parcel of
madcaps?"—"It's only James, madam."—"I have a prodigious footman!" thought Pomona.

Another day my lady's maid came up all in tears
to do something for her mistress, and could scarcely
speak.

"What's the matter, Lucy?"

"Oh, James, madam!"

Her lady blushed a little, and was going to be angry.

"I hope he has not been uncivil?"

"Oh, no, ma'am; only I could not bear his being turned
out o' doors!"

"Turned out of doors!"

"Yes, ma'am; and their being so cruel as to singe his
white head."

"Singe his white head! Surely the girl's head is
turned. What is it, poor soul?"

"Oh, nothing, ma'am. Only the old king in the play,
as your ladyship knows. They turn him out o' doors, and
singe his white head; and Mr. James did it so natural
like, that he has made us all of a drown of tears. 'Tother
day he called me his Ophelia, and was so angry with me,
I could have died."

"This man is no footman," said the lady. She sent for
him upstairs, and the butler with him.

"Pray, sir, may I beg the favour of knowing who you are ?"

The abruptness of this question totally confounded our hero.

"For God's sake, madam, do not think it worth your while to be angry with me, and I will tell you all."

"Worth my while, sir! I know not what you mean by its being worth my while," cried our heroine, who really felt more angry than she wished to be ; "but when an impostor comes into the house, it is natural to wish to be on one's guard against him."

"Impostor, madam!" said he, reddening in his turn, and rising with an air of dignity. "It is true," he added, in a humbler tone, "I am not exactly what I seem to be ; but I am a younger brother of a good family, and "—

"A younger brother!" exclaimed Pomona, turning away with a look of despair.

"Oh, those d—d words!" thought Vertumnus ; "they have undone me. I must go ; and yet it is hard."

"I go, madam," said he in a hurry. "Believe me in only this, that I shall give you no unbecoming disturbance ; and I must vindicate myself so far as to say that I did not come into this house for what you suppose." Then giving her a look of inexpressible tenderness and respect, and retiring as he said it, with a low bow, he added, "May neither imposture nor unhappiness ever come near you."

Pomona could not help thinking of the strange footman she had had. "He did not come into the house for what I supposed." She did not know whether to be pleased or not at this phrase. What did he mean by it ? What did he think she supposed ? Upon the whole, she found her mind occupied with the man a little too much, and proceeded to busy herself with her orchard.

There was now more caution observed in admitting new servants into the house ; yet a new gardener's assistant

came, who behaved like a reasonable man for two months.
He then passionately exclaimed one morning, as Pomona
was rewarding him for some roses, "I cannot bear it!"
—and turned out to be our hero, who was obliged to
decamp. My lady became more cautious than ever, and
would speak to all the new servants herself. One day a
very remarkable thing occurred. A whole side of the
greenhouse was smashed to pieces. The glazier was sent
for, not without suspicion of being the perpetrator; and
the man's way of behaving strengthened it, for he stood
looking about him, and handling the glass to no purpose.
His assistant did all the work, and yet somehow did not
seem to get on with it. The truth was, the fellow was
innocent, and yet not so, for he had brought our hero with
him as his journeyman. Pomona, watching narrowly,
discovered the secret, but, for reasons best known to herself, pretended otherwise, and the men were to come again
next day.

That same evening my lady's maid's cousin's husband's
aunt came to see her,—a free, jolly, maternal old dame,
who took the liberty of kissing the mistress of the house,
and thanking her for all favours. Pomona had never
received such a long kiss. "Excuse," cried the house-
wife, "an old body who has had daughters and grand-
daughters, ay, and three husbands to boot, God rest their
souls! but dinner always makes me bold—old and bold,
as we say in Gloucestershire—old and bold; and her
ladyship's sweet face is like an angel's in heaven." All
this was said in a voice at once loud and trembling, as if
the natural jollity of the old lady was counteracted by her
years.

Pomona felt a little confused at this liberty of speech;
but her good nature was always uppermost, and she
respected the privileges of age. So, with a blushing
face, not well knowing what to say, she mentioned something about the old lady's three husbands, and said she

hardly know whether to pity her most for losing so many
friends, or to congratulate the gentlemen on so cheerful
a companion. The old lady's breath seemed to be taken
away by the elegance of this compliment, for she stood
looking and saying not a word. At last she made signs
of being a little deaf, and Betty repeated as well as she
could what her mistress had said. "She is an angel, for
certain," cried the gossip, and kissed her again. Then
perceiving that Pomona was prepared to avoid a repetition
of this freedom, she said, "But lord! why doesn't her
sweet ladyship marry herself, and make somebody's life a
heaven upon earth? They tell me she's frightened at the
cavaliers and the money-hunters, and all that; but God-a-
mercy, must there be no honest man that's poor; and
mayn't the dear sweet soul be the jewel of some one's
eye, because she has money in her pocket?"

Pomona, who had entertained some such reflections as
these herself, hardly knew what to answer; but she
laughed, and made some pretty speech.

"Ay, ay," resumed the old woman. "Well, there's
no knowing." (Here she heaved a great sigh.) "And so
my lady is mighty curious in plants and apples, they tell
me, and quite a gardener, lord love her! and rears me
cart-loads of peaches. Why, her face is a peach, or I
should like to know what is. But it didn't come of itself
neither. No, no; for that matter, there were peaches
before it; and Eve didn't live alone, I warrant me, or we
should have had no peaches now, for all her gardening.
Well, well, my sweet young lady, don't blush and be
angry, for I am but a poor, foolish, old body, you know,
old enough to be your grandmother; but I can't help
thinking it a pity, that's the truth on't. Oh, dear! Well,
gentlefolks will have their fegaries, but it was very
different in my time, you know; and, lord! now to
speak the plain *scripter* truth: What would the world
come to, and where would her sweet ladyship be herself,

I should like to know, if her own mother, that's now an
angel in heaven, had refused to keep company with her
ladyship's father, because she brought him a good estate,
and made him the happiest man on God's yearth ? "

The real love that existed between Pomona's father
and mother being thus brought to her recollection, touched
our heroine's feelings ; and looking at the old dame, with
tears in her eyes, she begged her to stay and take some
tea, and she would see her again before she went away.
"Ay, and that I will, and a thousand thanks into the
bargain from one who has been a mother herself, and
can't help crying to see my lady in tears. I could kiss
'em off if I warn't afraid of being troublesome; and so
God bless her, and I'll make bold to make her my curtsey
again before I go."

The old body seemed really affected, and left the room
with more quietness than Pomona had looked for, Betty
meanwhile showing an eagerness to get her away which
was a little remarkable. In less than half an hour there
was a knock at the parlour door, and Pomona saying,
"Come in," the door was held again by somebody for a
few seconds, during which there was a loud and apparently
angry whisper of voices. Our heroine, not without agitation, heard the words, " No, no ! " and " Yes," repeated
with vehemence, and then, "I tell you I must and will;
she will forgive you, be assured, and me too, for she'll
never see me again." And at these words the door was
opened by a gallant-looking young man, who closed it
behind him, and advancing with a low bow, spoke as
follows :

"If you are alarmed, madam, which I confess you
reasonably may be at this intrusion, I beseech you to be
perfectly certain that you will never be so alarmed again,
nor indeed ever again set eyes on me, if it so please you.
You see before you, madam, that unfortunate younger
brother (for I will not omit even that title to your sus-

picion), who, seized with an invincible passion as he one day beheld you from your garden wall, has since run the chance of your displeasure by coming into the house under a variety of pretences, and, inasmuch as he has violated the truth, has deserved it. But one truth he has not violated, which is, that never man entertained a passion sincerer; and God is my witness, madam, how foreign to my heart is that accursed love of money (I beg your pardon, but I confess it agitates me in my turn to speak of it) which other people's advances and your own modesty have naturally induced you to suspect in every person situated as I am. Forgive me, madam, for every alarm I have caused you, this last one above all. I could not deny to my love and my repentance the mingled bliss and torture of this moment; but as I am really and passionately a lover of truth as well as of yourself, this is the last trouble I shall give you, unless you are pleased to admit what I confess I have very little hopes of, which is, a respectful pressure of my suit in future. Pardon me even these words, if they displease you. You have nothing to do but to bid me—leave you; and when he quits this apartment, Harry Vernon troubles you no more."

A silence ensued for the space of a few seconds. The gentleman was very pale; so was the lady. At length she said, in a very under tone, "This surprise, sir—I was not insensible—I mean, I perceived—sure, sir, it is not Mr. Vernon, the brother of my cousin's friend, to whom I am speaking?"

"The same, madam."

"And why not at once, sir—I mean—that is to say— Forgive me, sir, if circumstances conspire to agitate me a little, and to throw me in doubt what I ought to say. I wish to say what is becoming, and to retain your respect;" and the lady trembled as she said it.

"My respect, madam, was never profounder than it is

at this moment, even though I dare begin to hope that
you will not think it disrespectful on my part to adore
you. If I might but hope, that months or years of
service "—

"Be seated, sir, I beg; I am very forgetful. I am an
orphan, Mr. Vernon, and you must make allowances as a
gentleman" (here her voice became a little louder) "for
anything in which I may seem to forget either what is
due to you or to myself."

The gentleman had not taken a chair; but at the end of
this speech he approached the lady, and led her to her
own seat with an air full of reverence.

"Ah, madam," said he, "if you could but fancy you
had known me these five years, you would at least give
me credit for enough truth, and I hope enough tenderness
and respectfulness of heart (for they all go together), to be
certain of the feelings I entertain towards your sex in
general; much more towards one whose nature strikes me
with such a gravity of admiration at this moment, that
praise even falters on my tongue. Could I dare hope
that you meant to say anything more kind to me than a
common expression of good wishes, I would dare to say,
that the sweet truth of your nature not only warrants
your doing so, but makes it a part of its humanity."

"Will you tell me, Mr. Vernon, what induced
you to say so decidedly to my servant (for I heard
it at the door) that you were sure I should never see
you again."

"Yes, madam, I will; and nevertheless I feel all the force
of your inquiry. It was the last little instinctive stratagem
that love induced me to play, even when I was going to
put on the whole force of my character and my love of
truth! for I did indeed believe that you would discard
me, though I was not so sure of it as I pretended."

"There, sir," said Pomona, colouring in all the beauty
of joy and love, "there is my hand. I give it to the

lover of truth; but truth no less forces me to acknowledge, that my heart had not been unshaken by some
former occurrences."

"Charming and adorable creature!" cried our hero,
after he had recovered from the kiss which he gave her.
But here we leave them to themselves. Our heroine confessed, that from what she now knew of her feelings, she
must have been inclined to look with compassion on him
before; but added, that she never could have been sure
she loved him, much less had the courage to tell him so,
till she had known him in his own candid shape.

And this, and no other, is the true story of Vertumnus
and Pomona.

XVI.

THE DESTRUCTION OF THE CENCI FAMILY.

FROM A MANUSCRIPT COPIED BY AN ITALIAN GENTLEMAN
FROM A LIBRARY AT ROME.

FRANCESCO CENCI was the only son of a Roman lord, who had been treasurer to Pope Pius the Fifth, and who left him a clear annual income of a hundred and sixty thousand scudi.[1] Besides this, our miserable inheritor of wealth and impunity married a rich woman. After the death of this lady, he took for his second wife Lucrezia Petroni, of a noble family in the same city. By the former he had seven children. By the latter none.

Francesco hated these children. It is a dreadful thing to say so in so many words; but the cause is easily seen through. He led a life of the most odious profligacy, and was as full of sullenness as vice. His children were intelligent; their father's example disgusted them; and he saw, and could not bear this contrast. The account of his ill-treatment of them begins with his refusing his sons enough to live decently upon, while pursuing their studies at Salamanca. They were obliged to return to their miserable home; and here he treated them so much worse, denying them even common food and clothing, that they applied in despair to the Pope, who made him allow them a separate provision, with which they retired

---

[1] We know not the precise value of this coin, which does not appear among the current money of Italy; nor can we refer to books for it at this moment. But there were scudi of gold; and Cenci's fortune was accounted enormous.

to another dwelling. Previously to this period, Cenci had been convicted of a crime twice over, and been suffered to compound for it with the Pope in two several sums of a hundred thousand scudi, nearly two-thirds of his annual income. His third mortal crime now took place, and the sons by this time were so embittered by the constant wretchedness and infamy in which he kept his family, that they entreated the Sovereign Pontiff to put an end to his life and villainies at once. The Pope, says the narrative, was inclined to give him the death he merited, but not at the request of his own offspring, and for the third time he allowed him to make his usual composition of a hundred thousand scudi.

The wretched man now hated his children worse than ever, as he had some better reason to do. But not content with cursing his sons, he visited his two daughters with blows, and otherwise so trampled upon their feelings, that, not being able to bear his treatment longer, the elder one applied to the Pope, begging him either to marry her according to his discretion, or to put her in a nunnery. The Pope took pity on the unhappy girl, and married her to a gentleman of rank named Carlo Gabrielli, making the father at the same time give her a suitable dowry.

This event so gnawed into Cenci's mind, that, fearing his other daughter Beatrice would follow her sister's example when she grew old enough, he cast in his diabolical thoughts how he might prevent it most assuredly, short of taking away her life.

.   .   .   .

About this period the terrible old man received news of the death of two of his sons, Rocco and Cristofero, who by some means or other both came to violent ends. He welcomed it with delight, saying that nothing could make him happier but to hear the same thing of all his children ; and that whenever the last should die, he would keep open house to all comers for joy. To show his hatred the more openly, he would not give the least pittance towards interring them.

Beatrice was now beyond despair. She collected her thoughts, and sent off a letter to the Pope, which was excellently written. Let us stop here a moment, to speak more particularly of the extraordinary girl. "Beatrice," says the close of the Narrative, "was of a make rather large than small. Her complexion was fair. She had two dimples in her cheeks, which added to the beauty of her countenance, especially when she smiled, and gave it a grace that enchanted all who saw her. Her hair was like threads of gold; and because it was very long, she used to fasten it up; but when she let it flow loosely, the wavy splendour of it was astonishing. She had blue eyes, very pleasing, of a sprightliness mixed with dignity; and, in addition to all these graces, her conversation, as well as all that she did, had a spirit in it, and a sparkling polish (*un brio signorile*) which made every one in love with her. She was then under twenty years of age."

The letter to the Pope had no effect; but it is supposed that it never could have been laid before his Holiness. The reader may be allowed, under all the circumstances, to suspect otherwise. Cenci was still rich and powerful; and there is no knowing how many thousands of scudi he may have had to pay now.

What renders the conduct of the Pope the more suspicious, is that the criminal somehow or other got intelligence of the application. It made him more furious than ever; and, besides locking up his daughter, he incarcerated in the same manner, and apparently in the same room, his wife her mother-in-law, who had already drunk largely of the family cup of bitterness. Finding every avenue of relief shut against them, and taught by the old man himself, as well as their own awful thoughts, to forego the ties of relationship, they finally resolved upon despatching him.

There was a visitor in the Cenci Palace, a young prelate of the name of Guerra, who was "a young man of an agreeable presence, well-bred, and one that easily accommodated himself to any proposal, good or bad." He was well acquainted with the wickedness of Cenci, who hated him for the attentions he paid his family; so that he used to come there at such times only as he knew the old man had gone out. How he gained admittance to the wife and daughter in the present instance does not appear; but he did; and finding their miseries augmented at every visit, his interest in their wretched state increased in proportion. He was not without a love for Beatrice; but it does not appear that she returned it. Be this as it may, having gathered their intentions about the old man from some words which Beatrice let fall, he not only approved them, but declared his willingness to co-operate in the catastrophe. The design was then communicated to Giacomo, one of her brothers, who instantly fell in with it. He had felt his father's ill-treatment still more than the rest of his sons, having a wife and children whom the stipend assigned him by the Pope was insufficient to support.

Cenci had taken for the summer residence of himself and his family a castle called the Rock of Petrella. The first plan of the conspirators was to hire a banditti to surprise and kill him in his way thither. The banditti were hired accordingly, but the notice of Cenci's coming was given them too late, and he got into the castle. Neither did they lurk in the thicket about the place to any purpose; for being now seventy years of age (and probably aware of the state of the neighbourhood, no unusual thing in those times), he never stirred out of doors. It was therefore determined to put him to death in the castle. For this purpose, they hired two of his vassals, named Marzio and Olimpio, who either had or thought they had cause of offence with him. The reward offered for the deed was a thousand scudi, one-third to be paid beforehand by Monsignor Guerra, and the remainder by the ladies when all was over. The assassins were introduced into the Rock on the 8th of September 1598; "but as it happened to be the day of the Nativity of the Blessed Virgin, Signora Lucrezia, restrained by her veneration for that solemn anniversary, put off the execution, with the consent of her daughter-in-law, till the day following." On the evening of that day, an opiate was put into Cenci's drink. He went to bed, and fell into a profound sleep; and at midnight, Beatrice herself took the assassins into his chamber. Having told them what to do, she retired into an ante-room where her mother was waiting. In a little while the assassins returned, and said that their compassion had overcome them, and that they could not conquer their repugnance to kill in cold blood a miserable old man who was sleeping. Beatrice heard them with scorn and indignation. "If you are afraid," said she, "to put to death a man in his sleep, I myself will kill my father; but your own lives shall not have long to run." The men, intimidated at this, returned to the chamber. In a little time they came back. The deed was done. The assassins received the rest of their reward; and to Marzio (for what reason does not appear; probably because he had been the least back-ward) Beatrice gave a mantle laced with gold. The body was thrown over a terrace into the garden, so that it might seem to have fallen by accident, while the old man was moving about in the night-time.

The women next day affected great sorrow. A sumptuous burial was given to the deceased; and the family, after a little stay, returned to Rome, where they are described as living in tranquillity for some time. In the meanwhile, the youngest son of Cenci died, so that there remained but two, Giacomo and Bernardo.

The Court of Naples, however, whose interference at

this point of time is not accounted for, unless the banditti, who were from that kingdom, had let the secret transpire, sent a commissioner to make inquiries into the nature of Cenci's death. The usual petty circumstances of suspicion came out, and were laid before the Court of Rome; yet the latter took no further steps for several months. Guerra, who was afraid that the assassins might turn evidence, hired others to get them out of the way; but Marzio escaped. He got imprisoned, however, at Naples; and, having made an ample confession, was sent to Rome. Here he was confronted with the Cenci, who denied all that he said, particularly Beatrice. Her extraordinary firmness and presence of mind is described as so astonishing the man, that he retracted everything he had deposed at Naples; and, rather than confess, chose to expire under the torment.

The law being now perplexed how to proceed, the Cenci were transferred to the Castle, where they lived uninterruptedly for several months. Unluckily, one of the bravoes who had killed Olimpio was taken up, and confessed that he had been employed by Monsignor Guerra. Timely notice, by some means or other, was given to the bishop, and he escaped. He had difficulty in doing so, because he was a remarkable-looking man, with a fair face and hair, and the officers were on the alert; but he contrived it. He changed clothes with a coal-man, smutted his face and shaved his head, and, driving two asses before him, with an onion and a piece of bread in his hand, passed out of the city under their very eyes. He encountered with equal good luck the officers who were on the look-out in the neighbourhood; and got safe into another country.

The flight of the prelate, however, together with the confession of Olimpio's murderer, brought the hand of the law heavily upon the Cenci. They were now put to the torture. The courage of the men was prostrated at once.

"Signora Lucrezia, a woman of fifty years of age and large in person, not being able to resist the Torment of the Cord—[Here the Original is wanting]—But not one single criminating word," continues the document, "either by fair means or foul, by threats or by tortures, could be got out of the lips of Beatrice. Her vivacity and eloquence confounded even the judges." One of them, Signor Ulisse Morcatti, represented the matter to the Pope, who suspected him of having been overcome by the sufferer's beauty, and appointed another in his room. The new judge ordered a fresh torture to be applied, called the Torture of the Hair; and when she was tied up ready for it, the rest of the family were brought in and entreated her to confess. At first she refused. "You would all die then," said she, "and extinguish our honour and our house? This ought not to be; but since it pleases you, so be it." She then turned to the officers to let her loose, and asked for copies of the several examinations; adding, "What I should confess, I will confess:—what I should approve, I will approve:—what I should deny, I will deny." After this fashion she stood convicted, though she did not confess.

The affair rested here again in a very extraordinary manner. Probably some money matters were under the consideration of his Holiness,—deep questions as to the difference of fines and confiscations. The parties were separated from each other for five months. They were then allowed to meet one day at dinner; and then again they were divided. At length, the Holy Father, after having seen them all confronted, and examined the confession, sentenced them to be drawn at the cart's tail and beheaded.

Great interest was made, by princes and cardinals, for allowing the criminals a legal defence. The Pope, who had shown himself hostile from the first, answered these requests with severity, and asked, "what defence Cenci

had, when he was so barbarously murdered in his sleep."
At last he yielded the point, and gave them five-and-
twenty days to look about them. The most eminent
advocates in Rome prepared the defence, and appeared
before him at the proper time with their respective
papers. The first that spoke was impatiently interrupted
by his Holiness, who said he was astonished to find in
Rome children so barbarous as to kill their father,
and advocates so bold as to defend such a villainy. At
these words all the council were struck dumb, with the
exception of the advocate Tarrinacci, who replied, "Holy
Father, we are not here at your feet to defend the
brutality of the deed itself, but to save the lives of such
as may be innocent nevertheless, if your Holiness will
listen to us." The Pope, upon this, listened patiently for
four hours. Tarrinacci's defence proceeded upon the only
possible ground, and appears to have contained a strength
and eloquence worthy of his spirit. He balanced the
wrongs of father and children against each other. The
sons were made out to be the least concerned, and the
weight of murder thrown purposely upon Beatrice, who
had been so atrociously and unspeakably outraged. The
Pope sat up all the following night with one of the
cardinals, considering the defence point by point; and
the upshot was, that he gave the criminals a hope of
escaping death, and ordered that they should again be at
comparative liberty.

Unfortunately for this new and unexpected turn in their
affairs, a nobleman of the name of Paolo Santa Croce
assassinated, at this point of time, his own mother, for
not bequeathing him her inheritance. This renewed the
Pope's bitterness against those who had set an example of
parricide; and what increased it, was the flight of Santa
Croce, who eluded the hands of justice. He sent for the
governor of the city, and ordered the Cenci to be publicly
executed forthwith. Many of the nobility hastened to

his different palaces to implore at least a private death for
the ladies; but he would not consent. They could only
obtain the pardon of Bernardo, whom the MS. calls "the
innocent Bernardo," and whose treatment both past and
to come is thus rendered inexplicable.

The sentence was executed next day, Saturday, the
11th of May 1599, on the bridge of St. Angelo. Beatrice,
on receiving news of the sentence, felt, for the first time,
her young heart fail her; and burst into bitter and wild
lamentations on the necessity of dying. "Oh, God!"
she cried out, "how is it possible to die so suddenly!"
Her mother-in-law, whose greater age and perhaps less
hope of escaping death, had softened more into patience,
comforted her in the most affectionate manner, and got
her quietly into the chapel. Beatrice soon recovered herself, and behaved with a gentle firmness proportionate to
the wildness of her first grief. She made a will, in
which she left fifteen thousand scudi to the Confraternity
of the Sacred Stigmas (the Wounds of Christ), and the
whole of her dowry to portion fifty female orphans in
marriage. Lucrezia left a will in the same spirit. They
then recited psalms, litanies, and other prayers; and at
eight o'clock confessed themselves, heard mass, and
received the sacrament. The funeral procession called
for them on its way, having already taken up the two
brothers, to the younger of whom the Pope's pardon was
announced, informing him at the same time that he must
witness the executions. Beatrice and Lucrezia were
habited like nuns. On their way to the scaffold a striking thing was observed. Lucrezia's handkerchief was
continually applied to wipe away her tears; Beatrice's
only to dry up the moisture on her forehead.

When the procession arrived at the scaffold, and the
criminals withdrew for a while to a chapel, the poor young
Bernardo, condemned to see his nearest relations executed
before his very eyes, fell into an agony and fainting fit,

and was recovered only to be placed opposite the block. The first who mounted the scaffold was Lucrezia. In preparing for death the drapery was discomposed about her bosom, which, though she was fifty years of age, was still beautiful. She blushed and cast down her eyes, but raised them again in prayer; and then adjusting herself to the block, was in the act of repeating the words, in the 51st Psalm, "According to the multitude of Thy tender mercies," when her head was struck off. While the block was being prepared for Beatrice, a place on which some of the spectators stood broke down, to their great hurt. Beatrice, hearing the noise, asked if her mother had died well, and being told she had, knelt down before a crucifix, and said, "Thanks without end be to Thee, O most merciful Redeemer, for having given in the good death of my mother a sure proof of Thy pity towards me." Then, rising on her feet, "all courage and devotion," she walked towards the scaffold, putting up prayers as she went with such a fervour of spirit, that all who heard her melted into tears. Having ascended the scaffold, she accommodated her head to the block, and looking up once more towards heaven, prayed thus:—"O most affectionate Jesus, who, abandoning Thy divinity, didst become human; and didst will, in Thy love, to purge from its mortal blot even this my sinful soul with Thy precious blood; ah, grant, I pray Thee, that that which I am now about to shed may suffice before Thy merciful tribunal to do away my great misdeeds, and to save me from some part of the punishment which is justly my due." Having said thus, she laid down her head again on the block and began the 130th Psalm—"Out of the depths have I cried unto thee, O Lord. Lord, hear my voice: let Thine ears"— At these words her head was severed from her body. The latter underwent such a violent convulsion, that one of the legs is said to have almost leaped up. At sight of his sister's death, Bernardo swooned away again, and did not recover his senses for a quarter of an hour. It was now the turn of the last sufferer, Giacomo. He first gave a steadfast look at Bernardo, and then said aloud, that, if he went into a state of bliss instead of punishment, he would pray for the welfare of the Pope, who had remitted the tormenting part of his just sentence and saved his brother's life; and that the only affliction he had in his last moments was, that his brother was compelled to look upon a scene so dreadful; "but," added he, "as it has so pleased thee, O my God, Thy will be done." He then knelt down, and was killed with a blow of a leaded club. The executions being over, Bernardo was taken back to prison, where he fell into a long and violent fever. He was kept there four months, "when, at the request of the Venerable Arch-Confraternity of the Most Holy Crucifix of St. Marcello, he obtained the favour of being set at liberty, after paying to the Hospital of the Most Holy Trinity of the Pilgrims the sum of 25,000 scudi." He lived to have a son, named Cristofero; but we know not how long the family stock survived.

Thus ended this dreadful tragedy of mistakes; in which the most privileged were made fiends, the most virtuous murderers, and the customs that undertook to punish them were the cause of all.

XVII.

PULCI.

WE present our readers with a prose abridgment of the beginning of the *Morgante Maggiore* of Pulci, the father of Italian romance. We would rather have given it them in verse; but a prose specimen of this author is a less unjust one than it would be of any of his successors; because, though a real poet, he is not so eminent as a versifier, and deals less in poetical abstractions. He has less of the oracular or voiceful part of his art, conversing almost exclusively with the social feelings in their most familiar language.

Luigi Pulci, the younger of three literary brothers, was born on the 15th of December (3rd, O.S.), 1431. His family was noble, and probably gave their name to the district of Monte Pulciano, famous for the supereminence of its wine. It was a fit soil for him to grow in. He had an enviable lot, with nothing to interrupt his vivacity; passing his life in the shades of ease and retirement, and "warbling his native wood-notes wild," without fear of hawks from above or lurking reptiles from below. Among his principal friends were Politian, Lorenzo de Medici, and the latter's mother, Lucrezia Tornabuona. He speaks affectionately of her memory at the close of his work. At Lorenzo's table he was a constant guest; and at this table, where it is possible that the future Pope, Leo the Tenth, was present as a little boy, he is said to have read, as he produced it, that remarkable poem, which the old Italian critics were not agreed whether to think pious or profane.[1]

The reader, at this time of day, will be inclined to think it the latter; nor will the reputation of Leo himself, who is said to have made use of the word Fable on a very remarkable occasion, be against their verdict. Undoubtedly, there was much scepticism in those days, as there always must be where there is great vivacity of mind, with great demands upon its credulity. But we must take care how we pronounce upon the real spirit of manners unlike our own, when

---

[1] Leo was born in 1475, forty-four years after the birth of Pulci; so that supposing the latter to have arrived at anything like length of days, he may have had the young Father of the Faithful for an auditor.

we consider the extraordinary mixture of reverence and familiarity
with which the most bigoted periods of Catholicism have been
accustomed to treat the objects of their faith. They elbow them, till
they treat them like their earthly kindred, expecting most from
them, and behaving worst by them. Popish sailors have scourged
the idols whom they have prayed to the minute before for a fair wind.
The most laughable exposure of the tricks of Roman Catholics in our
own language is by old Heywood the Epigrammatist, who died abroad
"in consequence of his devotion to the Roman Catholic cause."—
"The bigotry of any age," says Mr. Hazlitt, "is by no means a test
of its piety, or even sincerity. Men seemed to make themselves
amends for the enormity of their faith by levity of feeling as well as
by laxity of principle; and in the indifference or ridicule with which
they treated the wilful absurdities and extravagances to which they
hoodwinked their understandings, almost resembled children playing
at blind-man's buff, who grope their way in the dark, and make
blunders on purpose to laugh at their own idleness and folly."—
Lectures on the Literature of the Age of Elizabeth, p. 192. It may be
added, that they are sometimes like children playing and laughing at
ghosts in daylight, but afraid of them at night-time. There have not
been wanting readers to take all Pulci's levity in good religious part.
This does not seem possible ; but it is possible that he may have had
a certain conventional faith in religion, or even regarded it as a sentiment and a general truth, while the goodness of his disposition led
him to be ironical upon particular dogmas. We must judge him in
charity, giving him the benefit of our doubts.

The specimen now laid before the reader is perhaps as good a one,
for prose, as could have been selected. The characteristics of our
poet are wildness of fancy, pithiness of humour, sprightliness of
transition, and tenderness of heart. All these, if the reader has any
congeniality of spirit, he may find successively in the outset about
the giants, the complaint made of them by the Abbot, the incipient
adventures of Morgante in his new character, and the farewell, and
family recognition of the Abbot and Orlando. The passages about
the falling of manna, and the eternal punishment of those who are
dear to us, furnish the earliest instance of that penetration into
absurdity, and the unconscious matter-of-course air of speaking of it
which constitute the humorous part of the style of Voltaire. The
character of Margutte, who makes his appearance in Canto xviii., and
carries this style to its height, is no less remarkable as an anticipation
of the most impudent portraits of professed worldliness, and seems to
warrant the suspicions entertained respecting the grosser sceptics of
that age, while it shows the light in which they were regarded by the
more refined. In Margutte's panegyrics upon what he liked, appear
to be the seeds of Berni and his followers. One of the best things to
be said of the serious characters of Pulci, and where he has the
advantage of Ariosto himself, is that you know them with more

distinctness, and become more personally interested in them as people like yourself; whereas, in Ariosto, with all his humanity, the *knights* are too much of mere knights,—warlike animals. Their flesh and blood is too much encrusted by their armour. Even Rubbi, tho quaint and formal editor of the *Parnaso Italiano*, with all his courtesies towards established things, says in distinguishing the effect of three great poets of Italy, that "You will adore Ariosto, you will admire Tasso, but you will love Pulci." The alliteration suits our critic's vivacity better :—"In fine, tu adorerai l'Ariosto, tu ammirerai il Tasso, ma tu amerai il Pulci."

PROSE TRANSLATION ÒF THE BEGINNING OF THE " MORGANTE MAGGIORE."

Twelve Paladins [saith the poet] had the Emperor Charlemagne in his court; and the most wise and famous of them was Orlando. It is of him I am about to speak, and of his friend Morgante, and of Gan the Traitor, who beguiled him to his death in Roncesvalles, where he sounded his horn so mightily after the Dolorous Rout.

It was Easter, and Charles had all his court with him in Paris, making high feast and triumph. There was Orlando, the first among them, and Ogier the Dane, and Astolfo the Englishman, and Ansuigi; and there came Angiotin of Bayonne, and Uliviero, and the gentle Berlinghieri; and there was also Avolio, and Avino, and Otho of Normandy, and Richard, and the wise Namo, and the aged Salamon, and Walter from Monlione, and Baldwin, who was the son of the wretched Gan. The son of Pepin was too happy, and oftentimes fairly groaned for joy at seeing all his Paladins together.

But Fortune stands watching in secret, to baffle our designs. While Charles was thus hugging himself with delight, Orlando governed everything at court, and this made Gan burst with envy, so that he began one day talking with Charles after the following manner :—"Are we always to have Orlando for our master? I have thought of speaking to you about it a thousand times.

Orlando has a great deal too much presumption. Here are we, Counts, Dukes, and Kings, at your service, but not at his; and we have resolved not to be governed by a boy. You began in Aspramont to give him to understand how valiant he was, and that he did great things at that fountain; whereas if it had not been for the good Gerard, I know very well where the victory would have been. The truth is, he has an eye upon the crown. This, Charles, is the worthy who has deserved so much! All your generals are afflicted at it. As for me, I shall repass those mountains over which I came to you with seventy-two Counts. Do you take him for a Mars?"

Orlando happened to hear these words as he sat apart, and it displeased him with Gan that he should speak so, but much more that Charles should believe him. He would have killed Gan, if Uliviero had not prevented him, and taken his sword Durlindana out of his hand; nay, he could have almost killed Charlemagne himself; but at last he went away from Paris by himself, raging with scorn and grief. He borrowed as he went, of Ermellina the wife of Ogier, the Dane's sword Cortana, and his horse Rondel, and proceeded on his way to Brava. His wife, Alda the Fair, hastened to embrace him; but while she was saying, "Welcome, my Orlando," he was going to strike her with his sword, for his head was bewildered, and he took her for Ganellone. The Fair Alda marvelled greatly, but Orlando recollected himself, and she took hold of the bridle, and he leaped from his horse, and told her all that had passed, and rested himself with her for some days.

He then took his leave, being still carried away by his disdain, and resolved to pass over into Pagan-land; and as he rode, he thought every step of the way of the traitor Gan; and so, riding on wherever the road took him, he reached the confines between the Christian countries and the Pagan, and came upon an abbey situate in a dark place in a desert.

Now, above the abbey was a great mountain, inhabited by three fierce giants, one of whom was named Passamonte, another Alabastro, and the third Morgante; and these giants used to disturb the abbey by throwing things down upon it from the mountain with slings, so that the poor little monks could not go out to fetch wood or water. Orlando knocked, but nobody would open till the Abbot was spoken to. At last the Abbot came himself, and, opening the door, bade him welcome. The good man told him the reason of the delay, and said that since the arrival of the giants, they had been so perplexed that they did not know what to do. "Our ancient fathers in the desert," quoth he, "were rewarded according to their holiness. It is not to be supposed that they lived only upon locusts; doubtless it also rained manna upon them from heaven; but here one is *regaled with stones*, which the giants rain upon us from the mountain. These are our nice bits and relishes. The fiercest of the giants, Morgante, plucks up pines and other great trees by the roots, and casts them on us." While they were talking thus in the cemetery, there came a stone, which seemed as if it would break Rondel's back. "For God's sake, cavalier," said the Abbot, "come in, *for the manna is falling.*"

"My dear Abbot," answered Orlando, "this fellow, methinks, does not wish to let my horse feed; he wants to cure him of being restive. The stone seems as if it came from a good arm."

"Yes," replied the holy father, "I did not deceive you. I think, some day or other, they will cast the mountain upon us."

Orlando quieted his horse Rondel, and then sat down to a meal: after which he said, "Abbot, I must go and return the present that has been made to my horse."

The Abbot, with great tenderness, endeavoured to dissuade him, but in vain; upon which he crossed him on the forehead and said, "Go, then, and the blessing of God be with you."

Orlando scaled the mountain, and came where Passamonte was, who, seeing him alone, measured him with his eyes, and asked him if he would stay with him for a page, promising to make him comfortable.

"Stupid Saracen," said Orlando, "I come to you, according to the will of God, to be your death, and not your foot-boy. You have displeased His servants here, and are no longer to be endured, dog that you are."

Non puo più comportarti, can mastino.

The giant, finding himself thus insulted, ran in a fury to arm him, and, returning to Orlando, slung at him a large stone, which struck him on the head with such force, as not only made his helmet ring again, but felled him to the earth. Passamonte thought he was dead. "What," said he, retiring to disarm himself, "could have brought that paltry fellow here?"

But Christ never forsakes His followers. While the giant went to disarm himself, Orlando recovered, and cried aloud, "Giant, where are you going? Do you think that you have killed me? Turn back, for unless you have wings, you shall not escape me, dog of a renegade." The giant greatly marvelled, turned back, and stooping to pick up a stone, Orlando, who had Cortana naked in his hand, cleft his skull; and, cursing Mahomet, the giant tumbled, dying and blaspheming, to the ground. Blaspheming fell the sour-hearted and cruel wretch; but Orlando, in the meanwhile, thanked the Father and the Word.

The Paladin went on, seeking for Alabastro, the second giant; who, when he saw him, endeavoured to pluck up a great piece of stony earth by the roots. "Ho, ho!"

cried Orlando; "what, you think to throw a stone, do you?" Then Alabastro took his sling, and flung at him so large a fragment as obliged Orlando to defend himself, for if it had struck him he would no more have needed a surgeon; but, collecting his strength, he thrust his sword into the giant's breast, and the loggerhead fell dead.

Morgante, the third giant, had a palace made of earth, and boughs, and shingles, in which he shut himself up at night. Orlando knocked, and disturbed the giant from his sleep, who came staring to the door like a madman, for he had had a bewildering dream. "Who knocks there?"

"You will know too soon," answered Orlando: "I am come to make you do penance for your sins, like your brothers. Divine Providence has sent me to avenge the wrongs of the monks upon the whole set of you; and I have to tell you that Passamonte and Alabastro are already as cold as a couple of pilasters."

"Noble knight," said Morgante, "do me no ill; but if you are a Christian, tell me in courtesy who you are."

"I will satisfy you of my faith," replied Orlando: "I adore Christ; and, if you please, you may adore Him also."

"I have had a strange vision," replied Morgante, with a low voice; "I was assailed by a dreadful serpent, and called upon Mahomet in vain; then I called upon your God, who was crucified, and He succoured me, and I was delivered from the serpent; so I am disposed to become a Christian."

"If you keep in this mind," returned Orlando, "you shall worship the true God, and come with me and be my companion, and I will love you with perfect love. Your idols are false and vain; the true God is the God of the Christians. Deny the unjust and villainous worship of your Mahomet, and be baptized in the name of my God, who alone is worthy."

"I am content," said Morgante.

Then Orlando embraced him, and said, "I will lead you to the abbey."

"Let us go quickly," replied Morgante, for he was impatient to make his peace with the monks.

Orlando rejoiced, saying, "My good brother, and devout withal, you must ask pardon of the Abbot, for God has enlightened you, and accepted you, and He would have you practise humility."

"Yes," said Morgante, "thanks to you, your God shall henceforth be my God. Tell me your name, and afterwards dispose of me as you will;" and he told him that he was Orlando.

"Blessed Jesus be thanked," said the giant, "for I have always heard you called a perfect knight: and, as I said, I will follow you all my life through." And so conversing they went together towards the abbey, and by the way Orlando talked with Morgante of the dead giants, and sought to console him, saying they had done the monks a thousand injuries, and our Scripture says the good shall be rewarded and the evil punished, and we must submit to the will of God. "The doctors of our Church," continued he, "are all agreed that if those who are glorified in heaven were to feel pity for their miserable kindred who lie in such horrible confusion in hell, their beatitude would come to nothing; and this, you see, would plainly be unjust on the part of God. But such is the firmness of their faith, that what appears good to Him appears good to them. Do what He may, they hold it to be done well, and that it is impossible for Him to err; so that if their fathers and mothers are suffering everlasting punishment, it does not disturb them an atom. This is the custom, I assure you, in the choirs above."

"A word to the wise," said Morgante; "you shall see if I grieve for my brethren, and whether or no I submit to the will of God and behave myself like an angel. So dust to dust; and now let us enjoy ourselves. I will cut off their hands, all four of them, and take them to these holy monks, that they may be sure they are dead, and not fear to go out alone into the desert. They will then be sure also that the Lord has purified me, and taken me out of darkness, and assured to me the kingdom of heaven." So saying, the giant cut off the hands of his brethren, and left their bodies to the beasts and birds.

They went to the abbey, where the Abbot was expecting Orlando in great anxiety; but the monks, not knowing what had happened, ran to the Abbot in great haste and alarm, saying, "Will you suffer this giant to come in?" And when the Abbot saw the giant he changed countenance.

Orlando, perceiving him thus disturbed, made haste and said, "Abbot, peace be with you! The giant is a Christian; he believes in Christ, and has renounced his false prophet Mahomet." And Morgante showing the hands in proof of his faith, the Abbot thanked heaven with great contentment of mind.

The Abbot did much honour to Morgante, comparing him with St. Paul; and they rested there many days. One day, wandering over the abbey, they entered a room where the Abbot kept a quantity of armour; and Morgante saw a bow which pleased him, and he fastened it on.

Now, there was in the place a great scarcity of water, and Orlando said, like his good brother, "Morgante, I wish you would fetch us some water."

"Command me as you please," said he; and placing a great tub upon his shoulders, he went towards a spring at which he had been accustomed to drink at the foot of the mountain. Having reached the spring, he suddenly heard a great noise in the forest. He took an arrow from the quiver, placing it in the bow, and raising his head saw a great herd of swine rushing towards the spring where he stood. Morgante shot one of them clean through the head, and laid him sprawling. Another, as if in revenge, ran towards the giant, without giving him time to use another arrow; so he lent him a cuff on the head, which broke the bone, and killed him also; which stroke the rest seeing, fled in haste through the valley. Morgante then placed the tub full of water upon one shoulder, and the two porkers on the other, and returned to the abbey, which was at some distance, without spilling a drop.

The monks were delighted to see the fresh water, but still more to see the pork; for there is no animal to whom food comes amiss. They let their breviaries, therefore, go to sleep awhile, and fell heartily to work, so that the cats and dogs had reason to lament the polish of the bones.

"Now, why do we stay here, doing nothing?" said Orlando one day to Morgante; and he shook hands with the Abbot, and told him he must take his leave. "I must go," said he, "and make up for lost time. I ought to have gone long ago, my good father; but I cannot tell you what I feel within me, at the content I have enjoyed here in your company. I shall bear in mind and in heart with me for ever, the Abbot, the abbey, and this desert, so great is the love they have raised in me in so short a time. The great God who reigns above must thank you for me, in His own abode. Bestow on us your benediction, and do not forget us in your prayers."

When the Abbot heard the Count Orlando talk thus, his heart melted within him for tenderness, and he said: "Knight, if we have failed in any courtesy due to your prowess and great gentleness (and, indeed, what we have done has been but little), pray put it to the account of our ignorance, and of the place which we inhabit. We are but poor men of the cloister, better able to regale you with masses, and orisons, and paternosters, than with dinners and suppers. You have so taken this heart of

mine by the many noble qualities I have seen in you,
that I shall be with you still wherever you go; and, on
the other hand, you will always be present here with me.
This seems a contradiction; but you are wise, and will
take my meaning discreetly. You have saved the very
life and spirit within us; for so much perturbation had
those giants cast about our place, that the way to the
Lord among us was blocked up. May He who sent you
into these woods reward your justice and piety, by which
we are delivered from our trouble; thanks be to Him
and to you. We shall all be disconsolate at your
departure. We shall grieve that we cannot detain you
among us for months and years; but you do not wear
these weeds; you bear arms and armour; and you may
possibly merit as well, in carrying those, as in wearing
this cap. You read your Bible, and your virtue has been
the means of showing the giant the way to heaven. Go
in peace, and prosper, whoever you may be. I do not
ask your name; but if ever I am asked who it was that
came among us, I shall say that it was an angel from God.
If there is any armour, or anything that you would have,
go into the room where it is and take it."

"If you have any armour that would suit my companion," replied Orlando, "that I will accept with
pleasure."

"Come and see," said the Abbot; and they went into
a room that was full of old armour. Morgante examined
everything, but could find nothing large enough, except a
rusty breastplate, which fitted him marvellously. It had
belonged to an enormous giant, who was killed there of
old, by Milo of Angrante. There was a painting on the
wall which told the whole story: how the giant had laid
cruel and long siege to the abbey; and how he had been
overthrown at last by the great Milo. Orlando seeing
this, said within himself: "Oh God! unto whom all
things are known, how came Milo here, who destroyed

this giant?" And reading certain inscriptions which
were there, he could no longer keep a firm countenance,
but the tears ran down his cheeks.

When the Abbot saw Orlando weep, and his brow
redden, and the light of his eyes become childlike, for
sweetness, he asked him the reason; but finding him
still doubly affected, he said, "I do not know whether
you are overpowered by admiration of what is painted in
this chamber. You must know that I am of high descent,
though not through lawful wedlock. I believe I may
say, I am nephew or sister's son to no less a man than
that Rinaldo, who was so great a Paladin in the world,
though my own father was not of a lawful mother.
Ansuigi was his name; my own, out in the world, was
Chiaramonte, and this Milo was my father's brother.
Ah, gentle baron, for blessed Jesus' sake, tell me what
name is yours!"

Orlando, all glowing with affection and bathed in tears,
replied, "My dear Abbot and kinsman, he before you is
your Orlando." Upon this, they ran for tenderness into
each other's arms, weeping on both sides with a sovereign
affection which was too high to be expressed. The
Abbot was so overjoyed, that he seemed as if he would
never have done embracing Orlando. "By what fortune,"
said the knight, "do I find you in this obscure place?
Tell me, my dear father, how was it you became a monk,
and did not follow arms, like myself and the rest of us?"

"It is the will of God," replied the Abbot, hastening
to give his feelings utterance. "Many and divers are the
paths He points out for us, by which to arrive at His
city: some walk it with the sword, some with the
pastoral staff. Nature makes the inclination different,
and therefore there are different ways for us to take;
enough if we all arrive safely at one and the same place,
the last as well as the first. We are all pilgrims through
many kingdoms. We all wish to go to Rome, Orlando:

but we go picking out our journey through different roads. Such is the trouble in body and soul brought upon us by that sin of the old apple. Day and night am I here with my book in hand; day and night do you ride about, holding your sword, and sweating oft both in sun and shadow, and all to get round at last to the home from which we departed—I say all out of anxiety and hope, to get back unto our home of old." And the giant hearing them talk of these things, shed tears also.

XVIII.

FARINETTA AND FARINONNA;

OR HOW TO MAKE FIVE PLEASURES OF ONE, AND BE IN FIVE PLACES AT ONCE.

A FAIRY TALE.

THERE were once two sisters, who lived near a forest haunted by Fairies. They were both young, handsome, and lively; only it was said that Farinetta was the more liked the more you knew her, while Farinonna seemed to get tired of one friend after another like a toy. If you went to see them, Farinetta would keep the same face towards you all day, and try all she could to make you happy. Farinonna would do as much for a time, and be exceedingly pleasant; but if anything crossed or tired her, she would exclaim, with a half pettish look, "Well, I've had quite enough of this, haven't you?" It was a look as much as to say, "If you haven't, you're a great fool; and whether you have or not, I shall do something else." Every one, accordingly, had their Buts for Farinonna. They would say, "Farinonna is a handsome girl, but— Yes, Farinonna is a very handsome girl, but"— People had also their Buts for Farinetta; but then it was only such people as had too many Buts of their own.

This difference in the tempers of the two girls was mainly attributed to Farinetta's acquaintance with the inhabitants of the forest. She was the more thoughtful of the two; and this led her to make herself mistress of

218

the Fairy language, which was the only passport necessary to a complete intimacy with the speakers. Farinonna, who had walked in the forest, yet never seen any Fairies, did not believe in them ; and she used to laugh at her sister for thinking that the language taught her to see more in what she read and observed than herself. " Do you think," said she, " that such fine writers as Homer, and Tasso, and Shakespeare, want any other key to their language than their own ? Do I not know a sword when I see it, or a horse, or a man, or a dance ? Is it necessary for me, when a gentleman is introduced to my acquaintance, to keep saying out loud the meaning of the word gentleman in Fairian,—gentleman, gentleman, gentleman, —like a great gawky school-girl at her lesson,—in order to have a proper sense of what he is ? Or is it requisite that I "—

" No, sister," said Farinetta, laughing ; " the power to translate a word into Fairian only gives you a very vivid sense indeed of the beauties of the original."

" Oh—my compliments pray to the very vivid sense, which appears to me—begging your pardon, sister—very like mighty fine nonsense. So, instead of saying gentleman out loud to the gentleman, I am to keep saying to my very vivid sense Generomildeasibol !—What is the horrid long word ?—Generomildeasiboldunsel—oh, it's no use. I can't see, for my part, why it is not quite as good to say gentleman at once, and not plague one's head about the matter. Every one knows a gentleman at sight, without any of your vivid senses. Do you think I want any language but my mother's to tell me the meaning of the words 'As I'm a gentleman'; or to help me to a passage in Shakespeare or Milton ? "

" Why now, sister," said Farinetta, " there was a passage the other day which was quoted from Hesiod, and which you said was unintelligible."

" Well, I know," replied the other; "it is unintelligible;

and would remain so were it translated into all the languages in Europe."

"No," said Farinetta; "if you could speak Fairian, you would see it has a meaning, and one of the finest in the world."

"Now there, sister," returned Farinonna, colouring, "you really make me angry. It doesn't follow that because à man's name is Hesiod, he could not say a silly thing. Wise men, say silly things sometimes, and so might he, for all he was a beardy old Greek. I'm sure he did a foolish thing when he let his brother cheat him of half his estate; and I cannot see that he proved his wits a bit better by adding that he was contented, because, forsooth, 'the half was greater than the whole.' The half greater than the whole! Is half this fan greater than the whole? Or half this peach? Or half the lawn there? Or half the dinner, my dear? which will be up in a quarter of an hour, and I'm prodigiously hungry."

"Yes," said Farinetta, laughing as good-naturedly as before, "half a dinner is greater than the whole, on many occasions. I tell you what now" (for she saw her sister getting more impatient);—"you know the flowers which the Fairy gave me."

"Yes, I do. Chuck half of them away, and see whether the rest will be doubled."

"No, sister, that is not the way of doubling in Fairyland. But since you admired them so yesterday, I intended one half for you, and there they. are in the window."

"Well, that's a good, kind, generous sister as ever lived; but hey! presto! why don't the others double."

"They do," said Farinetta. "I feel a double perfume from them: I see a double red in the roses, and a double fairness in the. lilies. And, what is more, I shall see your flowers when they have gone out of the room."

"Oh," returned Farinonna, "I forgot the knowledge of

Fairian was to double one's eyesight as well as one's knowledge. I suppose it doubles one's presence too?"

"Why, it might as well, sister," said Farinetta, "while it's about it; and it does accordingly."

"Sister, sister," reiterated the other, with a reddening gravity, and forgetting her flowers in her impatience; "you know I love you; for the truth is, you are very generous, and, when you don't take these freaks into your head, very sensible. But the more I love you, the more angry you make me at seeing you let yourself be so imposed upon by this nonsense about Fairies. Do you think one's common senses are to be deceived? Why, upon this principle of a double presence, you ought yourself to be able to be in five or six places at once, enjoying yourself."

"My dear sister," said Farinetta, with a pleasant earnestness, "give me a kiss, and don't spoil your beautiful mouth. You see that new gown of mine, worked all over with curious imagery. I say nothing to you but what I will prove,—this very evening, if you please;—but if I do certain things, and then put on that fancy dress, I can be in five or six places at once, and enjoy myself in all. I will give away, for instance, half the peaches off my best tree, send them in portions to five or six of your friends and mine, and go the same day and enjoy them with every one."

Farinonna wept outright at this assertion, partly with impatience, partly at her sister's being so extravagant, and partly from a lurking notion how silly and uninformed she must be herself, if all this were true. After a variety of Pshaws! Nonsenses! and Now Positivelys! the upshot was, that she agreed to let her sister make the experiment, and to write letters to the receivers of the fruit all round, in order to see what they would say in answer. "But then," said she, recollecting herself, "supposing this impossibility of yours to be possible, we shall not have

half the peaches we should have had to eat for the next
fortnight : that will be very foolish."

" Well, but, dear Nonna, for the sake of the experiment,
you know."

" Well, well, for the sake of the experiment."   So half
laughing, and half blushing at being so ridiculous, Farinonna helped her sister to put the peaches in green leaves
and baskets, and send them off with their several letters.
Farinetta then put on her fancy dress, and, saying,—

> " Fairies, Fairies, wise and dear,
>   Send me there and keep me here,"

sat down very quietly at the window, to the equal amusement of herself and her sister ; of the latter for seeing her
still remain where she was, and of the former for seeing
the amusement of the latter.

Farinetta, though the more thoughtful of the two, had
as much or more animal spirit occasionally; and she
entertained herself excessively in the course of the evening with her sister's extreme watchfulness over her.   The
latter, knowing the other's love of truth, and seeing her
at once so confident and so merry, began to have a confused and almost fearful notion that there was more in
the business than she fancied.   "Perhaps," thought she,
as the dusk of the evening gathered in, and she recollected
the ghost stories of her childhood, "these Fairies are evil
spirits who have put a phantom here in my sister's shape;"
and, creeping towards her with as much courage as she could
muster, she put forth her trembling hand and touched
her.   Farinetta guessed what she was thinking about,
and burst into a fit of laughter.   This set the other off
too, and they both laughed till the room rang again, the
one at her sister's fears, and the other at her own.

Farinonna, all that evening, walked about with her
sister, sat with her, talked with her, played music with
her, sung with her, laughed with her, nay, was silent and

looked grave with her; and at last went to bed with her. She would not suffer her out of her sight. "'Tis plain flesh and blood, you goose," said Farinetta, seeing the other look wistfully at her hand, which she jerked against her cheek as she spoke.

"So is this, for that matter," said Farinonna, and was peevishly lifting her own to give her sister a little harder smack, when it suddenly smote herself on the cheek.

"My dear sister!" exclaimed the other gravely, and at the same time embracing her,—"Thank you for that. You were angry with yourself for intending me a little bit of a twinge, and so resolved to let it recoil on your own cheek. I hail the omen."

"Hail the omen?" cried her sister, half in alarm, and half angry: "I did feel a little as you say, but I assure you I know not by what odd sort of palsy or convulsion I gave myself a blow."

"Enough!" returned Farinetta, embracing her still more warmly; "I see how it is: the Fairies have begun with you: you will know and love them soon." So saying, she blessed her and went to sleep. Enough! thought Farinonna, rubbing her cheek; but she kept silent, and shortly after dropped asleep too.

The next morning the answers to the letters were brought to Farinonna all at once. She snatched them from the servant's hand, exclaiming, "Now then!"

"A good phrase," said Farinetta, "that same Now then:—you will believe in another presently,—Here, there."

It was true enough. The first letter ran as follows:—

DEAR FARINONNA,—What do you mean by asking whether your sister was with us yesterday? To be sure she was. She joined us during the *desert*, in her beautiful fancy dress, and was the merriest among the party. Didn't she tell you?—Yours,   L. Y.

Letter the second :—

DEAR FARINONNA,—What has come to you? Your
sister told us at the *desert* yesterday that she had just
parted with you. Her fancy dress and her peaches were
the admiration of us all. You would have thought we
should devour one as we did the other. I am learning
Fairian.—Yours,   B. R.

The third letter was from a fine lady :—

MY DEAR CREATURE,—Was ever such a whimsical
being as thou? Why, thou dear giddy thing, one would
think that you had not seen your sister for ages, just as
we have not seen you. It's a week now, I declare, since
Monday. I die to see you. Don't you die to have a
fancy dress like your sister's? I do. I quite die. I die
to learn Fairian on purpose : only it's so hard, they tell
me. Lord ! here is a quantity of Dies: Well, you must
have another, for, do you know, Lady Di said she blushed
for me yesterday ; upon which that witty thing Lady Bab
said, loud enough for her to hear, " And the paint for her
Ladyship." Wasn't that good now? Quite charming.
If Lady Bab were but good-looking, she would be quite
charming. Excuse faults and all that,—Yours ever, my
love,   G. F.

The fourth was from Lady Bab :—

PRETTY ONE,—" Divinest " was with us yesterday,
looking, I really must say, like her name, in her fancy
dress. I only think it a little too crowded with imagery
to look quite reasonable. How came you not to know?
I thought I heard her say she had just seen you, but that
doll Lady Di and that stupid pretender Mrs. F. were
gabbling away at the time. Brilliante will tell you, she
says, that I sported one of my best things yesterday; but,
entre nous, it was not very happy, I think ; at least, not
so happy as many foolish things I said the day before.

But " I'm tired," as you say. They are all threatening to learn Fairian, so I must get it up in mere self-defence. Is not this hard upon one who has taken the trouble to know all the genteel languages already, and who is, dear Pretty-Protty, your obedient, humble servant, B. Q.

" An affected, ill-natured thing !" said Farinonna. "I wonder what she always takes the liberty of calling me Pretty-Protty for? I think I see her odious puckered mouth grunting it. What next? Oh, here's poor Trady."

DEAR MADAM,—Received yours of to-day. Saw your sister, as hope you did afterwards; for she had the finest fancy dress on I ever saw, much better than Miss Jones's, and Miss Jones's was the finest ever seen. Excuse running hand, not having time to write text. Should like to know, if you have time to write, why you ask about Miss Farinetta, as she said she saw you; but suppose she was mistaken. Excuse haste. Also, blots; and the way of writing the letter r, which Miss Jones says is best.—I have the honour to be, dear madam, your very obedient and humble servant, A. T.

P.S.—Miss Jones lives next door.

" What a pack of nonsense about Miss Jones !" said Farinonna ; "I've no patience with such stupid worship of nobody. Ah, here's dear Toady's hand."

DIVINEST,— Other Divinest was with us yesterday, sharing her peaches with us, and looking really celestial in her fancy dress. She reminded me so of you, that I quite longed to see you. Why didn't you come? And why, pray, do you write to know about your sister, after having just seen her? That is what we all want to know; but you know it is no new matter to want to know everything which you do, however whimsical and witty. Adieu, Divinest ! Pray learn Fairian, and get the dear, delightful creatures in the wood to get you an Imagina-

P

tion,—for so, you must know, we call Farinetta's dress on account of its imagery. All the world is beginning to believe in 'em. We don't quite understand about it. The mixture of such odd things as language and knowledge, being here and being there, etc., confuses one; but I've no doubt it's true, because they say so. However, I shall never learn Fairian myself, that's certain; because you know I'm such a lazy creature. And *entre nous, ma belle*, I've another reason, which is, that I am quite happy and contented as long as I can see such places as Green Bower, and the fairer than fairies that live in it. Adieu, adieu! Parting is such sweet sorrow, etc. *Mille graces* for your kind present of the box.—Believe me to be your ever obliged and affectionate friend, with esteem,

E. T.

P.S.—I shall come to spend a day or two next week at Green Bower; but don't get anything particular, there's a love.

Farinonna was now as impatient in her wish to enjoy the privileges of her sister, as she had been in doubting and contradicting her. She had heard the latter say, that the first and greatest step towards obtaining them, was a good hearty will; and that instances had been known in which it superseded all the other means, and gifted the wisher with the power of speaking Fairian at once. She, therefore, borrowed her sister's manuscript grammar, and, blushing, asked her to lend her the gown too. Farinetta guessed what she was going to do; but said nothing. She only kissed her very kindly, and gave them her. Farinonna hurried up into her room, locked the door, threw the grammar on the floor, slipped on the gown, and cried out as fast as she could, "I want to be in five places at once." However, she did not find herself anywhere else. "I want, I say," cried she, stamping her foot angrily, "to be in five places at once." Not a step

did she budge. Enraged at her disappointment, she began
to tear off the gown; when lo! for every rent which she
made in it, she hit herself a great thump in the face.
She wept bitter tears for fear and vexation. She did not
dare to exclaim that it was shameful to treat a person so;
but she thought it, and wished she could smack the
Fairies' faces all round. Suddenly she recollected that
her sister called that involuntary self-punishment a good
omen; and this recollection brought to mind another,
namely, that one of the first steps towards favour with
the Fairies, was to do something not entirely for yourself,
but for somebody else too. "I will give away half my
box of sweetmeats," cried she, clapping her hands. She
put half of them accordingly into another box, thrust the
lid to, threw up the window, and called out to a little
boy who was going by, "Hallo, there, little boy!" The
child looked up, and gaped. "There's a box of sweetmeats for you, little boy." The boy looked at the box, as
if doubtfully, and then looking up at the young lady,
gaped again. "Don't stand gaping there, you ninny,"
said Farinonna; "take up the box, and go and eat the
sweetmeats directly. I'll come and eat 'em with you
presently. There, go: — make haste; — make haste, I
say."

"Where, ma'am?" asked the boy, after taking up the
box.

"Anywhere, you dolt," said Farinonna, slamming down
the window. "Now then," cried she, "I shall do it.
Oh, I forgot the charm before:—I shall do it certainly
now;" and she half-said and half-sung, in the requisite
manner—

> "Fairies, fairies, wise and dear,
> Send me there and keep me here."

Not a jot did they send her anywhere. Farinonna was
bewildered. "The sweetmeats perhaps," said she, "were
not valuable enough. I'll give away half—what? let's

see—anything valuable—oh, my shelf of books; I'll give away half my shelf of books."

She rang the bell violently, and the old deaf house-keeper appeared: "Lord bless us!" said the good old dame; "why, what's the matter with my young lady; I heard the bell ring, and I should never forget the sound of that bell, ma'am, if I was to live a hundred."

"Ay, ay," said Farinonna. "Well, never mind what you shall never forget; but here—take these valuable books, Judith, and keep 'em, and read 'em, and—there, go."

Judith, not hearing a word, bent her ear to understand the orders.

"Take these valuable books," bawled Farinonna, "and keep 'em, and read 'em, and GO."

She uttered the last word so fiercely, that the good old gossip started, with another "Lord bless us!" muttering after her, "Keep 'em, and read 'em, and GO! Why, Lord, miss, how am I to read 'em?"

"They cost I don't know how much," answered Farinonna.

"But how am I to understand 'em?" returned Judith.

"They are bound in morocco," bawled the lady.

"But I tell you, dear Miss Nonna, I can't read; and what's more, I can't hear anybody read; and what's more, I"—

"Then give 'em somebody who can," interrupted the sister.

"Give 'em!" cried Judith, doubting her ears; "give 'em who!"

"Any one," shouted Farinonna; "and tell 'em I'll come and read 'em with 'em directly."

"Read 'em with 'em," repeated the housekeeper. "Why, you would not read 'em with the cook, or the hostler, or the footman, or the scullion, would you, miss?"

"Mark me, Judith," said Farinonna, suppressing her anger: "Take these books to my sister, and tell her"—

"Mister who?" asked the deaf woman.

"My sister," re-echoed the young lady; "and tell her that she must read 'em directly, because I want to stop here and read 'em there; and now go:—You can go, can't you, if you can't do anything else?"

"Oh, yes," returned the dame proudly, "I can go. Blessed be heaven, I can go fast enough, considering I'm seventy-eight; but I tell you what, Miss Nonna, if you take infirm old people by the shoulders in this manner, and make 'em go faster than Heaven wills, you'll not live to be old yourself; and now I'm in the mind, I tell you what, Miss Farinonna; and I'll tell you nothing but what all the house says; and that is, I don't know what you mean by these mad pranks, but you are not a bit like your sister, for all you're almost as handsome; and I don't love you half so well as I did, Heaven forgive your mother's old nurse for saying so!" (and she shed tears) "for all I dandled you in these arms; for one of your kindest things (when you do 'em) an't the value of anything that Miss Netta does, she does everything so sweetly and good-natured. You trample upon us, as a body may say, even when you help us to get up; but kind's kind, I say; and a man may ride from here to Land's End, and be no horseman:—yes, no horseman, Miss Nonna; and, I grieve to say it, but you're no horseman."

Farinonna, who had a turn for the ludicrous, and who was not naturally bad-hearted (who is?), could neither help smiling at, nor pitying, her old nurse, as she went out of the room lamenting over and over again, that so sweet a creature to look at was no horseman. The honest, involuntary ebullition had an effect on her, which even her sister's sweetness would have failed in, and which certainly no grave advice would have produced. She sat down with a feeling of shame and regret; and after a while exclaimed gently, "I see I must be patient,

and learn Fairian regularly, or I shall never be like my
dear sister." Now, the latter, who had been alarmed by
old Judith, and just come in, turned her sister's head
round affectionately with her two hands, and said, "Ah,
my dear Nonna, you will be a greater favourite with the
Fairies than I, if you keep in this mind; for I was less
strong than you, and was made patient earlier, and you
will have had more to conquer." So saying, she kissed
the tears out of her eyes. Farinonna took her sister's
hand, and kissed it; and looking up, she saw a group of
beautiful creatures in the room, who stood like friends
about her sister, and smiled upon herself; and one of
them said, in the most enchanting manner in the world,
" To be able to see us, is to be able to hope everything."

XIX.

A YEAR OF HONEYMOONS.

INTRODUCTION.

"A YEAR of honeymoons! We never heard of such a thing! impossible! incredible! We have heard of 'eleven thousand virgins.' That may be; but a year of HONEYMOONS!! Why, the word 'honey-moon' (month of honey) was expressly invented to illustrate the impossibility of the existence of anything honeyed *beyond* the month. It is as much as to say that the first month of a marriage is honeyed, and the first *only;* and everybody knows it. Talk of a year of honeymoons! You might as well speak of a year of Twelfth Nights or of Christmas Days! of cakes and mistletoe all the year round!"

My dear readers, I am aware of the rarity, both real and supposed, of such a year as the one I speak of. I know how the months run—after the common fashion. Let me see. They may be reckoned perhaps as follows :—First (as the little children say "A by itself A"), there is the *honeymoon* by itself *honeymoon*, with not a day beyond it. Then comes a month which may be designated the *sugar-moon*—something less sweet than honey, but still not without its dulcitude. Then comes, they tell me, the *treacle-moon* — somewhat cloying. Then the *raspberry-vinegar-moon*—a mixture of sweet and sour; and then, according to circumstances, the *vinegar* or the *water-gruel-moon*—the sour or the insipid; after which, vinegar or water-gruel, or a mixture of both, occasionally sweetened and made sickly, prevails to the end of the chapter.

Seeing then, ladies and gentlemen, that I may proceed, I shall do so without further preface, and inform you that I was married two years ago, all but a month—to wit, on the first of January, and that I have had therefore nearly two years of honeymoons, instead of one.

Readers—Come, that is going too far.

Writer—It is a fact, upon my honour.

Readers—We shall never believe it, unless you tell us something very extraordinary indeed. Who are you, sir ? and what are your pretensions ? Are they superhuman ? My good young gentleman, you are either a horrible fibber, or horribly afraid of your wife, and must say just what she pleases. We knew a pleasant fellow, who understood your sort of husband well. He had a favourite phrase in his mouth, of "*You must say so.*" A wife would call upon her husband to bear testimony to her conduct in such and such a matter, and the husband would do it ; upon which our friend would turn to him, in his knowing way, and say, "*Ah! you must say so.*" He would find fault with a lady's tea, upon which she would say to her husband, "That isn't fair, is it, my love, for I always make excellent tea, don't I ?" "You do, my love." "*Ah !*" quoth my friend, "*you must say so.*" Another lady, going to the opera with a cousin, would say to her husband, "Well, my dear, I am sorry you are engaged elsewhere, and cannot go with us." "Oh, he can go well enough, if you like it," quoth our friend. "How monstrous !" quoth the lady ; "it is not so, is it, my love ?" or "I am sure you know how delighted I should be to have you with us." "I am sure of it, my love," quoth the husband. "*Ah!*" said our pleasant friend, "*you may say so.*"

Writer—Very pleasant, indeed, where the parties did not deserve it ! Very horrible, where they did. It does not affect Harriet and me.

Readers—Ah ! you must say so.

Writer (laughing)—I am glad to see we are all in such good humour. I shall therefore proceed to convince you. Truth will easily be known from falsehood. You will perceive that it is quite impossible I should invent all the pleasant days I am going to describe, and the enjoyment I have had of them. At least, the invention would have such a counterpart in people's feelings that it would prove their possibility, and show that the enjoyment is not peculiar to myself.

Readers—Proceed, sir. We have great faith in you for our parts, for we all think we deserve to be happy, depend upon it, and most people would be so, if circumstances had been as favourable to them as to yourself and us.

Writer—Charmingly said ! and many thanks. To proceed then. You will probably expect me to give a description of my bride's beauty, but this I shall avoid, partly because I do not wish to excite differences of opinion about tall and short, fair and brown, black eyes, blue eyes, and grey eyes, and partly because beauty has little to do with the matter. Harriet's face is the most beautiful to me in the creation, because I love it most and have seen it look the most loving, yet I have heard others describe it as being only "very agreeable." Suffice it to say, that it is agreeable enough to attract the kind and respectful look of strangers ; in short, that it is a true woman's. Her shape, without entering into particulars, may be designated as of the same character. A gardener very well described it to me, as she was stepping about his parterres, choosing some flowers. "Sir," said he, " it is plumpness upon a stalk of lightness." Her laugh is such a quintessence of pleasure and goodwill, that a gentleman, overhearing it one day on an inn staircase, as I was standing in a room below, said, "God bless that laugh ! it makes me know the face without having seen it."

" Do you take it to be fair or brown, sir?" said I, smiling.

"I know nothing of that," returned he; "but I'll be sworn it is a face you have reason to love, sir, if you know the lady."

Harriet came in as he was uttering these words, and I said to her, "Here is a gentleman, my love, who has been panegyrizing your face, though he says he never saw it."

"Perhaps," observed Harriet, with a passing inclination of her head, and a smile between archness and modesty, "that is the reason."

"I can only say, madam," returned the gentleman, with a bow full of thanks, very serious, "that I really am surprised at the sort of face I had pictured to myself, and the wonderful exactness with which the fancy has been borne out."

This likeness between an abstract idea in the stranger's mind, and the realization of it in my charmer's face, gave me a high opinion both of his intelligence and his habitual good feeling, and I was not deceived, for, though I am not in the habit of making sudden intimacies, yet truth and right feeling are mighty; and from this little incident sprang a friendship which makes me seem as if I had known Jack Sutton these twenty years;—but more of him by and by.

A *History of Courtships* would be a curious book—I mean a selection of *real* specimens of the way in which married people first became acquainted with each other, and how the wooer thrived and the lady consented. What a number of things should we be made aware of—that we guess already! And yet what interesting surprises there would be for us! What a courtship of conveniences! what passions of estates! what headlong youthful credulities; what maturer artifices; what folly! what knavery! what *virtue!* What disinterested generosity should we not sometimes find under the most worldly appearances! —what worldliness under the most generous! What a nauseous heap of coldness and commonplace! What frightful disgusts ! What prospective ill-treatment! What selfish imprudence ! What prudence most horrible ! What awful unfitness ! What enchanting truth, good-heartedness, and love ! How should we not feel for the youth or the maiden about to be sacrificed to the worst passions in a mask ! How not laugh, and yet feel pity, for the poor fool who takes the most ridiculous airs for a bewitching elegance, and the wretched imposition upon him for a delightful compliment! How not be ready to cry out in a horror of warning, when we see a good and sensible heart, in a moment of weakness or vanity, about to ally itself to some dull wretch of wealth or family, whose want of all grace, perhaps of all goodness, will pollute even the pity it shall afterwards take upon its misfortune, in the doubt whether it had a right to mistake so far !

But I shall be moralizing on people's misfortunes, instead of recording my own luck. For, be it observed, I attribute my good fortune to nothing but itself. I can see where other people are deceived and taken in, but well do I know that I might have been taken in myself. I have too good an opinion of the sex in general to be secure against a mistake in the particular. The truth is, I have been in love three times before, but circumstances hindered the inclination from coming to anything. In one instance, I trust, there was no great demerit on either side ; in the two others, I would fain intimate, in as polite and modest a manner as possible, that I think I had an escape. I make these allusions with the less scruple, because I write under a feigned name, and nobody will know who I am. I am at once anonymous and tender— the very Junius of a soft secret.

But why do I talk of escapes ? Was not everything an escape that procured me the bliss of my present connection ? Could anybody but Harriet have made *me* so entirely happy, whatever happiness they might have bestowed upon others ? Could any one else have been

so considerate to what is defective in me, as well as
suitable to what is better ! You may call this the language
of a lover, but I care not. I am a lover; and what does
that prove but that my case is made out, and that Harriet
has a husband who is in love with her in the twenty-third
month of his marriage ? I have acknowledged to you,
dear, kind, listening, and trusting readers (whose attention
does honour to your hearts), that good luck has had the
main hand in constructing this marriage. I must add,
that circumstances were every way lucky for me, and that
the extreme resemblance of our fortunes, in many particulars, was no mean part of it. We both thought very
much alike, were both orphans, both disposed to the same
kind of life, and our incomes were pretty nearly of a size
—mine, by good luck, was somewhat the larger; and
Harriet's aunt, with whom she lived, was a good soul, with
a moderate ambition, and heartily content to put an end
to her anxieties for her niece's welfare by consigning her
to the care of a man she thought honest.

Readers—This was, indeed, a combination of circumstances, and takes off a little of the edge of our astonishment. But still the *two* years of honeymoons! *One* is
prodigious; but TWO !!

Writer—You will be pleased to recollect I have only
undertaken to describe one; but it is much to have got
you to allow that. I will tell you the secret, however,
at once. It consisted, first, in our being the sole additional advantage to one another, in our change of life;
and, secondly, in our mixing up the pleasures of one
another's society with such as were independent of
vanity and fashion, and grounded in what is eternal.

You will have partly seen what I mean by the first
part of the secret, in what I have said about the equality
of our incomes. This made us look for no change in
our mode of living, except what love bestowed upon us;
and we began our intimacy, from the first moment of it,

in the spirit of this feeling. We did not think about it, but we acted upon it instinctively; and good fortune assisted us. My courtship was one of the quietest in the world. Harriet lived with her aunt, and I used to spend every evening with both of them, reading and playing music, or sometimes we went to the play, and in the morning we visited exhibitions, or rode and took walks out of town. I saw very little of her alone; and, in truth, though I desired it passionately, I loved her so, that I did very well without it. I cannot describe the transport, the internal feeling of haste and buoyancy, the *mentem prætrepidantem*, with which I used to hurry off to Wimpole Street after dinner; or the amazing mixture of rapture and tranquillity with which, on advancing to the parlour door towards me (for she always did that when she heard my knock), she held out both her hands, and looked happiness into my eyes; or the perfect sympathy with which we used to fall to our books and music after tea, or talk of her flowers, or recollect our walks; or, lastly, the mere bliss of being in her presence, and sitting next her. Never did she quit or enter the room but, if I did not follow her with my eyes, I did with my heart. I had a great regard for her aunt (heaven rest her kind soul!), but when the old lady and I were left alone, the room appeared like an empty well.

We had no expensive establishments to talk of. There was no *trousseau*. I had no title to give her (I own sometimes I wished I had); I had no box of diamonds. I once regretted to her that I had no diamonds. Never shall I forget her look and manner to me. We happened to be alone. "*Diamonds!*" said she, looking at me with such beauty in her face, such love and satisfaction, such an indescribable mixture of liveliness, tenderness, and bewitching pleasure! She was going to add something, but the words faltered on her lips. It was as if she had kissed me, and could not speak for love.

From this kind of life I bore her off to a house a little nearer the country. There was no change in our ordinary habits. The very neighbourhood was the same. Her aunt was more with us than at home. And we made no ostentation of our marriage. We did not proclaim what a wonderful thing it was for two persons who loved one another, to come together; nor set the neighbours and the country-people staring and making themselves of our party, with the flare of our white ribbons. People might think as they pleased. Thought is free, and I did not wish to repress it. But with the leave of those who insist in this manner upon calling aloud for it, they are incompetent to the intensity of their pleasures, or even to the imagination of them. It is not as if all the world were made up of people with good taste and real sympathy, or presented a very golden age of ostlers and landladies. Too many witnesses to the marriage are summoned, and people taught to suspect that the happiness can neither be very delicate, which encourages so many people to inquire into it, nor very abundant, which must needs piece itself out with ostentation.

Thus my bride (so to speak) received nothing from me in marriage but myself,—no title, no riches, no glare; nothing opposed to our present or future happiness; and I from her received only herself,—the greatest, it is true, of all treasures: but I mean we had nothing in our fortunes calculated to divert ourselves artificially from one another, or to compete the mastery with us in our hearts: nor, on the other hand, were we forced upon the sole idea of each other for happiness, without its being secured by the endless resources of intellectual pleasures, and the love of nature.

But, above all, we knew, and did justice to what was

good in one another, and we had good tempers. I have the advantage of my wife, in being able to argue better, and to give reasons for what I think; but, on the other hand, as I frequently tell her, with an amazed kind of delight, she seems to me to have an instinctive perception of truth and right, quicker than anybody I know, and not standing in need of reasoning. She cannot describe it so well, nor say so many words about it, but there is nobody whose opinion I would sooner ask in a matter of importance than hers, even if she were not the woman I love. She feels what is best to be done, before she has time to think it. It is a kind of intuition, which I have observed in other sweet natures, particularly among females, and seems to result from some perfection of organization, both physical as well as moral—something that has no contradiction in it, and furnishes no wrong bias. They go direct to the matter like the sunbeams. They make peace and happiness, as the bees make honey.

Female Readers (aside)—Upon my word, a very knowing young gentleman, and one who understands us. Ah! if Mr. Jones did but understand as well!

Ah! if Mr. Smith did but understand!

Ah! if Mr. Tomkins!

Ah! if Mr. Jeffs!

Male Readers—Well, sir, all this is very pretty, but you have yet to give us your proofs. We hope they may be real ones, and convince us that you are not likely to find yourself deceived. You are of the faction, we perceive, of the Addisons, Sir Richard Steeles, and others, who believed in a certain *beau ideal* of humanity, particularly among the ladies.

Writer—The *faction!* Congreve, I think, was not much of their faction, to judge by his plays; and yet, in one of the few instances where he is known to have spoken seriously on the subject in his own person, he

has said one of the loveliest things about a woman ever
uttered by man.   I used hardly to believe it possible
that the author of the *Way of the World* and the *Double
Dealer* could have said it, but a perusal of his affectionate
dedication of Dryden's plays to the Earl of Newcastle
convinced me that he really could utter fine sentiments.
The saying I allude to is this, and it is a volume of gold.
I would apply it to Harriet :

"To love her is a liberal education."

Male Readers—Well, sir, we will allow it to be very
prettily said, and that there are ladies, no doubt, who
would make very pretty schoolmistresses.   But the proof,
the proof is the thing.   You have yet got to describe us
your *year of honeymoons!*   The whole twelve months
is before you, and you really propose to fill it up!   All
with honey !

Writer—It is not I that shall fill it up; it is love,
nature, and the love of books.   Our honey is still made
after the fashion of the bees.   It comes from a thousand
flowers.

JANUARY.

I have informed the reader that I was married in
Scotland, on the first of January, one thousand eight
hundred and thirty-one (I love to write the words at
full length).   Harriet and her aunt had been on a visit
there to some relations, and I joined them, and brought
my charmer away.   The indifferent formality of the
ceremony, and the presence of total strangers, enabled
me to go through the task with proper self-possession ;
nor, indeed, should I have been deficient in that respect
anywhere, for something of the like reasons.   But, on
coming away to the carriage, I seemed to forget everything but my happiness; nor was Harriet, whose words

were almost inaudible, and who, with her hand trembling in mine, relied on me for self-possession enough for both of us, in a more collected state. All that I remember is, that I was delightfully acquiescent with everything. I mechanically paid everybody treble what was expected, and believe I should have given my hat away, had any one chosen to ask me for it. Somebody saying it was fine weather, I replied, "By all means;" and Harriet, receiving a knock and an apology from a great girl, who came running into the doorway as we were leaving it, said, "I am much obliged to you."

These mishaps were maliciously told us by our good aunt, when she came to town. She had not overlooked the smallest particular connected with the day, down to the very shoes of the officiator's daughter; and indeed astonished me by the extent of her information. She was an excellent soul, but, having so much knowledge, and wanting a little more, she did not always know what to do with the knowledge she had. She had harangued me so long that morning upon affairs of love and marriage, and the difference of Scotch and English customs, that, happening to speak of novels, I was tempted to object to the formality of Sir Walter Scott's heroines, and said I should have felt it an absolute indelicacy to marry them. This she could not comprehend; and, notwithstanding what I had been just before observing, she exclaimed, not without some look of alarm, "Dear me! Then I suppose, Mr. Dalton, you could not at all have put up with such people as Sophia Western, or Miss Darnel, or Amelia, or Mrs. Coventry's ladies, much less any in Mrs. Bage's or Madame Riccoloni's novels?" I saw it would lead us into an awkward discussion to undeceive her, so I parried the question. She would not, however, let the subject drop, but plagued poor Harriet with it for near an hour, and I never saw my charmer's sincerity or address put

Q

so hard to the test, or come off with more delightful
colours.

I did not feel in a real world, till I got into the
post-chaise, and was fairly on the road home with my
bride.   Everything else seemed a dream and an impertinence.

.   .   .   .

(Here a thousand reflections are left out.)

I shall not say what pictures we drew of our present
and future felicity, and our past secret feelings towards
each other.   Our spirits required a poise, and we resorted
to poetry and the landscape.   Poetry was prose compared with our feelings.   Harriet was versed in all the
romance of the road, and we lived in succession with the
borderers, and hermits, and Robin Hood, and the Babes
and Robin Red-breast, and Milton's Arcades, for every
fresh county, or quarter of the compass, brought its
story with it.   I daresay we lived in this sort of company
each day for an hour.

In the evening, when we thought it was a little after
dark, we found ourselves arrived at a seven o'clock dinner,
and our first stage for the night.   Our house of reception
was one of these delightful solid old inns which are made
out of ancient private houses, with thick walls, warm
oak wainscots, huge old screens, noble mantelpieces, fine
ample staircases, and a mixture of large and little rooms,
with seats in the windows, and a great tree here and there
to look upon.   There was a glorious fire on the hearth,
and a carpet like a double one to one's feet.   A brief and
elegant dinner was quickly displaced by tea, with little
cups, that looked as old as the time of Lady Suffolk.
Mistress Millet, aunt's own woman, and Tom Hand, my
valet, an hereditary secret-keeper, piqued themselves upon
saying nothing about a wedding-day ; and after tea arose
a good handsome tempest out of doors, just enough to put

an end to all noise but its own, and only noisy enough to make winter music at intervals, and to seem as if it bound the fine old stout house closer together and all that it contained.

. . . .

(Here a thousand pages are omitted.)

The poets are understood to know more about love than other people, and very fine things they have said about it, but I am not aware of any one of them who has done justice to a bridal. Indeed, it is not to be expected they should. The world is not honest enough to hear them, or perhaps a little spice of the "ineffable," or the " *dicere nefas* " is necessary to our human conceptions of happiness. The angel in Milton,

> "With a smile that glow'd
> Celestial rosy red, love's proper hue,"

parried the inquiries of Adam himself, in his state of innocence, relative to love-making in heaven. Take all the passages, however, from the poets who have touched upon the subject, whether professed amatory poets, or epical, or philosophical, or in whatever spirit of gaiety or sentiment they wrote,—Homer, Theocritus, Catullus, Ariosto, Boiardo, Spenser, Shakespeare, Milton, Beaumont and Fletcher, Thomson, Burns, Ramsay, Shelley, Keats, and a hundred others,—and the imagination may arrive at some faint glimpse of a remote notion of the borders of the felicity of an espousal. Some afford a hint of the vivacity, others of the gravity, others of the pride, the dignity, the religion. For no happy feeling, of whatsoever sort, grave or gay, is missed in a genuine love. I once heard a red-faced fellow in a tavern (Lord S.) compare a kiss with a bottle of wine, and laugh it to scorn in comparison. "What is the touching of a lip," quoth he, "to the real, solid, masculine, manifest satisfaction of a bottle

of good port ?" and having said this with an air of logical
triumph, he tossed off another glass, and then stamped
the foot of it on the table, and smacked his lips with a
" Hah !" as if he had settled the matter for over. A man
of gallantry might with equal good argument have reversed
the question, and smacked the lips of the barmaid. But
the truth is, his lordship should first have taken out of
the bottle of port almost all that gives value to it—genuine-
ness, sociality, its effects on the spirits, etc. A man of
pleasure of this sort is not competent to his own appellation. All the lips he has known have been lips, and
nothing else—at least, to him. There was no love in
them, and consequently little in the kiss. Now, a lip
that has love in it has heart and soul, and a certain
portion of grace and imagination ; and a true lover, in
kissing the lip, kisses all these qualities. A fellow like
this stupid lord talks of a peach without flavour in it, or
without sense to perceive the flavour, and then says,
" What is a peach ? "

Allow me to say that the greatest of our old poets,
probably out of a sense of their inability to say enough,
have overlaid their bridal narrations with too much
" pomp and circumstance." Spenser's famous " Epi-
thalamium," full of beauties, is too loud and splendid, and
calls for too many witnesses, like our white ribbons and
public marriages. There are too many " angels" at his
altar, and too much clergyman ; and he sets the bells
ringing too ostentatiously. He makes even the church-
organ "*roar*" (which is a fine daring word, too, and with
great truth in it) ; but he is so full of his triumph that,
upon the principle of extremes meeting, the very excess of
his worship and humbleness becomes a part of it. We
may say to him, as Villanor, in the tragedy of "Bren-
noralt," says to one who is describing the charms of a
young beauty with pertinacious minuteness : "Tyrant !
tyrant ! tyrant !" He invests his bride with all sorts of

beauty, and glory, and superiority, purely that he may sacrifice her the more victoriously to his will. It is a fine poem, and by no means to be "curtailed," as Dr. Aikin would have had it; but there is more of the pride than of the felicity of a wedding in it; and I will venture to add, without using the word in a bad sense, more of sensuality than affection. The virtue he most insists upon in his bride is her modesty, which he pampers like an epicure. The angelical hierarchy and his earthly happiness are brought too much together; yet with how much beauty! The following picture is a mixture of Rubens and Raphael :—

> "Behold, whiles she before the altar stands,
>   Hearing the holy priest that to her speaks,
> And blesseth her *with his two happy hands*,
>   How the red roses flush up in her cheeks,
> And the pure snow, with goodly vermill stayne
>   Like crimson dyde in grayne :
> That even the angels, which continually
>   About the sacred altar doe remaine,
> Forget their service, and about her fly,
> Oft peeping in her face, that seems more fayre,
>   The more they on it stare.
>
> "But her sad eyes, still fastened on the ground,
>   Are governed with goodly modesty,
> That suffers not one look to glance awry,
>   Which may let in a little thought unsound.
> Why blush ye, love, to give to me your hand,
>   The pledge of all our band !
> Sing, ye sweet angels, alleluya sing,
> That all the woods may answer, and your echo ring."

The evening star rises with all its beauty in the following lines :—

> "Ah! when will this long weary day have end,
>   And lende me leave to come unto my love !
> How slowly do the hours theyr numbers spend
>   How slowly does sad Time his feathers move !
> Haste thee, O fayrest planet, to thy home
>   Within the westerne fome

Thy tyred steedes long since have need of reste.
  Long though it be, at last I see it *gloome;*
And the *bright evening star with golden creaste*
    Appeare out of the west.

"Fayre childe of beauty! glorious lampe of love!
  That all the host of heaven in rankes doost lead,
And guidest lovers through the night's sad dread,
  How cheerfully thou lookest from above,
And seemst to laugh atween thy twinkling light,
  As joying in the sight
Of these glad many, which for joy do sing,
That all the woods them answer, and their echo ring."

I must give another passage, exquisitely Spenserian.
It is a quintessence of him :—

"Now day is deon, and *night* is *nighing* fast,
  Now bring the bryde into the brydall bower;
The night is come, now soon her disaray,
  And in her bed her lay;
Lay her in lilies and in violets,
  And silken curtains over her display,
And odourd sheets, and arras coverlets.
Behold how goodly my fair love does ly,
In proud humility!
Like unto Maia, when as Jove her took
  In Tempe, lying on the flowery grass,
  'Twixt sleepe and wake, after she weary was,
With bathing in the Acidalian brooke."

Having ventured to qualify my praises in this matter,
of a poet whom I reverence, I will grow still bolder, and
hazard an objection to the bridal in *Paradise Lost.* This
also has too much angelic circumstance about it; and we
can never fairly rid ourselves of the important event
hanging upon the fate of the married couple. They are
crushed between the weight of heaven and earth. Milton
writes about love and beauty like a proper poet; but,
with reverence be it spoken, something of the Puritan is
superadded, something too much of the "head matri-
monial," the lord and master. The "schoolmaster" had
begun to walk "abroad" in his time, and Adam is a little

too much of one. There is a bit of the celestial pedagogue in him. I am afraid Milton talked somewhat too much in the same style to his first wife, who ran away from him. There is a time for all things. It has been thought strange that Apollo, the god of poetry, was the most unsuccessful wooer in Olympus; but if he always talked as he did to Daphne, about his knowledge and his physic, it is no wonder.

> "Inventum medicina est, opiferque per orbem
> Dicor," etc.
>
> —*Metamorph*. lib. i.

What pleasant poet is it who, writing on this passage, says :—

> "As he spoke the word *physic*, she darted outright;
> At the dreadful word *physic*, she hastened her flight."

I fear that Sir John Suckling's honest "Ballad on a Wedding" was thought more to the purpose by the gravest ladies of that time, though the change of manners will not allow a quoter to make much use of it in this.

> "Her finger was so small, the ring
> Would not stay on, which they did bring—
> It was too wide a peck;
> And, to say truth (for out it must),
> It look'd like the great collar (just)
> About our young colt's neck.

> "Her feet beneath her petticoat,
> Like little mice stole in and out,
> As if they feared the light,
> But oh! she dances such a way!
> No sun upon an Easter day
> Is half so fine a sight.

> "Her lips were red, and one was thin,
> Compared with that was next her chin,
> Some bee had stung it newly."

We are not to think the possessor of this lip could not talk as fine sense, or listen to it, as any woman in the

land, or be as truly loving and affectionate. Nay, we
may suppose it the more. One good quality is apt to
imply another. Harriet had just such a lip, with a little
chin under it, and a dimple, and may I never think of a
bee again when I look at it, if I ever heard more sensible
things uttered by any female in town. Certainly I never
heard half so many affecting ones, or playful. Her mouth
is so expressive, that I know by the least movement of
it what sort of thing she is going to say, even if I do not
see her eyes. If I see those at the same time, and they look
at me, she is apt to forget what she was going to say.

I will finish these quotations with a homely, I should
rather call it a domestic, copy of verses, written by an
amiable man (Dr. Cotton the physician), which are
excellent of their kind, and sufficiently suggestive to a
good, handsome imagination; nor will I apologize, *to the
highest circles*, for the cat or the tea-kettle. I could
mention "Squares" and "Places," in which it would be
necessary to excuse these appendages of a fireside fifty
years back; but firesides of true refinement do what
they please in these matters. I have drunk tea as early
as seven o'clock, with Lady L——, made out of a kettle
on the very fire before us, when, if I had gone a little
farther eastward, and said I liked such a thing, I should
have been asked if I had come out of Wapping.

> "The hearth was clean, the fire was clear,
>   The kettle on for tea;
> Palemon in his elbow chair,
>   As blest as man could be.
>
> "Clarinda, who his heart possest,
>   And was his new-made bride,
> With head reclined upon his breast,
>   Sat toying by his side.
>
> "Stretched at his feet, in happy state,
>   A fav'rite dog was laid,
> By whom a little sportive cat
>   In wanton humour play'd.

"Clarinda's hand he gently press'd;
   She stole an amorous kiss,
And, blushing, modestly confess'd
   The fulness of her bliss.

"Palemon, with a heart elate,
   Pray'd to almighty Jove,
That it might ever be his fate
   Just so to live and love.

"De this eternity, he cried,
   And let no more be given;
Continue thus my loved fireside,
   I ask no other heaven."

I should grudge these quotations about other people's happiness, even on such a subject, if I had not enjoyed them a thousand times with Harriet. I have told the reader that one of the great secrets of our happiness is the enjoyment of many things in common, poetry, music, painting, riding, and walking, etc. Each of us felt that the other's presence and love were sufficient for happiness, but each had a diffidence as to the power of making it so, and was willing to aid the attractiveness of love with whatever else is lovable. Even Angelica and Medoro in Ariosto, who are a personification of young love and its absorptions, wandered forth into the woods, and invested themselves with the charms of nature.

"Se stava a l'ombra, o se del tetto usciva,
   Avea di e notte il bel giovine allato:
Mattina e sera, or questa or quella riva
   Cercando andava, o qualche verde prato.
Nel mezzo giorno un antro li compriva, etc.

"In doors and out of doors, by night, by day,
   She had the charmer by her side for ever:
Morning and evening they would stroll away,
   Now by some field, or little tufted river,
They chose a cave in middle of the day."

Our landscapes in January are not like those of a southern summer. But nature never fails those who do not fail her; and my bride and I no sooner got home, than we continued our daily exercise. Our house, being near the Regent's Park, commands both town and country. If it was fine, we enjoyed the clear frost, and the warm looks of the farm-houses with their haystacks; and we noticed the birds, and the trees (always beautiful, even with the leaves off), and the red holly-berries. If the weather barely allowed a walk or a ride, we made a merry boast of our courage; and I delighted to see Harriet wrapped up in her furs, or even returning home with her lovely curls dabbled with wet. Oh, ye common-place, effeminate, inactive voluptuaries! How little do ye know what you are about; or what a sharpness and swiftness of delight exercise puts into the blood! Besides, I had her arm in mine all the way; she was a part of me; and she occasionally pressed my arm to her side, with a stolen look such as only true love can give. If on horseback, I had the pleasure of taking care of her, for she is not a bold rider; only she says that when she is on horseback with *me*, she seems to be "included in my security." In fact she looks so, and dances away on the saddle as confidently as the best. The motion sometimes forces her to raise her voice in speaking, in order that I may hear her; and, among the innumerable charms which affection helps us to discern in those we love, I have noticed what a peculiar beauty there is at such times in the elevation of a voice naturally soft and low. The sound comes dancing to my ears across the road, as the sight of her does to my eyes. I have observed that people on the footpath sometimes give a smiling look of admiration, and seem to think how happy we are. The poet truly says of one of his heroines—

"Her voice was ever soft, gentle, and low,
   An excellent thing in woman."

But, with regard to the lowness, he should have added, "except occasionally on horseback."

As we said little at first of our return to London, our friends left us almost entirely together for several weeks; and partly out of dislike of proclaiming ourselves we scarcely went into town. Our time passed much in the following manner. We had not yet chalked out any system : Harriet had her music, and books, and work to attend to, and I my books and writing; for not being of any profession, and having found the inconveniences of it, I had long been getting together materials for a volume of criticism upon such subjects as had pleased me at the University. The feelings already alluded to had made each of us resolve, in a half-conscious way, to prosecute our respective occupations without intermission; but somehow they came to nothing. We were always going to begin; and did, in fact, do so; we began, and re-began : but, I know not how it was, the time fled, and we found ourselves together again, almost as soon as we parted. After breakfast, having seen to the household arrangements for the day, we looked at the garden and greenhouse to see how the crocuses, lilacs, lilies of the valley, roses, hyacinths, arbutus, hollies, and pyracantha, went on; and this took us more time than we expected. Harriet then touched her pianoforte, or drew, or took up a book, or worked, and I went to my study; but one of us had some question to ask, or some little notice of the weather, or a book to recommend; and this, besides the time it took in going backwards and forwards, led to other questions which required discussion; and so the hour came for going out, and then I was obliged to put up my papers, because health was the first thing to be attended to ; and so we went out; and then came dinner; and after dinner we did not profess to work ; and then came tea; and then a book, one page of which sometimes took us up a wonderful time; and then came a duet; and so the days went round and round, and it required an effort of reflection to recollect that all the world was not made up of idleness, and happiness, and being grateful for it.

Christmas and Twelfth Night we absolutely forgot. Harriet's maid reminded her of the latter, and we sent out, and got a huge cake, just as the shops were about to close; for we love old holidays: so we gave it to the servants to make merry with, first having cut off a good lump, over which we were as merry as they, though there were but two of us.

I laughed at the notion of our being king and queen by ourselves, without having a court; but my charmer said she would be no queen, she would be Viola, in the play of "Twelfth Night," and I should be the duke. "Oh ho!" quoth I insolently; "a pretty Viola you for 'concealing' your love, and having a 'green and yellow melancholy.'"

"No," said she, "it shall be the play with a new reading, all happy and only pretending to concealment, in order to be more candid;" and then, shaking her curls at me, with the greatest mixture conceivable of archness and tenderness, she repeated,—

> "My father had a daughter loved a man,
> As it might be, were I a woman,
> I should your lordship."

Next day the servants were very grateful, and said so many things about our "thinking of them," that Harriet blushed. Dear soul! she amply deserved their praise; for one of the great reasons why I love her is, that she thinks of others as well as of herself, thus paying me the highest of all compliments—that of individual preference, in the midst of an unbounded sympathy.

FEBRUARY.

It was fine to see how my charmer and I triumphed over the bad weather of February. We treated it with a

pleasant spite. We had our revenge of it. The worse
it was out of doors, the better we made it within.
Ours was truly the "sunshine of the breast," none the
worse for a good fire, great thick curtains, huge cushioned
sofas, books, music, pictures, and good health. When I
looked through the window and found the whole scene
before us a mass of rain, mistiness, chillness, and mud,
I would turn to Harriet, with her warm heart in her
warm dress, and think of the blessed climate I had
within doors. Some such dialogue would then ensue as
the following :—

"It is impossible to go out to-day, Harriet."

"Impossible, Charles."

"Impossible even to take the carriage—the horses
would suffer."

"And the coachman."

"He would. We'll take our walk then in-doors,
shan't we ?"

"That will be just the thing."

"People might oftener walk in-doors if they chose.
It is very healthy ; it is *exercise*, you know."

"Yes ; and so *convenient*, Charles."

This word "convenient," the reader must know, is a
piece of insolence in Harriet. She means that I can
walk in-doors with my arm round her waist, which I
have sometimes complained I cannot do abroad. So I
punish her for it.

Our walk is only through a suite of three rooms, but
two of them are long ; all are hung with paintings, and
part of the delight of our promenade is to enjoy the
paintings as we go, and live in their scenery. By this
means we take excursions into Italy and Arcadia, and
call upon some divine friends, who have eyes and
expressions of countenance equalled only by one of their
visitors, and to whom we have been introduced by
Giorgione, Guido, and others. I am not rich enough

to possess more than two or three originals of the great
masters, but we have many excellent copies, some of
them by the masters themselves when they were young;
and with these, and the landscapes around them, we are
as intimate as if they were old friends, and Italy was
next door. Our paintings are windows, through which
we look upon a bluer climate, or rooms with their
partition walls thrown down, and bringing us in company with some of the noblest and most beautiful of
their inmates. The only fault, as far as concerns our
walk, is that we sometimes stop too long, and that
some sweet speech or natural remark of Harriet's makes
me forget every prospect before me, but that of her true,
sweet face.

Then, of an evening, during this dreary month, we
used to read the most beautiful descriptions of summer
time and rural enjoyment in the poets, not because we
needed them, for we needed nothing, but partly out of
a pretence that we did so, partly because so intoxicating
a love as ours was too good to drink every moment, and
partly from a feeling already mentioned, of a pleasant,
wilful spite to the bad weather. Sometimes it was I
that read, sometimes Harriet, but, merry as she is, the
dear creature's voice would falter too often in some of
the passages. There is a famous one in Thomson, in
which she could not get further than the word " beings."

> "But happy they! the happiest of their kind!
>   Whom gentler stars unite, and in one fate
>   Their hearts, their fortunes, and their *beings* blend.
> 'Tis not the coarser tie of human laws,
>   Unnatural oft, and foreign to the mind,
>   That binds their peace; but harmony itself,
>   Attuning all their passions into love;
>   Where friendship full exerts her softest power;
>   Perfect esteem enliven'd by desire
>   Ineffable, and sympathy of soul;
>   Thought meeting thought, and will preventing will,
>   With boundless confidence."

We persevered, however, in going out when the weather allowed us no real excuse. I thought, besides the reasons before mentioned, that a certain manly respect for the exercise was proper on my side, and that Harriet would think the better of me for it; and, for her part, she had a similar instinct for the preservation of health· and its graces. Out, therefore, we went, as in January,—often when we met not a single *out-of-doorer* besides, at least none equally bent upon exercise for its own sake. We spared the servants and horses when we did not spare ourselves. In the milder days of February there are some glimpses of spring, which we did not fail to notice. We hailed the "pale primrose" in sunshine almost as pale. We agreed that it was a pity the *Lamium purpuerum* in the hedges had no better English name than the "dead nettle," and that it was foolish to give pretty things disagreeable appellations;—a word with no meaning but one may be as uncouth of sound as it pleases, provided it belong to something pleasant; but why associate melancholy ideas with agreeable objects? We felt grateful for the warmth of the crocus in the cottage gardens, and loved the new daisies, and vindicated the claim of the elder-tree to a more general admiration. The sight of the first buds on the trees was a treasure to us. We saw the whole spring and summer in them. Harriet made such a panegyric on the hue of the crocus, when she first saw it, that we fell into some very pretty, poetical, pictorial, classical, romantic talk upon Hymen and the ancient poets, and his saffron or crocus-coloured vest; and I will venture to say there was not a bit of pedantry in our discourse, though I quoted Latin and Greek. Love and learning go well together, provided there is as much love in the learning, as learning in the love. My charmer, as I conversed about Hymen and the crocuses, and gradually got into other loving quotations full of tenderness and domestic pleasure, felt the truth of this maxim so strongly, that she resolved to become acquainted with both languages, and read their most beautiful poems under my direction, in order, as she prettily said, that there might be " *no heart in a meaning,* into which she could not thoroughly enter with me." But we agreed to say nothing about the new accomplishment, unless questioned on the subject, or to very select people, who could give her credit for remaining as much a woman as ever, and wearing as unaffected *stockings !* So we are very particular on this point, and I must hereby give notice that this part of my present writing is a kind of *stage-whisper,* to be heard by none but such as have a right to hear it; people who have too much merit of their own to be jealous of a little addition to the stock of others, and who can distinguish the *graces* from the *airs* of scholarship. Harriet was already a good Italian as well as French scholar, of the lighter sort; and if her stockings are now somewhat blue, I can assure the reader it is the tenderest and handsomest blue in the world,—the sweetest violet-colour in Theocritus. The greatest ignoramus of a man need not be afraid of her company, for she is too good-natured to mortify any one knowingly, and her accomplishments she keeps for those who like them. She is of opinion with myself, that women who are unpleasant in consequence of a little unusual scholarship, would be as unpleasant, perhaps more so, without it, and that it is as bad a symptom to grow less agreeable, from an acquaintance with the beauties of the ancient poets, as it would be for a young face to look the less attractive for being adorned with the roses and vine-leaves of which they speak.

Behold us, then, on one of the worst days in February, varying our usual occupations with a sudden heap of *Excerpta* and *Delectuses ;* and Harriet, half in jest, half in earnest, with a pretty mixture of confidence and mis-

giving, and a breath in her voice saying, "*Amo, I love,*"
and "*Vocative, o.*" We soon, however, exchanged that
plan for Jacotot and other maturer systems. We talked
of Eloisa and Madame Dacier, and other ladies who
united learning with love; and, I must confess, got on
very slowly. It is but of late that my friend reckons
herself able to encounter a reasonable Idyll or Anacreontic,
with a dictionary by her side, and she can manage a bit
of Anacreon better than Horace; for after a little trial
of Latin, we resolved upon making our serious commencement with Greek, which, we are convinced, is the more
loving, as well as the wealthier language. The Latin,
however, has pretty pickings, as, for example, the following, which I made haste, among others, to lay before my
pupil for her opinion—

> " At Acme leviter caput reflectens,
> Et dulcis pueri ebrois ocellos
> Illo purpureo ore suaviata,
> Sic, inquit, mea vita, Septimille,—
> Huic uno domino usque serviamus,
> Ut multo mihi major acriorque
> Ignis mollibus ardet in medullis.
> > Hoc ut dixit, Amor sinistram ut ante,
> > Dextram sternuit approbationem."

It is part of a bridal picture in Catullus. There is a
beautiful version of it by Cowley, but, as I cannot
remember all his lines, I must piece them out with
inferior ones—

> "But she her purple mouth with joy "—

(The ancient *purple* is to be taken for the quintessence of the modern *red.*)

> " But she her purple mouth with joy
> Stretching to the delicious boy,
> Kissed his reeling, hovering eyes,
> And 'Oh, my love, my life!' replies, .
> 'So may our constant service be
> To this divinest deity,

R

As with a transport doubly true
He thrills your Achme's being through.'
   She said; and Love, on tip-toe near her,
   Clapped his little hands to hear her."

My charmer took a dislike to Ovid for his "artifice,"
and "want of heart." Her dear honest nature had not
yet enabled her to suspect that there could be a sort of
professional sincerity in a writer, apart from a more
native impulse, and that Ovid, like so many good-natured
men after him, often wrote verses for the mere sake of
enjoying his reputation, and meant nothing but to be a
poet and wear laurel. I merrily completed her disgust
at the time, by quoting the beginning of Dryden's
translation of one of his elegies, addressed to a married
lady—

   " Your husband will be with us at the treat;
   May that be the last supper he shall eat."

The plain-spoken, malignant force of this second line
forced her to laugh out of pure astonishment and indignation.

I remember the circumstances particularly well, because,
in a minute or two, after a thoughtful silence, she rose
up to lead me into one of our promenades up and down
the room; and in something which she said, introduced
the mention of the word "husband," in the tone of
especial tenderness, as if to relieve it from the insult
put upon it by the two court poets, Ovid and his translator. And it was just after she had uttered this, that,
in casting my eyes out of the window, I saw something
which induced me to break gently away from her with
pretended gravity, and say, "Are you aware, madam,
that this affection of ours is very unbecoming, and that
we have no longer a right to be happy."

She looked a little startled in spite of her consciousness of its being some jest, and said, "How so pray,—if
you please, Mr. Dalton?"

"Madam," quoth I, "it is at this precise time of day, five weeks ago, by a certain ceremony in Scotland, that I was made the happiest man on earth, and here is your aunt's carriage at the gate, bringing her to tell us that our honeymoon is over by full seven days, and therefore it is becoming in us to receive visits, and be proper married people, and not pretend to be happier than our neighbours."

"Was it, Charles?" cried she; "then I will say of that day, in the words of the sonnet we were reading last night,—

> "Benedetto sia il giorno, e 'l mese, e l'anno,
> E la stagione, e 'l tempo, e l'ora"—

nay, I must say in plain English, May God for ever bless the day, and you, and both of us, and all the world!"

It is thus that, in some of her most affectionate moments, the gratitude which she feels to heaven for the pleasure of loving breaks out into a blessing on all the creation.

I took her overflowing heart to mine, which she had filled with a flattery so delicious; and she had scarcely recovered from her transport when her aunt came in, dressed in the height of punctilious visitation, and after vainly essaying to pay some formal compliment, threw her arms about her neck with "My dear, dear Harriet," and burst into a mingled passion of gaiety and tears. Had she been less amiable, we should have had a great deal of these tears, for she felt the loss of her niece's company, and was prone enough by nature to indulge herself in the luxury of self-pity. But an excellent breeding, of the old school, had taught her, on these occasions, to see fair play between what was due to herself and to others, and she quickly fell into the old track, and was as much at home as if she had been in

her own house. Still there was a slowness of understanding about her, that did not enable her to see into
the nicety of matters quite as well as the generality of
her kindred, and Harriet was accustomed at times to
manifest a little confusion in her society, as she did at
this moment, which made her aunt observe, " Well,
child, you do not think me in a hurry, I hope. It is
now a good five weeks since dear Mr. Dalton took you
away, and you know you are now ranked among old
married people, and need not object to seeing all the
world."

"Dearest aunt, I am sure I am most heartily glad to see
you, and I am sure that you know it."

"Do I *not* ?" (with a kiss of great tenderness) ; "and it
is a blessing to me, I am sure, to think you are so well
matched, for she is a very good girl, is she not, Mr.
Dalton ? and very well behaved, and quite after your own
heart, and will make a most exemplary "—"mother," she
was going to say ; but Harriet playfully clapped her
hand upon her mouth, and said, " You will make me
blush, dear aunt, if you praise me so much."

Blush she did, indeed, already, enough to make her
aunt stare. The truth is, that neither the word "mother,"
nor any other connected with it, had yet been mentioned
between us. We had seemed, somehow, too blithe in our
very tenderness, to think of it with reverence enough,
and had instinctively waited in silence for the proper
time.

Yet from these and other evidences of what may be
called *seasonableness* of nature, which prompted Harriet
to speak or be silent according as the occasion warranted,
I discovered that Mrs. W. had set her down for "a very
good girl and affectionate, but cold ;" and it seems that I
partook largely of the same suspicion, and that the discourse about the heroines of novels, mentioned in my
last, had completed it. The good lady was full of con-

ventional decorums, and would have been shocked at
what she thought the least real impropriety ; but between
friends, especially females, she was apt to be a little freer
of her thoughts than occasion demanded ; and if this
communicativenes was not responded to, she set down her
own coldness, which enabled her to talk so, to the account
of the more genial persons who kept their thoughts for
those to whom they belonged.

As our good kinswoman broke up the regularity of our
tête-à-tête life, and took us abroad, and brought us our
visitors, I will take the opportunity of observing that
Harriet manifested an exquisite propriety of feeling in
her new state before strangers, and in company. Not
because she studied it, but because the habits of behaviour
partly occasioned in her by the very inferiority of her
aunt's understanding, and partly by the moral grace of
her own happy, harmonious nature, made her do so
without effort. ·Nothing could be more touching to me
than her conduct to myself before others. And I hope I
deserved it, by doing my best to show how well it was
understood by me. She neither fell into the idle and
perilous mistake of treating me with affected indifference
or superiority, and allowing herself to use undervaluing
language about men and marriage ; nor was she at all
formal or prudish ; neither did she proclaim her triumph
or her self-will, and make others participators in the
interior of her feelings by turning privacy into publicity,
and thus spoiling and rendering equivocal the lovingness
of fond looks. She paid me the compliment of dividing
attention to me with others, secure that neither she nor I
should doubt the reality of the preference ; and when her
attention was more immediately directed to myself, so
perfectly beautiful and womanly was the respect without the ostentation of it, the sweet gravity in general, and
the cordial and happy, yet somehow unparticular delight
when I said anything which pleased the company, that

her very abstinence from any more special manifestation
of her love became the counterpart of her reverse of it at
other times; and my heart was often melting within me
(as the rogue knew) when people were least suspecting
anything of the matter. The only way in which her
feelings would sometimes escape her, so as to hazard the
discovery of a nice observer, was in the depression of her
voice towards the close of her speeches, if she had to say
much to me; and I do not· deny that, now and then, if
there was no possible chance of detection, she would
contrive to lay her hand upon mine in passing, or
whisper something that would rather have surprised
Mrs. W.

Thus did Harriet behave to me in the second, third,
fourth, and fifth months of our union, and thus does she
behave to me now, in the thirteenth. And thus, therefore, grew our year of honeymoons, which I undertake
to say were better and better, if possible, as the year
advanced; for, the more I knew of her heart, the more
reason I had to love it; or, rather, the more it answered
the expectations I had formed of it as a lover.

But I am obliged to break off here, much against my
will, for I was going to take her to the theatre, to hear
some music.

MARCH.

If the rains of February did not keep my bride and
myself in-doors, still less were we kept in by the glad
winds of March, which dried up for us the winter
moisture, and prepared our paths through the green
meadows and our walks by "hedgerow elms." We had
no objection to a little of that "blowing about," which in
robust geniality tossed the arms of the trees, and set the
new flowers dancing. Harriet felt a difficulty sometimes
in retaining her look of self-possession, without colouring,

when the wind set violently against her as a stranger passed, drawing somewhat too beautiful an outline of her figure; but it is part of the sweetness of her nature never to be provoked by things inanimate, or where there is no intention of offending her, and the next minute she would half laugh, half talk away her blushes, the wind, as if in gaiety, beating back the words into her mouth, like doves into their nest.

We cared nothing for those *east* winds of which sedentary people talk, except when the air was very cutting indeed; and then for luxury's sake we had a favourite walk against a long sunny garden wall, over which looked the scarlet-flowering maple, and the blossoms of what is called the laurel—a name profanely usurped by that glossy and handsome species of *prunus;* and in the tree inside the garden we heard the rooks in motion, building their nests. This wall (which is a resort of ours still on the like occasion; indeed I might write the account of all our months in the present tense as well as the past, and in reading how we passed our time then, you may pretty well guess how we pass it now) belongs to a large square garden on a hill, the east side of which is finely peppered when the wind sets in that way, and now and then we would go round the other three sides, purely to get a good sharp blow, and enjoy with double delight the sense of quiet and warmth on the sunny western side. Here there is a country road, a good deal lower than the path, from which it is separated by a rail as well as bank, and on the other side of the road are some more garden-walls with their gates, and an outhouse or two, with a little belfry or pigeon-house, frequented by doves. It is pleasing to see how full of beauty are the earliest smiles of spring, and how well even the leafless trees and the outhouses look in the fine weather, merely because the sun shines upon them. Indeed we have noticed the same effect in the middle

of winter, especially if the twigs of the trees be of a
reddish hue.   A poplar in a suburb garden will show it.
It is not spring alone which, in the beautiful language of
the poet,

" *Kindles* the birchen spray."
—*Shelley's Fragment from Goethe.*

We have seen this bit of country road, with its railed
path, its wall, its pigeon-houses, and its winter trees,
present a combination of natural and artificial elegance,
which would agreeably surprise many an eye that little
dreams of it, for want of a hint from those who have
been more fortunately instructed.   And be it observed,
that outhouses and pigeon-houses may be handsomely
built, and in fine architectural taste.   (This reminds us
that we must look at Mr. Loudon's book upon Cottage
Architecture, and see what he has to say on that
matter.)   There is a coach-house, or some building of
that kind, in a lane leading from the north-western side
of Hampstead Heath to a place called the Potteries (a
favourite spot of ours), which, though nothing but a
simple brick building with a blind face to the road, is a
real pleasure to the eye, and beats all to nothing the
mansion to which it belongs.

A dry-looking Reader with a red face—And so part of
your "Year of Honeymoons," Mr. Dalton, is passed in
looking at pigeon-houses and garden walls!

Author—It is.   We lose none of the pleasures that art
or nature has made us acquainted with, and the mutual
enjoyment of which serve to endear and enrich us to one
another.   I told you so in my introduction.   Hence it is
that we enjoy every moment of our existence; and by
this means (*aside*), if you had known it, you might have
attained to better things in life than that doubting face
of yours, and that after-dinner complexion.

Part of Harriet's pleasure in our March walks consisted
in her detecting the early violet, for which she would let

go my arm now and then as we passed a sunny bank, and
by degrees get me a good handful. She carried a phial
of water in her reticule, and thus preserved them. One
day she came down to dinner with a profusion of them
for a crown to her head, and with a sauciness peculiar to
herself, very charming for a certain air of deference
which she contrives to mix with it, thrust head and all
into my face to let me see "how sweet they were."
"Sweet indeed!" cried I, detaining her cheeks in my
hand, and kissing the beautiful back of her neck. Whatever ornament she puts on she only makes me think the
more of herself—herself the ornament of the ornament.
She repays the grace she receives from it with a double
return, moral and intellectual. There is the wish to please,
and the exquisite knowledge how to please. I noticed on
this occasion, as on a thousand others, how very beautiful
is the flowing line of the throat and neck to the shoulder,
especially when bending in this manner, with that gentle
acquiescent look natural to a woman, and showing to
perfection the contrast of its white colour, and its firmness, with the meek, floating locks. Milton seems to
imply, though he does not expressly mention it, in the
passage where he describes Eve sitting and leaning
towards Adam "in meek surrender." And Akenside
notices a neighbouring beauty—the only poet, I believe,
who has—

> " Hither, gentle maid,
> Incline thy polish'd forehead: let thy eyes
> Effuse the mildness of their azure dawn;
> And may the fanning breezes *waft aside*
> Thy radiant locks; disclosing, as it bends
> *With airy softness from the marble neck,*
> The cheek fair-blooming, and the rosy lips."
> —*Pleasures of Imagination.*

" Effuse the mildness of their azure dawn "

is a beautiful line. I have sometimes looked at a grace
of this sort in a woman,—I mean a beautifully-turned

throat and bend of the neck,—and wondered how she could
have a face not entirely answering to it in sweetness of
expression.   But she *would* have had it, if education
and pre-existent circumstances would have let her.   Contradiction of appearance in offspring implies contradiction
in progenitors of their fortunes.

There are moments when the very earliest indications
of spring in March have something in them almost
superior to the bursts of beauty in April and May.   We
poetical pedestrians are grateful to the first peepings of
the buds, in proportion to their long absence.   This is
particularly the case on a fine quiet day, when the winds
are silent, and the sun strikes warm upon one's cheek
or shoulder; and when in some pretty secluded spot,
abundant in evergreens, and not without indications of
the new shrubs, you hear the thrush for the first time,
or the cooing of doves, or catch the miniature dinning
of the gnats.   If the bee comes in with his richer
murmur, and plunges into some panting blossom, the
charm is complete.   It is a boast of ours that we are
the first of all our acquaintances who hear the bee and
the cuckoo.   We may add, all the other vernal and
summer voices; for there is nobody else, to our knowledge, who makes it a point to enjoy all the luxuries of
nature, great and small, throughout the whole of the
year.   Harriet or myself, as it happens, will suddenly
stop during our walks, and with finger up, and a happy
face, bid the other listen.   It is the first sound of the
thrush, or the nightingale, or the cuckoo, the lark, or
the bee; or it is the dove aforesaid, or the gnats.   None
of the music of nature is lost upon us; nor a picture.
We reckon even the departing fieldfare a sight worth
hailing.   And happy is the one who first points it out;
only it is sometimes "inconvenient," as my companion
says; for there is such a charming mixture of luxury
and innocence in her countenance when listening on

these occasions, such absorption in the sound, and yet
such inclusion of me in the absorption,—with a pressed
arm and a little closer creeping to my side,—that I long
to thank her with a kiss. Now lips are apt to look
most beautiful in leafy and sequestered spots; but from
the very love you bear them, which is mixed with an
inconvenient thing called "respect," and a jealousy lest
they should be lightly thought of by others, you cannot
always reckon upon the safety of the salutation in consequence of the thickness of the leaves about you. The
thicker they are, the more safely they may include some
prying neighbour. Your Scotch heath is the place for
salutation out of doors—the *Cowdenknowes,* or the *Bush
aboon Traquair;* where there is just enough foliage or
floweriness to screen you from the idea of publicity,
while your eye has the range of the country round about,
so that you are sure of nobody's being near. *Vide*
Burns, Allan Ramsay, Allan Cunningham, and all the
tribe of Scotch poets, who love a heath as surely as
Horace says other poets do a wood. But I shall be
anticipating my own seasons of heath and hayfield.

The first sight of human occupation in the fields is
very pleasant after its long absence; such as the plough-
man with his team, and the sower stalking with his basket.
The unweaned lambs would be more so, but for a bitter
thought which it requires further thinking to reconcile,
and the meditation is painful, and to youth not very
easy. Fortunately at that time of life it makes no great
impression. But as long as it lasts it is unpleasant, the
more so from being mixed up with the tenderest feelings
and the most common - place wants. Maternity, and
innocence, and helplessness, and the permission of pain
and suffering, and the homely intrusion of the thoughts
of one's dinner, make up a strange and provoking perplexity of ideas. The imagination of young and gentle
womanhood sees but the most affecting of these images,

and the shadow of evil for a moment passes over her
sunshine.

> "A tear bedews my Delia's eye
> To think yon playful kid must die,"

says the poet, in an artificial but not untouching strain.
I have already said that the thoughts of motherhood had
never yet been expressed between my bride and myself;
nor were they now; but one day, as we passed a field in
which, to use the finer language of another poet (Dyer),
there was many a new-born lamb who

> "Tottering with weakness by his mother's side,
> *Feels the fresh world about him,* and each thorn,
> Hillock, or furrow, trips his feeble feet,"

Harriet looked suddenly another way, and I knew by her
silence there were tears in her eyes. I did not say anything; but in the evening, without laying any particular
stress upon it, I read her, among others, the following
passage from a greater poet, who had just made his
appearance in print. Never, surely, were pain and evil
more sweetly reconciled to good, or briefness of suffering
to the predominance of pleasure :—

> "The ox
> Feeds in the herb, and sleeps, or fills
> The horned valleys all about,
> And hollows of the fringed hills,
> In summer heats, with placid lows,
> Unfearing, till his own blood flows
> About his hoof. And in the flocks,
> The lamb rejoiceth in the year,
> And raceth freely with his fere,
> And answers to his mother's calls
> From flower'd furrows. In a time
> Of which he wots not, run short pains
> Through his warm heart; and then, from whence
> He knows not, on his light there falls
> A shadow; and his native slope
> Where he was wont to leap and climb,
> Floats from his sick and filmed eyes,
> And something in the darkness draws
> His forehead earthward, and he dies."
>
> —*Poems of Alfred Tennyson.*

When I had finished this lovely passage, Harriet, who had been loud and profuse in her expressions of delight at the others, said simply at this, in a low voice, "How *very* sweet!" and stooping down on my hand, kissed it. It was to thank me for all the thoughts which she knew had passed between us on the subject, though we had not spoken, and for the relief I had afforded her by means of the poet. She is exquisite at this kind of *womanly gallantry*, if I may so call it, without degrading the feeling by the word. She never would allow from the first (indeed I never contested the point with her), that all the manifestation of courtesy, and deference, and gratitude should be on the man's side; and she says there are moments of exceeding fulness of heart, understood on both sides, when it is a grace in a woman to be foremost in manifesting her feelings. I know that, from a person of her exquisite taste, it is a very exquisite compliment.

Taste is the perception of what is appropriate, and the relish consequent upon the perception. By some persons it is acquired or greatly improved; with others it seems to be born, like the common properties of health and a good palate. Certainly there are many who study to obtain it without much success; while others, without studying at all, say, do, and think the best things by a certain harmonious perfection of their nature. In Harriet it is a mixture of instinct and consciousness. The shapeliness of her soul naturally inclines her to move in a right direction, and the cultivation of her thoughts makes her aware of it without vanity. She would be called romantic, but only by those who do not see far enough into the interior of good sense, and who are not aware how much reasonable pleasure is to be extracted out of a thousand things that never enter their heads for want of a little fancy. I reckon therefore that she passes her days quite as much in a round of good sense as of elegant

enjoyment, the one indeed being the soul of the other.
Knowing how I value the first evidence of spring, and
how I hail the very name of March, harsh and rude as
it is, because the winter months are gone, and it is the
"piping time" of the coming flowers, she covered our
first breakfast-table in the month with a profusion of
hyacinths and narcissus, intermingled with roses, tulips,
and violets, and surmounted with the beautiful pink
blossoms of the mezereon, and some branches of maple.
We hail the first new leaves of the year with quite as
much, nay, more joy than the flowers, because flowers we
have all the year round, but green leaves we have not.
There is also a very vital look in them, with their tender,
expanding folds, and the redness of many of them next
the bough. The young crinkled leaves of the currant
and gooseberry bushes are like miniature fans put forth
by invisible fairies.

It was beautiful to see my charmer, with her own
rosy smile and "hyacinthine locks," sitting looking at
me through the foliage of this flowery table, like the soul
of my domestic paradise ; for we allow of no "curl-papers"
at breakfast, nor of a cap. She knows I cannot see too
much of her face and its ornaments in their natural state ;
and therefore she withholds them from me as little as
possible. We have always some flowers on our table of
a morning, and the monthly roses all the year round.
Harriet says that people do not think well enough of
the Chinese, considering that they found out tea for us,
and that they are also, after their small fashion, a poetical,
flowery people ; and she looks upon the "Chinese rose"
as belonging to the teacup, and likes to see them together.
I am reminded of this Chinese turn of sentiment by a
quotation she made on this morning of the first of March,
when I was expressing my thanks for the manner in
which she had set out the table. I observed that it was
a picture of herself—"all freshness, and grace, and pro-

mise, and present joy." "Nay," said she, "it is an
emblem of my fate;—you remember the passage we
noticed among others in the Chinese novel: only I have
had the light without the previous darkness."

The passage she alluded to is striking for the excessive
piece of brightness and colour with which it terminates,
and which is rendered so by this "previous darkness."
It is a prose version of a Chinese bit of poetry in the
novel of *Ju-kiao-li*—

> 'These disasters were not the mistakes of fate;
> These cross-purposes were the result of misunderstanding.
> Who would have foreseen, that from so many mistakes and
>   disappointments
> Would result, in the end, *a fate brilliant as flowers?*"

We have flowers on our dinner as well as breakfast-
table; for as nature is always profuse of her beauties, we
see no reason why we should not always acknowledge
her beneficence, and have some of them about us. If
this is not reason enough, we have the great authority of
Lord Bacon on our side, of whose dinner-table the same
custom is recorded. A late noble poet said he "could
not bear to see a woman eat." It was the infirmity of
his ultra-sensual turn of mind, and the debasing habit of
satire. The former inclined him to see everything grossly,
and the latter to subject "the greater to the less." A
true lover of a woman, when at table with her, does not
think of her *eating.* He only thinks (if he thinks of the
matter at all) of her health and good humour, and of the
grace with which she goes through even so common a
thing. They both think just as much of it as it is worth,
and no more. I confess I hate to see a woman *given* to
eating. That is coming round to his lordship's inversion
of the matter, and forgetting every kind of feminine grace
and propriety in the indulgence of a gross will. If a
lover thinks of eating or drinking at all when his mistress is before him, it ought to be either in the spirit of

Fielding's Amelia, when she set one of her little suppers
before her husband, and delighted to see him cheerful
over it, or in that of the Greek poet so well rendered by
the English—

> " Drink to me only with thine eyes,
>   And I will pledge with mine,
> *Or leave a kiss within the cup,*
>   *And I'll not ask for wine.*"

Real love, instead of degrading either a great pleasure
or a small, can take the most commonplace of enjoyments, and convert it into a ground of refined sympathy.

When my wife and I found the morning fine enough
to allow of taking a long walk, and spending a good
many hours in the country, we were not fond of concluding our day with town amusements, such as going to
the play or the opera.   At any rate, we did not like to
look forward to such a termination of it, though we had
no system to the contrary.

We let our feelings guide us, modified by circumstances,
and by the wishes of our friends.   But the enjoyment of
rural scenery, its tranquillity and silence, begets a wish
to continue that sort of life ; and as we were in the habit
of staying at home of an evening, we seldom found ourselves going out, after spending a morning in the country.
From the quiet and lovingness of the fields, we returned
to the quiet and lovingness of our book and fireside.   It
was different if we rode.   There is something of comparative noise and bustle and the town in horses and
equipages.   It seemed natural enough that the carriage
which wafted us through doubtful or bleak weather of a
morning, should take us to the opera after dinner.   When
I knew that we were going out in this way, I sometimes
made a whole town day of it ; and if Harriet had nothing
to do with drapers and milliners (for though she likes to
dress well, she is not fond of shopping), I took her to my
bookseller's or the music-shop, or some exhibition.   The

exhibitions, however, we preferred in fine weather, when the days were at their clearest, and no fire was wanted. But great was our pleasure at taking home in the carriage some new book of poetry (like the one just mentioned), or some old poetry in a new edition, or some exquisite print or etching, or new air, which had delighted us at the opera; and yet half of our enjoyment of it was pretence. We felt ourselves so sufficient to one another, and were at heart so much inclined to do without anything but our own company, that, had we given ourselves up to impulse, we should have done nothing but walk and talk together, or sat like a pair of lovers at a stolen interview. But from a lucky instinct already explained, each of us, without running into a strain of systematic reflection on the subject, doubted the ability to confer that entire happiness, which neither doubted to receive; and thus we availed ourselves of all those collateral helps to good-will, those little external diversions, and objects of intellectual sympathy, which at once suspended the intensity of our feelings, and kept us more surely together. To this day the neighbourhood of her cheek to mine, while we are reading the same book, makes me long to touch it; and when I catch a little of her breath upon me, as she half turns to say something, I seem to feel, with all the freshness of a first sensation, "the fragrance of her heart."

To divert the passionate state of my emotions, I would sometimes endeavour to reflect metaphysically on the nature of *love*; and it was in one of these meditations I discovered in what the highest state of it exists, which I am convinced is *gratitude for pleasure given by intellectual, moral, and personal grace, and an extreme desire to give pleasure in return for it.* The love is perfect in proportion to the perfection of these three graces in the object, or to the imagination of them in the lover's mind, or to the abstract and candid appreciation

of them in the mind of the person beloved, so as to show
that the nature merits to be as externally as it is intrin-
sically graceful. Disinterestedness of *wish* is not to be
expected in a lover, because it is among the conditions of
our being (and a very delightful and useful one it is, and
looks like something angelical), that the bestowal of
happiness, and consequently the very idea of its bestowal,
is unavoidably connected with that of receiving it. But
the lover is reasonably to be called disinterested, in proportion as he can *act* disinterestedly where the happiness of the beloved object is concerned ; and doubtless
that love is the truest, which can so act in the highest
degree, and which can receive the greatest amount of
consolation from the knowledge of the beloved person's
happiness, apart from its own contribution to it. It is
not everybody, I fear, that is capable of real love at all,
in however small a degree. Some portion of generosity
and imagination is necessary to it ; and there are people,
whose ignorance or bad habits, or a nature derived from
unfit or unloving parents, have rendered them so destitute
of both that they know nothing of love but the animal
passion, and not even that with any admixture of grace.
The rest is as unintelligible to them, as Paradise at
present is to us ; and, by the way, it would be amusing
to know what sort of idea of Paradise theirs can be,
supposing them to believe in it, for this degradation
even of the animal passion does not allow them to
include that in their sense of dignities ; and they know
so little of affection, except to make a tool of it, and
exact it from others, that they must be equally at a loss
in the more spiritual part of the conjecture. *We* may be
allowed to guess a little. On the other hand, the capa-
bilities of being in love are of various sorts, and of almost
every degree of amount ; and while nothing tends to
exalt and perfect it so much as an admission of its
identity with the wish to see another happy, all the

perplexities and inconsistencies of it are to be accounted for and guarded against, in honourable and estimable natures, in proportion to the doubt they conceive of their own sufficiency for another's happiness, and the generosity of that doubt; that is to say, in proportion to its freedom from that impatience, which sets the will up above moral grace, and ends in caring for nothing, so that it produces a strong sense of itself and its desires; in other words, in proportion to its love of love, and not its love of power. For it is easy to desire the best things, but far less easy to deserve them; and if the desire is put stubbornly forward, and the deserve not half so much cared to be made out, the end will be, that in proportion as the best things are wished for, they will be lost; and this is the way in which will is for ever defeating itself. Pitiable is the state of those whose wilfulness obscures the real portion of love which they feel; especially as the love, though great enough to torment them, is seldom sufficient to work out their cure, by leaving the reason strong enough to compare notes with it, and come to the most loving conclusion. When it does, there is no nature worthier of cultivation, or more likely to stamp a lasting affection; for, in the present imperfection of humanity, the very habit of pity for imperfection in others helps to render a generous nature capable of being satisfied with the love, out of a sense of its own imperfections, provided the affection really succeeds in getting rid of what does not belong to it.

I will add one word more, in all delicacy, to this digression upon love; and that is (agreeably to what has been hinted before), that as the animal part of it is not to be set up as the only or more desirable portion, so neither is it to be unfeelingly or hypocritically debased into what it is not; for all impulses are good and graceful, provided they be reasonable and in good taste; and it is an impertinence and even a grossness in love, if there be not a lively sense in it of all its faculties, equally remote from an ungenial coldness and an unaffectionate self-revolvement.

The opera season in the spring of 1831 was not a good one. We missed Pasta and others; and the rest of the theatres were in no good condition. But we are so fond of music, and are so willing to find ourselves sitting together in the midst of any collection of human beings, assembled for a common pleasure, that we went even to the oratorios; not the most lively of entertainments. We had the pleasure of seeing others pleased, and more think themselves pleased, and of hearing some of the divine strains of Handel and Winter,—divine whether the subject be sacred or profane; for all sweet music is like the sound of the tongues of Paradise. It seems like a heavenly language which we hear without knowing the words, and as if it must have a meaning far beyond the words which are sometimes given to it. Love, pleasure, pity, speak to us in it beyond all question, and in their loveliest manner, and yet we know not by what secret. It is upon this principle that we understand what Mozart meant when he professed to have an indifference or contempt for "words," and did not care how poor they were. He knew that it must be very wonderful poetry indeed which should not be beaten, and *ultra*-expressed, by the mere notes of his music. No words are required to give the most enchanting and even the most definite effect (as far as particular emotion is concerned) to parts of the instrumental compositions of that great master,— to some of the overtures of Handel and Gluck, or the delicate inventions of Haydn. These beautiful echoes of our most indescribable feelings, my bride and I enjoyed with a pleasure as indescribable, sitting side by side, conscious of the enjoyment around us, and fancying a quintessence of it concentrated in our persons. And it was the same at the opera when Italian passion was pouring forth its triumph, with an intensity in every breath ; or when the music seemed to wake up and to warrant the ostentatious fervour of the dance, and the castanets sounded like the very thrill of its bones.

And then our carriage wafted us to a blissful home.

APRIL.

What does the reader think that Harriet had the face to do to me on the first of April, the moment I sat down to breakfast ?

Reader—First of April—I see it.

Ah, but *how?* She had too much taste to make a fool of her husband in a really ridiculous manner ; she respected both him and herself too much, and yet she would forego none of the privileges of playfulness. She even contrived to pay herself a compliment out of an exquisite instinct of converting a pretended joke upon me into a congratulation—a loss of dignity into a gain.

What, therefore, does my lady as soon as she has taken her chair, but get up with a little hurried air of affected gravity, go to a chiffonier, open and shut it so as to make me hear the sound, and then, coming behind me, with a tap on the shoulder, asked me what I thought of this " new honey she had bought me ? "

I turned round, and received a laugh and a kiss, with the inquiry if I knew what I was *on the first of April ?*

" The wisest man in England," quoth I, " as sure as I am the happiest. Nay, Harriet, this, I must say, is a complete failure ; I never knew you make a failure before, but when you begin, I suppose you must do everything completely. You propose to make me a fool, and you bring me the very bond and seal of my charter to the title of wise."

I waive the pretty compliments we proceeded to bandy with one another, and also the divers instances in which I had my April-day revenge. Our discourse fell upon bees, and then upon April, and then on the bees again ; and we

never had a breakfast more full of mirth and poetry.
Harriet said that people did not do enough honour to the
works of the bees in thanking them for their honey only ;
for they gave them tapers for their love-letters, and lights
to read them by. And hereupon she became .poetical
upon the subject of wax, describing its beauty and purity,
and saying that it was the " fit *second* manufacture of
such fairy creatures. It is proper," continued she, " that
the beings who make honey should make wax ; it is the
only kind of insipidity they could condescend to, and is
turned into twenty elegant things. There is the *seal* as
well as the taper. To think that I should forget *that /*
And the bee himself often furnishes a device for the seal.
Come now, Charles, I will prove your words, and make
you a *complete* case out of this. I meet you with some
fine honey in my walks, and send you a pot of it with a
note. The note, of course, is on the subject of honey,
and therefore of the bees. I seal it with a substance
made by the bees ; the taper that helps to make the seal
is of a substance made by the bees ; and the seal is
stamped with a bee's likeness. No ; my case is not complete after all, for the pen ought to have been connected
with bees, and the paper."

"It is complete, Harriet," said I, " though not in the
way you designed it. It is a specimen of that complete
sincerity, and desire for truth in small matters as well as
great, which is one of the things for which I love you,
and which makes you sweeter than all the sweets you can
describe. But not having seen so much of France and
Italy as I have, there is one application of this waxen
elegance of yours which has not made so strong an
impression upon you, though you have witnessed it in
Catholic chapels. You see to what I allude—the use of
it on Catholic altars, where those huge waxen pillars (for
such they are rather than candles), lighted with the beautiful mystery of fire, and flaming away in a world of devotion

and music and sublime paintings, are understood to
typify the seraphical ministrants before the divine throne,
burning with love. You remember the Italian poem on
bees, out of which we read some pages one day last June,
in the little hayfield near the pines. The Catholic poet,
be sure, has not forgotten this and similar uses of wax by
his fellow-worshippers, though he mentions it in a way to
startle a Protestant's ear, describing the tapers as things
made in honour of ' God's image '—

> ' Odorate cero
> Per onorar l'immagine di Dio.' "
> —*Rucellai.*

"Ah!" said Harriet, "I remember one word in particular that struck me in that poem, and your saying how
modern it was, and how impossible for a pagan to have
written it; it was *angelette.* I remember the whole line.
He calls the bees

> ' Vaghe angelette de le erbose rive.' "

" Say it again," quoth I.

She repeated it in one of her pretty, saucy styles,
between self-derision and display ; and I pelted a rose at
her lips across the table because she spoke the Italian
so well. If one cannot reward people for charming us,
one must punish them. There is no alternative. The
feelings must be vented somehow.

The imagination sometimes has involuntary caprices of
association, not unfounded in truth. April, compared
with March, always appears to me a female contrasted
with one of the rougher sex ; and compared with May,
she is a female dressed in white and green, instead of
white, green, and rose-colour. Her fingers also seem as
cold as they are delicate, and she is slender compared
with the buxomness of her sister. In other words, she
is a personification of her slender stock of green, her
blossoms, her chillness, her lilies of the valley, and her

white clouds and rains. She has colours, it is true, in her garden—the jonquil, the stock, the glowing peony, and many others; and there is the rose always. But a lover of nature is accustomed, in his first thoughts of a new season, to paint to himself its appearance in general; its skies, fields, and woods, before its gardens. I confess I think I ought to admit blue and yellow among my April colours, on account not merely of the skies, but of the charming profusion of primroses and wild hyacinths to be found in the woods. But these do not appear on the *face* of things; they are *in* the woods, and you must go there to find them. A mock-heroic poet would call them "April's under-petticoat."

What an exquisite carpet these and the other wild flowers of the season make, in a wood at all worthy of the name, with a good mossy ground! Harriet and I, who are not rich enough to have large grounds of our own, are acquainted with all the sylvan places within twenty miles of London; and in the particular April we went several days in succession to a spot called Combe Wood, near Wimbledon, which was the nearest for our purpose, and there enjoyed the blue and yellow tapestry to our eyes' content, and ate divers pretty little dinners at an inn in the neighbourhood. I shall beg the reader's company to one of these dinners by and by, in the course of the summer, as I take them to be highly sensible things, and deserving imitation; but at present I must content myself with saying that they are the reverse of everything pretending and public, and can be adapted to the cheapest capacities, provided there be no real spirit of stinginess in the parties. The fortunes of the Daltons are just good enough to afford them a few handsome luxuries, and therefore we order certain of them at the inn, quite as much to gratify the people of the house as ourselves. But I am surer of nothing upon earth than I am of this, that I could have a room to myself in one of these inns, and eat a chop and a potato with Harriet, and be as happy, and make the waiter as satisfied with me to boot, as if I had come in a carriage and four. The reader shall have my secret when time serves. In returning from one of these excursions, we saw for the first time the swallow darting about with that incredible velocity of his, that apparent *weight* of swiftness (for there seems as much weight in his plumage as speed in his circuit), which gives the look of him, as he passes, such a remarkable union of substance and evanescence. The idea of a knife is not more cutting than that of his wings. Spenser must have taken from him his feeling of the "sharp-winged shears," which he gives to one of his angels. A tropical-blooded friend of ours, who does not stop to explain his phrases, or to suit them to the colder consideration of our northern criticism, calls the swallow "a pair of scissors grown fat."

But a more wonderful bird comes in April than the swallow—the nightingale. How different from the other! He all so public, so restless, and so given up to his body; this all so hidden, so stationary, so full of soul! We hear him to singular advantage where we live. I verily believe that ours is the last house, near the metropolis, to the garden of which he comes. It is an old practice of mine, taught me by my father, who was a studious cultivator of what he called "nature's medicine," to open one of my chamber windows with the dawn of light, and so let in upon my last slumbers the virgin breath of the morning. Never shall I forget the first time I heard the nightingale in company with the dear creature who is the delight of my life. The tears come into my eyes to think of it. Is this from effeminacy? from weakness? Oh, God, no! It is from that secret sense we feel in us of the power of man to perceive and appreciate the wonderful beauty of the universe, mingled with an unconscious regret of our mortality—of the weakness and shortness of our being, compared with the strength of our affections. But far was a tear from my eyes at the time. The fulness of the sweet burthen of beauty was on us, without the weight. Harriet heard the nightingale first. "Hark!" said she. The sound was not to be mistaken. It was one of those passages of his song, not the finest, but still exquisite and peculiar, in which he chucks out a series of his duller notes, as if for the pleasure of showing how rich he is in the common coin of his art, as well as in the more precious. I rose and opened the window. The most divine of all sounds rewarded us— that low, long-drawn, internal, liquid *line of a note*, the deepest and sweetest ever heard, for which it seems as if the bird resorted to the innermost core of his soul, and meditated as he drew it along, over I know not what celestial darkness of delight. It is the meeting with the extreme of pleasure—with the gratitude which melancholy only can express. The sound mingled with our waking dreams, and heaven and earth seemed to enfold us in their blessing.

Mr. Coleridge, in one of those sallies of his genius, in which he has so often startled and instructed one's commonplaces, informed the world some time ago that it was wrong to designate the nightingale by the title "melancholy," there being "in nature nothing melancholy;" and the song of the bird being full of quick, hurried, and lively notes, anything but sorrowful; in short, he concluded, we ought to say, not the melancholy, but the "merry nightingale."

I regret that I have not his beautiful lines by me to quote.

The critics, at Mr. Coleridge's direction, inquired into this matter, and pronounced him in the right; and it is now the fashion to say, that the talk of the melancholy of the nightingale is an error, and that he is a very gay, laughing, merry fellow, who happens to be out of doors at night like other merry fellows, and is not a whit more given to pensiveness.

Nevertheless, with submission, I think that the new notion is wrong, and that the nightingale of Milton,

"Most musical, most melancholy,"

is still the real nightingale, and that the old opinion will prevail. Not that the bird is sorrowful, as the ancient legend supposed, though many of his notes, especially considering the pauses between them, which give them an air of reflection, can never be considered as expressing pleasure by means of gaiety, much less mirth. There is no levity in the nightingale. We know not what complication of feelings may be mixed up in the mystery of his song; but we take it for granted, and allow that, upon the whole, it expresses a very great degree of pleasure. I grant that to the full. But the truth is, that this pleasure, being not only mixed up with an extreme of gravity, as I have just been showing, but bringing with it an idea of loneliness, and coming at night-time, when the condition of the whole universe disposes us to meditation, the very pleasure, by the contrast, forces us more strongly upon the greater idea of the two; and hence the effect of the nightingale's song has been justly pronounced to be melancholy. It may be allowed to Mr. Coleridge, that in some very energetic and comprehensive and final sense of the assertion, there is "nothing melancholy in nature," although to our limited faculties there may seem to be enough of it to contend with, as the world goes; but upon the same principle, melancholy itself is not melancholy, and so we come round again to the natural opinion. Shakespeare has made one of his characters in "The Merchant of Venice" account partly for the reason why music, generally speaking, produces a serious impression—

"I'm never merry" (says Jessica to Lorenzo) "when I hear sweet music.
The reason is" (says her lover), "your spirits are attentive.
For do but note a wild and wanton herd,
Or race of youthful and unhandled colts,

> Fetching mad bounds, bellowing and neighing loud,
> Which is the hot condition of their blood :—
> If they but hear perchance a trumpet sound,
> Or an air of music catch their ears,
> You shall perceive them make a mutual stand,
> Their savage eyes turn'd to a modest gaze
> By the sweet power of music."

And such, no doubt, is partly the case with all creatures capable of attending to musical sounds. But with the human being the consciousness is mixed up with a thousand unconscious feelings to the effect already mentioned. There falls upon them a shadow of the great mystery of the universe. If a party of glee-singers were to become aware of a nightingale singing near them at one o'clock in the morning, and upon a pause in his song were to strike up a jovial catch by way of answer, they would be thought in bad taste, and a parcel of simpletons. The feeling, in any real lover of music, would be serious— voluptuous, if you please, and enchanting, but still full of the gravity of voluptuousness—serious from its very pleasure.

MAY and JUNE.

The May morning of 1833 broke beautifully, before we cast a look out of window to see whether it was beautiful or not. " 'Tis May," said Harriet, looking as she were the goddess of it. The month was in her eyes. I did not say to her, with the poet,—

> " Get up, sweet slug-a-bed, and see
> The dew bespangling herb and tree;
> Each flower has wept, and bowed towards the east,
> Above an hour since ; yet you not drest."

Harriet is a very reasonable getter-up ; and as goddesses as well as mortals have bedrooms, and my charmer was now representative of the goddess Maia, or month of May, it struck us that May does not leave her chamber quite so soon as people fancy ; but that she ought to make her appearance about nine o'clock, full-grown and blooming, after having collected all her poetry about her, and drest her loveliness at the glass of divinest thoughts. Harriet's toilet, therefore, took a long time on May morning, purely to do honour to the month; and when at last she descended, you might really have taken her for a personification of the month, she looked so exuberant of sweetness.

On coming down myself to the breakfast-table (for she always sees it in proper condition before I make my appearance), I found it covered with a profusion of May-blossom, daisies, roses, and cowslips, together with boughs of fruit trees and sweet-brier. Pinks came afterwards, and morning after morning we had a succession of novelties, the scabious, the scarlet lychnis, Solomon's seal (an exquisite nest of white bells lurking in green leaves), the sweet pea (that delicate, winged thought of red and white), the orchis, the lily of the valley, and the marigold. Our May-day, in point of weather, did not turn out so fine a one as we deserved to have; and old May-day (the 12th of the month), which we keep when the other disappoints us, was not much better. What signified? We kept them both, and all the days between them, partly out of doors, and more in; and we hoped for better days, and we had some, and enjoyed them to the full. Harriet was ever my best part of the month, whether it was poor weather or fine. The dull days were bright with her, and the bright ones thrice beaming.

There is a commonplace on the subject of nature and its aspect as modified by love and poetry, which takes itself for a mighty profundity, and yet is one than which nothing can be more shallow. The poets are laughed at for saying that nature mourns, and the flowers hang their heads for the death or absence of a mistress, and that *vice versâ* she laughs and sparkles, and the rose blooms again for the lady's return.

Dr. Johnson (whom I beg leave to say I think as

highly of over a dinner-table or a criticism on Pope, as I
am obliged to differ with when he comes to speak of still
greater men) thinks he has the laugh against Milton,
when he ridicules him for talking of fauns and satyrs in
his elegy on a friend. And a French wit has written an
amusing banter on these sympathies between inanimate
nature and the poets, in which he turns their delicate
sentiments into flaring matter-of-fact, and makes the
woods literally nod and the mountains groan at the
request of some lamenting gentleman, the flowers at the
same time bending their heads as he goes by, and the
rivers murmuring the name of his fair one. This is very
good ; and is deserved by *bad* poets, or those who affect
a sympathy with nature which they do not feel, and who
therefore cannot be supposed to see external objects in a
sadder or gayer light at one time than another. But the
most extreme fictions of good poetry are but subtle aspects
of truth ; nay, of truths felt by everybody, though not
in the same definite manner. A man who has lost his
mistress says, "I have no comfort now ; my days are
dull ; I take nothing of the pleasure I used to do in the
most beautiful objects ; mirth, flowers, sunshine, are
insipid to me ; nay, melancholy ; for they only remind
me of her loss ; everything is black and gloomy." This
is the ordinary language of a real affliction, and this
contains all that the poet tells us in other words. The
flowers "remind him of her loss : " what is this but
making them take a part in the grief, and absolutely
assisting in bringing her image before him? "Everything
is black and gloomy : " what is this but saying that the
roses have lost their colour ; that nature puts on a
funeral dress ; and that all beauty has departed with his
mistress, and left nothing but tears and mourning? And
so it has. To *his* eyes such is the *fact*. We have no
proof of the existence of anything but in our perception
of it ; and if to our perception it exists in a melancholy

manner, it is melancholy.   So in Milton's talk about the
fauns and satyrs which he laments that he should no more
see in company with the friend whom he mourns under
the name of *Lycidas*.   Fauns and satyrs abound in the
books which Milton and his friend delighted to read;
their imaginations were full of them, and of the poetry
to which they belonged; and therefore, in talking about
fauns and satyrs in his elegy, and lamenting that he and
his friend should no more play their " pastoral reed"
together, he talked about real subjects of deprivation;
just as much as if a musician should lament that he and
his friend could no more play the flute together, or a
huntsman that the fox would be no longer hunted in his
company.   I am sure, if I had the misery of losing my
bride (which I could not bear to think of, if she were not
as young and healthy as she is), the most beautiful objects
in the creation would seem to me the most melancholy.
I should scarcely be able to look at them; and when I did,
they would drip with the tears through which I beheld them.

Therefore I say, and say again, that with Harriet
beside me, the darkest day is bright, and the brightest
thrice beaming—

> " What pleased at first, tor her now pleases more,
> She most; and in her look seems all delight."
>   —*Paradise Lost.*

Shakespeare, in one of his sonnets, says that the very
birds grow dumb when his mistress is away; that is to
say, he hears them no more than an absent man does; or
if he does hear them, he tells us that their songs have
grown dull.   And doubtless he *literally* felt them to be
so.   They sang to him, not of present pleasure, but of
absence and loss—

> " For summer and his pleasures wait on thee;
> And thou away, the very birds are mute;
> Or if they sing, 'tis with so dull a cheer,
> That leaves look pale, dreading the winter's near

They who do not see the literal truths contained in these fancies of love and poetry, only proclaim that they are unacquainted with the refinements of either.

A pleasant banter is so different a thing from this cold, critical objection, that it often arises, not from any want of faith in the thing which is supposed to be made ridiculous by it, but the reverse. It may either be resentment of its abuse, for very love of it, or a liberty taken with the object of its love for the same reason. The Italian poets are equally famous for their faith in romance and their jokes upon it. The author of *Don Quixote* had himself the soul of a knight-errant, and wrote heaps of romantic stories in as grave and childlike a tone of belief as can be. It has been thought no detriment to the fame of Homer to suppose him the author of the *Battle of the Frogs and Mice*. I remember, when I was travelling in Italy, I was awakened one morning at a place near Florence by a sound of guitars and singing. It was May morning. The air played on the guitars was simple, graceful, and fervid ; as old, perhaps, as the time of Lorenzo de Medici ; and there was a joke mixed up with the graver enjoyment, which consisted in hailing everybody by name as he made his appearance out of doors or at a window, and attributing the coming beauties of the season to *him !*

Had Harriet and I not been able to make our own May-time within doors, it would have been provoking to see how we were kept at home, day after day, by the rain. There was a succession of drenching weather (I think) for ten days, during which the water ran down the windows at such a rate, that it seemed as if poor May was crying her heart out. But we laughed, and vowed to have a double portion of pleasure when the sun came ; and come it did, so stoutly, for several days together, that the roads and fields grew dry as in summer-time, and there was such an exuberant burst of green

and white in the hedges, and of flowers in the grass, that
it seemed as if we had been held back by the rain,
purely that we might enjoy the season to double advantage. In the south of Europe I have seen broad-leaved
myrtle growing wild, and the hedgebanks covered with
cyclamen and tulips; but never have I seen a lovelier,
fresher, or more vernal sight than is exhibited by a full,
sunny, luxuriant May-day in England, when the bushes
are thick with blossom, and the fields with daisies and
buttercups, and the lower meadows with cowslips, and
the hedgebanks glitter with the blue speedwell and the
white anemone, and the butterflies are seen, and the bees
heard, and the cattle stand, heavy and placid, in midst
of the juicy grass. I do not say much in these papers
about gardens. Everybody knows something about them;
but it is astonishing how many people, who are fond of
reading about the beauties of the country in books, and
who could really double the pleasure of their existence
if they would but consent to realize what they read of,
suffer the most beautiful seasons of the year to pass by
without enjoyment. For magnificent, astounding views,
you must go to Alps and glaciers; for sierras and chestnut woods to Spain; for vines and olives to Italy; for
picturesque rivers to Germany; for enormous waters and
trees to America; for Elysian scenes on a large scale
(mixed with wild beasts) to Africa; for icebergs and
northern lights (a sight worth a peril) to northern seas;
for pretty homesteads, occasionally knocked on the head
by an avalanche, to Switzerland: but for homesteads
equally pretty and more safe; for scenes of perfect rural
beauty between homeliness and elegance; for fields
"shut in," sylvan lanes, bosky and flowery meadows, tree-
clumps with cottage smoke, and gentle intermixtures of
vale and upland, commend us to green, old, grassy, village-
dotted England, with its verdure all the year through,
and its fair faces of red and white. Would to heaven

T

they were a little less sulky! But the Reformers must
see to that. "Maids and Milk" is, or was, according to
Drayton, the motto of the county of Suffolk—

"As Essex hath of old been named 'Calves and stiles,'
 Fair Suffolk 'Maids and Milk,' and Norfolk 'Many wiles,'
 So Cambridge hath been called 'Hold nets, and let us win,'
 And Huntingdon, 'With stilts we'll stalk through thick and
     thin,'" etc.   —*Polyolbion*, Song 23.

It seems, to my fancy, to have been the motto of all
England in old times during the month of May. At all
events, the milkmaid's garland was the prettiest of the
May-day shows. It has long gone out, and left us nothing
but the chimney-sweepers! melancholy emblem of our
fireside cares! I am not more convinced, however, of
anything on this side certainty than I am of the re-
vival of the best things in our old holidays when England
has done paying for her game at soldiers, and mirth re-
vives upon a new ground of wisdom. Then will come
back the milkmaids, announcing the vernal overflow of
their store; and Robin Hood will be had in double esti-
mation; and the chimney-sweepers will vanish with the
poor stage-coach horses before some triumphant piece of
machinery; and the plough will be at strange work in
the fields; and all will enjoy them. Do we think that
nature made such beautiful things for people to know
that they are beautiful, and yet do nothing but sigh at
the thought? Is *that* the poor jest, of which we suppose her guilty? Depend upon it, there is not a pleasure
within the possibility of being hoped for by the human
race, which they are not destined to realize.

But I am philosophizing and thinking of others, forgetful of my own exemption from the necessity. Such
are these impertinent times, which force even the rich
and the young to reflect, and will not allow a gentleman
to be happy with his bride without remembering that
other people would like to be happy too. Dear Reformers,

"there is a time for all things," and positively I will
think no more about you during these my "Honeymoons."
Surely if a man has a right to forget you, it is when—
hark !

The cuckoo !

I heard it just this moment; for I am writing of one
month of May during another, and scribbling a piece of
this article in a little rustic inn half an hour before
dinner, while Harriet is talking with the hostess, and
charming her by dandling her infant. I know by her
leaving off speaking that she hears the cuckoo as well as
I do, and that she is thinking I am thinking so. She
would have come to tell me of it, but the fact is we
heard it before; and this reminds me that I forgot to
mention the cuckoo in my article on April. We heard
it often enough then, and I wonder how it could have
escaped me. I suppose the reason was, that I got talking about the nightingale, who is a very absorbing
personage.

The cuckoo is an odd bird, with strange privileges of
grafting his children upon other people's nests. I suppose he has a licence from nature for it, in order to
enable him to play his part better as a hiding songster
and pleasant rambling mystery. It has fallen, however,
to the lot of Harriet and myself to know him not only
as a "wandering voice," but to see him many times as
plainly as a pigeon, and in the very act of singing,—nay,
singing as he flies. I confess it does not injure the
pleasure which I take in his seclusion. Nor does Harriet
wish him to have been less visible. We have enough
imagination to afford to see him; the invisibility may be
necessary for the many; to us who have such endless
faith in nature, it is otherwise. We never find a limit
to our perceptions of beauty.

There is an old belief that it is fortunate for lovers to
hear the nightingale before the cuckoo. Judge, if we

who are so loving and so believing, choose to give up this notion; and how pleased we have been these two seasons in succession to have fortunate ears. Milton speaks of this once popular notion in one of his sonnets, and entreats the nightingale to favour him accordingly. Spenser, who loves to make traditions of his own, provided they be accordant with nature, and who contradicts even the old mythologies whenever it suits him, not only vindicates the right of the cuckoo to a good name, calling him

> "The merry cuckoo, messenger of spring,"

but says that he is the herald of lovers, and summons them to wait upon their king, whom he fancies coming out of the woods, crowned with flowers, and opening the choirs of the birds.

Chaucer gives in to the old notion, upon which he has written a whole poem, called "The Cuckoo and the Nightingale." But nature is stronger than her greatest favourites; and, in spite of Chaucer and Milton, the old notion has gone out, and the cuckoo is considered pleasant. Chaucer's feeling with regard to the month of May is, as usual, beautifully expressed in this composition, in the course of which he indulges himself in one of his beloved pictures of daisied grass and bushes in blossom. (I drop the old spelling. The rhythm is of the dancing order, measured by the cadence.)

> "Then I thought anon, as it was day,
> I would go somewhere to assay
> If that I might a nightingale hear,
> For yet had I none heard of all that year,
> And it was then the third night of May.

> "And anon as I the day spied,
> No longer would I in bed abide,
> But unto a wood that was fast by
> I went forth alone, boldly,
> And held the way down by a brooke side.

> "Till I came *to a land of white and green,*
> So fair one had I never in been ;
> The ground was green ypowder'd with daisies,
> *And the flowers and the groves like high,*
> *All green and white ; was nothing else seen.*"

By "the flowers and the groves *like high,*" he means
that the flowers were the May-blossoms, and therefore as
high as the bushes on which they grew.

If anybody wishes to enjoy the May-bush in perfection,
he should go to Richmond Park, on the side sloping down
to Ham Common, where there is a hill as thick with them
as an orchard with apple-blossom.   Harriet has christened
it May-Bush Hill; and therefore I beg that this name
may be respected and brought into use by all who value a
pretty mouth and taste for nature.

June.—I cannot help thinking there is much expression
in the sound of the word June,—perhaps from association
of ideas, but something on its own account too.   It is
deeper and closer and warmer than that of May; more
spicy and pungent.   It is brown and red, compared with
red and white ; the deep rose and the marigold compared
with the May-blossom.   May has a silver sound.   She is
played, too, as it were, on a guitar of ivory, and with a
fair hand.   June's music is golden, deeper in the wire.
It is noontide, the under-current of the brooks, the tune
of bees.   But something like this has been said elsewhere
in verse, and I hate repetitions.   If twenty pictures of
spring and summer are painted, it is fit that they should
all be different, though all in accord.

When June is fine, it is a very fine month indeed—
perhaps the finest in the year.   Spring is not quite
gone ; there are some trees to fill up yet; and yet summer
is confirmed, while we have the greater part of it before
us.   The skies are blue ; the clouds small, sailing, and of
silver; the fields thick and dry—you may lie in them;
the hedges full of wild roses ; the gardens rich with gold

and red, roses, marigolds, wallflowers, nasturtiums, and red
lilies; and the trees are still fresh, yet beginning to
brown. By degrees the leaves get browner, the daisies
begin to be lost in the superabundance of buttercups, the
elder trees in the hedgerows are rich with blossom, and
shearing-time is come. We see nothing of it within
the limits of our excursions. In the course of a year or
two we mean to take a summer tour through the finest
parts of England, and see every beauty we can think of.
Meanwhile, thinking must content us, as sight is not to be
had. What we can witness for ourselves we do; what
we cannot we enjoy in the green fields and Elysian pictures
of the poets—

> "Softly mixt
> With every murmur of the smiling wave,
> And every warble of the feather'd choir;
> Music of Paradise; which still is heard,
> *When the heart listens.*"
>   —*Dyer's Fleece.*

This is beautifully said; and then the poet speaks of the
paradisiacal scenes which are within the power of almost
every one to enjoy who can walk, and the idle regrets
they utter at not having enjoyed them!

> "Yet we abandon these Elysian walks
> *Then idly for the lost delight repine.*"

Get up, for God's sake, ladies and gentlemen, and
believe that the creation does not consist only of the
"West End," nor even of your parks. How many of us
have no parks, nor even gardens, and yet sigh over the
recollection of a common field-walk in our youth, *as if it
were not to be had still !*

I speak against my interest; for, the fact is, the less you
take my advice, the quieter the fields will look, and
Harriet and I have them more to ourselves. At present
we meet a pale-faced student now and then with a book,
and a few lovers; but not enough to make us cease
wondering at the want of imagination and animal spirits

which keep so many people at home. It does not become us to say anything against marriage ; but the reader may recollect a couple of prints in the shop windows,—popular, I am sorry to say,—the one representing a gentleman helping a lady over a stile, and called " *Courtship*," the other the lady getting over by herself, and the gentleman walking on before her, and this is " *Marriage.*" I confess we have witnessed both these spectacles, and wondered what the latter did in the fields at all. I suppose they were going "the shortest way" somewhere. The lovers you may always know by a certain conscious look as you pass them—the lady sometimes affecting to appear nonchalant, the gentleman smiling but ceasing to speak, and turning away his face, which has just been earnestly fixed on hers as she looked down. Sometimes the lady is more candid, and cannot get rid of an expression of pleasure, somewhat bashful. For our parts, we endeavour to think that some of these lovers are married, but pique ourselves upon perplexing them with regard to what they think of *us*. Were they to catch us at a stile, they would feel no doubt on the subject, for they would find me (if I did not see them) lifting my charmer over as if she did not possess the use of her limbs. I sometimes beg her pardon for it, for she is as light and active as she is plump; but it is not always that married ladies must be permitted to jump, and at other times I cannot resist the opportunity of giving her the thanks of a clasp for the sweetness she is ever evincing. When we meet others, . however, I neutralize my countenance in a wonderful manner, between seriousness and happiness, complacency and respect; and Harriet's, unless speaking to me, is always in the state so exquisitely touched by our restorer of the drama—

> "A gentleness that *smiles without a smile.*"
> —*The Wife.*

A very delicate observer (such as this poet, for instance)

would, I think, detect us, but I defy common eyes.
They take us, I suspect, for a highly reputable brother
and sister; affectionate, nay, edifyingly so, thus to walk
out with one another, which is not a very brother and
sister-like thing; but they do not conclude us to be lovers
—we do not blush or simper enough, or affect enough
indifference.

I do not know a more entire piece of rural enjoyment,
an hour uniting greater complacency with delight, or that
quiet sense which one ought to have of the quiet and
gentleness of the country, combined with a greater portion
of inward transport, than in taking a walk, towards an
evening in June, through a series of fields full of clover
and buttercups, with hedgerow elms and wild roses, the
path leading from stile to stile, the bee buzzing, and the
cuckoo heard at intervals, while the scenery, as it shifts,
presents now a cottage, and now a farm, now a group of
cattle with their white and coloured bodies, and now the
tower of an old village church above the trees. To
complete the thing, the stiles should be good liberal
stiles, fit to make a seat of, in order to receive the air in
your face, or read a passage out of some favourite author;
and there should be a brook with a bit of plank over it,
and a corner of bushes; and children should be seen
occasionally, gathering the wild-flowers. Here you scent
a beanfield, such as threw Thomson into a fit of rapture—

> "Arabia cannot boast
> A fuller gale of joy, than liberal, thence
> Breathes through the sense, and takes the ravished soul."

The feeling of abstract or moral delight, received
through the medium of the scent of flowers, and other
impressions on the sense, is an interesting phenomenon,
and terminates, like all conscious impressions pursued to
their utmost, in leading from the material into the
spiritual. Our very grossest perceptions would fail us

without that intellectual mystery, the brain. Milton
speaks of an odour arising from fields and flowers—

> "Able to drive
> All sadness but despair.'

And there you hear the scythes of the mowers. In the
next field you catch glimpses of their white shirts through
the russet elm trees; in the next you come upon them;
and at due distance, and provided it be not a very
frequented field, you seat yourself with your companion
against one of the haycocks, perhaps under an oak tree,
which shades you from the sun, while the western air
comes breathing upon you. Haymakers are not uncivil
if they see you are respectable, and mean no harm to
their labours. For my part, who can afford it, I cannot
pass their careworn faces, especially in these happy-look.
ing spots, without giving them something for drink;
which brings upon my head and Harriet's lovely countenance a world of poetical Irish blessings. But this is no
precedent for those whose pockets are in less easy condition. Civility itself is money;—the common coin of
justice.

A seat of this kind sets one upon visions of happy
times and golden ages, and of what the world might come
to under wiser management. My friend and I, however
(I delight, amidst the variety of appellations which I
have for her, to call Harriet "my friend"), do not spoil
the pleasure of such a moment by too much regret on
this point. We hope the best, and resolve to do what
we can to aid it; and then we reward the virtue of our
good resolutions by present enjoyment. We chat, we
laugh, we fancy ourselves birds and butterflies; we take
out some delicate little volume, and read a bit, perhaps
on something we know as familiarly as our names; but
we read it because of the spot and the occasion, and
because we *do* know it. We literally make a companion

of our author, and turn to him to ask what he thinks of
the fine weather and the country; though we know very
well what he will say. There are passages in Spenser,
and Milton, and Theocritus, and Ovid, and Ariosto, in
Palmerin of England, the *Arcadia*, and twenty other
books, which I have read over hundreds of times in this
way, though I know them as intimately as the pictures
that hang in my sitting-room. They are the pictures
that hang in a reader's walk.

What a thing is a book,—that a man should have
written it hundreds of years ago, perhaps in Italy or in
Greece, and that by means of it we should have his
immortal company with us on the grass in an English
hayfield in June, doubling the delights of the landscape,
and increasing those even of love itself!

JULY.

July is a dumb, dreaming, hot, lazy, luxurious, delightful month for those who can do as they please, and who
are pleased with what they do. The birds are silent; we
have no more cuckoo, no more nightingale; nature is
basking in repose; the cattle stand in the water; shade
is loved, and rest after dinner. We understand, in July,
what the Spaniard means by his *siesta*. A book and a
sofa in the afternoon, near a tree-shaded window, with a
prospect of another room, seen through folding-doors, in
which the hot sun comes peeping between Venetian
blinds, is pleasant to one's supineness. The sensible
thing is to lie on your back, gently pillowed 'twixt head
and shoulders, the head resting on the end of the sofa,
and to read—listening at intervals to the sound of the
foliage, or to the passing visit of the bee. The thing,
more sensible, is to have a companion who loves your
book and yourself, and who reads with you, provided

you can let her read. I must not come, however, to my
afternoon before my morning; though July, being lazy,
makes us think of it first. July and August are afternoon and evening months; May and June are morning
months; September and October are day months; the
rest are night months, for firesides, unless we except
April, and that is as you can get it. You may experience
all the seasons in it, and must catch the sunshine as you
can, betwixt the showers.

July, however, though a lazy month, is not lazy from
weakness. If nature reposes, it is the repose of affluent
power and sovereign beauty. The gardens are in purple,
and golden, and white splendour (with the lily); the
trees in thickest exuberance; the sky at its bluest; the
clouds full, snowy, and mountainous. The genial armies
of the rain are collecting against the time when the hot
sun shall be too potent. The grandest, and at the same
time the loveliest of the wild-flowers, the convolvulus, is
lording it in the hedges. In the garden, the nasturtium
seems a flower born of fire. There is an exquisite flavour
of something burning in its taste. The daughter of
Linnæus found out that sparks are emitted from the
nasturtium in warm evenings. It was a piece of observation fit for the daughter of the great botanist, and has
associated her memory with one of the most agreeable
secrets of nature. Female discoveries ought to be in the
region of the beautiful and the sprightly. No disparage-
ment to Miss Martineau, who unites poetical and philosophical feeling to a degree hitherto displayed by none
of her sex; and whose sphere of the useful, being founded
on sympathy, contains in it all the elements of enjoyment. I mention this, because it has been strangely
supposed of *me*, Charles Dalton, husband of Harriet D.
that I have thrown divers stones, yclept paragraphs, at
the head of my wife's namesake; which I should as soon
think of doing as being angry with the summer sky.

"Do you like Harriet?" said a learned lord to me the other day, no less remarkable for the vivacity of his good-nature than his wit. He was speaking of Miss M., whom I have not the pleasure of knowing. The question startled me; for, besides the identity of the Christian name, it is manifestly impossible not to like "Harriet." Harriet is all womankind. A female name, thus put in question, *ad hominem*, stands for the whole sex. I knew not which I liked better at the moment, the lady or the interrogator.

Harriet, by the way, is a very sprightly name. It is the female of Harry, and is identified, in my imagination, with I know not what of the power of being lively and saucy, without committing the sweetness of womanhood. I have told my bride so a hundred times, and it is astonishing what a talent she has at corroboration. I believe if you were to put the same case to her twenty times an hour, she would meet you with twenty new illustrations of it. It is perfectly amazing to me, how these extremely gentle and quiet women, who present the same mild, unruffled, unaffected manners from morning to night, and who seem (as the phrase is) as if "butter would not melt in their mouths," can open upon you a world of feeling and fancy inexhaustible, and which would seem to have been secreted in a marvellous manner from everybody but myself. But I shall get into a discussion. I suspected, however, from the first time I saw her, that Harriet had a great deal of vivacity lurking under that soft eye of hers. It is an eye that looks *into* you, not *at* you; or rather, which has an inward look in itself, so that if it looks at you at all, you take the depth from which it speculates for a proportionate insight into the depth of your own feelings. And this insight she has when she chooses. Her very glance conveys the strongest impression of the idea passing in her mind, accompanied by an equally strong recognition of what is passing in yours. It was thus that I knew she returned my love, before a word of it was said on either side. She had been remarking the day before to her aunt, in answer to a sort of apology which the latter had made for giving a more peremptory opinion than usual upon some doubtful matter in which her niece was concerned, that she knew nothing more desirable than to be delivered from a painful state of hesitation by a kind friend, and that she always desired it "in proportion as she loved." "I wish she would desire it of me," thought I; "this would be true female love, looking for the help of man." Next day an application for charity was made to her, which she wished to accede to, but was not quite sure of her right. Her aunt and I were both present, but she instinctively looked first at me, with the dear question in her eyes, and then blushed like scarlet, and turned to the old lady. *Conobbi allor* (to make a grand quotation from an exquisite sonnet of Petrarch)—

> "Conobbi allor sì come in Paradiso
> Vede l'un l'altro."

> I knew her then, as spirits in Paradise
> See one another.

We sometimes got up early of a morning in July, going to bed proportionately soon at night, and laughing to think how some of our fashionable acquaintances would suppose they had the laugh on their side, for our reasonable and happy life. Sometimes we took the carriage, and, leaving it with the servants, walked into some thick lane of trees, or little wood, seeing what flowers were left us, and listening to the silence, which was swept at intervals by the gentle morning wind. We then returned to breakfast, went to our tasks, met at an early dinner, had the dessert laid in another room, and, retiring there, passed a delicious afternoon. Harriet was now in that condition which the eye of every

gallant man respects, and the soul of love encircles with
its tenderest protection. I have a theory,—no, not a
theory, it is a conviction, founded upon all that I ever
read, thought, or saw upon the subject,—that the character
of the human offspring is modified at a period much
earlier than the earliest of its observers are apt to
suppose, and that it is delightful to see the future
mother passing her time in security, and with a double
portion, if possible, of sense and cheerfulness. A
suspicion, partly to this effect, has, in fact, always
existed, but not often to very sensible purpose. An
expectation of good sense from the lady has been raised
at the precise time that she most needs it, and ladies,
not very sensible in general, have availed themselves of
the privilege to be more than usually absurd. Hence,
because the frames of children are affected by sudden
impressions on the part of the mother (a fact not to
be doubted) have risen all sorts of fantastic wants
and pretences, with their pleasing accompaniments of
hysterics, faintings, rages, remonstrances, and additions
to tradesmen's bills; and hence (for the minds of children
are affected as well as their bodies, though the apparently
obvious deduction is never thought of) the children come
into the world squalling and to squall, and the foolish
parents who helped to make them what they are hasten
to make them worse by scolding or indulgence, till they
wonder what perverse brats they have engendered.

Fortunately for me, and for the little creature that has
just been crowing at me with a voice of sugar, and a
face full of dimples, Harriet understood the philosophy
of this matter at a glance, and estimating the perils of
her condition at their proper amount, and no more, and
feeling herself joyfully secure from them as far as her
own temper and mine were concerned, her goodness and
taste were never more evinced than at this period.
Never did I know her more delightful. She volunteered

no dangers, nor imagined any, where there was no
ground for them. She renounced horseback, and was
cautious enough not to walk the street without a veil,
or with eyes unprepared, lest she should encounter any
of those frightfully pitiable objects which luckily are
not so common in England as in some other parts of
Europe. For the rest, she was as gay as a lark, and
tender as gratitude, had no fancies, because she had no
wilfulness or folly, and walked (to the last) in the garden
as if she had been an Amazon. Yes, one fancy she had,
but she was doubtful whether she should indulge it,
purely because it was a fancy. She had read accounts
of the supposed origin of the beauty of the ancient
Greeks, and of imaginations affected by paintings and
sculpture, and she asked me whether I should think the
wish whimsical, or whether she ought to wish me to
hasten the purchase of a couple of statues I had talked
of—the celestial Venus and the Apollo of the Vatican.
I said I rejoiced in seizing the opportunity to get them,
for that I had delayed it for no other reason than
because we had been ruralizing so much of late that I
had almost forgotten the town. They were procured
the next day, and installed in the two farthest corners
of our principal sitting-room, where they looked beauty
and tranquillity at us from morn till night, and disposed
my charmer's mind to repose on her idealism made
visible. She said she had no fear of unpleasant
thoughts, but was willing to render pleasant ones more
than usually distinct to her imagination. "And these
beautiful strangers," said I, smiling, "will not displace
me in your thoughts?" "Displace you!" cried she,
rising from the chair in which she was sitting near me,
as I reclined on the sofa, and coming towards me with
an air of gay revenge, then added, in a lower tone, and
with exquisite tenderness, and gently pressing herself
against my heart, "How *could* they?"

But I ought to have an audience made on purpose, and safe from the chance of unworthy listeners, before I could indulge my pride with recording more of these speeches. To others I leave it to imagine the evenings we passed; —how attentive without exaction,—how reposing on certainty,—how full of past, present, and future—making my July as well as my January a true honeymoon, if ever there was sweetness in truth and love.

AUGUST.

The month of August, owing to the heat of the weather, and the interesting circumstances mentioned in my last, passed much in the same manner with us as that of July. But we oftener went out in the carriage, because Harriet could walk less.   Not that she did not walk as often as she could; for she was religious upon that point, and proposed to gift her offspring with the peripatetic principle before it was born.   But the weather was so hot that, in order to keep up our country pleasures at any distance, we were fain to be carried; she out of necessity, and I because I chose to be as near her as possible.   I do not much like riding at any time by the side of a carriage, and talking with a lady inside of it, when I can sit with her,—she straining her voice, and the horseman bobbing up and down, and losing it in the sound of gravelly roads, and the whisking of the wind; and Harriet's "situation" (to use one of the numberless unmeaning, yet understood words, by which gossips express delicate circumstances) attracted my arm around her with fresh force every day,—the more so, as, though she depended as much as possible on herself, and made no fuss about it, she could not conceal the comfort it gave her, and the gratitude that sighed for every felicity as I drew her within it.   It may be an odd word to use, but many a man will sigh from a very different feeling at hearing it, when I say, that one of the most excellent reasons which I have for loving Harriet consists in her being one of the *unfussiest* of women. She never exacts, nor fidgets, nor *maunders*, nor is ill-timed, nor makes mountains of mole-hills, nor insists upon attention to herself by any of those numerous petty and restless manœuvres, by which inferior understandings think to make themselves of consequence, while they betray their want of right to it. The result is, as in all cases where people unaffectedly disclaim attention, that one gives it her in double portion, and is grateful that she thinks it worth acceptance. Good heaven! what straws become precious between those who know how to love! and what caskets of jewels one could pitch into the river when they are only the go-betweens of a mistake! I do not pretend that I, Charles Dalton, however justly I lay claim to the title of the most "bridal" of men, have not, in my time, "loved," yea, and been "made love to" by divers fair persons, before (to speak Hibernically), I knew what love was! And doubtless there are many honest people who know not what love is all their lives, and would have taken it for very good love. You read of such in the works of the Duke of Buckingham and the Count de Buffon. Nor do I mean to disparage it after its fashion. The very best love, I confess, would be puzzled to know how to do without it, yet I will venture to say, to those who have heart and understanding enough to allow of its being said to them, that the least touch of the cheek, loved by that best love, is a greater pleasure even to the senses than all which Madame du Barri brought to the hero of the *Parc aux Cerfs*. The delight of holding the very tips of Harriet's fingers, as I lead her to the carriage, is greater to me, with all my town experience (such as it is), than if I had the run of the Grand Turk's seraglio. And there are very lovable persons there, nevertheless, I dare-

say, and such as might give him a sensation, if he knew
how to be less of a sensualist and more of a *voluptuary.*
I use the term "advisedly," as the discreet say; for, between the "knowing reader" and myself, these poor
people,—your Grand Turks, and your "men of pleasure
about town," are ignorant of the very trade they profess,
and never make Cupid laugh so heartily as when they
think they know him best, taking him for a sorry little
devil, who ought to be whipped! But I fear I have said
this before!

I took Harriet in August to see some glorious harvests
on the borders of Middlesex, Hertfordshire, and thereabouts, including the famous Perivale, recorded by Drayton, and eminent among "exalted valleys," for having
produced the bread that was set on Queen Elizabeth's
table. They say there is a family living there in the
rank of yeomen who have cultivated the same spot of
ground ever since the time of Edward the Confessor!
What a respectable family must that be (if it is not the
dullest in the world); and what sturdy principles of dura-
tion and conduct must be in it! It is the next thing
to a man's living for ever. I have heard of such families
in Kent and Sussex, but never before on this side of
London; though I have been told of one not half so far
from town, who have kept their carriage for twenty years,
and never seen the metropolis! This seems incredible;
though there is no saying what freaks people may take
into their heads, or how far the conduct of one obstinate
misanthropical or even amiable but morbid person may
affect a generation of jog-trot old coach-horses and good-
natured aunts. Ought I to be ashamed to say, that I
could live twenty years with Harriet without going to
London,—content to receive my books by the coach, and
to wander with her in the same old woods, and be snug by
the same fireside? This may be thought a bridal fancy;
but I am sure I could. I know it from what I used to

feel when a child,—a time of life at which novelty is loved for its own sake. I had two favourite houses which I visited for a series of years, and I know not what it was to desire a third. I could have passed to and fro betwixt the gardens of the one and the picture-galleries of the other for ever, desiring only what I did desire, namely, somebody to love, as Ariosto's lover did, in a picture which hung up in one of the parlours, of Angelica and Medoro. And this somebody I have found. Why need I then wander? It is true, chance has thrown me on the borders of the metropolis, and I am fortunate enough, so situated, to like both town and country; but the former is not necessary to me. Love only is necessary, with imagination and a green tree. My world is so large with imagination, and so rich with love, that it is more easy to me to contract than to extend it. I can find, as the Jew of Malta saw in his gem,

"Infinite riches in a little room;"

but take away one or two things that are in it, and the richest and busiest streets in London would become a poverty-stricken solitude. I should take a lodging (if I could get no better) near some bit of a tree, perhaps half dead with smoke, and sit in a churchyard; but it would be a visible bit of nature, and remind me of something larger than all the cities of the earth. Or I would stick up a few flowers in my window, and take refuge with those. Something to love, or to represent what we love, is the thing, or any thing that any way resembles its beauty, its grace, or its good-nature.

Harriet was now the more willing to exchange her walks for the carriage, inasmuch as her "situation" made her less easy at being stared at. When Catherine the Second of Russia grew corpulent, she set a fashion, or took upon herself the exclusive privilege (I do not mention which) of wearing a long loose gown, of such a

make as to conceal the deformity of her shape, without
hurting what was left of the grace and dignity of her
movement.   I wish Mrs. Dalton were an empress for a
day or two, so that she might set a fashion which should
do justice to shapes of a certain kind,—not deformed,
God knows,—but such as women do not willingly subject to the chance of being looked upon by common eyes.
She has invented such a one, and would look charming
in it; but she would not wear it, even before acquaintances, lest she should be thought eccentric.   So hard it
is for society to add a little bit to their reasonableness.
It is of a rich, heavy, deep-coloured texture, hanging
directly from the bosom to the ground, after the fashion
of the fair autocrat, and would form at once an understood veil and a majestic ornament.   But the ladies of
Almack's do not set such fashions, and therefore their
husbands must have them indecently stared at.   I know
not by what unrefined instinct it is, but I have seen men
in theatres and other places, and indeed in rooms, fix
their eyes, with so strange and apparently so stupid an
absorption, upon women in this condition, that I have
been astonished how anybody in the rank of a gentleman
could be guilty of so manifest an outrage, and have been
ready to get up and chuck a glass of wine in his face.
The imagination of these starers must be wondrously
matter-of-fact, and require a world of proof to set them
going.   When ladies are

"As ladies wish to be who love their lords,"

I suppose these gentlemen take the spectacle for the only
proof positive that there has been any love in the case.
They are sure of nobody else.   Existence, for aught they
know, may be the dullest thing possible from here to
China, with all the rest of the world; but here, they
think, "be proofs."   They require ocular demonstration
that the earth is to continue peopled; and, of course, are

in like doubt upon all other desirable points. They question whether there is any laughter going forward in France itself, unless they occasionally meet with some native of that country ready to split.

"My *soul*, turn from them;" and let us acknowledge that the above line of the poet's is a very pretty one, albeit repeated quotation has done it a mischief. Poets have said less on this subject than might have been expected, probably because they doubted whether they should find "fit audience." Shakespeare has touched it —scarcely, I think, with his usual delicacy—in a passage in the "Midsummer Night's Dream" (act ii. scene 2). Spenser has an exquisite line about it, calculated to make every mother love him—

> "The loving mother, that nine months did beare,
> *In the dear closet of her painful side,*
> Her tender babe," etc.

I cannot venture to say anything to the same purpose after this. The perfection of humanity is in it—the tenderest, thoughtful mixture of pain and pleasure.

When we got among the rich lanes and cornfields of Perivale, I told Harriet that she looked like the goddess of the month, and that if she had had her proposed gown on, I could have led her forth like the splendid personification of its Plenty in the "Faerie Queene"—

> "The sixth was August, being rich arrayed,
> In garments all of gold, doune to the ground,
> Yet rode he not, but led a lovely maid
> Forth by the lily hand, the which was crown'd
> With ears of corn, and full her hand was found."

After laughing, with a pretty saucy blush, at a double mistake I had made in this quotation, and giving praise to this and other beautiful passages in her wonted style, such as crying out, "Now—how very beautiful that is!" "Now—how lovely!" "Now, Charles, if you repeat any more such, I will do you a mischief,

because, as you say, I do not know how to vent
my satisfaction." Harriet began to raise a hundred
ludicrous images of our playing the part of August and
Plenty, and astonishing the rustics and little children in
the lanes,—I looking gravely at her sideways, leading
her by the "lily hand," and she looking as gravely right
forward, not at all heeding the little children ; and then
she fell into a strain of grateful tenderness towards nature,
and me, and mirth, and tenderness, and everything. By
this time we had got back into the carriage,—the happiness she felt made her more and more serious ; till at
length, as it led her by degrees into the indulgence of
every affectionate thought, and the tenderest consciousness of her hopes, it produced the softest shower of tears
I ever beheld, part of which, as she leant her forehead
against mine, fell from her downcast, but willing eyes,
like drops of consecration.

A honeymoon only the first month ! as well might it
be said that the bees make honey but one month in the
year ; or that the moonlight is not as sweet in summer
as in spring. I may repeat here a saying I met with the
other day, out of good-natured Boccaccio : " Bocca baciata
no perde ventura anzi rinuova, come fa la luna : "

> How can lips by kissing lose?
> Like the moon, the mouth renews.

Here is a series of honeymoons described by the author
of the "Decameron," without his knowing it ; but I grant
that it is true love only which is gifted with the power
of renovation.

Apropos of the word Honeymoon : I happen to have
just been reading in two different anonymous authors,
both very clever ones, and both, I understand, ladies, that
the metaphor took its rise from a custom among our
Saxon ancestors, of drinking wine made from honey
during the first wedded month. How could these ladies
do such injustice to the poetry and the sweet thoughts

that are in them. At least they might have added a protest as to its non-importance; for what signifies a Gothic accident like that, granting it even to have happened. Honey is thought to be the sweetest food in the world, and marriage is thought to be at once the sweetest and briefest bliss that is entered upon. There is a mònth, it is calculated, of right good marriage, and that month is, of course, a month of honey. The word honey has been used to express the sweetest of sweets all over the world, and in all ages. "Sweeter than honey and the honeycomb," says a reverend authority. "By the honey - sweet!" exclaimed an ancient of Mount Hybla, swearing by Goddess Proserpina. "Honeyed eyes," quoth the Latin poet—*mellitos oculos;* not that the lover drank hydromel in their honour, and so made them sweet by authority, but because he drank honey out of their own sweetness, and grew intoxicated with love.

XX.

A TALE FOR A CHIMNEY CORNER.

A MAN who does not contribute his quota of grim story now-a-days, seems hardly to be free of the republic of letters. He is bound to wear a death's head as part of his insignia. If he does not frighten everybody, he is nobody. If he does not shock the ladies, what can be expected of him?

We confess we think very cheaply of these stories in general. A story, merely horrible or even awful, which contains no sentiment elevating to the human heart and its hopes, is a mere appeal to the least judicious, least healthy, and least masculine of our passions—fear. They whose attention can be gravely arrested by it, are in a fit state to receive any absurdity with respect; and this is the reason why less talents are required to enforce it, than in any other species of composition. With this opinion of such things, we may be allowed to say, that we would undertake to write a dozen horrible stories in a day, all of which should make the common worshippers of power, who were not in the very healthiest condition, turn pale. We would tell of Haunting Old Women, and Knocking Ghosts, and Solitary Lean Hands, and Empusas on One Leg, and Ladies growing Longer and Longer, and Horrid Eyes meeting us through Keyholes, and Plaintive Heads, and Shrieking Statues, and shocking Anomalies of Shape, and Things which when seen drove people mad; and Indigestion knows what besides. But who would measure talents with a leg of veal or a German sausage?

Mere grimness is as easy as grinning; but it requires something to put a handsome face on a story. Narratives become of suspicious merit in proportion as they lean to Newgate-like offences, particularly of blood and wounds. A child has a reasonable respect for a Raw-head-and-bloody-bones, because all images whatsoever of pain and terror are new and fearful to his inexperienced age; but sufferings merely physical (unless sublimated like those of Philoctetes) are commonplaces to a grown man. Images, to become awful to him, must be removed from the grossness of the shambles. A death's head was a respectable thing in the hands of a poring monk, or of a nun compelled to avoid the idea of life and society, or of a hermit already buried in the desert. Holbein's Dance of Death, in which every grinning skeleton leads along a man of rank, from the Pope to the gentleman, is a good Memento Mori; but there the skeletons have an air of the ludicrous and satirical. If we were threatened with them in a grave way, as spectres, we should have a right to ask how they could walk about without muscles. Thus many of the tales written by such authors as the late Mr. Lewis, who wanted sentiment to give him the heart of truth, are quite puerile. When his spectral nuns go about bleeding, we think they ought in decency to have applied to some ghost of a surgeon. His little Grey Men, who sit munching hearts, are of a piece with fellows that eat cats for a wager.

Stories that give mental pain to no purpose, or to very little purpose compared with the unpleasant ideas they excite of human nature, are as gross mistakes, in their way, as these, and twenty times as pernicious; for the latter become ludicrous to grown people. They originate also in the same extremes, of callousness, or of morbid want of excitement, as the others. But more of these hereafter. Our business at present is with things ghastly and ghostly.

A ghost story, to be a good one, should unite, as much as possible, objects such as they are in life with a preternatural spirit. And to be a perfect one,—at least, to add to the other utility of excitement a moral utility,—they should imply some great sentiment,—something that comes out of the next world to remind us of our duties in this; or something that helps to carry on the idea of our humanity into after-life, even when we least think we shall take it with us. When "the buried majesty of Denmark" revisits earth to speak to his son Hamlet, he comes armed, as he used to be, in his complete steel. His visor is raised; and the same fine face is there; only, in spite of his punishing errand and his own sufferings, with

> "A countenance more in sorrow than in anger."

When Donne the poet, in his thoughtful eagerness to reconcile life and death, had a figure of himself painted in a shroud, and laid by his bedside in a coffin, he did a higher thing than the monks and hermits with their skulls. It was taking his humanity with him into the other world, not affecting to lower the sense of it by regarding it piecemeal or in the framework. Burns, in his "Tam O'Shanter," shows the dead in their coffins after the same fashion. He does not lay bare to us their skeletons or refuse, things with which we can connect no sympathy or spiritual wonder. They still are flesh and body to retain the one; yet so look and behave, inconsistent in their very consistency, as to excite the other.

> "Coffins stood round like open presses,
> Which showed the dead in their last dresses:
> And by some devilish cantrip sleight,
> Each, in his cauld hand, held a light."

Reanimation is perhaps the most ghastly of all ghastly things, uniting as it does an appearance of natural interdiction from the next world, with a supernatural experience of it. Our human consciousness is jarred out of its

self-possession.   The extremes of habit and newness, of
commonplace and astonishment, meet suddenly, without
the kindly introduction of death and change ; and the
stranger appals us in proportion.   When the account
appeared the other day in the newspapers of the
galvanized dead body, whose features as well as limbs
underwent such contortions, that it seemed as if it were
about to rise up, one almost expected to hear, for the
first time, news of the other world.   Perhaps the most
appalling figure in Spenser is that of Maleger ("Faerie
Queene," b. ii. c. 11) :—

> " Upon a tygre swift and fierce he rode,
>   That as the winde ran underneath his lode,
>   Whiles his long legs nigh raught unto the ground :
>   Full large he was of limbe, and shoulders brode,
>   But of such subtile substance and unsound,
> That like a ghost he seemed, whose grave-clothes were unbound."

Mr. Coleridge, in that voyage of his to the brink of all
unutterable things, the " Ancient Mariner " (which works
out, however, a fine sentiment), does not set mere ghosts or
hobgoblins to man the ship again, when its crew are dead ;
but reanimates, for awhile, the crew themselves.   There
is a striking fiction of this sort in Sale's *Notes upon the
Koran.*   Solomon dies during the building of the temple,
but his body remains leaning on a staff and overlooking
the workmen, as if it were alive ; till a worm gnawing
through the prop, he falls down.—The contrast of the
appearance of humanity with something mortal or supernatural, is always the more terrible in proportion as it is
complete.   In the pictures of the temptations of saints
and hermits, where the holy person is surrounded, teased,
and enticed, with devils and fantastic shapes, the most
shocking phantasm is that of the beautiful woman.   To
return also to the poem above-mentioned.   The most
appalling personage in Mr. Coleridge's "Ancient Mariner"
is the Spectre-woman, who is called Life-in-Death.   He

renders the most hideous abstraction more terrible than
it could otherwise have been, by embodying it in its own
reverse. "Death" not only "lives" in it, but the "unutterable" becomes uttered. To see such an unearthly
passage end in such earthliness, seems to turn commonplace itself into a sort of spectral doubt. The Mariner,
after describing the horrible calm, and the rotting sea in
which the ship was stuck, is speaking of a strange sail
which he descried in the distance :—

> "The western wave was all a-flame,
>   The day was well nigh done !
> Almost upon the western wave
> Rested the broad bright sun ;
> When that strange ship drove suddenly
> Betwixt us and the sun.

> "And straight the sun was flecked with bars,
>   (Heaven's Mother send us grace!)
> As if through a dungeon-grate he peer'd,
> With broad and burning face.

> "Alas ! (thought I, and my heart beat loud)
>   How fast she neers and neers !
> Are those *her* sails that glance in the sun
> Like restless gossameres ?

> "Are those *her* ribs, through which the sun
>   Did peer as through a grate ?
> And is that Woman all her crew ?
> Is that a death ? and are there two ?
> Is Death that Woman's mate ?

> "Her lips were red, her looks were free,
>   Her locks were yellow as gold,
> Her skin was as white as leprosy,
> The Night-Mare Life-in-Death was she,
> Who thicks man's blood with cold."

But we must come to Mr. Coleridge's story with our
subtlest imaginations upon us. Now let us put our
knees a little nearer the fire, and tell a homelier one about

Life in Death. The groundwork of it is in Sandys'
Commentary upon Ovid, and quoted from Sabinus.[1]

A gentleman of Bavaria, of a noble family, was so
afflicted at the death of his wife, that, unable to bear the
company of any other person, he gave himself up to a
solitary way of living. This was the more remarkable
in him, as he had been a man of jovial habits, fond of his
wine and visitors, and impatient of having his numerous
indulgences contradicted. But in the same temper,
perhaps, might be found the cause of his sorrow; for
though he would be impatient with his wife, as with
others, yet his love for her was one of the gentlest wills
he had; and the sweet and unaffected face which she
always turned upon his anger, might have been a thing
more easy for him to trespass upon, while living, than to
forget when dead and gone. His very anger towards her,
compared with that towards others, was a relief to him.
It was rather a wish to refresh himself in the balmy feeling of her patience, than to make her unhappy herself, or
to punish her, as some would have done, for that virtuous
contrast to his own vice.

But whether he bethought himself, after her death,
that this was a very selfish mode of loving; or whether,
as some thought, he had wearied out her life with habits
so contrary to her own; or whether, as others reported,
he had put it to a fatal risk by some lordly piece of self-
will, in consequence of which she had caught a fever on
the cold river during a night of festivity; he surprised
even those who thought that he loved her by the extreme
bitterness of his grief. The very mention of festivity,
though he was patient for the first day or two, afterwards
threw him into a passion of rage; but by degrees even
his rage followed his other old habits. He was gentle,

[1] The Saxon Latin poet, we presume, professor of belles-lettres at
Frankfort. We know nothing of him, except from a biographical
dictionary.

but ever silent. He eat and drank but sufficient to keep him alive; and used to spend the greater part of the day in the spot where his wife was buried.

He was going there one evening, in a very melancholy manner, with his eyes turned towards the earth, and had just entered the rails of the burial-ground, when he was accosted by the mild voice of somebody coming to meet him. "It is a blessed evening, sir," said the voice. The gentleman looked up. Nobody but himself was allowed to be in the place at that hour, and yet he saw with astonishment a young chorister approaching him. He was going to express some wonder, when, he said, the modest though assured look of the boy, and the extreme beauty of his countenance, which glowed in the setting sun before him, made an irresistible addition to the singular sweetness of his voice; and he asked him with an involuntary calmness, and a gesture of respect, not what he did there, but what he wished. "Only to wish you all good things," answered the stranger, who had now come up, "and to give you this letter." The gentleman took the letter, and saw upon it, with a beating yet scarcely bewildered heart, the handwriting of his wife. He raised his eyes again to speak to the boy, but he was gone. He cast them far and near round the place, but there were no traces of a passenger. He then opened the letter, and by the divine light of the setting sun, read these words :—

"To my dear husband, who sorrows for his wife—

"Otto, my husband, the soul you regret so is returned. You will know the truth of this, and be prepared with calmness to see it, by the divineness of the messenger who has passed you. You will find me sitting in the public walk, praying for you, praying that you may never more give way to those gusts of passion and those curses against others, which divided us.

"This, with a warm hand, from the living Bertha."

Otto (for such, it seems, was the gentleman's name) went instantly, calmly, quickly, yet with a sort of benumbed being, to the public walk. He felt, but with only a half-consciousness, as if he glided without a body, but all his spirit was awake, eager, intensely conscious. It seemed to him as if there had been but two things in the world—Life and Death; and that Death was dead. All else appeared to have been a dream. He had awaked from a waking state, and found himself all eye, and spirit, and locomotion. He said to himself, once, as he went: "This is not a dream. I will ask my great ancestors to-morrow to my new bridal feast, for they are alive." Otto had been calm at first, but something of old and triumphant feelings seemed again to come over him. Was he again too proud and confident? Did his earthly humours prevail again, when he thought them least upon him? We shall see.

The Bavarian arrived at the public walk. It was full of people with their wives and children, enjoying the beauty of the evening. Something like common fear came over him as he went in and out among them, looking at the benches on each side. It happened that there was only one person, a lady, sitting upon them. She had her veil down, and his being underwent a fierce but short convulsion as he went near her. Something had a little baffled the calmer inspiration of the angel that had accosted him, for fear prevailed at the instant, and Otto passed on. He returned before he had reached the end of the walk, and approached the lady again. She was still sitting in the same quiet posture, only he thought she looked at him. Again he passed her. On his second return, a grave and sweet courage came upon him, and in an under but firm tone of inquiry, he said, " Bertha ?"—" I thought you had forgotten me," said that well-known and mellow voice, which he had seemed as far from ever hearing again as earth is from heaven. He

took her hand, which grasped his in turn ; and they
walked home in silence together, the arm, which was
wound within his, giving warmth for warmth.

The neighbours seemed to have a miraculous want of
wonder at the lady's reappearance. Something was said
about a mock funeral, and her having withdrawn from
his company for awhile ; but visitors came as before,
and his wife returned to her household affairs. It was
only remarked that she always looked pale and pensive.
But she was more kind to all, even than before ; and her
pensiveness seemed rather the result of some great internal
thought, than of unhappiness.

For a year or two the Bavarian retained the better
temper which he acquired. His fortunes flourished
beyond his earliest ambition ; the most amiable as well
as noble persons of the district were frequent visitors ;
and people said that to be at Otto's house must be the
next thing to being in heaven. But by degrees his self-
will returned with his prosperity. He never vented
impatience on his wife, but he again began to show that
the disquietude it gave her to see it vented on others
was a secondary thing, in his mind, to the indulgence of
it. Whether it was that his grief for her loss had been
rather remorse than affection, and so he held himself
secure if he treated her well, or whether he was at all
times rather proud of her than fond, or whatever was the
cause which again set his antipathies above his sympathies, certain it was that his old habits returned upon
him ; not so often, indeed, but with greater violence and
pride when they did. These were the only times at
which his wife was observed to show any ordinary
symptoms of uneasiness.

At length, one day, some strong rebuff which he had
received from an alienated neighbour threw him into such
a transport of rage that he gave way to the most bitter
imprecations, crying with a loud voice, "This treatment

to *me* too! To *me!* To me, who if the world knew all"— At these words, his wife, who had in vain laid her hand upon his, and looked him with dreary earnestness in the face, suddenly glided from the room. He and two or three who were present were struck with a dumb horror. They said she did not walk out, nor vanish suddenly, but glided as one who could dispense with the use of feet. After a moment's pause, the others proposed to him to follow her. He made a movement of despair, but they went. There was a short passage which turned to the right into her favourite room. They knocked at the door twice or three times, and received no answer. At last one of them gently opened it, and, looking in, they saw her, as they thought, standing before a fire, which was the only light in the room. Yet she stood so far from it as rather to be in the middle of the room; only the face was towards the fire, and she seemed looking upon it. They addressed her, but received no answer. They stepped gently towards her, and still received none. The figure stood dumb and unmoved. At last, one of them went round in front, and instantly fell on the floor. The figure was without body. A hollow hood was left instead of a face. The clothes were standing upright by themselves.

That room was blocked up for ever, for the clothes, if it might be so, to moulder away. It was called the Room of the Lady's Figure. The house after the gentleman's death was long uninhabited, and at length burnt by the peasants in an insurrection. As for himself, he died about nine months after, a gentle and childlike penitent. He had never stirred from the house since, and nobody would venture to go near him but a man who had the reputation of being a reprobate. It was from this man that the particulars of the story came first. He would distribute the gentleman's alms in great abundance to any strange poor who would accept them, for most of the neighbours held them in horror. He tried all he could to get the parents among them to let some of their little children, or a single one of them, go to see his employer. They said he even asked it one day with tears in his eyes. But they shuddered to think of it; and the matter was not mended when this profane person, in a fit of impatience, said one day that he would have a child of his own on purpose. His employer, however, died in a day or two. They did not believe a word he told them of all the Bavarian's gentleness, looking upon the latter as a sort of ogre, and upon his agent as little better, though a good-natured-looking, earnest kind of person. It was said many years after, that this man had been a friend of the Bavarian's when young, and had been deserted by him. And the young believed it, whatever the old might do.

XXI

CHARLES BRANDON, AND MARY QUEEN OF FRANCE.

THE fortune of Charles Brandon was remarkable. He was an honest man, yet the favourite of a despot. He was brave, handsome, accomplished, possessed even delicacy of sentiment; yet he retained the despot's favour to the last. He even had the perilous honour of being beloved by his master's sister, without having the least claim to it by birth; and yet instead of its destroying them both, he was allowed to be her husband.

Charles Brandon was the son of Sir William Brandon, whose skull was cleaved at Bosworth by Richard the Third, while bearing the standard of the Duke of Richmond. Richard dashed at the standard, and appears to have been thrown from his horse by Sir William, whose strength and courage, however, could not save him from the angry desperation of the king.

> "But Time, whose wheeles with various motion runne,
> Repayes this service fully to his sonne,
> Who marries Richmond's daughter, born betweene
> Two royal parents, and endowed a queene."
> —*Sir John Beaumont's Bosworth Field.*

The father's fate must have had its effect in securing the fortunes of the son. Young Brandon grew up with

Henry the Seventh's children, and was the playmate of
his future king and bride. The prince, as he increased
in years, seems to have carried the idea of Brandon with
him like that of a second self; and the princess, whose
affection was not hindered from becoming personal by
anything sisterly, nor on the other hand allowed to waste
itself in too equal a familiarity, may have felt a double
impulse given to it by the improbability of her ever being
suffered to become his wife. Royal females in most
countries have certainly none of the advantages of their
rank, whatever the males may have. Mary was destined
to taste the usual bitterness of their lot; but she was
repaid. At the conclusion of the war with France, she
was married to the old king Louis the Twelfth, who
witnessed from a couch the exploits of her future husband
at the tournaments. The doings of Charles Brandon
that time were long remembered. The love between him
and the young queen was suspected by the French court;
and he had just seen her enter Paris in the midst of a
gorgeous procession, like Aurora come to marry Tithonus.
Brandon dealt his chivalry about him accordingly with
such irresistible vigour, that the Dauphin, in a fit of
jealousy, secretly introduced into the contest a huge
German, who was thought to be of a strength incompar-
able. But Brandon grappled with him, and with seeming
disdain and detection so pummelled him about the head
with the hilt of his sword, that the blood burst through
the vizor. Imagine the feelings of the queen, when he
came and made her an offering of the German's shield.
Drayton, in his "Heroical Epistles," we know not on what
authority, tells us, that one occasion during the combats,
perhaps this particular one, she could not help crying out,
"Hurt not my sweet Charles," or words to that effect.
He then pleasantly represents her as doing away suspicion
by falling to commendations of the Dauphin, and affecting not to know who the conquering knight was;—an

ignorance not very probable; but the knights sometimes disguised themselves purposely.

The old king did not long survive his festivities. He died in less than three months, on the first day of the year 1515; and Brandon, who had been created Duke of Suffolk the year before, reappeared at the French court, with letters of condolence, and more persuasive looks. The royal widow was young, beautiful, and rich; and it was likely that her hand would be sought by many princely lovers; but she was now resolved to reward herself for her sacrifice, and in less than two months she privately married her first love. The queen, says a homely but not mean poet (Warner, in his " Albion's England "), thought that to cast too many doubts

> " Were oft to erre no lesse
> Than to be rash: and thus no doubt
>   The gentle queene did guesse,
> That seeing this or that, at first
>   Or last, had likelyhood,
> A man so much a manly man
>   Were dastardly withstood.
> Then kisses revelled on their lips,
>   To either's equal good."

Henry showed great anger at first, real or pretended; but he had not then been pampered into unbearable self-will by a long reign of tyranny. He forgave his sister and friend; and they were publicly wedded at Greenwich on the 13th of May.

It was during the festivities on this occasion (at least we believe so, for we have not the chivalrous Lord Herbert's life of Henry the Eighth by us, which is most probably the authority for the story; and being a good thing, it is omitted, as usual, by the historians) that Charles Brandon gave a proof of the fineness of his nature, equally just towards himself, and conciliating towards the jealous. He appeared, at a tournament, on a saddle-cloth, made half of frieze and half of cloth of gold,

and with a motto on each half.   One of the mottos ran
thus :—

> " Cloth of frize, be not too bold,
>   Though thou art match d with cloth of gold."

The other :—

> " Cloth of gold, do not despise,
>   Though thou art matched with cloth of frize."

It is this beautiful piece of sentiment which puts a
heart into his history, and makes it worthy remembering.

XXII.

GILBERT! GILBERT!

THE sole idea generally conveyed to us by historians of Thomas à Becket is that of a haughty priest, who tried to elevate the religious power above the civil. But in looking more narrowly into the accounts of him, it appears that for a considerable part of his life he was a merry layman, was a great falconer, feaster, and patron, as well as man of business; and he wore all characters with such unaffected pleasantness, that he was called the Delight of the Western World.

On a sudden, to everybody's surprise, his friend the king (Henry the Second) from chancellor made him archbishop; and with equal suddenness, though retaining his affability, the new head of the English Church put off all his worldly graces and pleasures (save and except a rich gown over his sackcloth), and, in the midst of a gay court, became the most mortified of ascetics. Instead of hunting and hawking, he paced a solitary cloister; instead of his wine, he drank fennel-water; and in lieu of soft clothing, he indulged his back in stripes.

This phenomenon has divided the opinions of the moral critics. Some insist that Becket was religiously in earnest, and think the change natural to a man of the world, whose heart had been struck with reflection. Others see in his conduct nothing but ambition. We suspect that three parts of the truth are with the latter; and that Becket, suddenly enabled to dispute a kind of

sovereignty with his prince and friend, gave way to the
new temptation, just as he had done to his falconry
and fine living.　But the complete alteration of his way
of life—the enthusiasm which enabled him to set up so
different a greatness against his former one—shows that
his character partook at least of as much sincerity as
would enable him to delude himself in good taste.　In
proportion as his very egotism was concerned, it was
likely that such a man would exalt the gravity and importance of his new calling.　He had flourished at an
earthly court; he now wished to be as great a man in
the eyes of another; and worldly power, which was at
once to be enjoyed and despised by virtue of his
office, had a zest given to its possession, of which,
the incredulousness of mere insincerity could know
nothing.

　　Thomas à Becket may have inherited a romantic turn
of mind from his mother, whose story is a singular one.
His father, Gilbert Becket, a flourishing citizen, had been
in his youth a soldier in the crusades; and being taken
prisoner, became slave to an Emir, or Saracen prince.
By degrees he obtained the confidence of his master,
and was admitted to his company, where he met a
personage who became more attached to him.　This was
the Emir's daughter.　Whether by her means or not does
not appear, but after some time he contrived to escape.
The lady with her loving heart followed him.　She knew,
they say, but two words of his language,—London and
Gilbert; and by repeating the former she obtained a
passage in a vessel, arrived in England, and found her
trusting way to the metropolis.　She then took to her
other talisman, and went from street to street pronounc-
ing "Gilbert!"　A crowd collected about her wherever
she went, asking of course a thousand questions, and to
all she had but one answer—Gilbert! Gilbert!—She
found her faith in it sufficient.　Chance, or her deter-

mination to go through every street, brought her at last
to the one, in which he who had won her heart in slavery
was living in good condition.   The crowd drew the
family to the window; his servant recognised her; and
Gilbert Becket took to his arms and his bridal bed his
far-come princess, with her solitary fond word.

XXIII

THE MOUNTAIN OF THE TWO LOVERS.

WE forget in what book it was, many years ago, that we read the story of a lover who was to win his mistress by carrying her to the top of a mountain, and how he did win her, and how they ended their days on the same spot.

We think the scene was in Switzerland; but the mountain, though high enough to tax his stout heart to the uttermost, must have been among the lowest. Let us fancy it a good lofty hill in the summer-time. It was, at any rate, so high, that the father of the lady, a proud noble, thought it impossible for a young man so burdened to scale it. For this reason alone, in scorn, he bade him do it, and his daughter should be his.

The peasantry assembled in the valley to witness so extraordinary a sight. They measured the mountain with their eyes; they communed with one another, and shook·their heads; but all admired the young man; and some of his fellows, looking at their mistresses, thought they could do as much. The father was on horseback, apart and sullen, repenting that he had subjected his daughter even to the show of such a hazard; but he thought it would teach his inferiors a lesson. The young man (the son of a small land-proprietor, who had some pretensions to wealth, though none to nobility) stood, respectful-looking, but confident, rejoicing in his heart that he should win his mistress, though at the cost of a noble pain, which he could hardly think of as a pain, considering who it was that he was to carry. If he died for it, he should at least have had her in his arms, and have looked her in the face. To clasp her person in that manner was a pleasure which he contemplated with such transport as is known only to real lovers; for none others know how respect heightens the joy of dispensing with formality, and how the dispensing with the formality ennobles and makes grateful the respect.

The lady stood by the side of her father, pale, desirous, and dreading. She thought her lover would succeed, but only because she thought him in every respect the noblest of his sex, and that nothing was too much for his strength and valour. Great fears came over her nevertheless. She knew not what might happen, in the chances common to all. She felt the bitterness of being herself the burden to him and the task; and dared neither to look at her father nor the mountain. She fixed her eyes, now on the crowd (which nevertheless she beheld not) and now on her hand and her fingers' ends, which she doubled up towards her with a pretty pretence,—the only deception she had ever used. Once or twice a daughter or a mother slipped out of the crowd, and coming up to her, notwithstanding their fears of the lord baron, kissed that hand which she knew not what to do with.

The father said, "Now, sir, to put an end to this mummery;" and the lover, turning pale for the first time, took up the lady.

The spectators rejoice to see the manner in which he moves off, slow but secure, and as if encouraging his mistress. They mount the hill; they proceed well; he halts an instant before he gets midway, and seems refusing something; then ascends at a quicker rate; and now, being at the midway point, shifts the lady from one side to the other. The spectators give a great shout. The baron, with an air of indifference, bites the tip of his gauntlet, and then casts on them an eye of rebuke. At the shout the lover resumes his way. Slow but not feeble is his step, yet it gets slower. He stops again, and they think they see the lady kiss him on the fore- head. The women begin to tremble, but the men say he will be victorious. He resumes again; he is half-way between the middle and the top; he rushes, he stops, he staggers; but he does not fall. Another shout from the men, and he resumes once more; two-thirds of the remaining part of the way are conquered. They are certain the lady kisses him on the forehead and on the eyes. The women burst into tears, and the stoutest men look pale. He ascends slowlier than ever, but seeming to be more sure. He halts, but it is only to plant his foot to go on again; and thus he picks his way, planting his foot at every step, and then gaining ground with an effort. The lady lifts up her arms, as if to lighten him. See : he is almost at the top; he stops, he struggles, he moves sideways, taking very little steps, and bringing one foot every time close to the other. Now—he is all but on the top; he halts again; he is fixed; he staggers. A groan goes through the multitude. Suddenly, he turns full front towards the top; it is luckily almost a level; he staggers, but it is forward :—Yes :—every limb in the multitude makes a movement as if it would assist him :—see at last : he is *on* the top; and down he falls flat with his burden. An enormous shout! He has won : he has won. Now he has a right to caress his mistress, and she is caressing him, for neither of them gets up. If he has fainted, it is with joy, and it is in her arms.

The baron put spurs to his horse, the crowd following him. Half-way he is obliged to dismount; they ascend the rest of the hill together, the crowd silent and happy, the baron ready to burst with shame and impatience. They reach the top. The lovers are face to face on the ground, the lady clasping him with both arms, his lying on each side.

"Traitor!" exclaimed the baron, "thou hast practised this feat before, on purpose to deceive me. Arise!"

"You cannot expect it, sir," said a worthy man, who was rich enough to speak his mind; "Samson himself might take his rest after such a deed!"

"Part them!" said the baron,

Several persons went up, not to part them, but to congratulate and keep them together. These people look close; they kneel down; they bend an ear; they bury their faces upon them. "God forbid they should ever be parted more," said a venerable man; "they never can be." He turned his old face streaming with tears, and looked up at the baron:—"Sir, they are dead!"

XXIV.

THE HAMADRYAD.[1]

An Assyrian, of the name of Rhæcus, observing a fine old oak-tree ready to fall with age, ordered it to be propped up. He was continuing his way through the solitary skirts of the place, when a female of more than human beauty appeared before him, with gladness in her eyes. "Rhæcus," said she, "I am the Nymph of the tree which you have saved from perishing. My life is, of course, implicated in its own. But for you, my existence must have terminated; but for you, the sap would have ceased to flow through its boughs, and the godlike essence I received from it to animate these veins. No more should I have felt the wind in my hair, the sun upon my cheeks, or the balmy rain upon my body. Now I shall feel them many years to come. Many years also will your fellow-creatures sit under my shade, and hear the benignity of my whispers, and repay me with their honey and their thanks. Ask what I can give you, Rhæcus, and you shall have it."

The young man, who had done a graceful action, but had not thought of its containing so many kindly things, received the praises of the Nymph with a due mixture of surprise and homage. He did not want courage, however, and emboldened by her tone and manner, and still more by a beauty which had all the buxom bloom of humanity in it, with a preternatural gracefulness besides,

[1] See the Scholiast upon Apollonius Rhodius, or the Mythology of Natalis Comes.

he requested that she would receive him as a lover. There was a look in her face at this request answering to modesty, but something still finer; having no guilt, she seemed to have none of the common infirmities either of shame or impudence. In fine, she consented to reward Rhæcus as he wished; and said she would send a bee to inform him of the hour of their meeting.

Who now was so delighted as Rhæcus? for he was a great admirer of the fair sex, and not a little proud of their admiring him in return; and no human beauty, whom he had known, could compare with the Hamadryad. It must be owned, at the same time, that his taste for love and beauty was not of quite so exalted a description as he took it for. If he was fond of the fair sex, he was pretty nearly as fond of dice, and feasting, and any other excitement which came in his way; and unluckily, he was throwing the dice that very noon when the bee came to summon him.

Rhæcus was at an interesting part of the game—so much so, that he did not at first recognise the object of the bee's humming. "Confound this bee," said he, "it seems plaguily fond of me." He brushed it away two or three times, but the busy messenger returned, and only hummed the louder. At last he bethought him of the Nymph; but his impatience seemed to increase with his pride, and he gave the poor insect such a brush, as sent him away crippled in both his thighs.

The bee returned to his mistress as well as he could, and shortly after was followed by his joyous assailant, who came triumphing in the success of his dice and his gallantry. "I am here," said the Hamadryad. Rhæcus looked among the trees, but could see nobody. "I am here," said a grave sweet voice, "right before you." Rhæcus saw nothing. "Alas!" said she, "Rhæcus, you cannot see me, nor will you see me more. I had thought better of your discernment and your kindness; but you were but gifted with a momentary sight of me. You will see nothing in future but common things, and those sadly. You are struck blind to everything else. The hand that could strike my bee with a lingering death, and prefer the embracing of the dice-box to that of affectionate beauty, is not worthy of love and the green trees."

The wind sighed off to a distance, and Rhæcus felt that he was alone.

XXV.

A NOVEL PARTY.

--" Hic ingentem comitum affluxisse novorum
Invenio admirans numerum."—VIRGIL.

O the pleasure that attends
Such flowings in of novel friends !

Spiritual Creations more Real than Corporeal—A party composed
of the Heroes and Heroines of Novels—Mr. Moses Primrose,
who has resolved not to be cheated, is delighted with some
information given him by Mr. Peregrine Pickle—Conversation of the Author with the celebrated Pamela—Arrivals of
the rest of the Company — The Party found to consist of
four Smaller Parties—Characters of them—Character of Mr.
Abraham Adams — Pamela's Distress at her Brother's want
of Breeding — Settlement together of Lovelace and Clarissa
—Desmond's Waverley asks after the Antiquary's Waverley
—His Surprise at the Coincidence of the Adventure on
the Seashore—Misunderstanding between Mrs. Slipslop and
Mrs. Clinker—The Ladies criticized while putting on their
Cloaks.

WHEN people speak of the creations of poets and
novelists, they are accustomed to think that they are
only using a form of speech. We fancy that nothing
can be created which is not visible ;—that a being must
be as palpable as Dick or Thomas, before we can take
him for granted ; and that nobody really exists, who will
not die like the rest of us, and be forgotten.   But, as we
have no other certainty of the existence of the grossest
bodies than by their power to resist or act upon us,—as
all which Hipkins has to show for his entity is his power

Y

to consume a barrel of oysters, and the only proof which Tomkins can bring of his not being a figment is his capacity of receiving a punch in the stomach,—I beg leave to ask the candid reader, how he can prove to me that all the heroes and heroines that have made him hope, fear, admire, hate, love, shed tears, and laugh till his sides were ready to burst, in novels and poems, are not in possession of as perfect credentials of their existence as the fattest of us? Common physical palpability is only a proof of mortality. The particles that crowd and club together to form such obvious compounds as Thomson and Jackson, and to be able to resist death for a little while, are fretted away by a law of their very resistance; but the immortal people in Pope and Fielding, the deathless generations in Chaucer, in Shakespeare, in Goldsmith, in Sterne, and Le Sage, and Cervantes,—acquaintances and friends who remain for ever the same, whom we meet at a thousand turns, and know as well as we do our own kindred, though we never set gross corporeal eyes on them, — what is the amount of the actual effective existence of millions of Jacksons and Tomkinses compared with theirs? Are we as intimate, I wish to know, with our aunt, as we are with Miss Western? Could we not speak to the character of Tom Jones in any court in Christendom? Are not scores of clergymen continually passing away in this transitory world, gone and forgotten, while Parson Adams remains as stout and hearty as ever?

But why need I waste my time in asking questions? I have lately had the pleasure of seeing a whole party of these immortal acquaintances of ours assembled at once. It was on the 15th of February in the present year. I was sitting by my fireside, and, being in the humour to have more company than I could procure, I put on my Wishing-cap, and found myself in a new little world that hovers about England, like the Flying Island of Gulliver.

The place immediately above me resembled a common drawing-room at the West End of the town, and a pretty large evening party were already assembled, waiting for more arrivals. A stranger would have taken them for masqueraders. Some of the gentlemen wore toupees, others only powder, others their own plain head of hair. Some had swords by their sides, others none. Here were beaux in the modern coat and waistcoat, or habiliments little different. There stood coats stuck out with buckram, and legs with stockings above the knees. The appearance of the ladies presented an equal variety. Some wore hoops, others plain petticoats. The heads of many were built up with prodigious edifices of hair and ribbon; others had their curls flowing down their necks; some were in common shoes, others in a kind of slippered stilts. In short, not to keep the reader any longer upon trifles, the company consisted of the immortal though familiar creatures I speak of, the heroes and heroines of the wonderful persons who have lived among us, called Novelists.

Judge of my delight when I found myself among a set of old acquaintances, whom I had never expected to see in this manner. Conceive how I felt, when I discovered that the gentleman and lady I was sitting next to were Captain and Mrs. Booth; and that another couple on my left, very brilliant and decorous, were no less people than Sir Charles and my Lady Grandison! In the centre were Mr. and Mrs. Roderick Random; Lieutenant Thomas Bowling, of the Royal Navy; Mr. Morgan, a Welsh gentleman; Mr. and Mrs. Peregrine Pickle; Mr. Fathom, a Methodist—(a very ill-looking fellow)—Sir George Paradyne, and Mr. Hermsprong; Mr. Desmond, with his friend Waverley (a relation of the more famous Waverley); a young gentleman whose Christian name was Henry—(I forget the other, but Mr. Cumberland knows), and Mr., formerly Serjeant, Atkinson, with his wife, who

both sat next to Captain and Mrs. Booth. There were
also some lords whose names I cannot immediately call
to mind ; a lady of rank, who had once been a Beggar-
girl ; and other persons too numerous to mention. In a
corner, very modest and pleasing, sat Lady Harold, better
known as Miss Louisa Mildmay, with her husband, Sir
Robert. From the mixed nature of the company, a
spectator might have concluded that these immortal
ladies and gentlemen were free from the ordinary passions
of created beings ; but I soon observed that it was otherwise. I found that some of the persons already assembled
had arrived at this plebeian hour out of an ostentation of
humility ; and that the others, who came later, were
influenced by the usual variety of causes.

The next arrival—(conceive how my heart expanded at
the sight)—consisted of the Rev. Dr. Primrose, Vicar of
Wakefield, with his family, and the Miss Flamboroughs ;
the latter red and staring with delight. The Doctor
apologized for not being sooner ; but Mrs. Primrose said
she was sure the gentlefolks would excuse him, knowing
that people accustomed to good society were never in a
flurry on such occasions. Her husband would have made
some remark on this, but seeing that she was prepared to
appeal to her son, "the Squire," who flattered and made
her his butt, and that Sir William Thornhill and both
the young married ladies would be in pain, he forebore.
The Vicar made haste to pay his respects to Sir Charles
and Lady Grandison, who treated him with great distinction, Sir Charles taking him by the hand, and calling
him his "good and worthy friend." I observed that Mr.
Moses Primrose had acquired something of a collected
and cautious look, as if determined never to be cheated
again. He happened to seat himself next to Peregrine
Pickle, who informed him, to his equal surprise and
delight, that Captain Booth had written a refutation of
Materialism. He added, that the Captain did not choose

at present to be openly talked of as the author, though he did not mind being complimented upon it in an obscure and ingenious way. I noticed, after this, that a game of cross purposes was going on between Booth and Moses, which often forced a blush from the Captain's lady. It was with much curiosity I recognised the defect in the latter's nose. I did not find it at all in the way when I looked at her lips. It appeared to me even to excite a kind of pity, by no means injurious to the most physical admiration; but I did not say this to Lady Grandison, who asked my opinion on the subject. Booth was a fine strapping fellow, though he had not much in his face. When Mr. and Mrs. Booby (the famous Pamela) afterwards came in, he attracted so much attention from the latter, that upon her asking me, with a sort of pitying smile, what I thought of him, I ventured to say, in a pun, that I looked upon him as a very good "Booth for the Fair"; upon which, to my astonishment, she blushed as red as scarlet, and told me that her dear Mr. B. did not approve of such speeches. My pun was a mere pun, and meant little; certainly nothing to the disadvantage of the sentimental part of the sex, for whom I thought him by no means a finished companion. But there is no knowing these precise people.

But I anticipate the order of the arrivals. The Primroses were followed by Sir Launcelot Greaves and his lady, Mr. and Mrs. Thomas Jones, Mr. and Miss Western, and my Lady Bellaston. Then came Miss Monimia (I forget her name), who married out of the old Manor House; then Mr. and Mrs. Humphrey Clinker (I believe I should rather say Bramble), with old Matthew himself, and Mrs. Lismahago; and then a whole world of Aunt Selbys, and Grandmamma Selbys, and Miss Howes, and Mr. Harlowes, though I observed neither Clarissa nor Lovelace. I made some inquiries about them afterwards, which the reader shall hear.

Enter Mr. John Buncle, escorting five ladies, whom he
had been taking to an evening lecture. Tom Gollogher
was behind them, very merry.

Then came my Lord and Lady Orville (Evelina), Mr.
and Mrs. Delville (Cecilia), Camilla (I forget her sur-
name), with a large party of Mandleberts, Clarendels,
Arlberys, Orkbornes, Marglands, and Dubsters, not omitting the eternal Mrs. Mitten. Mrs. Booby and husband
came last, accompanied by my Lady Booby, Mr. Joseph
Andrews and bride, and the Rev. Mr. Adams, for whom
Mrs. B. made a sort of apology, by informing us that
there was no necessity to make any,—Mr. Adams being
an honour to the cloth. Fanny seated herself by Sophia
Western (that was), with whom I found she was intimate; and a lovelier pair of blooming, unaffected creatures, whose good-nature stood them instead of wit, I
never beheld. But I must discuss the beauties of the
ladies by and by.

An excuse was sent by Mr. Tristram Shandy for his
Uncle Tobias, saying that they were confined at home,
and unfit for company, which made me very sorry, for I
would rather have seen the divine old invalid than any
man in the room, not excepting Parson Adams. I
suspect he knew nothing of the invitation. Corporal
Trim brought the letter; a very honest, pathetic fellow,
who dropped a tear. He also gave a kiss, as he went
out, to one of the maid-servants. The Rev. Mr. Yorick,
friend of the Shandy family, sent his servant La Fleur to
wait on us; a brisk, active youth, who naturalized himself among us by adoring the ladies all round. The poor
lad manifested his admiration by various grimaces, that
forced the Miss Flamboroughs to stuff their handkerchiefs
in their mouths. Our other attendants were Strap, Tom
Pipes, Partridge, and two or three more, some of them in
livery, and others not, as became their respective ranks.
The refreshments were under the care of Mrs. Slipslop;

but underwent, as they came up, a jealous revision from Mrs. Lismahago and Mrs. Humphrey Clinker, who, luckily for her, differed considerably with one another, or none would have been worth eating.

I have omitted to observe that the meeting was of the same nature with assemblies in country towns, where all the inhabitants, of any importance, are in the habit of coming together for the public advantage, and being amiable and censorious. There the Sir Charles Grandison of the place meets the Tom Jones and the Mrs. Humphrey Clinker. There the Lady Bellaston interchanges courtesies and contempt with the Miss Marglands; and all the Dubsters, in their new yellow gloves, with all the Delvilles.

Having thus taken care of our probabilities (or verisimilitude, as the critics call it), to which, in our highest flights, we are much attached, we proceed with our narrative.

We forgot to mention that Mrs. Honour, the famous waiting-maid of Sophia Western, was not present. Nothing could induce her to figure as a servant, where that "infected upstart," as she called her, Mrs. Humphrey Clinker, fidgeted about as a gentlewoman.

The conversation soon became very entertaining, particularly in the hands of the Grandisons and Harlowes, who, though we could perceive they were not so admired by the rest of the company as by one another, interested us in spite of ourselves by the longest and yet most curious gossip in the world. Sir Charles did not talk so much as the others; indeed he seemed to be a little baffled and thrust off the pinnacle of his superiority in this very mixed society; but he was thought a prodigious fine gentleman by the gravest of us, and was really a good-natured one. His female friends, who were eternally repeating and deprecating their own praises, were pronounced by Hermsprong, as well as Peregrine Pickle, to be the greatest coxcombs under the sun. The latter said something about Pamela and Covent Garden which we do not choose to repeat. The consciousness of doing their duty, however, mixed as it might be with these vain mistakes, gave a certain tranquillity of character to the faces of some of this party, which Peregrine, and some others about him, might have envied. At the same time, we must do the justice to Peregrine to say, that although (to speak plainly) he had not a little of the blackguard in him, he displayed some generous qualities. We cannot say much for his wit and talents, which are so extolled by the historian; nor even for those of his friend, Roderick Random, though he carries some good qualities still further. Roderick's conversation had the vice of coarseness, to the great delight of Squire Western, who said he had more spirit than Tom himself. Tom did not care for a little freedom, but the sort of conversation to which Roderick and his friends were inclined disgusted him, and, before women, astonished him. He did not, therefore, very well fall in with this society, though his wit and views of things were, upon the whole, pretty much on a par with theirs. In person and manners he beat them hollow. Sophia nevertheless took very kindly to Emily Gauntlett and Narcissa, two ladies rather insipid.

We observed that the company might be divided into four different sorts. One was Sir Charles Grandison's and party; another, the Pickles and Joneses; a third, the Lord Orvilles, Evelinas, and Cecilias, with the young lady from the old Manor House; and a fourth, the Hermsprongs, Desmonds, and others, including a gentleman we have forgotten to mention, Mr. Hugh Trevor. In this last were some persons whose names we ought to have remembered, for an account of whom we must refer to Mrs. Inchbald. The first of these parties were for carrying all the established conventional virtues to a high pitch of dignity; so much so as to be thinking too much of the dignity, while they fancied they were absorbed in the virtue. They were very clever and amusing, and we verily believe could have given an interest to a history of every grain of sand on the sea-shore; but their garrulity and vanity, united, rendered other conversation a refreshment. The second were a parcel of wild, but not ill-natured young fellows, all very ready to fall in with what the others thought and recommended, and to forget it the next moment, especially as their teachers laid themselves open to ridicule. It must be added, that their very inferiority in some respects gave them a more general taste of humanity, particularly Tom Jones, who was as pleasant, unaffected a fellow, and upon the whole perhaps as virtuous, in his way, as could be expected of a sprightly blood educated in the ordinary fashion. The Camillas and Evelinas were extremely entertaining, and told us a number of stories that made us die with laughter. Their fault consisted in talking too much about lords and pawnbrokers. Miss Monimia, too, from the old Manor House, ridiculed vulgarity a little too much to be polite. The most puzzling people in the room were the Desmonds and Hugh Trevors, who had come up since a late revolution in our sphere. They got into a controversy with the Grandisons, and reduced them sadly to their precedents and authorities. The conclusion of the company seemed to be, that if the world were to be made different from what it is, the change would be effected rather by the philosophies of these gentlemen than the seraphics of the other party; but the general opinion was, that it would be altered by neither, and that in the meantime, "variety was charming;" a sentiment which the Vicar of Wakefield took care to explain to his wife.

But how are we forgetting ourselves! We have left

out, in our divisions, a fifth set, the most delightful of all,
one of whom is a whole body of humanity in himself—to
wit, Mr. Abraham Adams, and all whom he loves. We
omit his title of Reverend; not because he is not so, but
because titles are things exclusive, and our old friend
belongs to the whole world. Bear witness, spirit of everything that is true, that, with the exception of one or two
persons, only to be produced in these latter times, we love
such a man as Abraham Adams better than all the
characters in all the histories of the world, orthodox or
not orthodox. We hold him to be only inferior to a
Shakespeare; and only then, because the latter joins the
height of wisdom intellectual to his wisdom cordial. He
should have been Shakespeare's chaplain, and played at
bowls with him. What a sound heart—and a fist to stand
by it! This is better than Sir Charles's fencing, without
which his polite person—virtue included—would often
have been in an awkward way. What disinterestedness!
What feeling! What real modesty! What a harmless
spice of vanity—Nature's kind gift—the comfort we all
treasure more or less about us, to keep ourselves in heart
with ourselves! In fine, what a regret of his Æschylus!
and a delicious forgetting that he could not see to read if
he had had it! Angels should be painted with periwigs,
to look like him. We confess we prefer Fanny to Joseph
Andrews, which will be pardoned us; but the lad is a
good lad, and if poor Molly at the inn has forgiven him
(which she ought to do, all things considered), we will
forgive him ourselves, on the score of my Lady Booby.
It is more than my Lady has done, though she takes a
pride in patronizing the "innocent creatures," as she calls
them. We are afraid, from what we saw this evening,
that poor Joseph is not as well as he would be with his
sister Pamela. When the refreshments came in, we
observed her blush at his handing a plate of sandwiches
to Mr. Adams. She called him to her in a whisper;

and asked him whether he had forgotten that there was
a footman in the room ?

The arrival of the refreshments divided our company
into a variety of small ones. The ladies got more together;
and the wines and jellies diffused a benevolent spirit
among us all. We forgot our controversies, and were
earnest only in the putting of cakes. John Buncle, however, stood talking and eating at a great rate with one of
the philosophers. Somebody asked after Lovelace and
Clarissa; for the reader need not be told that it is only in
a fictitious sense that these personages are said to have
died. They cannot die, being immortal. It seems that
Lovelace and Clarissa live in a neighbouring quarter,
called Romance, a very grave place, where few of the
company visited. We were surprised to hear that they
lived in the same house; that Lovelace had found out
he had a liking for virtue in her own shape as well as
Clarissa's, and that Clarissa thought she might as well
forget herself so far as to encourage the man not to make
a rascal and a madman of himself. This, at least, is the
way that Tom Gollogher put it, for Tom undertook to be
profound on the subject, and very much startled us by
his observations. He made an application of a line in
Milton, about Adam and Eve, which the more serious
among us thought profane, and which, indeed, we are
afraid of repeating; but Tom's good nature was so evident,
as well as his wish to make the best of a bad case, that
we chose to lay the more equivocal part of his logic to the
account of his "wild way"; and, for all that we saw to
the contrary, he was a greater favourite with the ladies
than ever. Desmond's friend, Waverley, asked us after
his celebrated namesake. We told him he was going on
very well, and was very like his relation—a compliment
which Mr. Waverley acknowledged by a bow. We
related to him the seaside adventure of Waverley's friend,
the Antiquary; at which the other exclaimed, "Good

God! how like an adventure which happened to a friend
of our acquaintance! only see what coincidences will take
place!" He asked us if the Antiquary had never noticed
the resemblance, and was surprised to hear that he had
not. "I should not wonder at it," said he, "if the
incident had been well known; but these Antiquaries,
the best of them, have strange grudging humours; and I
will tell him of it," added he, "when I see him." Mr.
Waverley anticipated with great delight the society of
his namesake, with his numerous friends, though he did
not seem to expect much from the female part of
them.

Before we broke up, tragical doings were likely to have
occurred between the housekeeper and Mrs. Humphrey
Clinker. Mrs. Slipslop sent up a message apologizing for
some of the jellies. She expressed a fear—which was cor-
rectly delivered by an impudent young rogue of a messenger,
—that the *superfluency* of the sugar would take away the
tastality of the jellies, and render them quite *inoxious*."
(If the reader thinks this account overcharged, we have
to inform him that he will fall into the error of the
audience about the pig.) Mrs. Humphrey was indignant
at this "infected nonsense," as she called it; and she was
fidgeting out of the room to scold the rhetorician when
her husband called her back, telling her that it was
beneath the dignity of a rational soul like hers to fret
itself with such matters. Winifred's blood began to rise
at the first part of this observation; but the words, "like
hers," induced her to sit down, and content herself with
an answer to the message. Peregrine Pickle, who was
sorry to see affairs end so quietly, persuaded her, however,
to put her message in writing; and Mrs. Slipslop would
have inevitably been roused and brought up-stairs, had not
Sir Charles condescended to interfere. The answer was
as follows :—

" Mrs. Slibberslop,

"Hit Bing beneath the diggingit of a rasher and sole to cumfabberate with sich parsons, I Desire that you wil send up sum geallies Fit for a cristum and a gentile wommun to Heat. We are awl astonied Att yure niggling gents. The geallys ar Shamful."

Peregrine begged her to add a word of advice respecting the "pompous apology," upon which she concluded thus :—

"A nuther tim doant Send up sich pumpers and Polly jeers and stuf ; and so no moar at present from
"Yure wel wisker,
"Winifred Clinker."

When the ladies had put on their cloaks, and were waiting for their carriages, we could not but remark how well Sophia Western—(we like to call her by her good old name)—looked in any dress and position. She was all ease and good-nature, and had a charming shape. Lady Grandison was a regular beauty, but did not become a cloak. She was best in full dress. Pamela was a little, soft-looking thing, who seemed "as if butter would not melt in her mouth." But she had something in the corner of her eye which told you that you had better take care how you behaved yourself. She would look all round her at every man in the room, and hardly one of them be the wiser. Pamela was not so splendidly dressed as her friend, Lady Grandison ; but her clothes were as costly. The Miss Howes, Lady G.'s, and others of that class, were loud, bright-eyed, raw-boned people, who tossed on their cloaks without assistance, or commanded your help with a sarcasm. Camilla, Cecilia, and Evelina were all very handsome and agreeable. We prefer, from what we recollect of them, Camilla and Evelina ; but they say Cecilia is the most interesting. Louisa Mildmay

might have been taken for a pale beauty; but her paleness was not natural to her, and she was resuming her
colour. Her figure was luxuriant; and her eyes, we
thought, had a depth in them beyond those of any
person's in the room. We did not see much in Narcissa
and Emily Gauntlett, but they were both good, jolly
damsels enough. Of Amelia we have spoken already.
We have a recollection that Hermsprong's wife (a Miss
Championet) was a pleasant girl, but somehow she had
got out of our sight. The daughters of the Vicar of
Wakefield were fine girls, especially Sophia, for whom,
being of her lover, Sir William's, age, we felt a particular
tenderness.

XXVI

THE BULL-FIGHT.

EVERYBODY has heard of the bull-fights in Spain. The noble animal is brought into an arena to make sport, as Samson was among the Philistines. And truly he presents himself to one's imagination as a creature equally superior with Samson to his tormentors; for the sport which he is brought in to furnish is that of being murdered. The poor beast is actuated by a perverse will, and by a brutality which is deliberate. He does but obey to the last the just feelings of his nature. He would not be forced to revenge himself if he could help it. He would fain return to the sweet meadow and the fresh air, but his tyrants will not let him. He is stung with arrows, goaded and pierced with javelins, hewn at with swords, beset with all the devilries of horror and astonishment that can exasperate him into madness; and the tormentors themselves feel he is in the right, if he can but give bloody deaths to his bloody assassins. The worst of it is, that some of these assassins, who are carried away by custom, are persons who are otherwise among the best in the kingdom. They err from that very love of sympathy, and of the admiration of their fellows, which should have been employed to teach them better.

The excuse for this diabolical pastime is, that it keeps up old Spanish qualities to their height, and prevents the nation from becoming effeminate. To what pur-

pose? And in how many instances? Are not the
Spanish nobility the most degenerate in Europe? Has
not its court, for three generations, been a scandal and a
burlesque? And would any other nation in Christendom
consent to be made the puppets of such superiors?
What could Spain have done against France without
England? What have all its bull-fights, and all its other
barbarities, done for it, to save it from the shame of
being the feeblest and most superstitious of European
communities, and having no voice in the affairs of the
world?

Poor foolish Matadore! Poor idle, illiterate, unre-
flecting *caballero!*—that is to say, "horseman!" which,
by the noble power or privilege of riding of horse (a
thing that any groom can do in any decent country),
came to mean "gentleman," as distinguished from that
of "centaur," can you risk your life for nothing better
than this? Must you stake wife, children, mistress,
father, and mother, friends, fortune, love, and all which
all of them may bring you, at no higher price than the
power of having it said you are a better man than the
butcher? Is there no sacred cause of country to fight
for? no tyrants to oppose? no doctrine worth martyrdom?
—that you must needs, at the hazard of death and agony,
set the only wits or the best qualities you possess on out-
doing the greatest fools and ruffians in your city? And
can you wonder that your country has no cause which
it can stand to without help or to any purpose? that your
tyrants are cruel and laugh at you? and that your very
wives and mistresses (for the most part) think there is
nothing better in the world than a flaring show and a
brutal sensation?

Bull-fights are going on now, and bull-fights were going
on in the wretched time of King Charles the Second, of
the House of Austria, whose very aspect seemed ominous
of the disasters about to befall his country; for his face

was very long, his lip very thick, his mouth very wide, his nose very hooked, and he had no calves to his legs, and no brains in his skull. His clemency consisted in letting assassins go, because passion was uncontrollable; and his wit in sending old lords to stand in the rain, because they intimated that it would be their death. However, he was a good-natured man, as times went, especially for a king of Spain; and it is not of public disasters that we are to speak, but of the misery that befell two lovers in his day, in consequence of these detestable bull-fights.

Don Alphonso de Melos, a young gentleman of some five-and-twenty years of age, was the son of one of those Titulados of Castile, more proud than rich, of whom it was maliciously said, that " before they were made lords, they didn't dine; and after they were made lords, they didn't sup." He was, however, a very good sort of man, not too poor to give his sons good educations; and of his second son, Alphonso, the richest grandee might have been proud; for a better or pleasanter youth, or one of greater good sense, conventionalisms apart, had never ventured his life in a bull-fight, which he had done half a dozen times. He was, moreover, a very pretty singer; and it was even said, that he not only composed the music for his serenades, but that he wrote verses for them equal to those of Garcilaso. So, at least, thought the young lady to whom they were sent, and who used to devour them with her eyes, till her very breath failed her, and she could not speak for delight.

Poor, loving Lucinda! We call her poor, though she was at that minute one of the richest as well as happiest maidens in Madrid; and we speak of her as a young lady, for such she was in breeding and manners, and as such the very grandees treated her, as far as they could, though she was only the daughter of a famous jeweller,

z

who had supplied half the great people with carkanets and rings. Her father was dead; her mother too; she was under the care of guardians; but Alphonso de Melos had loved her more than a year; had loved her with a real love, even though he wanted her money; would, in fact, have thrown her money to the dogs, rather than have ceased to love her; such a treasure he had found in the very fact of his passion. Their marriage was to take place within the month; and, as the lady was so rich, and the lover, however noble otherwise, was only of the lowest or least privileged order of nobility (a class who had the misfortune of not being able to wear their hats in the king's presence, unless his majesty expressly desired it), the loftiest grandees, who would have been too happy to marry the lovely heiress, had her father been anything but a merchant, thought that the match was not only pardonable in the young gentleman, but in a sort of way noticeable, and even in some measure to be smilingly winked at and encouraged; nay, perhaps, envied; especially as the future husband was generous, and had a turn for making presents, and for sitting at the head of a festive table. Suddenly, therefore, appeared some of the finest emeralds and sapphires in the world upon the fingers of counts and marquises, whose jewels had hitherto been of doubtful value; and no little sensation was made on the gravest and most dignified of the old nobility, by a certain grandee, remarkable for his sense of the proprieties, who had discovered "serious reasons for thinking" that the supposed jeweller's off-spring was a natural daughter of a late prince of the blood.

Be this as it may, Don Alphonso presented himself one morning as usual before his mistress, and after an interchange of transports, such as may be imagined between two such lovers, about to be joined for ever, informed her that one only thing more was now remaining to be done, and then—in the course of three mornings—they would be living in the same house.

"And what is that?" said Lucinda, the tears rushing into her eyes for excess of adoring happiness.

"Only the bull-fight," said the lover, affecting as much indifference as he could affect in anything when speaking with his eyes on hers. But he could not speak it in quite the tone he wished.

"The bull-fight!" scarcely ejaculated his mistress, turning pale. "Oh, Alphonso! you have fought and conquered in a dozen; and you will not quit me, now that we can be so often together? Besides"— And here her breath began already to fail her.

But Alphonso showed her, or tried to show her, how he must inevitably attend the bull-fight. "Honour demanded it; custom; everything that was expected of him;" his mistress herself, who would "otherwise despise him."

His mistress fainted away. She fell, a death-like burden, into his arms.

When she came to herself, she wept, entreated, implored, tried even with pathetic gaiety to rally and be pleasant; then again wept; then argued, and for the first time in her life was a logician, pressing his hand, and saying with a sudden force of conviction, "But hear me;" then begged again; then kissed him like a bride; reposed on him like a wife; did everything that was becoming and beautiful, and said everything but an angry word; nay, would have dared perhaps to say even that, had she thought of it; but she was not of an angry kind, or of any kind but the loving, and how was the thought to enter her head? Entire love is a worship, and cannot be angry.

The heart of the lover openly and fondly sympathized with that of his poor mistress; and, secretly, it felt more even than it showed. Not that Don Alphonso feared for consequences, though he had not been without pangs and thoughts of possibilities, even in regard to those; for, to say nothing of the danger of the sport in ordinary, the chief reason of his being unpersuadable in the present instance was a report that the animals to be encountered were of more than ordinary ferocity; so that the caballeros who were expected to be foremost in the lists in general now felt themselves to be particularly called on to make their appearance, at the hazard of an alternative too dreadful for the greatest valour to risk.

The final argument which he used with his mistress was the very excess of that love, and the very position in which it stood at that bridal moment, to which he in vain appealed. He showed how it had ever and irremediably been the custom to estimate the fighter's love by the measure of his courage; the more "apparent" the risk (for he pretended to laugh at any real danger), the greater the evidence of passion and the honour done to the lady; and so, after many more words and tears, the honour was to be done accordingly, grievously against her will, and custom triumphed. Custom! That "little thing," as the people called it to the philosopher. "That great and terrible thing," as the philosopher justly thought it. To show how secure he was, and how secure still it would render him, he made her promise to be there; and she required little asking; for a thought came into her head, which made her pray with secret and sudden earnestness to the Virgin; and the same thought enabled her to give him final looks, not only of resigned lovingness, but of a sort of cheered composure; for, now that she saw there was no remedy, she would not make the worst of his resolve, and so they parted. How differently from when they met! and how dreadfully to be again brought together!

The day has arrived; the great square has been duly

set out; the sand, to receive the blood, is spread over it; the barricadoes and balconies (the boxes) are all right; the king and his nobles are there; Don Alphonso and his Lucinda are there also; he in his place in the square, on horseback, with his attendants behind him, and the door out of which the bull is to come in front; she where he will behold her before long, though not in the box to which he has been raising his eyes. All the gentlemen who are to fight the bulls, each in his turn, and who, like Alphonso, are dressed in black, with plumes of white feathers on their heads, and scarfs of different colours round the body, have ridden round the lists a quarter of an hour ago; they salute the ladies of their acquaintance; and all is still and waiting. The whole scene is gorgeous with tapestries and gold and jewels. It is a theatre in which pomp and pleasure are sitting in a thousand human shapes to behold a cruel spectacle.

The trumpets sound; crashes of other music succeed; the door of the stable opens, and the noble creature, the bull, makes his appearance, standing still a while, and looking as it were with a confused composure before him. Sometimes when the animal first comes forth, it rushes after the horseman who has opened the door, and who has rushed away from the mood in which it has shown itself. But the bull on this occasion was one that, from the very perfection of his strength, awaited provoking. He soon has it. Light, agile footmen, who are there on purpose, vex him with darts and arrows, garnished with paper set on fire. He begins by pursuing them hither and thither, they escaping by all the arts of cloaks and hats thrown on the ground, and deceiving figures of pasteboard. Soon he is irritated extremely; he stoops his sullen head to toss; he raises it, with his eyes on fire, to kick and trample; he bellows; he rages; he grows mad. His breath gathers like a thick mist about his head. He gallops, amidst cries of men and women,

frantically around the square, like a racer, following and
followed by his tormentors; he tears the horses with his
horns; he disembowels them; he tosses the howling dogs
that are let loose on him; he leaps and shivers in the
air like a very stag or goat.   His huge body is nothing to
him in the rage and might of his agony.

For Alphonso, who had purposely got in his way to
shorten his Lucinda's misery (knowing her surely to be
there, though he has never seen her), has gashed the bull
across the eyes with his sword, and pierced him twice
with the javelins furnished him by his attendants.   Half
blinded with the blood, and yet rushing at him, it should
seem, with sure and final aim of his dreadful head, the
creature is just upon him, when a blow from a negro who
is helping one of the pages, turns him distractedly in that
new direction, and he strikes down, not the negro, but
the youthful, and, in truth, wholly frightened and helpless
page.   The page in falling loses his cap, from which
there flows a profusion of woman's hair, and Alphonso
knows it in the instant.   He leaps off his horse, and would
have shrieked with horror; but for something which
seemed to wrench and twist round his very being, and
in a sort of stifled and almost meek voice, he could
only sobbingly articulate the word, "Lucinda!"   But
in an instant he rose out of that self pity into frenzy;
he hacked wildly at the bull, which was now spurning
as wildly round; and though the assembly rose, crying
out, and the king bade the brute be despatched, which
was done by a thrust in the spine by those who knew
the trick (ah! why did they not do it before?), the
poor youth had fallen, not far from his Lucinda, gored
alike with herself to death.

As recovery was pronounced hopeless, and the deaths
of the lovers close at hand, they were both carried into
the nearest house, and laid, as the nature of the place
required, on the same bed.   And, indeed, as it turned

out, nothing could be more fitting. Great and sorrowful was the throng in the room; some of the greatest nobles were there, and a sorrowing message was brought from the king. Had the lovers been princes, their poor insensible faces could not have been watched with greater pity and respect.

At length they opened their eyes, one after the other, to wonder—to suffer—to discover each other where they lay—and to weep from abundance of wretchedness, and from the difficulty of speaking. They attempted to make a movement towards each other, but could not even raise an arm. Lucinda tried to speak, but could only sigh and attempt to smile. Don Alphonso said at last, half sobbing, looking with his languid eyes on her kind and patient face—"She does not reproach me, even now."

They both wept afresh at this, but his mistress looked at him with such unutterable love and fondness, making, at the same time, some little ineffectual movement of her hand, that the good old Duke de Linares said, "She wishes to put her arm over him; and he too — see — his arm over her." Tenderly, and with the softest caution, were their arms put accordingly; and then, in spite of their anguish, the good Duke said, "Marry them yet;" and the priest opened his book, and well as he could speak for sympathy, or they seem to answer to his words, he married them; and thus — in a few moments, from excess of mingled agony and joy, with their arms on one another, and smiling as they shut their eyes—their spirits passed away from them, and they died.

XXVII.

THE MARRIAGE OF BELPHEGOR.

"There he arriving round about doth flie,
    And takes survey with busie curious eye:
    Now this, now that, he tasteth tenderly."
                                        —SPENSER.

[This is "the renowned tale of Belfagor," as Mr. Dunlop justly calls it. It came originally from a Latin manuscript, and has been told by Giovanni Brevio, an Italian novelist, by the famous Machiavelli, by Straparola, La Fontaine, and the old English dramatists. It is repeated here, with the usual differences practised on these occasions. We thought of introducing it with Ariosto's preface to a superfluous story in the "Orlando:"

"Ladies, and you who hold the ladies dear,
    For God's sake take no notice of this story:"

but a moment's reflection told us, that our fair readers need not be hurt with a satire, which, in order to see fair play between the two sexes, we have traced to its proper causes in both. We expect, on the contrary, that amiable women of all classes, and really good wives in particular, will show a just partiality for it.]

As Pluto was taking his rounds one day in the infernal regions, to see that all was right and miserable, he thought he observed a parcel of fellows, in a particularly hot corner, giggling and making merry. Upon looking more narrowly, his astonishment was confirmed: the rogues had discovered his presence, and changed the expression of their countenances to a most doleful and hypocritical sorrow.

Pluto sent for his chief overseers.

"Gentlemen," said he, "here is a very extraordinary case," and related what he had seen.

The overseers looked at each other in confusion, for in fact they had noticed some such phenomenon themselves, but had scarcely dared to think of it. They did not know what comfort might happen, if enjoyment was to be found even in Tartarus.

As the case, however, was not to be compromised, it was agreed, after much consultation, to examine the offenders apart. The examination took place after the ordinary forms of law; but nothing appeared to account for their behaviour. They protested, upon oath, that they had no secret about them for escaping pain. They were put to various torments described in Dante, and gave proofs of what they said : only the familiars observed, that in the midst of all their sufferings, there certainly was an irrepressible something about the mouth which looked like self-congratulation.

A chief counsellor was now directed to compare the examinations, and see if by narrow inspection he could make anything out of them. He did so, for the space of three days and nights, and reported that he could discover nothing. The prisoners had offended on earth like other men,—loved a good deal too much, doubted the triple nature of Diana, thought hell unfair, etc. : "but," said the lawyer, "I can find nothing which at all explains the enormity in question, unless it is" (and here he put on the facetious smile, usual on such occasions), "unless it is, my lords, that they have all been married."

The court laughed at this sally; but one of Minos's under-clerks begged leave, with great deference, to offer himself to their lordships' attention, having a few words to say, which nothing but the urgency of the question could have compelled him to intrude upon their consideration. He said that the learned gentlemen had

laughed, and that learned gentlemen might laugh; but
that, with great submission, it was no laughing matter.
The learned gentleman modestly supposed that he had
uttered nothing but a commonplace joke; and he would
concede (if he might use the expression) to that learned
gentleman's modesty, that the joke was commonplace;
nay, emphatically so. "But," continued he, "let me
ask your lordships, with all becoming humility, how
such a very ungallant and unconjugal jest came to be
commonplace; and whether in the discovery of that
secret, we might not discover the more important secret
now before us."

This address made a considerable sensation. The
counsel, who had inspected the examinations, was the
only one on whom it seemed to make no impression.
He rejected, with a dignified impatience, the compliments paid to his modesty, and yet was proceeding to
throw out some other sarcasms in a style equally con-
descending, when Minos, who had fallen into a study, said
he had a proposition to make, which would settle the
matter beyond all doubt or equivocation. It was this,
that some ingenious devil should be selected and sent on
earth, with injunctions to enter into the state of matrimony, and in due time come back and report the
consequences. Rhadamanthus suggested that the task
should be assigned to one of the criminals, both on
account of his previous knowledge, and as the best
punishment that could be awarded to his offence. But
the suggestion was overruled. The criminal, it was
argued, however loth he might be to undergo the return
to his wife, would not dare, even under all the circumstances, to affect a disinclination, conscious that the rest
of the offenders would insist upon his becoming a sacrifice
to the general welfare, and that he had the certainty of
coming back to his old quarters. To keep such offenders
upon earth always was impossible, or humanity must

change its nature, and Pluto would lose subjects.
Besides, marriage might be altered, and so make a
heaven upon earth, and then the very damned would
become blest; which was a thing too profane to be
thought of.

Unfortunately, a new dilemma now occurred; for the
story having got about, no devil was found hardy enough
to undertake the adventure. No, no, said they; we
have a bad life enough of it here; and it has long been
a good diabolical maxim, to let ill alone. Promises of
as many enjoyments as possible were lavished in vain;
wine, riches, rank, beauty, influence, knowledge, and
ices every day. Some started at the ices, but, on reflection, they agreed with the rest. The prisoners, they
said, had had experience of all these, and yet they
preferred the hell under the earth to their hell upon it.
As a last temptation they were promised a considerable
amendment of their condition upon returning, and at
this they again hesitated, till Pluto unluckily offered to
ratify the promise by his royal word: upon which they
immediately shook their heads, and declined pursuing
the question any further.

At length a very daring, ambitious devil, of the name
of Belphegor, said he would go. The whole infernal
public were astonished; but they agreed that if it were
possible for any devil to do such a thing, Belphegor was
he. It was thought that he had a private commission
from Proserpine, and that Pluto was not sorry to wink
at the cause of his departure. He was a sprightly devil,
who could play on the serpent, and wrote verses with a
great deal of fire: accomplishments, which got him
occasional admittance to Pluto's table. He would make
experiments upon the flames about him, and was suspected of holding an heretical opinion upon the possibility
of getting used to anything.

The credit of his orthodoxy was not strengthened by

his actually setting out. Pluto conferred on him the shape, in which a devil of his agreeable turn of mind would have appeared had he been a man. It was something betwixt the jovial and melancholy, — very amiable. He looked like one of the most agreeable gentlemen of the time. The public waited with some impatience for his appearance out of Proserpine's apartments, whither he had gone to kiss hands on leaving Pandæmonium. At last my gentleman comes forth. The spectators set up a shout, like that of a myriad of coal-heavers. Belphegor takes off his hat, with an air as if he had been used to it all his life; and it is observed universally, that if Belphegor is not happy in wedlock, there must be something worse than the devil in it.

It was settled, in order to do everything fairly, first, that if our hero lit upon a wife more than usually wifely, she should die with reasonable celerity, and leave him another chance; secondly, that he should not return to hell without orders, upon pain of some rare punishment; and thirdly, that he should emerge in England, as the place where marriage was held in the gravest repute. Accordingly, he made his appearance in the British metropolis, as a young gentleman of fortune; and soon found that an alliance with him would be regarded in a very estimable point of view.

After admiring the beauty of the women, which he thought nevertheless a little too cold-looking (a fancy at once odd and pardonable in a devil), the thing that most astonished him in this exemplary and very married nation, was to find, that the sarcasm of Pluto's counsel was as common here as elsewhere,—that nothing was of such ordinary occurrence as the ridicule of wedlock, sometimes bitter, sometimes merry, often between both. A grave and seemingly approving ear was leant in public when it was praised;—a panegyric on it in a sentimental

comedy met with applause; but the applause was double
when another comedy abused it. Husbands and wives
joked each other upon their bonds, with the air of people
who break the force of a satirical truism by meeting it.
In the shops were pictures of Before Marriage and After
Marriage, the former exhibiting a lover helping his
mistress over a stile, the latter the same gentleman
walking on, and leaving the lady to get over by herself.
Belphegor overheard a knot of persons one day disputing
whether this was a caricature; but they all agreed that the
spirit of it was like enough. "Generally like," said one,
"eh, Jack?" Jack seemed to be the melancholy wag of
the party, and said, that the present company always
excepted, he thought, for a general resemblance, it was
particularly like.

These symptoms were not at all encouraging to our
hero; so that having been told to do what others did,
he availed himself of the letter of his instructions somewhat beyond the spirit of their intention, and amused
himself as much as possible in the character of a bachelor.
He dressed, dined, lounged in the coffee-houses, went to
the theatres, visited in the most respectable circles, and
was understood to be well acquainted with a description
of ladies, whom nevertheless it was not proper to mention.
It was even supposed probable that he had furnished his
quantum of maid-servants and others to that class of
persons, and scattered a considerable portion of misery
about town, without at all diminishing his receptibility
among the said circles; a phenomenon, which in so grave
and reputable a nation he would have placed to the
account of an error of charity, had he not observed, as
we have just hinted, that if the most serious ladies
showed no contempt for himself, they evinced a good
deal for the class whom he was thought likely to have
increased. He also saw that they would expect very
different conduct from him, should one of them honour

him with her hand; and that if he might like the worst,
and deceive the very best of the sex now, it would go
hard with him should he then desire to evince a grateful
sense of the most admirable of women.

Captain Lovell however (for he had purchased a com
pany under this name) had received a due portion of
man's nature with his shape; and he was induced to
hasten the period of matrimony, partly by an express
from Pluto, and partly by his falling in love with a
young lady of reasonable beauty and accomplishments,
who appeared to him as likely as anybody "to render
the married state happy,"—a phrase indeed which was
often in the mouths of her parents.

The captain married, and for three or four months
was the happiest devil existing. He met with occasional
instances of petulance and self-will; but these, he thought,
were pardonable in one who made him so happy in the
main : and he was resolved not to be the first to create
a rupture. If the lady could not bear him out of her
sight, it only proved the excess of her fondness; and if
she began by degrees to bear it better, he was convinced
that she did it solely for his comfort, by the sweetness
with which she received the new dresses and trinkets he
bestowed upon her to make amends.

You must know that Captain Lovell, being a devil (as
the ladies occasionally startled his ear by calling him),
had acquired by dint of suffering what humanity often
attains to by the same means. He hated monopoly, and
loved to see fair-play both in the distribution of pains
and pleasures. The first thing that gave him a seriously
uneasy sensation about his wife, was to see so gentle a
creature capable of scolding her servants. He remon-
strated, and was scolded himself. The next night he
stayed out longer than usual, and was welcomed home
with a long lecture, which perfectly stunned him. The
words he could chiefly distinguish, all but one, were,

creatures—honest wife—is this usage?—tender heart—
plagues of servants—other women (with great stress on
other—my husband (with still greater stress on my)—
duty—decency—lawful—usual fate—defy anybody—
religion—and chastity. The one word in particular was
virtue, which she used in common for the last-mentioned
quality. He afterwards found that whenever she charged
him with any vice, or was guilty of any herself, she had
a special taste for repeating the same synonym. If he
looked with fondness on any lady with a frank, good-
humoured face, his wife was sure to doubt the lady's
"virtue," and to remind him of her own. If she
exhibited any petty selfishness in eating and drinking,
or laying out money, or exacting too much of others,
and suspected that he observed it, she sighed at the
fate which denied the least privilege or consolation to
"virtue." If she was a little insincere with him, or
pettish with others, and he reproved her for it (for he
began now to reprove, on his own side), she delighted to
tell him, with a very malignant aspect, that such petty
fault would not be found with anybody but a person of
"virtue." If she was in the mood to be fond with
him, and he had not quite got over her last peroration,
she wept and said that love was no longer considered
a duty; no longer a holy tie; no longer the reward of
"virtue."

He was one day so provoked by her harping
upon this favourite word, that he turned on his heel,
and exclaimed, with great gusto of utterance, "Damn
virtue!" The lady sat down, pale, smiling, and satisfied.
"Well!" she exclaimed; "if"—The captain did not
stay to hear the rest. He knew what that Well
portended, too well.

Captain Lovell fell into conversation with his brother
officers on the subject of this virtue. He had laid as
much stress on it as any man, particularly as he had led

a very gay life, and thought it very difficult to keep.
But he now began to suspect, that the difficulty was no
such great matter, if ladies made up for it with all these
privileged vices;—that if it were, it put on a very
unpleasant aspect, so managed;—and that at all events,
the system deserved inquiry, which made so many
virtuous men and women disagreeable as well as respectable, so many vicious women pleasant and despised,
and such numbers of both descriptions extremely miserable. He started the question at the mess, but the
officers, though incorrigible profligates, were equally
inexorable in their theories of virtue. If their wives
and mistresses, they said, were not faithful, they could
shoot them through the head.

"But," said Lovell, "suppose they become disagreeable."

"Oh, damn it," said the colonel, "there are plenty of
agreeable women, for that matter;" upon which they all
laughed, and toasted a favourite demirep.

"But," returned Lovell, "is that fair in us? Is it
fair in us to make our wives disagreeable with our
theories, to insist that they shall remain so for our
credit forsooth, and then to leave them for those whom
we teach them to despise?"

The mess all stared at him, as widely as the port in
their eyes would permit.

"Oh, pray go home, and instruct yours, Tom," said
the colonel; "you are much too profligate for us.—My
compliments, however. And I say"—(hallooing after
him)—"remember,—in the event of a reformation,—I'm
your man."

Lovell went home, much more ruffled than became a
demon of his vivacity; but his earthly nature clogged
him, and he began to wish himself heartily rid of it.
He sat down opposite his wife, and though he had a
grudge against Milton for what he called his trucklings

about Pandæmonium, could not help repeating after
him,—

> "O shame to men!   Devil with devil damned
> Firm concord hold, men only disagree."

The lady did not at all relish this apostrophe; but she
had been unexpectedly softened by his coming home so
soon; and asking him to read a little to her out of that
"truly divine poet," she went to the book-case and took
down a volume of him, intending (we must own) that he
should shame himself with reading the conjugal loves of
Adam and Eve.   Unluckily, she happened to hit upon
one of his prose instead of poetical works; and what
was more unlucky, the captain, opening it at random,
hit upon a passage in his *Doctrine and Discipline of
Divorce*, where, in spite of his divinity, he says that
personal infidelity in a woman is not so good a ground
for separation as ill temper and other vices of antipathy,
because she may still remain a very pleasing and even
affectionate woman in the main, whereas the other vices
totally cut up the happiness of a wedded life.—After
sitting dumb with astonishment at hearing such a quotation from Milton (which the captain maliciously showed
her, to convince her eyes), the lady ended a long and
vehement dispute by charging him with wishing to
corrupt her virtue, in order to furnish excuses for himself.   There had been little peace before.   There was
now an uninterrupted cannonade of hard words.   The
gentleman was "the most wonderful, the most amazing,
the very meanest of mankind for deliberately wishing to
pander to his own dishonour:—she was astonished at
him—she was overwhelmed; she—in short, for the first
time in her life, she wanted words."   On the other hand,
the lady was "the most provoking of women for eternally
beginning the question, to indulge her own silly mistakes, .
cursed ill-humours, spleen, vanity, envy, hatred, and
malice, and all uncharitableness."   ·

The captain, not having been used to this sort of torture in the other world, had much the worst of it. His wife could talk, though she said nothing. She also piqued herself more than ever upon her "virtue," whereas he had nothing to boast on that score. By degrees he neglected his affairs, and grew melancholy and slovenly. His creditors came upon him, but the lady would not go out of the house, because she said he did it on purpose to get rid of her. At length he sold his commission and absconded.

Our hero looked hard at every person he met in black, hoping that he brought him the summons to return to hell; but he was disappointed. He was therefore obliged to content himself with hiding from his creditors; for, though he had lived so long in the infernal regions, he could not bear the idea of bailiffs and lock-up houses. One day, being hot pressed with the pursuit, he made known the earthly part of his history to a countryman. The peasant, in spite of his deaf wife's objections, who saw she knew but half the secret, concealed him faithfully, and the captain, in return, undertook to make his fortune.

The rustic laughed at this. "Nay, nay, Muster Lovell," said he, "there's no making a zilk purse of zow's ear. I judge I beez better able to make fortunes nor you; and God He knows, I'm as poor as Job; and for that matter," added he, winking towards his wife, "as patient too; ch, captain?"

Belphegor (for so we shall again call him) did not much relish this sally, for obvious reasons; not to mention that his natural pride, as a devil, began to return upon him from a comparison with mortals. However he adhered to his promise. He therefore disclosed his real quality to the terrified countryman, whom he had much ado to encourage. A good deal of ale, and some toasts given to the church (which made the man think him too good-natured a devil, considering the tithes), succeeded in reassuring him. Our hero undertook to go to the continent, and possess a German prince, whom the farmer was to follow and cure. The latter gave out, that in consequence of some experiments with dogs, he had found a marvellous remedy for disorders connected with phrensy; and as a previous step, Belphegor pitched himself into a censorious old lady in the village, who began talking of the farmer with such extraordinary fondness, that it was thought better to send for him in his new capacity. He came accordingly, and wrought a cure which was reckoned the more surprising, inasmuch as the old lady, from that day forward, became extremely charitable in her discourse. On the day of the cure, Belphegor crossed sea, and pitched himself into the German prince. His Majesty was taken with a very odd fancy. He was a huge, fat man, very profligate; and yet fell into long discourses on his exceeding thinness and integrity. Nothing relieved him so much as making him presents of shoes and gloves too small for him, measuring waists to see which was the larger, and making bold to say, that, if anything, he was somewhat too slender and amiable for a man. He had already been seized with a notion, that his wife (a sort of harum - scarum, but excellent-hearted person) was not as genteel and virtuous as himself; and for this Belphegor had a pique against him, both on account of the mistake, and of the man's making it so ridiculous. He accordingly entered him in all his triumph, and rendered his behaviour so exceedingly fantastic and absurd, that his very courtiers were ready to die with laughter.

The rustic doctor, as he anticipated, was sent for. His fame had spread rapidly by means of the newspapers; and his second cure, being upon a prince's understanding, of course outdid in reputation his first.

His method electrified the physicians. He merely
approached the royal ear, whispered something in it
which nobody heard, and the evil spirit departed. His
words were these: "Captain, I am come: remember
your promise."—"I do," answered the spirit; "and to
make you still richer, I shall go and possess the Czar
of Muscovy, who undertakes to be a moral fop, and is
my aversion."

"Good," said the peasant, who was growing rich with
prosperity; "but have a care, my dear captain, that you
don't tell 'un any o' your theories, as you calls 'em, or
you'll never get at 'un."

Now the reader must know that our hero, besides the
pride above-mentioned, had a vice in him more befitting
in practice, if not in theory, a good orthodox Christian,
which was revenge. Besides, his temper had been embittered by his earthly sojourn. He therefore condescended to be piqued with the farmer's airs of
superiority; he was also annoyed by the sight of a
happiness which he could not taste, and he determined
upon ruining the poor dolt. The Czar of Muscovy
doated at such an extravagant rate, that the famous
English doctor was sent for with all speed. He came,
dressed in the extremity of the medical fashion, humming
and hawing with great pomposity. Belphegor chuckled
at the sight. The farmer whispered as usual; but what
was his astonishment when the Czar read him a grave
lecture on his presumption? He entreated his dear
captain, his excellent Mr. Lovell, his kind good master, etc.
etc., all to no purpose. Belphegor would not move, and
the Czar went on, making both himself and the mock-
doctor ridiculous. The poor peasant, whom despair
rendered ingenious, remembered hearing from the village
pulpit that the devil could not abide the presence of a
clergyman. He requested that four priests might be
sent for. They were, and mass performed to boot, after

the fashion of the Greek church; but Belphegor was inexorable. He even made the Czar fall a-laughing, to his Majesty's own exceeding horror.

The farmer was now giving himself up for lost, when a buffoon came bursting through the crowd, mimicking the poor doctor's manner so irresistibly, that the assembled thousands could not refrain from bursting into shouts of laughter and approbation.

"What the devil's that?" said Belphegor.

"Oh, my dear captain," answered the peasant, "there is your wife coming in search of you."

At these words, Belphegor, without waiting even to kick the Czar and the doctor, leaped out of the royal person, and in the teeth of his instructions to the contrary, made the best of his way to hell.

XXVIII.

THE GENEROUS WOMEN.

> " There he arriving round about doth flie,
> And takes survey with busie curious eye:
> Now this, now that, he tasteth tenderly."
>
> —SPENSER.

[The ground-work of the following story is from the old French and Italian novelists, and has been turned to good account in his "Albion's England" by William Warner. Nothing can exceed the general cast of nature in his homely account. One of his touches of painting is extremely beautiful:—

> " He took her in his arms, as yet
> So coyish to be kist,
> As maids that know themselves beloved,
> And yieldingly resist."]

A GENTLEMAN of Tours, of the name of De Lorme, had a wife whom he had courted with extreme ardour, and whom he still loved as his chosen companion. She had perceived, however, for some time past, that his gallantry towards her was more constrained than it used to be, and this surprised the lady. In truth, it might well do so, for she was still young and handsome, her accomplishments were many, and if anything, the love on her own side was greater than ever.

It must be confessed at the same time, that she had not been aware of this last circumstance, till her husband's love had appeared to decline; it must be added, that she had for some time been accustomed to regard his tenderness as a matter of course; and it must be further acknowledged, that M. De Lorme had given grounds for this persuasion, both in the excess of his first ardour, and in his happy and delicate imitation of it when it began to cool. Our heroine, in short, forgot that there was such a thing as imagination in love, or the necessity of being meritorious in the person beloved.

Still Madame De Lorme was far from being destitute of merit. She had even more virtue than she was aware of, but too secure in the conventional forms of it, and in her own good opinion, her husband's altered behaviour began to turn her surprise into resentment. She insinuated his fickleness, and nobody likes insinuations. What is more, he did not deserve them. She took to being prouder, when she was too proud already. She wept at intervals, with the air of an ill-used person; and this contrasted but ill with the pride. At last, she mentioned her "virtue," and this, as our readers know, is the devil.

M. De Lorme had informed his wife that she might not be, perhaps, quite so perfect or amiable as she supposed; but this she regarded as a resentful speech, and her own resentment was heightened accordingly. She looked about her, to consider what could have induced him to spend less time with her, or to enjoy less the time that he did spend. He did not game; he did not drink; he was not fond of hunting; there was no lady with whom she could compare herself; and yet, from some instinct or other, she thought it must be a lady who had beguiled him; not so handsome or virtuous, she thought, as myself; but neither virtue, nor even beauty, can fix the men in these degenerate days. If Madame De Lorme had called her own virtue in question, she might have been nearer the mark; but she thought of everyone's faults instead of her own.

These jealous inquiries helped to produce the catas-

trophe she dreaded. M. De Lorme, though full of natural
sentiment, was not aware that the customs and exactions
of his own sex had helped to spoil both women and men,
and, tired with canvassing a subject which he almost
knew as ill how to handle as his lady, he was left open
to the first impressions he should receive from a handsome and good-tempered female. At that time Henry
the Fourth was upon the throne. The example of the
monarch had not tended to make the gallantry of his
loving subjects more scrupulous. His virtues, at the
same time, helped to divest it of hypocrisy, without
letting it run into impudence. At least, this was the
effect at a distance from him, where his example fell
upon a soil worthy of him. What it was in the old
and corrupt hot-bed of the court, it is not our business to inquire. The country lasses were certainly
very amiable at that period; and M. De Lorme found
them so.

There was a lively good-humoured girl on a farm
which he had about eight miles from Tours, whose
reputation was none of the austerest, but who was so
kind to the old, and so choice of her kisses to the
young, that she enchanted the whole neighbourhood.
She supported an old uncle and aunt with her industry,
would help anybody, when she had done her work, in
field or dairy, and then led off the evening dance under
the elms with a mixture of grace and good nature,
which nobody would have dared to treat with disrespect,
had he been inclined. You might hear her, early in
the morning, singing

"Mignonne, allons voir si la rose,"

with the spirit and sweetness of a lark. She made it a
sort of chivalrous thing to obtain a kiss of her; always
gave the best to the kindest and most courageous; was
strangely coy to the lacqueys and other wise men of the

world, who sometimes instructed the neighbourhood; but said that if Monsieur the Poet Ronsard ever came into those parts, she was afraid she should kiss him before he thought of it. In short, Fanchon had a born genius for the amiable; and by proper cultivation among the wits of those times, would have become a wit herself, and much less agreeable.

M. De Lorme visited his farm one day after a long absence, and was riding very thoughtfully into the hamlet, when he saw one of the prettiest figures in the world before him, walking the same way with a milk-jug on its head, and singing under the lime trees. His horse happened to give a snort, and Fanchon, turning round (for it was she), dropped a curtsey, and then continued her way silently.

"She looks too much in earnest," thought M. De Lorme, "to have seen me before she stopped singing.— You seem very happy, child," said he aloud, looking at her as he rode by her side.

"Oh yes, sir," said the girl, with an impulse she seemed to repress. She then dropped a more respectful curtsey, and began to loiter behind him. He loitered in his turn.

"Are you all so happy, my dear?" asked the gentleman, who would have said a prettier thing, had her countenance struck him less.

"Yes, sir," replied she,—"I think so—most of us."

"And what is it, pray, that makes most of us so happy?" rejoined the horseman, repeating her words, for the sake of the air of sincerity with which she spoke them.

"I beg your pardon, sir," answered the fair peasant, "but I am sure you must know."

She said this with much more gravity than archness; yet M. De Lorme somehow or other coloured.

"I beg your pardon, sir," she repeated, apparently dis-

covering that she ought to say more; "but I recollect
Monsieur's face, and my aunt says he makes everybody
happy as well as his tenants."

Not exactly everybody, thought M. De Lorme, nor
myself neither.   But the answer enlivened him.

"If I make everybody so happy, my fair one," said
he, "I think it is their business to make me so, is it
not?"

Fanchon perceived that he was talking gallantly: she
had also heard that he was not so happy at home as he
used to be; and what with her superiority to the common
gallantry which there might be in this speech, her
sympathy nevertheless with the sentiment of it, and her
cordial respect for the Seigneur, she was confused in her
turn.

She said, "Yes truly, sir," with a gravity which made
him smile.

"I will not distress you, my love," said M. De Lorme,
"but you have a fine face of your own, and I would beg
one kiss of it, if it would not alter it."

At these words he leaned from his horse; Fanchon let
her face move towards him, with the sweetest and gravest
want of prudery in the world; she gave him even her
lips instead of her cheek; and a better-hearted kiss on
both sides had not been taken under a milk-jug, with the
lime trees over it, for many a day.

As soon as our gentleman got to his farm, he made
inquiries respecting the fair peasant.

"Oh, sir," said the steward, smiling, "that is Mademoiselle Fanchon.   She must be courted, I can tell you,
as much as if she were a fine lady."

M. De Lorme, accustomed to the more sophisticated
loves of Paris, was astonished to find, in the person of
a country-girl, such union, as he called it, of the modest
and the liberal.   Modesty, where it was to be found, was
generally in the possession of wives, and by no means

liberal in anything. Liberality, on the other hand, was exclusively in the possession of the mistresses, and by no means modest.

M. De Lorme was told, among other anecdotes of Fanchon, that she was a great ballad-singer and early riser. The next morning he found himself up very early, singing as he arranged the feather in his hat. He walked down the green lane, in love with everything he saw, and came to the residence of Fanchon's uncle and aunt. It was one of the thickest and most sylvan nests on the banks of the Loire. One window alone was seen looking out of the trees. The rest of the cottage seemed almost built up with green. The birds in the boughs overhead made a morning concert of the fullest and most sparkling description, but M. de Lorme did not hear Fanchon.

"She is not up," said he to himself; "the jade is so pleasant, she gets a character given her for anything. Perhaps some dream has detained her:—if it were only now about a well-looking gentleman on horseback."

M. De Lorme, as he thought this, had got into the inner part of the little homestead, and there he saw Fanchon, not singing, not doing anything, but standing with her back towards him and her hand upon a churning-stick, thinking.

"Her very boddice," thought he, "is worth all the dresses at court."

A pang came over him as he remembered his wife playing the milk-maid once in this very neighbourhood, and he asked himself whether they might not still be happy and constant; but he had been disappointed so often, that her image began to look rather like a sour interference with his comfort, than a kindly appeal to his affection; and stepping softly onwards, he was about to tap Fanchon on the shoulder, when a feeling more respectful withheld him, and he contented himself with bidding her good morning.

Our dairy-maid, colouring, turned quickly round, and returned his salutation, adding somewhat abruptly, but evidently without design, "I hope madame is well."

She followed it up instantly with as cordial a welcome as her inferiority of condition would allow her to give, and suffered herself to be more familiar than she might otherwise have been, out of a feeling that her thoughts on this occasion ought not to have spoken out loud. She had an instinct against pedantry of all sorts, and hated to seem interfering and didactic. Not that she knew a word about such words as didactic, which puzzled her sometimes in her friend Ronsard; but, as we have before observed, Fanchon was a charmer by nature, and the early necessity of feeling and working for others had preserved her character, and bred thoughts in her deeper than she was aware of. If she ever wished to give pain, it was only when some proud or malignant pain had been given. Her propensity both to give and receive pleasure was so great, that she often said, if she married, she would love her husband, provided he would let her, better than anybody on earth, would be his best companion, would die for him, would starve for him, would be torn to pieces for him, if necessary; but that husbands must have a care, for though not of their opinion in thinking it proper to scold others for what one did one's self, she would not undertake to say that she should not feel a little bit grateful to those who had the same charming qualities as the man of her heart.

It was the face, accustomed to be animated with these thoughts, that was now turned upon the kind lord of the manor. The kiss under the limes was repeated and repeated again. M. De Lorme at once flattered and relieved her by saying, that all the accounts he heard of her were much to his taste; and Fanchon thought, that setting aside this, he deserved a kiss for every good thing he had done to the neighbourhood, which, to say the truth, would have made a very considerable series. The upshot was, that the steward above mentioned, having been very petulant at finding his master come to the farm, and not a little sarcastic upon " Mademoiselle Fanchon," was removed to another estate, and the uncle and aunt put in care of La Grange.

The steward, finding his master never came down, had usurped a good part of the house; but M. De Lorme insisted that his new housekeepers should share it with him; and if Fanchon's apartment was at a different corner from his, it befits the truth of our history to say, that the passage to it was not difficult, provided she chose to let it lie open, especially as the good people, after lecturing their niece a little sharply, as they would sometimes do, upon the over-vivacity of her abstract opinions, always slept very soundly.

Fanchon fairly blushed now and then when they talked to her, and the lower they bowed and curtsied before M. De Lorme, she blushed the more; but as his respect for herself increased, his quiet indifference towards them seemed to do so likewise; and after the tribute of a flood of tears to the many unhappy hours in which she had formerly struggled against her ill-opinion of those for whom she laboured, she agreed with him that such meanness ought not to distress her.

The steward, when removing his goods from La Grange, had taken care to lay his hands upon every item he could, so that M. De Lorme found his residence very barely provided. Fanchon, however, would not suffer him to furnish it as he wished. The goods for the housekeeper's side were of the plainest kind; and he could not persuade her, when she admitted him to a visit, that he had acquired a foolish love for certain kinds of tapestry and other bed-chamber ornaments. She even insisted (for she would get into strange subjects of conversation, such as mistresses, of all others,

are supposed to avoid) that he only slept the pleasanter
for it, when he was at home; and what is more, she
thought as much; and would be froward with him, if
he did not sleep there often.

"How much virtue," thought he, "in my wife is
obscured, and turned into vice, by the single fault of
intolerance; and how very like the virtue my wife
wants, does vice—I believe they call it—look in this
village girl!"

One day Fanchon received him with a particularly
sparkling face.

"Well," said she, "my dear M. De Lorme, they say
that the ladies are fond of you; and fond they must be,
to do things for you in secret."

"How now, real one?" said M. De Lorme, for so he
delighted to call her.

"A cart," she resumed, "came this morning with a
heap of good things for you, and the man knew nothing
of the person that sent them, except that a lady gave him
the order, and paid for it."

"What sort of a lady?"

"Oh, now," cried Fanchon, "see the vain gratitude
in his eyes! We must find her out for him! A lady
in a veil."

M. De Lorme went up-stairs, and found the bedroom
hung with a new piece of his favourite tapestry. It
consisted of stories from the Provençal poets. There
were also pictures of Joan of Arc, and of Agnes Sorel;
a couple of noble arm-chairs hung with crimson velvet;
and a toilet, carved in silver with shepherds and shep-
herdesses, and containing everything that a country
beauty could desire, of combs, bodkins, and laces.

"And it is not for me only," said M. De Lorme,
doubly delighted and perplexed.

"I shall die till you can thank her for both of us,"
said Fanchon: "I mean," added she, lowering her voice,

"till you can add my grateful respects, if you think she will like it." And the tears stood in her eyes.

M. De Lorme, whose popularity among the Parisian ladies, and his acquaintance with their manners both bad and good, rendered his vanity more than pardonable, considering the life he led betwixt Tours and La Grange, thought his fair farmer was growing jealous; but the way in which she exhibited this new passion was so amiable, that he kissed the tears from her eyes with great affection, and said there was not a lady in the land with whom Fanchon need be afraid of standing face to face.

The truth is, that during his absence, Fanchon, who never looked upon herself as destined to be his chief companion, and had heard much of the former qualities of his wife, was wondering whether he stopped longer than usual on account of a termination of their coldness, when a lady in a veil (the same, she had no doubt, who afterwards sent the goods) came unexpectedly into her sitting-room, and after accepting a chair, and holding a silence unaccountably long, asked her somewhat haughtily whether she was the steward's niece.

Fanchon, though a little abashed, contrived to answer with her usual mixture of sweetness and respectfulness that she was.

The answer was followed, after a less silence, with another abrupt remark, though in a less haughty tone.

"If this is your sitting-room," said the lady, "it is very plainly furnished for so—handsome a possessor."

The tone of the concluding words was not at all sarcastic; yet Fanchon coloured. In fact, she guessed who was before her, or she might have thought proper to show a greater self-possession.

"Not plainer, madame," she replied, "than I trust is becoming."

The stranger seemed to doubt the sincerity of these words, for she added in a less gentle manner —

"M. De Lorme (M. De Lorme, mademoiselle, is an old friend, and I happen to be just now particularly interested in his comfort), M. De Lorme is happier, I am told, in this place than he is at home?"

Now this was a little too hard of Madame De Lorme, for she, of course, it was. She had heard a great deal of Fanchon to her credit, and what she heard was corroborated, as far as it could be, by what she now saw; but whether she judged her insincere in her last answer, or whether that very corroboration gave her a passing wound that irritated her, we cannot say.

Fanchon, thus pushed home, did not think of attacking in turn; but she forgot for a moment that there was anybody to be defended but herself, and said with an air of great simplicity, betwixt enthusiasm and exculpation, that M. De Lorme was so kind and forgiving, and did so much to make others happy, that everybody must wish him to be happy, wherever he was.

"And you contribute, of course," said the stranger, "all you can to make him so."

She said this with the more pointedness, inasmuch as she was struck with the truth of the observation, and angry with herself for feeling the very anger.

Fanchon turned very red, then pale, then blushed out in all the natural beauty of her truth and good-heartedness, and said, —

"Without meaning to inquire, madame, what right you have to question me in this way, but supposing it to be the best and oldest right in the world, perhaps you will pardon me for hoping, that a friend of M. De Lorme will not be offended with me, when I say, that neither my wishes nor my endeavours for M. De Lorme's happiness have been confined to the neighbourhood in which I now have the honour of seeing you."

The lady appeared greatly agitated at this. It was evident, through her veil, that the tears were pouring down her cheeks.

"You seem ill, madame," said Fanchon, in an altered tone full of naïveté and humility. "May I do anything for you."

She stood aloof, ready to approach, or to run anywhere.

The stranger rose, went towards her herself, and pressed her hand in the most affectionate manner.

"You cannot do more for me," said she, "than you have done. Only keep this visit a secret from M. De Lorme. I know it will pain you to do so, if he makes many inquiries; but it will be a kindness to all parties, and that seems to be your motto." She paused here a little, and resumed. "I told you truly when I said I was an old friend of M. De Lorme; and I will prove to you that I have that right in common with yourself by sending you a few things to adorn the apartment he likes best with."

Fanchon made no scruples, as she might have done had she been less generous. She felt what was due to a generous woman. She kissed the stranger's hand, who lifted her veil a little, and kissed her on the mouth.

"You are a charming creature," said the lady, "that is certain. We shall be friends, though you never see me again."

"Ah, madame," said Fanchon, "if we are friends, it is hard if you will not see me again. I could walk barefoot and alone to meet you, wherever you pleased."

The lady put her finger on her lips, as if to remind her of the secret, and departed. It was about a week or two from this visit that the tapestry came, and M. De Lorme after it.

Madame De Lorme, by dint of suffering and reflection,

2 B

and what helped her reflection not a little, the accounts
that she heard of Fanchon,—not omitting an increasing
though dispassionate delicacy of attention on the part
of her husband, — was determined to encourage some
very romantic resolutions she had formed, by going and
judging for herself of the fair rustic. She anticipated,
we must own, that her resolutions might possibly be
somewhat dashed by what she saw; but how was she
first angered, then softened, and then confirmed in them
all, by what she actually beheld! A long darkness
seemed melted from her eyes.

The reader sees to what the tapestry led. But it
was weeks, and even months first. Fanchon thought
of putting the new furniture into M. De Lorme's own
bed - chamber; but at sight of the toilet, she saw for
which room it was intended, and she acted accordingly.
As for M. De Lorme, whether it was owing to his being
such a favourite with the ladies, or to the habitual
notion of marriage which had grown upon him, we
must leave the ladies to determine; but his wife was
certainly the last woman whom he thought of as the
unknown lady. Perhaps he would not have guessed
the truth as soon as he did, had he not been helped
by the guesses of Fanchon; and they had both to
ascertain the matter, after all. What staggered him
was, that on his first return home after the receipt of
the tapestry, Madame De Lorme certainly appeared
more reserved than usual, though he must confess that
afterwards, there was a something in her conduct,—a
patience, as it were,—a sort of—he might say—winning
sweetness and dignity;—he did not quite know how to
finish his description, especially as it appears to have
baffled his behaviour, which was a thing on which he
piqued himself. The upshot of the conversation was,
that he set out for Tours that very day, and surprised
the lady with an unexpected visit.

It was twilight; but madame was still poring over a desk, writing. She left off at his entrance, and said with a tone of equal kindness and sincerity, "Dear M. De Lorme, is it you? Had you forgotten anything when you last went away."

"Yes, Manon," said he.

It was the first time for many months that he had called her Manon. She turned pale, and trembled.

"I forgot," continued he, "that one of the kindest of wives was treating me with all sorts of gentleness and good-humour, and that I was one of the most insensible of men."

"Not so,—Alain," returned she, hesitating before she uttered the Christian name; "my forgetfulness began before yours."

"May I ask what you are writing here?" said M. De Lorme, taking up the paper as he spoke, and endeavouring to break the confusion by resorting to commonplaces.

Madame De Lorme turned paler. A fine lady at Paris, whether "virtuous" or not, would have sworn that madame had been about to have her "revenge," and that the manuscript was a billet-doux. It was the commencement of some verses on her husband's birthday, hoping that others would make him as happy as he and they deserved, though it was not in her own power. She was in his arms the next minute. What a long and dreary mistake vanished at the heaven of that caress!

"But Fanchon?" the reader may say. This is the very thing Madame De Lorme said about half an hour after that embrace. Fanchon, it was agreed, who had helped to make so much happiness, was never to be made unhappy, was never to be treated but as a friend and companion, was never to be spoken to, or spoken of, or spoken about, but as a delightful and noble-hearted creature, whom everybody should make as happy as possible. We will not say how often M. De Lorme was at the farm afterwards, especially when Fanchon was married; but it is certain that he was not only there sometimes, but that Fanchon was as often at Tours; and Madame De Lorme and she have been seen laughing with all their might, on a summer's day, to the great scandal of an old maiden lady, who thought they were laughing at her, which they certainly were not.

FINIS.

MORRISON AND GIBB, PRINTERS, EDINBURGH.

www.ingramcontent.com/pod-product-compliance
Lightning Source LLC
Chambersburg PA
CBHW021324110726
47900CB00005B/1345